# NOW
# I
# SEE
# YOU

# NOW I SEE YOU

## LAUREN TREVAN

**TRIGGER WARNING**

This book includes references and descriptions of domestic abuse and child sexual abuse that some readers may find distressing. Please practice self-care whilst reading.

First Published in 2022 by Laneway Press
Re-published in 2023 by Lauren Trevan
https://laurentrevan.com/
admin@laurentrevan.com

A catalogue record for this book is available from the National Library of Australia
www.trove.nla.gov.au

Cover Design & layout: Working Type
Cover Photography: Elizabeth Harrington

ISBN:978-0-646-88715-9 (print)
978-0-646-88736-4 (epub)

LAUREN TREVAN
AUTHOR

*To all victims and survivors of domestic and child sexual abuse.*
*Your voice matters. You are worth so much more*
*than how you have been treated. I believe you.*

*Gerard, Taylor and Harvey, I love you infinitely.*
*And to all those teachers who*
*helped me navigate the in-between.*

# *Spring 2003*

I wasn't meant to be here.

My knuckles white, gripping the bungy cord as we rose higher. For one long, terrifying moment, I lost sight of the horizon before the boat smacked down between the waves. Salty water spattered over me, invading my nostrils and mouth, and I bounced uncomfortably on the trampoline. But I didn't care. I threw back my head in glee, exploding with laughter as my friend, Carrie, scrambled to regain her grip.

"You ladies hang on tight, won't you?" called Julian, our skipper, flashing us a smile. Even though we only met Julian this morning on the catamaran, it was like we'd been friends for years. He made us feel welcome, part of the team. Now, his smile broadened as Carrie and I continued to flail around, struggling to keep our balance on the trampoline. All the while, he stood steadily, steering the boat along the coastline like it was the easiest thing on earth.

But I wasn't meant to be here. I should have been having lunch with Matt, celebrating our three-year anniversary. He called last night, saying, "Sorry babe. I know I promised, but I have an assignment due Monday and they offered me an extra shift at the pub." Blah blah blah ... I'd stopped listening. His excuses were getting old. He was studying agriculture at a university that was a three hour drive away, working towards saving the planet by implementing sustainable farming techniques. "I'm doing this for us babe," he told me, saying it was all part of our dream future together. Fat lot of good that did me now.

I should be glad he was so focused, but it had been a hard six months without him. At the beginning, we were both so eager to make long-distance work. He promised he'd be home most weekends. But he hadn't been home for three weekends in a row, and now, he cancelled on our anniversary.

When I arrived at my six am shift this morning at Kendall's Bakery, Carrie took one look at my face and said, "What's his excuse this time?"

"Matt has to work." I avoided her gaze as I tied the knot on my apron. "And he has an assignment due."

Carrie patted me on the shoulder and started filling the cabinet with baked treats.

"I booked Marshall's ages ago," I said. "What a waste." I picked up a tray of sourdough rolls and started stacking the shelf. "Hey, why don't you and I go to lunch? I've wanted to go there forever."

"Oh, I'd love to," Carrie said, "but I'm going sailing at Rochford." She cocked her head. "Why don't you come with me?"

My eyebrows rose. Despite growing up in the rural coastal town of Darvo River, I had never sailed before. Carrie always came to work with crazy sailing stories, telling me how fun it was. What did I have to lose? I'd take any distraction from Matt at this point.

So after our four-hour shift, we headed to Rochford Sailing Club, and before we knew it, we were sailing out of the river mouth into the ocean.

Not much was required of us on the boat, so Carrie and I

bounced around on the trampoline while the crew went about winding ropes and changing sails at Julian's command.

"Is it normally this rough?" I called to Luke, one of the crew.

Luke threw me a goofy smile. "You ain't seen nothin' yet! Don't worry, we'll make sure nothing happens to you. Julian's the best of the best. Just sit back and enjoy the ride."

I glanced over at Carrie. Even though she kept a firm grip on the bungy, Carrie was glowing. There was a contented calmness I had not previously seen in my perpetually busy friend. It was clear how much it meant to her to be back on the water. She had grown up sailing but stopped when she got pregnant at nineteen.

I was nineteen and couldn't imagine being pregnant now. But Carrie had taken it all in her stride. Now at twenty-nine, she had returned to university to complete her Bachelor of Business. It was a wonder how she managed it all: working at Kendall's Bakery, studying, wrangling children, staying fit, keeping her house showroom tidy and now, taking up sailing again. I'd never seen her look so happy.

I echoed her smile. Something about this experience was making me feel more alive. Life had become a cycle of balancing work, study and a long-term relationship. The ease and joy of high school seemed a distant memory, where I spent afternoons surfing with friends or downing milkshakes at the surf club. I had not realised my life lacked excitement until now, out at sea, where all my synapses seemed to be firing in sensory overload.

My attention was pulled to a flock of sea birds, fluttering metres above the water. They took turns dive bombing what I assumed were bait fish. They squawked and screeched as they darted amongst each other in semi-organised chaos.

But amidst the tumult at sea, there was a calmness, too. The whoosh of the wind picking up a sail. Waves smashing between the hulls. Figures and cars dotted the shoreline, but they seemed a world away. Gone was the everyday hustle and bustle of life; I existed now in a simpler space, where moving forward was at its most primitive. A piece of cloth and a float, essentially. I marvelled at its simplicity and complexity.

"How do you two like it so far?" The skipper, Julian, lowered himself to sit at Carrie's side. He looked in his late twenties and was a solid brick of a man, built like a rugby forward, standing just taller than me. Normally, I was attracted to taller guys, but his smile grabbed my attention. It was the smile of a Hollywood movie star; white and gleaming on a tanned face.

I turned to see Luke at the helm. His lanky build and toothy grin was a stark contrast to Julian's rugged appeal.

"I've missed this so much!" Carrie said.

"What about you ... Jess is it?" Julian directed his warm smile at me, causing another neuron flourish.

"This is my first time," I said. He raised his eyebrows, which made me unaccountably giddy. "It's far better than I ever imagined." I had barely even thought about Matt since I boarded, for one thing.

"We might see a sailor in you yet." Julian said, and my stomach leaped at the prospect.

Later, Julian pulled the boat into the mooring so masterfully I didn't notice we were docked at first. I stepped onto the stationary jetty, soggy and cool. It took a few seconds for my legs to notice I was not on a moving boat anymore.

Luke walked towards us. "Okay, time to put you two to work. Jess, follow me to the bow and hold this rope for a minute." I did as instructed, watching as the others packed away the sails. Luke disappeared to show Carrie to the stern. I'd never noticed what a bustling marina this was. There were people and boats everywhere, but it all appeared to work seamlessly.

Julian approached me, his lips spread broad, showing his perfect smile. "Let me show you what to do with this." He took the rope from my hand and gently wrapped it around a metal cleat on the jetty. "Now you try."

I squatted next to him and fiddled with the rope, trying to replicate what he'd done. Julian chuckled and leaned in so close our shoulders touched. He placed his hands on mine and led them in perfect figure eights to secure the vessel.

When he was done, he didn't immediately let go of my hands. He leaned closer to my face, causing a tiny flutter in my chest. "So, what do you think? Are you sold?"

For a moment, I thought about how this day would have played out if Matt hadn't cancelled on our anniversary lunch. It didn't last. "Absolutely."

9

I sat cross legged on my bed, opening and closing my flip phone, undecided on whether to make the call. Matt had left two messages of apology today.

*I'm sorry babe, I should have been there x*

I was still angry he let me down but I wasn't going to ignore him forever, so I opened the phone and called him.

"Hey babe," Matt said. "I'm glad you've called me back. I'm so sorry about yesterday." He took a deep breath. "That was a shit thing to do. I should have just blown the shift and handed the assignment in late."

"It's okay," I said. "I understand." I fiddled with the threads of my cut-off denim skirt. "I was just looking forward to Marshall's. And I really want to see you. It felt crappy, that's all."

"No, it's not okay, babe. I love you so much. I should have come. I was stressed about rent and my results. You know. Wondering if it's all worth it ..." His voice trailed off.

"Of course it's all worth it, Matt. This is your passion. It's everything you've dreamed of." My shoulders sagged; all my anger had dissolved. I wanted to reach through the phone and hug him.

"I just miss all our friends. And I miss you and my family." His voice was quiet. "It's feeling hard at the moment."

I felt a pang of guilt. "I miss you too."

"I promise I'll make it up to you."

I smiled, even though he couldn't see it. "Well, the whole day wasn't a total waste." I told him about the day spent sailing with Carrie at Rochford Sailing Club. I didn't mention Julian, the skipper with the nice smile. The omission bothered me, but I couldn't reason why.

"I'm thinking of doing a course and joining the club." I waited for a negative response. He was responsible with money and had made so many sacrifices for our future. But it's not like I didn't do my part. On top of weekend shifts at the bakery, I worked part time at Darvo Animal Hospital whilst studying veterinary nursing. The money was not great, but it was fine while I was still at home with Mum and Dad. Still, I felt a tad guilty spending money on hobbies when he struggled to pay his rent.

To my surprise, he sounded interested. I told him the cost and what was involved. "Once I'm a member, I can get involved in the evening social races and formal regattas."

"Well, I'm glad *someone* will have a good time."

I bristled at the sarcasm. "It's not all beer and skittles here, you know!"

"You sound like your dad." His voice lightened again.

I laughed despite myself. I did sound like Dad.

"Seriously ... I'm happy for you," he said. "A little jealous, that's all. Have you caught up with anyone from school?"

We had a close bond with our group from school. All of us tried hard to maintain it despite many splitting off in different directions to follow their dreams. I still caught up every week with my best friend, Rose, and some others at Darvo Surf Club.

"Yeah, most of us were at the club Thursday."

"Cool. I wish I could have come." I heard longing in his tone.

"I know. Me too."

"Hey sorry, babe. My shift starts in ten, I better hit the road. I promise I will make it up to you soon. Love you."

"I love y–" He hung up before I could finish.

I sighed. This long-distance relationship deal was harder than I ever imagined.

We were sipping on wine spritzers after our first official race as crew members. Now, Carrie and I stood on the balcony at Rochford Sailing Club, watching as the sun dipped over the headland past the centre of town.

The marina was a flurry of action as people cleaned and locked up the last of the vessels before nightfall. There was always something happening in this stretch of the river and Rochford sat in prime position to view it all. No wonder the restaurant attached to it got away with charging exorbitant prices, boasting the best view in town.

I couldn't wipe the smile off my face. The race had been a success, but even if it hadn't, it didn't matter. It wasn't about winning or losing. There was something about being out on the water and returning to the dock with sinuses clear, face sticky from sea spray and licking the salty residue off my lips. I felt alive.

"I'm getting chilly," Carrie said. "Should we head inside?"

I nodded and we walked towards the bar, where the room was a hum with music and members sprawled about, chatting about the race. Friendly banter could be heard as we passed different groups. I loved the inside of the club almost as much the view outside. The white-washed floorboards and wood panelled walls had an elegant but beachy feel, completely different to the daggy old surf club. I'd gone there less since I joined Rochford. I missed my old friends, but the surf club made me miss Matt more.

While Carrie refilled our drinks, I strolled around the room, checking out the club photos spread on the walls. Most faces I didn't recognise, but there were a few I did. I found myself drawn to Julian, who featured in many, proudly holding trophies, Luke often by his side. He must have been a member for years, as there were photos of him at around my age, maybe younger. Since then, a few lines had appeared, and his physique had thickened, but his smile remained the same.

My eyes lingered until Carrie distracted me by handing me another wine spritzer.

The music stopped.

"Can I have everyone's attention please?" Julian stood on the stage next to the bar. He held a Peroni stubbie in one hand and ran his other hand through his dark hair.

Everyone gathered closer and quietened.

His voice was loud and confident; no need for a microphone. "On behalf of our club president, Mr Crowlers, I would like to take this opportunity to officially welcome our newest members to Rochford Sailing Club." He lifted his drink to his lips and took a long gulp before continuing. He had the room. No need to hurry.

He continued: "Seven people have successfully completed our sailing course over the last three weeks and tonight, two are here proving how much they've learnt by crewing for me in the third of the friendly series." He cleared his throat and gestured to Carrie and me. I flushed, trying to ignore the many pairs of eyes looking our way.

"These ladies were fantastic aboard tonight, with *almost* no mistakes." I turned redder remembering I had headed to the wrong block and tackle before Luke rescued me, steering me in the right direction. I had dipped my head in embarrassment for my petty mistake, but Julian had laughed it off. He had lowered his sunglasses to shoot a wink in my direction, his dark eyes momentarily blocking a chest valve.

"I would like everyone to make an effort to introduce yourselves to Carrie and Jess tonight." He slugged his beer. "Now, can everyone please raise their glasses. Cheers to Carrie and Jess!" He drained the rest of his beer and stepped off the stage.

"Your face has gone bright red," Carrie said, chuckling.

"You're one to talk," I said. "Go find a mirror. That was so embarrassing."

A woman approached us. She wore a warm smile that reminded me of Mum's. Nothing fake about it. "Hi, I'm Bridget Smith." She shook hands with both of us. "Welcome to Rochford." After we introduced ourselves, Bridget dived into stories of who's who within the club, pointing out members as she went. "That's my husband, Oliver." She pointed to an older man with a serious face chatting in a group with Julian, Luke and a few others. "And over there is Rhonda and Frank. They're second generation members. Big contributors to the club ... a lot of dough to flash about." She rubbed her thumb and index finger together.

"That's Sarah and Tony Robinson over there." She pointed towards a man and woman I assumed to be in their late twenties. Sarah's hand rested on her back as if to hold the spinal curve caused by her enormous belly. "I'm surprised she's here, she's due any day. And, of course, you know Julian." I followed her finger, pointing towards Julian. He was laughing with Luke again, his arm slung over an attractive twenty-something blonde.

"Is that his girlfriend?" I blurted before thinking.

"Oh yes. That's Kayla. They've been dating going on ..." She tapped her finger to her lower lip. "Three years now." She took a sip of wine. "Julian has been with Rochford since his late teens. We've seen quite a few girlfriends come and go, but Kayla is his longest relationship I've seen."

"He seems like a nice guy," Carrie added.

"Oh, he is. No one gives more time to this club than Julian. He's on the committee, but I think he even gives more time than the president himself. He's so generous. Always helping everyone. He's wonderful with the juniors. Always goes above and beyond."

I nodded towards Luke, who had left Julian and was now animating a funny story to Oliver. "What's Luke's story?"

"Oh, Luke is almost joined at the hip with Julian. He's a great guy, too. Both know their stuff. Really talented sailors." The group around Julian erupted in laughter again. "Oliver gets frustrated competing against Julian. He says it's like Julian knows what the wind will do before even the wind does." She laughed and sipped again.

I put my wine on a nearby table. "I'm just ducking to the loo."

As I dried my hands in the bathroom, I looked at my reflection in the mirror. There was a lightness I'd never noticed before. A slack in my facial muscles. My eyes seemed brighter. Gone was the usual furrowed, heavy brow.

I couldn't help but smile to myself as I left the bathroom. In the hall, I spotted Julian heading in my direction. He stopped before me.

"What are you smiling about?" he said, reflecting my smile. He ran a hand through his hair, making it sit up in messy tufts, which just added to his rugged appeal.

"I'm just enjoying the night," I said, my grin spreading wider. "That's all."

"Sorry if I embarrassed you earlier. I was being honest, though. You two are doing great. Particularly you, Jess, having never sailed before." He placed his hand on my shoulder. I felt the weight of his heavy, muscular arm. Despite being shorter, Julian's arms were twice the size of Matt's. I felt a stab of guilt acknowledging it, but it was quickly shadowed by the warmth of Julian's touch. It spiralled to my fingertips, turning them to fire.

"Thanks," I murmured, looking at the carpet, unable to hold his gaze. "It's a whole new world to me." I risked a glance up. "I'm loving it!"

His smile broadened when my eyes landed on his again. "That's great, Jess. You have a lot of potential. I can help you out with improving your technique, if you like. I'm more than happy to do

11

some coaching sessions with you to help with your confidence." He rubbed his thumb lightly on my shoulder before removing his hand.

I inhaled deeply. It was like I stopped breathing when his hand landed on my shoulder. I tried to steady my voice and said, "That would be great, thanks Julian."

He smiled and walked away. I stared at his back until he disappeared into the men's room.

Was he flirting with me? Surely not. He was just being friendly. He was in a long-term relationship, and he knew I was, too.

Did I just flirt back?

I brushed my teeth with too much vigour for comfort, hands shaking with fury. What the hell did Matt expect? So, he could cancel on me whenever he saw fit, but expected me to drop all my plans without warning?

I was invited to crew on Oliver's boat in the Darvo River Classic, one of the biggest races of the season. I didn't want to miss it. I'd worked so hard to prepare for it. Over the past few weeks, Julian had helped me with one-on-one training. And Matt wanted me to give it up just because he decided to bless me with his company for a weekend!

I returned to my bedroom to find Matt laying on the bed, facing away from me. Any closer to the edge and he'd be on the floor.

I rolled my eyes and yanked the covers back hard enough to make a point. I got into bed, my back to him. I snatched at my book and read, turning the pages loudly. This was not how I envisaged us going to bed the first night he had been home in almost two months.

Only a few pages in, I felt Matt roll over. He slid his hand onto my right hip. I was not even wearing my nice pyjamas; a passive show of upset.

I didn't speak, letting him fill the silence, for once.

"Look Jess, I'm sorry, okay?" He pulled his body up against mine, barely a breath between us. "I don't want to argue. I just thought that you might want to spend the day with me tomorrow."

"Of course, I do," I said. "But I'm not going to drop everything to accommodate you when it suddenly suits. I've worked *so* hard at this. I finally found something I enjoy doing. I'm not missing tomorrow's regatta for anything."

Matt squeezed my hip. "I get it. I was probably a bit selfish. I just wanted you all to myself for the weekend." He nudged closer, kissing my neck, his hands rediscovering what he'd missed. What we'd both missed. I let my book drop and turned to face him.

"I'll tell you what, why don't you come down to the club for a drink after the race? I'll introduce you to the friends I've made. You'll love Luke. And Bridget will adore you." There was one name I didn't say. Would he like Julian? I couldn't see why not, but for some reason, the idea of Matt and Julian being in the same room together made me uncomfortable. I forced myself to refocus on Matt. "Jim and Carrie are going to bring Meghan and Amelia along for the afternoon, too."

"That sounds great. I'll catch up with the boys for a surf in the morning." He swept me onto my back and placed light kisses all over my neck and chest. "Now, to make it up to you." I grinned and brought his mouth to mine realising how much my body had missed his.

— ⚓ —

Julian stood on the stage, holding a huge trophy. He waited patiently for the room to quieten. It didn't take long; his presence rarely went unnoticed. He let the room simmer in silence for a moment, eyes brushing over different club members in turn. His eyes met mine. Did they linger a little longer with me?

I blushed, glancing at Matt standing next to me. We were at the edge of the room, near the balcony outside. I pulled him closer, wrapping my arm through his. When I looked back at Julian, he had fixed his attention to a blonde at the front of the crowd; his girlfriend, Kayla.

"Thanks, everyone," Julian said. "I just wanted to say a huge thank you to Luke, Kayla and the rest of my crew today for being so instrumental in taking out yet another Darvo River Classic. The next round is on me. Cheers!"

Everyone cheered, but no one louder than Luke, who immediately launched towards the bar.

Matt put his arm over my shoulder. "Well, babe, I'm impressed. You've done a great job to be part of a nearly winning team." He kissed the top of my head.

I beamed. My cheeks were growing sore from smiling so much, but I'd worn a huge grin since the race ended. I didn't expect my team to place, let alone come second, in my first big race. But the truth was, I'd been smiling since I joined Rochford. Carrie and I had spent a lot of time around the club over the past month; it had almost become a home away from home. It was the only thing helping me deal with the long-distance thing.

"And you too, Carrie, even if you came last," Jim chuckled, tapping Carrie's backside.

She swatted him away. "It wasn't last!" She opened her mouth to say more to her husband, but her attention was diverted by the sight of her girls leaning over the balcony rail. They were spotting fish in the brackish water below. "Meghan! Amelia! Be careful. Don't lean over the railing."

The oldest, Meghan, pouted but stepped away from the rail. She was ten but had the maturity of a girl much older. The eight-year-old, Amelia, just giggled, ignoring her mother in favour of mimicking the sea gulls.

Both girls were spitting images of their mother, Carrie, sharing her auburn locks. But while Meghan's hung in perfect curls, like Carrie's, Amelia's spilled down her back in unruly waves.

I'd gotten to know Carrie's daughters even better over the past few weeks since I started helping Julian with the junior training sessions. They joined the junior program not long after Carrie and I became members. Amelia brought cheek and laughter to every training session, while it was amazing to watch their eldest, Meghan; her steadfast focus and competitive nature foretelling a fierce racer in the future. I loved being a part of it and couldn't help imagining my future children learning to sail here one day, too.

Julian approached us and headed straight to Meghan and Amelia. He dropped to one knee. "Are you both coming to training tomorrow morning?"

Meghan smiled, nodding in response, but Amelia hopped from the rail, shouting, "Definitely!"

A wide smile spread on Julian's face. "Right answer!" He high fived them both and winked at Carrie, who looked happy watching the exchange.

Julian stood and joined our group. He shook Jim's hand. "Good to see you again, Jim."

"You too," Jim said. "Good win today."

"Julian," I said, "this is Matt, my boyfriend I told you about."

Matt offered his hand, smiling.

Julian shook Matt's hand, nodding absently, before darting away to join another group.

Matt raised an eyebrow at Julian's speedy departure. I shrugged; he must have had a million people to greet tonight, being the leader of the winning team.

Luke dived into the middle of our circle, beer in hand, trophy high, singing 'We Are the Champions'. He didn't seem to care he was out of tune.

I laughed, shaking my head at my nutty friend.

Carrie grabbed Luke's shoulders, cutting off his song, and pressed him to help her get on a better boat for the next race. Luke sent pleading eyes my way, but I could only shrug. There was no stopping Carrie once she decided to do something.

I left the group to refill my drink. Julian stood by the bar with Kayla. Our eyes met, but his expression was unreadable. I turned away, ordering my drink. As I waited, Julian enveloped Kayla, kissing her passionately.

I couldn't look away. Kayla was his girlfriend; they were drunk and in love. I didn't know why I stood there, transfixed. But there was something in the way he had looked at me that gave me pause. I was used to him smiling, joking around and exchanging banter. But he had barely said anything to me this afternoon.

Abruptly, he let go of Kayla, his eyes meeting mine for the briefest moment before he grabbed the attention of the bartender.

I walked away, holding my drink, racking my brain to explain his odd behaviour. He had been so nice to Jim when Carrie introduced

16

them, but he practically ignored Matt when I introduced him. He was probably just distracted celebrating his win. So many new faces to meet, it must have been overwhelming. He was usually much nicer when he met people, trying to sell them on the sport. More often than not, he succeeded.

I rejoined the group, glancing back at Julian. Matt, Carrie and Jim were discussing our country's political climate. Carrie made a comment about the need for more women in politics.

I sipped on my drink, nodding and half listening to the conversation, my mind wandering to my training sessions with Julian. The time I'd spent with him in the dinghy had been some of the most fun I'd had in months. I put it down to availability. My friends were drifting away and Matt was barely around; it was great to make a friend and spend my free time *doing* something.

It was nothing to do with Julian.

But my eyes subconsciously wandered in Julian's direction throughout the night, and I was hyper aware every time he was in my vicinity. Like a silent alarm causing my heart rate to climb and my body temperature to rise a degree.

I forced my brain back to the moment, back to Matt. I was in love with Matt. The only problem with Matt is that he was gone most of the time.

I stared at the empty chair with disdain. I had been looking forward to Rochford's annual fundraiser since I'd joined three months ago. I didn't know why I got my hopes up again. Another day, another

Matt no-show. But even though I'd grown used to his last-minute cancellations, it didn't make them any easier.

The member's bar was packed with round, white-clothed tables. Fairy lights wound around the banister of the balcony and candles flickered on the tables in the barely there summer breeze. It was beautiful, welcoming, magical; but I couldn't enjoy any of it.

The table erupted in laughter as Jim told another joke. I forced a chuckle, though I had barely heard it.

"Come on Jess, snap out of it!" Carrie tugged on my arm. "Don't let him wreck tonight. You've had your hair and makeup done. You look *amazing*. But your sad face is undoing all that hard work."

I leaned back into my chair, wanting to sink into it. Something in me snapped. "You know what," I said through gritted teeth, "You're right!" I sat up and filled my wine glass well above the recommended pour line and drunk a large mouthful, heedless of the fact I'd had a couple of glasses already. "I'm not going to let him spoil my night. I worked so hard for this. And I *do* look good." I chuckled, but my face soured again. "I'm just pissed I wasted fifty bucks on his ticket. But he'd promised he would come!" My last words came out a whine and I teared up with disappointment again.

"Right," said Carrie. "That's it." Carrie pushed her chair back with gusto, dragging me up with her. "We're going to dance."

The next few hours went by in a blur. Someone ordered cowboy shots. I had three, at least. I stopped counting. I danced and mingled; Matt barely on my mind. Julian disappeared for a while but emerged later on the dancefloor. In between shots, Julian's hands landed on my waist, and he shimmied playfully against me before Luke took my hand and spun me around the room.

At one point, after another round of shots, I realised the music had stopped and the crowded room had thinned, many had called it a night. I wasn't ready for the night to end.

"Time to go Jess," Carrie said, dragging me away from the bar. "Our cab's on the way."

I took the glass Carrie was walking out with and put it back on the bar. We locked arms and held firm to each banister heading down the stairs, giggling incessantly. We spilled out the door and waved as people pulled away in cars.

"I don't want to go," I slurred. "I'm not tired." I rubbed my forehead, damp with sweat. I spun around; the boys were trailing behind us, laughing at something Luke had said. "Hey! Let's go to another bar."

"I think you'd regret that one Jess!" Jim said, taking Carrie off my arms and leading her to a cab. "Besides, we have to relieve the sitter." Jim opened the door to the cab.

"I'm not ready for bed either Jess," Luke said, his words running into each other. "Let's find somewhere to get a drink." He looped his arm around mine and steered me away from the cab. "Come on Julian, we're going out!"

Julian watched us, an amused expression on his brow. He looked completely sober, which was not possible; he'd drunk as much as I had out on the dancefloor. He looked at Jim and said, "I'll make sure she gets home safe."

Jim nodded and headed into the cab, but Carrie hovered by the door. "Jess, are you sure?" she hiccupped.

"I'll be fine," I said. "See you at brunch tomorrow!"

Carrie shrugged and climbed into the back seat.

I waved them off and headed towards Main Street with Luke, Julian trailing behind. Darvo River was not a large town but in the warmer months it was a tourist hot spot, so the main strip had a few bars that stayed open late.

"I hate to burst your bubbles," Julian said, "but there is no way either of you are getting in to one of those bars."

Luke and I turned to each other and simultaneously burst out laughing.

"Come on." Julian waved for us to follow. "I'll walk you both home. Neither of you need another drink."

I wanted to protest, but my stomach churned a little at the mention of another drink. How long ago was that last shot? So we followed behind Julian along the water's edge, zigzagging along the path that led towards their apartments.

"Hey Luke," I said, leaning on him as I walked, "how long have you been a plumber?"

"Since I left high school." He leaned on me just as much, doing our bit to keep the other upright.

"Is it hard?"

"Nup, all you gotta know is two things; pay day's on Thursd'y an' shit runs downhill."

We erupted in laughter again and Julian turned to smirk at us.

"Why don't you have a girlfriend?" I asked Luke.

"I'm too young and spritely to be held back by the ol' ball and chain." He laughed. "Seriously though, I've had girlfriends. None could live up to my high standards, that's all." I looked up to see if he was being serious and with a grin, he said, "Gotcha!"

His legs buckled, and we both toppled to the pavement laughing hysterically.

"Alright, that's enough," Julian said. "Up you get." He heaved Luke to his feet before taking my hand and doing the same. He

20

helped Luke all the way to his apartment door.

"Catcha later, Jess," Luke said and he disappeared with Julian into his home.

I leant against the door jamb wondering if I should try to get a cab. It was only a twenty minute walk, and it was a beautiful night.

Julian sauntered back to me. "Now, to get you home." He smirked at me before turning my shoulders towards the path. "Do you know the way?"

"Yes, of course!" I took a few moments to gather my bearings. "It's this way." I pointed and stepped forward. The communication between my brain and feet proved sluggish, it took concentration to step straight. "I'll be fine on my own though." I gestured at the apartment blocks surrounding us. "Isn't this where you live?"

Julian's forehead crinkled. "If you don't mind, Jess, I'd rather see you home safe. That way I won't sit up and worry if you got there or not."

I pressed my lips together trying to think of a response to his kind words. None came to me, so I nodded and followed him. We headed along the river path in the opposite direction we came. Julian's shoulder bumped gently with mine every couple of steps.

"Hey," I said, "where did Kayla end up tonight?"

"She puked and I walked her to my place a couple of hours ago to sleep it off."

I nodded, hoping I wasn't going to do the same.

"Where was Mike?" Julian asked, after a pause.

"It's *Matt* actually, and he cancelled last night."

"Bridget was saying that's not the first time he's done that." I nodded, letting the sour thought back in. My face must have showed it. "That's pretty fucked up, if you ask me. He shouldn't treat you like that. You deserve better."

My eyes prickled with fresh tears. "I don't want to talk about him." I murmured. "Let's talk about something else." My foggy brain ticked for a few seconds. "Did you grow up around here?"

The rest of the way home, he told me his life story, with me shooting constant questions. I found out he had always lived at Darvo River and went to the elite boy's school on the hill. The one with the fancy uniforms I used to make fun of. I didn't tell him that. I learnt he got a business degree after finishing high school and now worked in middle management for an insurance firm. I was surprised to learn he had just turned thirty-one.

"What about you, Jess?" Julian said. "What's your story?"

"I'm only nineteen, I don't have much of a story yet."

"You have more of a story than you think. I already know a bit of it."

My stomach flipped, and not with nausea.

"I know you are studying veterinary nursing," he continued, "so that means you have a caring nature." His arm stayed flush with mine. "I know you are intelligent because you picked up sailing so quickly."

My cheeks must have been scarlet and I was thankful for the cover of darkness.

He stopped walking and turned to me. "I know you are patient because you're good to your boyfriend. Even though he treats you like shit." His strong hand took mine in a tender grasp. "I know you are a good friend because I see you make sure everyone else is happy before making sure you are yourself." The back of his hand lifted and stroked my cheek. Each epithelial awakened under his touch and my face involuntarily turned towards his hand, almost touching my lips to his fingers. "And now I know you have the softest skin of anyone I've ever met."

"Julian ... I ..."

He leaned in, gently brushing his lips to mine. He paused there. Barely a millimetre from my face.

This was wrong. He had a girlfriend. And I had Matt. I loved Matt.

Why wasn't I moving away?

Julian lingered so close that my voice of reason faded. So faint, it may as well have been someone shouting from the moon. All I heard was my body screaming at me to kiss him back.

And I did.

<hr />

I headed through the side gate of Carrie and Jim's suburban home, following the scent of bacon, where Jim was cooking up a storm on the barbeque. Meghan, was bouncing on the trampoline while Amelia sat at the table by the pool, where Carrie was applying her sunscreen.

Carrie greeted me with a peck on the cheek and an unsympathetic smile. I took a seat and she pointed to a coffee, which I cradled like it was the source of life. I needed all the coffee and bacon I could get. Waking up that morning had been hard. Not even pain killers helped. Punishment for being such a terrible person.

"So," Jim said cheerily as he flipped mushrooms. "Spill it. Where did you end up last night?"

I stared at him through my dark glasses, disbelieving. He looked completely fine. Why was I the only awful, cheating, hungover idiot here? I rubbed my temples; someone was engraving a long message into the back of my eyes. I deserved it.

"It's a funny story, really," I said. "All that happened was Julian convinced us we wouldn't get into a bar, so we walked Luke home." I took a sip of my coffee, refusing to meet either of their eager-for-gossip eyes.

Amelia was restless to get on the trampoline and Carrie hurriedly finished applying her sunscreen.

"Hurry up, Mummy!" Amelia cried.

Carrie rubbed a bit more in before declaring, "Oh, that'll do." Amelia darted across the lawn with white smudges over her freckled cheeks, joining her older sister on the trampoline.

"So, where did you sleep last night, Jess?" Jim said, eyes twinkling.

"At home," I said in a bored tone.

"What happened?" Carrie whispered, so Jim couldn't hear.

"I'll tell you later."

Meghan sat by my side, rosy cheeked from the trampoline, as Jim piled the food to the centre of the table.

"I lost a tooth this morning, Jess!" she said, puffing her chest with pride.

"Oh wow! That's exciting, Meghan. Show me."

"See, look." She dug the bloodied tooth from her pocket and shoved it so close to my eyes, I was taken aback.

"I meant your mouth!" I said, chuckling. "I don't need to see your grotty old tooth ... gross!"

After brunch, I stood too fast and sat immediately, head spinning. Jim laughed and walked away to tidy the kitchen.

The girls returned to tumbling on the trampoline. I felt a pang

24

of envy of their young, untroubled lives. The hardest decision they had to make was to either keep a tooth or give it up to the tooth fairy and get paid.

"Come on," Carrie said, finally. "Spill it."

I sipped my coffee, praying for fortitude. "Julian kissed me last night." I paused as her eyes widened. "And I kissed him back."

Carrie's eyebrows shot north. "Well ..." A small grin crossed her lips. "What was it like?"

I rolled my eyes and couldn't help smiling at the thought of it again. "It was amazing, actually." I slouched back into my chair.

After a moment, Carrie asked what I had been dreading: "What are you going to do about Matt?"

I slapped my hand to my forehead and instantly regretted it. "I don't have a clue what to do. I don't even know how I feel."

"Do you want my advice?"

I nodded.

"Well, I have none!" She laughed. "This is a bit of a sticky mess you're in. The way I figure is, you can act like it never happened. Or you can tell Matt and apologise profusely. Or you can give him the flick and pursue Julian."

I huffed, rubbing at my eyes. "I love Matt. I do. He's my first love and all I've ever known."

"And how do you feel about Julian?"

"He's exciting," I admitted. "Mostly because he's nothing I've ever known."

"You have some thinking to do." She smirked. "It's not the worst thing in the world to have to decide between two men, you know."

"I don't even know if that's something I get to decide." But if I did, who would I choose? I loved Matt; I had planned to spend my life

25

with him. I couldn't decide if that life still looked desirable. Matt let me down again and again while Julian was there for me. I kept replaying last night's kiss with Julian. Kissing Matt didn't feel like that. My stomach backflipped with a rush of tiny butterflies as I imagined his lips on mine. The bristles of his stubble pressed firm against my skin. The woody scent of his aftershave lingering on his jacket collar. I got goosebumps then. I got goosebumps now.

I couldn't linger on that kiss without Kayla taking over my thoughts. I was hungover but sickened mostly with guilt. We both cheated on our partners. It was only a kiss, but that was enough. Maybe we were just drunk, and it really was just a kiss. But it didn't explain the things he said.

I left Carrie's and drove home, my mind a mess as I pondered my situation.

The moment I stepped inside the house, Mum appeared, her round face lit up. "Matt must be feeling guilty for cancelling on you yesterday." She ushered me into the kitchen.

"Why?" I said. "Did he call?" I rounded the doorway, and my question was answered. On our dining table was a large bunch of red roses.

"Oh my God!" My hand flew to my mouth. Matt was never romantic like this.

"Don't blaspheme," Mum said, automatically like she normally did whenever someone took the Lord's name in vain. Mum was like that. She tolerated swearing, but God forbid we blaspheme! I always thought it was strange, as she barely went to church except at Christmas.

"Go on," Mum said, rubbing her hands together. "Read the card."

"No, I'm taking them to my room."

Her face deflated. "But Jess ..."

"Leave her be, Eve. It's none of our business." Dad walked in, holding his favourite coffee cup, a gift I gave fifteen years ago that said, 'World's Best Dad'. The letters were worn, but still legible.

I picked up the roses and headed to my room, sick with a new wave of remorse. There Matt was, studying and working hard, preparing for our future, while I was off at a fundraiser, kissing a hot older sailor.

I laid the flowers on my chest of drawers, kicked off my sandals and headed to the bathroom. I was stalling. Dying to know what the card said but terrified it would confirm what a terrible person I was. Finally, I could stand it no longer and ripped the envelope open.

My hand flew to my mouth, stifling a squeal.

*Hopefully you don't feel too bad today.*

*I can't wait to see you again.*

*Julian x*

❦

After a restless night of little sleep, I forced myself to get up and go to work at the animal hospital. My mind everywhere but on task. One minute I was near tears thinking I may have ruined things with Matt forever. Next minute I was lost in rapture reliving that kiss. Finally, a putrid smell from the cage with the blue heeler pulled me from my daze, and I got to cleaning, welcoming the unpleasant distraction. Anything to stop me from thinking about Matt and Julian.

Later that afternoon, I drove to Rochford Sailing Club, where I sat in my car outside, staring at the overcast summer sky. I couldn't bring myself to leave the car, unsure if the training session with Julian was a good idea. We had arranged it last week. Before the kiss. I wanted to go. But the thought of Matt flooded me with guilt.

I buried my face in my hands for the umpteenth time.

Tap. Tap. Tap.

I looked up. Julian's smiling face was outside my window. He gestured for me to wind it down.

"You're not going to learn anything in there," he said, pulling up the lock and opening my door. "Come on."

I followed him through the boatyard. As we pushed a dinghy towards the boat ramp, I said in a quiet voice, "Thanks for the flowers."

"You deserve nice things," he said simply.

Once in the water, we climbed into the hull, donned our safety gear and prepared the sail.

"We're going to practice a standard windward leeward course again today," he said.

I nodded, forcing my brain to concentrate.

"But you are at the helm, Jess. You're calling all the shots." He patted his hand on my thigh.

"You'll correct me though, right?" My head was not in the right space for this.

"You're in charge, Jess. You call the shots."

I couldn't take my eyes off those lips as he smiled and pointed in the direction we were headed. We passed a marker buoy and Julian pointed to the next I needed to aim towards.

"The plan will be to head windward for a beat," he said, "reach to the spreader mark and a run to the leeward mark. Off you go."

I took the tiller and it all went to plan for a while. We moved fast with a stronger breeze than I was used to. I was reaching too broad and before my brain could focus on the correction, a gust took the sail and I was catapulted headfirst into the water.

I was flailing, searching for a way up. Millions of tiny alveoli in my lungs screaming for air. I kicked hard towards the surface and the back of my head exploded with a sharp pain. The world turned dark.

The next thing I knew, I was coughing and spluttering. Little razors were tearing at my airways. Julian encircled me with one strong arm, holding firm to the upturned hull with the other. Our life vests working to keep us afloat.

"You're alright," he said, his voice surprisingly calm. "It'll be alright. Take some deeps breaths."

I finally drew in a full breath.

"That's it, keep breathing. You'll be okay."

White caps lapped at our faces as we bobbed, holding firm to the boat. My gasps were replaced with sobs as I took in what had happened. Julian had pulled me out from under the boat. I'd capsized before, but never so fast and with such force.

Julian hugged me into his body. I clung to him and sobbed into his neck. It took a few minutes to pull myself together and my heart rate to stabilise.

Julian pulled back and looked into my raw eyes. He pushed the hair plastered to my cheeks back with a soft sweep of his thumb. "See, everything's fine. You're safe. I won't let anything happen to you. You're safe."

We embraced, bobbing in the water for some time. The absurdity of the situation, with him holding me, speaking words of comfort, finally calmed me. I took long breaths, feeling safe in his arms. I couldn't speak and didn't want him to let me go. His arms were firm and felt secure around me. The sudden rush of adrenaline had sent my mind in a spin. I stared into his dark eyes. He slid some wet hair from my face behind my ear, letting his index finger trail my jaw line. I leant in and kissed him. Gently, at first, but in mere seconds, we were completely entwined. Our lips eager and firm, moving with each other's. I didn't want to stop. I couldn't.

⁹

"Jess, dinner's ready," Dad called.

I took a moment to collect myself and straighten my face before going downstairs to the dining room.

"Have you got hay fever?" Mum asked as I took my seat at the dinner table.

I adjusted my chair, taking a napkin and unfolding it. "No." I didn't look up. "This looks good, thanks Mum." I feigned cheer, reached for the peas and spooned a few on my plate. I ignored Mum eyeballing me from across the table.

We ate in silence for a few minutes. I moved food around my plate without bringing much to my mouth. My appetite sapped. I sensed the unspoken conversation playing out between Mum and Dad.

Finally, Mum slapped her cutlery to the table. "Jess, what's wrong?"

I gritted my teeth. Best to get it over with. "I broke up with Matt."

"What? Oh, my goodness. Why?" Her brow squashed inwards. She looked at Dad before searching my face again.

"Mum, it's not working out. I don't feel the same way I used to." Tears crept at the corners of my eyes. "He's so far away. It's hard." My voice petered off. I focused on my plate, pushing carrots around. I'd cried over the phone when I told Matt this. That it was all because he was so far away. It wasn't a lie, exactly. But I didn't mention Julian.

"Jess ... I don't know what to say." Mum's voice cracked.

"Oh, Mum, don't you start crying."

"I'm not," she said, her voice suddenly high. "It's just– you've been together so long. He's part of the family." Her knife and fork lay forgotten as she blotted her eyes with a napkin.

"Come on, love." Dad put his hand over Mum's. "I think it's smart, Jess. You two have been serious for a long time. You shouldn't necessarily settle with your first love. Even if he is a good guy like Matt. If it's meant to be, it will be." He patted Mum's hand again before returning to his meal.

"Thanks, Dad."

Mum stayed flat throughout the meal. I hadn't expected Mum to take the news so poorly. I didn't want to upset her, but I was glad it was over and she knew. Before I went upstairs, she gave me a comforting hug. "It'll be alright," she said. I didn't know if she was trying to convince me or herself.

In my room, I sat on the edge of my bed and texted Julian.

*I broke up with Matt. I feel like shit.*

The reply was fast:

*I've broken up with Kayla too. Don't feel bad, you have done nothing wrong Jess x*

I nodded, trying to convince myself, but the guilt sat heavy and relentless.

Moments later, another text arrived, this time from my closest

31

friend from high school, Rose.

*Tell me it's not true. This is so sad Jess, why?*

Matt had obviously made some calls.

I typed back: 'It wasn't meant to be' before shaking my head, deleting it and typing: 'It's none of your business' before deleting that, too. I couldn't deal with other people's disappointment. It was sad enough for me, let alone taking on board other people's sadness. I hadn't realised how invested my friends and family were in our relationship.

In the end, I didn't reply.

<hr />

I sat on Julian's balcony, enjoying the river views from his third-floor vantage. He handed me a coffee and sat by my side, his hand gravitating to my thigh. We'd been inseparable for three weeks now; an intimate comfort in each other's company grew daily.

"How was work?" he asked, his words sending a warmth through my chest. The same feeling I got every time we talked. He stayed attentive, waiting on my answers. I never felt that with Matt. Sometimes I still felt bad about the breakup, but in moments like this, I knew I made the right decision. Julian made me feel important, interesting, loved. When I thought of it like that, my guilt washed away. Or at least washed over.

"Work was alright," I said. "We had a crazy lab with a hot spot that needed to be sedated before I could shave him. What about you?"

He pressed my thigh and told me about his day. I smiled at the

32

mundanity of our conversation. I'd missed these simple conversations about life's daily happenings and rituals when I was with Matt; when we spoke, it was over the phone, normally short and to the point. But with Julian, we spent almost every spare minute together, telling each other every little thing.

I heard the door open. "Hey Julian, what are you up to?" Luke appeared at the balcony door. He still had his grubby work clothes on but his steel caps were off. When he saw me, a smile spread across his face. "Oh, hey Jess, how's it goin'?"

"Good," I said, matching his smile. Luke, Carrie and Rose from school were the only ones that knew Julian and I were dating. Luke seemed happy for us.

My phone chimed. Mum was calling. I darted towards Julian's bedroom. I had not told my parents about Julian yet. They still grieved Matt.

"Hi, Mum," I said in a bright tone.

"Hi. I'm just checking if you'll be home for dinner tonight?"

"Sorry, I should have called. No, I'm going out to dinner."

Julian opened the bedroom door and I motioned for him to stay quiet. He smirked and closed it again.

"Oh, okay." There was a pause. "Who with?"

"Just some friends from the yacht club. I'll probably stay at Carrie's." I felt silly lying to my Mum. I was nineteen, not a child. But she wouldn't be able to handle news of Julian yet. Dad might have, maybe, but not Mum.

"Alright, well, have fun. We'll see you tomorrow."

"See ya." I flipped the phone shut and went back to the balcony to join the boys.

"I thought we were going to the club?" Luke said to Julian.

"I'm going to give it a miss tonight and get some dinner with Jess." Julian smiled in my direction.

Luke shrugged and walked to the kettle, grabbing himself a coffee.

I sat next to Julian, who lent over and kissed me. "You're going to have to tell them soon, Jess."

"I know. I just feel guilty moving on so fast and Mum was so upset when we broke up."

"I understand. It's hard. But you don't want them to find out through anyone else." He brushed his lips against my neck, causing my insides to warm. He lowered his voice so Luke couldn't hear, saying, "And I'm not keeping you a secret much longer."

"I promise. Soon."

His face broke into a smile. "Hey, I was going to surprise you later, but I've booked a night in the city for us. I thought we could head in after the race on Saturday, in time to have dinner."

My eyes lit up. "I've never stayed overnight in the city before! It sounds expensive, though. Can I put in?"

He frowned. "I've got it." He kissed my lips firmly, sending me bouncing off the walls inside.

My phone vibrated with a message. "Sorry. It's Rose again." I couldn't keep secrets from her.

*I just think you're making a mistake. Why don't you come out with us tonight and we can talk about it?*

I searched for the best response. 'I've already fallen for him, it's not a mistake'. Or 'If I come, you might try to talk me out of it.' My mind raced for answers, but none satisfied.

Julian waited patiently for me to finish. His patience seemed endless. If Rose and the others met him, they would understand why I chose him.

34

I flicked the phone shut. She could wait.

Luke joined us on the balcony, sipping gingerly at his fresh pour. "Jess, I hear you're joining our crew this Saturday?"

I looked at Julian with my eyebrows raised. "Really?"

Since Kayla left, Julian had asked others to fill in for her over the last few weeks. Everyone coveted the position; his crew were the best at Rochford.

"Yeah, of course," he said. "You're on my team now."

This was where I belonged.

# *Winter 2004*

**"W**hat are you staring at?" Julian quizzed from the driver's seat of his BMW sedan. We were on our way to his parents' house for dinner, something we tried to do every week or so.

"You," I said. "I love you."

"I love you too, sweetie." He patted my leg; still making me tingle.

"How much do you love me?" I asked with a cheeky smile, caressing my fingers down his neck.

"A lot. So much that ... Jess, I've been thinking. I think you should move in with me."

I bolted upright. "What! Are you serious?"

"I've thought about it for a while. What do you think?" His eyes flickered between me and the road, expectant.

I beamed, relishing his dark eyes, strong jawline, wide lips. Lips that I still craved after six months together. I could never tire of looking at him, especially now, his face aglow with anticipation; with love for me.

How did I get so lucky?

Julian spoilt me rotten. Flowers sent to my work. Sweet phone messages. Luxurious presents. On my birthday, he'd surprised me with a trip to Hawaii. Five nights of cocktails, swimming, sunbathing and lovemaking. It felt like a honeymoon.

Six months together and we'd barely had an argument. Except one night, a few weeks into dating, when I had my period, so did not feel like making love.

"Are you not attracted to me anymore?" he'd said, face contorted. "Already?"

"Of course, I am," I'd said in surprise. "I'm more than attracted to you."

"Well, it worries me to start a relationship with someone who doesn't like sex."

"Julian, I'm sorry. You've got it wrong. I've got my period, that's all. I just don't feel like it tonight."

I had expected sympathy, understanding, but instead, he rolled his eyes and slept facing away from me. That was the first night he hadn't spooned me to sleep. I'd lain awake for hours, worried he would break up with me. The next morning, I apologised again. He'd just pulled me into a hug and told me there was nothing to be sorry about. Since then, there had barely been a ripple in our connection; we were so closely bonded.

I had spent countless days with him sailing at Rochford, and countless nights at his apartment. I had basically moved in, spending more time there than at home. I loved staying over at his house, ready for the time when I could fully move out of my parents'.

So, when it came down to it, the answer was already there, waiting.

"Yes," I said. "Hell yes! I love you so much!" I stretched my seatbelt, planting kisses all over his face and neck.

He nodded, showcasing his brilliant smile, my favourite part of him.

He was still smiling as we pulled into his parents' drive for dinner.

He turned the car off and we kissed in the front seat like a couple of loved-up teenagers, until Julian pulled away gently, saying, "Come on. They're expecting us at six thirty. If Mum says be there at six thirty, arrive late at your own peril." He threw me a look of faux warning.

His dad, Greg, met us at the front door, still in his work suit. I rarely saw him without a suit or some kind of formal attire. Julian told me he was a workaholic, working late hours and often bringing work home with him. Today, though, he seemed relaxed, holding a glass of scotch.

"Good to see you, Jess," Greg said. "Come on in. Hello, son." He patted Julian on the shoulder as he passed through the doorway.

I was blown away the first time I entered the Rundell home; it oozed opulence and perfection. To such a degree that it caused me mild discomfort. I attributed it to my upbringing. It's just not what I was used to. Mum and Dad kept a comfortable home, well lived in, with dishes left drying on the sink, magazines on the coffee table, family photos lining every wall, every surface. But at the Rundell home, nothing looked out of place; every surface bare, except for the occasional bowl or sculpture, carefully placed like it was a museum display. Framed artworks lined the walls, and even though I didn't know who the artists were, I could tell they were expensive. It was odd there were hardly any family photos, except on the fridge. Even then, it was just one of Julian at graduation, posing formally with his parents.

I followed Julian and Greg to the kitchen where Lyn was drying her hands on a tea towel. She hurried forward for her standard flamboyant greetings. I subtly wiped my cheek after she kissed it when I noticed the bright red spurge left on Julian's. Every time I met Lyn, she was dressed to perfection with a full face of makeup.

Always with an opaque slick of bright red or pink lipstick. She didn't need it; she looked great for her age.

"Greg, can you get the drinks?" Lyn said. Both of his parents tended to throw me a vodka and soda or wine on my way in the door. It was a welcome gesture; a drink took the edge off my nerves. While his parents were easy enough to be around, I still felt like I had to be on my best behaviour.

Lyn gave me a lengthy rundown of her hectic day while she prepped her green salad. All I really had to do was nod and smile; she did the talking for all four of us. "Honestly," she sighed, "between the tennis club and keeping the house up, I don't know how I ever had time to work."

Lyn once told me 'in another lifetime' she worked as a personal assistant before marrying her first husband and raising two sons. After her first husband died, she married Greg and gave birth to Julian and his brother, Karl. She hadn't worked professionally since.

We were on our second glasses of wine – though it might have been Lyn's third – when she dove into humorous stories about young Julian. I laughed along while Julian smiled, or maybe grimaced, at being the butt of Lyn's funny stories. Greg was nowhere to be seen, having been ordered to cook steaks on the barbeque outside a while ago.

"So," Lyn said, "when I took him to the emergency room after falling from the roof again, I said to Greg, 'You have *got* to do something about the fence. Julian could die if he falls from that height again!'"

"Okay, Mum," Julian said, finally breaking his stoic silence. "Can we give the young daredevil stories a rest for a bit? Jess and I have some news."

39

"What news?" she said absentmindedly, heading to the fridge.

"I've asked Jess to move in with me." Julian took a sip of his beer; a picture of calm while he waited for Lyn to process the news.

Lyn paused, her head still in the fridge. She closed the fridge door, returning empty-handed, rubbing her hands over her apron. For a long, torturous moment, she stared at Julian, expression unreadable. In the blink of an eye, she broke into a smile. She rounded the bench and gave each of us a kiss on the cheek. "Well, isn't that just *wonderful* news."

After the big news died down, I excused myself for the bathroom. I took my time; readjusting my thick ponytail, fixing flyaway strands, wiping the residual red smudge off my cheek. I made sure I didn't have mascara clumped in the corner of my eyes, like Lyn. It used to distract me, but I'd grown used to it.

Beaming, I leaned on the sink, my feet bouncing up and down on my tiptoes like a child. This was actually happening. I was moving in with the man of my dreams. When I woke up this morning, I didn't expect my whole life to change, but a new chapter of my life was about to start. This was everything I ever wanted. I contained a squeal and left the bathroom.

Nearing the kitchen, I heard Julian's hushed voice. "Just keep your voice down, will you?" I stopped, holding my breath; I wasn't meant to hear this conversation.

"Oh, all right." Lyn's voice was barely above a whisper. "All I'm saying is that you should get her to sign a rental contract and pay you rent."

"Do you think?"

"You just don't want her to have any right to your apartment, Jules. I mean, how well do you really know this one? Leave it with me and I'll get some legal advice."

What sort of person did she think I was? I forced myself to look unfazed as I rounded the corner.

"Oh, Jess." Lyn's voice returned to her normal, honeyed tone. "Could you please pop these onto the table?" She handed me the salt and pepper.

"Sure, no problem." I matched her smile.

Later that night, lying in bed with Julian, I could not stop replaying the conversation in my head. When Julian leaned in to kiss me, I stiffened. I knew where he wanted this to lead but my earlier elation was tainted. All I could think about was Lyn's warning. I closed my eyes, willing myself to forget it.

"Jess, is something wrong?" Julian said.

I opened my eyes. Julian's face hovered above me, full of concern.

"I heard the conversation you had with your mum earlier," I finally said. "I didn't mean to, but I heard it coming back from the bathroom. Sorry."

He laid on his side facing me, his arm wrapped over my waist. "No, I'm sorry. I should have warned you. She can be a bit overprotective at times. She hasn't had an easy life."

"I would never do that to you. You know that, right? I love you for you."

His fingers stroked my side. "I know. I should probably explain a bit. Mum grew up watching her dad beat the shit out of her mum. I think it made her tougher in a lot of ways. Anyway, her first husband died of a heart attack when my older brothers were toddlers."

"Oh god, I can't imagine."

"That's not all. She married Dad and gave birth to Karl and me in quick succession. He raised all of us as his own." He paused for a few minutes, winding his fingers through mine. When he finally spoke, his voice was flat. "Louis, my eldest brother, died in a car accident when he was twenty-four."

I squeezed his hand, unable to find the words.

"It was pretty bloody horrendous. Anyway, Roger, my next brother, went off the rails after Louis died, putting just about anything into his body chasing his next high. Mum and Dad did everything they could, but he pushed everyone away. We don't even know where he lives now. Karl, my brother that's just older than me, threw himself into his studies and is now a medical scientist working in the city."

"Karl's the only brother I've heard you talk about before." I kept a firm grip on his hand, glad he was confiding in me, but realising we still had so much to learn about each other.

"Yeah. So can you understand now? I'm the only one left, really. It's why she tends to smother me a bit."

"I understand."

"I love you, Jess. Don't let my mum worry you. She thinks you're as wonderful as I do." As he spoke, he moved on top of me, kissing me hungrily as our hands roamed each other's bodies.

Now, I was distracted in all the right ways.

# Spring 2004

The comforting smells of Mum's cooking filled my nostrils. We were gathered around Mum's dining table, steam rising from the feast before us, a welcome sight on a cold night.

"Eve, these potatoes are delicious," Julian said. "What have you done to them?"

"I par cook them before roasting," Mum said. "They are so much crispier that way."

"Jess, you should take some cooking tips from your mum." He threw me a crooked smile.

Dad butted in before I could retort. "How is work going, Julian?"

"Great, actually. I just got a promotion."

"Yeah, Senior Management now," I said, beaming, my annoyance at his comment forgotten.

Mum and Dad gushed, offering their congratulations. Julian picked up the plate of potatoes and offered the last to Mum and Dad before popping it into his mouth. Mum watched him eat with a satisfied smile; she loved compliments on her cooking, and Julian was always full of them. He complained it was always the same at his parents' house; salad and meat. I thought it strange to put such effort into a spotless gallery type home and little thought or energy into sustenance. Mum had long ingrained a love of good food and

43

cooking. Julian always looked forward to dinners here. It would be hard to live up to.

Later in the kitchen, I helped Mum wash the dishes while Julian and Dad continued chatting. The nights often ended this way; they seemed to have struck up a nice alliance over the time I'd been with Julian. I liked to leave them to it.

"Do you think the two of you might look to make things 'more official' one day?" Mum asked, as casually as if she was asking for me to pass the soap.

"Mum, it's not even been a *year*," I said, but my stomach did a somersault at the thought. I dreamt of marrying him all the time; it was surreal to hear someone else say this fantasy aloud.

Mum was silent as she rinsed a plate and placed it in the dishwasher. After a moment, she said, "Does he make you happy?" Her voice had lost its casual tone.

"So happy."

Mum's face broke into a relieved smile. "We should have his family over for a barbeque one day."

I made a noncommittal sound. Our parents had only met once, for Julian's birthday dinner at a restaurant, and as much as they got along I would be uncomfortable inviting them here. Our house was nice, but it was no gallery.

"I can't believe my course is almost over," I said, eager to change the subject. I'd been studying for two years, but it felt like forever.

"That's an idea!" Mum said. "We can have Lyn and Greg over for a joint celebration. Julian's promotion and your graduation."

"Mum, please!" I exclaimed.

She recoiled, a mix of hurt and confusion crossing her face.

"Sorry," I said quickly. "It's just ... they're ..."

Mum patted me on the back with a small smile. "It'll be great to go full time, I bet. You've been at the bakery for so long."

"Yeah," I said, sighing, the tension releasing from my body. "It will be amazing to have my Saturday mornings back."

"Oh, by the way, I have a box of your things."

Mum pointed to a box I must have missed when moving into Julian's place. She returned to the dining room while I rifled through the box. All my old diaries, notes from school friends, even the ticket stub from my first Pearl Jam concert, all safely contained in a floral hat box. The soft rabbit Mum and Dad gave me when I got my tonsils out and an embroidered cushion from Gran.

I was fighting back tears when I walked in the dining room. Mum and Dad were laughing at something Julian had said.

I gave Mum a peck on the cheek before sitting.

I felt like a horrible daughter. I grew up here, created so many wonderful memories. It might not be as opulent as the Rundells', but it was my home.

?

I threw the front door open, stepped into the living room, and cried. "Guess who's qualified?" I almost squealed like one of Carrie's girls; I could barely hold back my excitement. Now I was fully qualified, I would get a promotion, including a handsome pay rise and all my tasks would purely be nursing related. Finally. No more drudgery and answering the bloody phones.

Julian swigged his beer, his attention on the television. "That's great."

I jumped onto his lap, straddling him. Palming his cheeks, I shoved my head towards his, hoping my enthusiasm rubbed off. "Don't you get it? This is a *big* deal!"

He looked around me to see the TV. "I'm excited ... my team's about to lose, that's all."

"Who gives a shit? It's just football." I climbed off him.

"I do, Jess! Not everything can be about you!" His eyes were daggers, meeting mine for a split second before returning to the TV.

I stared at him, but he refused to meet my glare. I stomped out of the room, taking refuge in the bedroom. I plonked on the edge of the bed, ripped my boots off and threw them on the floor.

I heard him swear, followed by a loud clack, like the remote being chucked onto the coffee table. Then, silence.

I thought over the last few days, tooth picking moments to see if I had done something to upset him. Nothing came to mind. Things had been going so well lately. I couldn't even remember the last argument we had.

I didn't leave the room, preferring to read a book than risk confronting him. Let him cool off and watch his football, if that's what he wanted. I was half asleep when he entered the bedroom, startled awake by him loudly banging the door shut. He didn't look at me as he stomped around the room, readying himself for bed. When he finally slipped into the covers, it was with his backed turned to me.

I reached for his shoulder. He didn't react to my touch.

"Hey," I said. "Sorry I got so shitty."

"It's okay." He didn't turn around.

"Have I done something wrong?"

He finally turned around, his dark eyes piercing right through me. "How long have you been back in contact with Matt?"

46

"What? I'm not."

"I saw the message on your phone."

I rolled my eyes, remembering the message of congratulations he had sent for completing my course. "Rose must have told him I was finishing this week," I explained, my voice soothing. "He was congratulating me, that's all."

He pulled the covers tightly over him and turned back around. I nestled closer to him, my lips brushing his ear as I spoke. "I am not back in contact with Matt. It was one message. I haven't even replied yet. Julian ..." I put my palm to his cheek and turned his face towards me. "I love you. I am with you." I kissed him on the lips. He nodded, his face unchanged, and rolled away from me.

The following morning, it was serendipitous that Carrie and I were working our last ever shifts at Kendall's together. We had met on my first shift so it was fitting we finished together. She had completed her degree and was hired a few weeks ago by a property developer. She started Monday, the same day I was to start full time in my new position at the Darvo Animal Hospital.

I was bittersweet the whole shift. I would miss the sweet heady scent of the pastries and cinnamon scrolls. I'd miss my colleagues, but more than that, I'd miss working with my best friend.

When the shift ended, we gave teary hugs goodbye to the staff and each other, even though we would see each other later that night.

I headed home. I hadn't seen Julian since last night, as he left for work before I woke up. I opened the door, unsure of what I would find, hoping his mood had lifted.

The place was empty. I found myself sighing with relief, glad I didn't have to walk on tiptoes. I didn't want his bad mood to ruin my night out later.

I went into the bedroom.

A small gift bag lay on the bed. I picked it up with shaking fingers before ripping open the tissue-wrapped gift. A bottle of far-too-expensive perfume.

I couldn't contain my smile. I picked up the note and read, in Julian's blockish scrawl:

*My Dearest Jess,*

*You are the best thing in my life, and I will love you to*
*eternity.*

*All my love,*

*Julian xxx*

I leaned back on the bed, my eyes closed, the smile not leaving my lips.

I opened the front door and Meghan and Amelia burst inside. "Hi Jess!" They sang in unison.

"Hi girls," I said and smiled at Carrie who was halfway up the stairs carrying their pillows.

"You two ready to go sailing?" Julian said as he walked into the living room.

"Yeah!" Meghan said.

Amelia tugged at his shirt. "Can we go in the fastest boat you've got?"

"That's the attitude Amelia, absolutely!" He smiled and high-fived the nine-year-old.

My smile grew watching him interact with the two girls. I dreamt of watching him play with our own little cherubs one day. He saw me watching and walked over, planting a soft kiss on my neck. I cherished those little moments, which were more frequent of late. Last week he took me out to dinner when he knew I'd had a taxing day at work. This morning, a gorgeous note on my pillow. Nice text messages throughout the day, telling me he was always thinking of me and wanted to know how I was. I was the luckiest woman alive.

"Thanks again Jess," Carrie said, handing me the pillows. "I'm so relieved to have friends like you two." She hugged me and I could tell she was itching to leave to get ready for her big night on the town with Jim.

"You have nothing to worry about Carrie," Julian said. "We'll take good care of them."

"Yeah, Mum, you can go now." Meghan ushered her out the door as Carrie landed a hurried kiss on each of their foreheads.

When Carrie had gone, Julian turned to the girls, clapping his hands together. "Now, who wants lollies?"

After an afternoon of sailing, Julian let the girls have three servings of dessert before reluctantly telling them to brush their teeth, after finally cottoning on to my disapproving stares. We settled them together into the spare bedroom. We said our goodnights, my heart melting at the sweetness of the young girls tucked up in bed. I had not given much thought to when I might want children but babysitting these two made me look forward to it.

We shut the door and smiled at each other for our brilliant work as babysitters.

In the kitchen, Julian pulled two glasses from the cupboard. "Sweetie, would you like a glass of red?"

"Yes, please." I patted him lightly on his back.

We took our glasses and nestled into the couch to watch a movie.

"I think we're quite good at this babysitting gig," he said.

"Me too. It suits us." I leant my head against his shoulder. "We haven't talked about children much ... how do you feel? You want kids, right?"

"I'd like to have a few. Two or three. No more than three. But I definitely see myself as a dad."

"You'd make a great dad."

"Yeah. Maybe we should do lots of practice for when the time comes." He gave me a cheeky grin and kissed my neck, moving up to the edge of my chin towards my mouth.

"Not here, the girls could come out!" I slapped at his groping hands which were making their way down my back.

He chuckled and rested back on the couch. I snuggled into his chest. Our future as parents couldn't come soon enough.

—9—

# *Summer 2005*

I stomped into the kitchen, making zero effort to be quiet. The lever on the kettle almost snapped, I pushed it with such force. I smacked a mug onto the counter and landed the coffee jar with just as much force.

I took a deep breath, palm pressing my forehead. I had such a headache. I needed coffee. Coffee, and the early morning sun on my face to help unjumble my brain.

I headed to the sun-drenched balcony, clutching my steaming mug. I leant over the balustrade, closing my eyes, letting the sun fill me with warmth.

I swore under my breath; the peace didn't last long.

I hoped Julian felt as sick as me. I'd left him sprawled spread-eagled on the bed, snoring loudly. Normally, our Sunday mornings involved opening the curtains and mellowing naked in the warm hues. It was usually a long lie-in, followed by a decadent breakfast at a café along the riverfront. I would not be getting my chilli scrambled eggs this morning. I certainly wouldn't be enjoying the tender cuddles I longed for after we made love. It was normally my favourite morning of the week. Chatting about our future. Planning our week. Making love again.

I wouldn't be touching him this morning. I couldn't even explain what happened. But I felt sick to my stomach thinking about the night before. I had been woken by a sudden influx of light. It had taken me a few moments to work out what was going on.

There he stood. Leaning against the door jamb.

I sat up, rubbing at my eyes. "What's going on?"

"Who's been here?" He boomed. His eyes black with rage.

"What?" My voice cracked; dry from the wine I had enjoyed the night before. We had been at a party at the club, celebrating Bridget's birthday. We all had a blast, and when the bar closed, Julian carried on at a pub up the road with a few other guys. I'd had enough to drink and went straight home to bed. I was woken by Julian, who'd clearly returned straight from the pub.

"I know someone's been here." He pointed at me, so aggressive I could almost feel it from across the room. Such disgust on his face. I recoiled at the sight; I had never seen that expression before.

"Nobody has been here," I said, pulling the covers a bit higher. "I'm alone."

"I *know*. The toilet paper is different!" His aggressive finger pointed frantically at the en-suite.

"What?"

"You would never leave the toilet paper hanging like that!"

I got out of bed to see what he was talking about, avoiding getting too close to Julian's fury on the way. The toilet roll hung limply in place, a few squares longer than perhaps normal.

"There is nothing wrong with the toilet roll." My voice croaked; my mouth so dry it hurt to talk. "No one has been here."

Julian shook his head defiantly.

I made my way back to my side of the bed. The clock mutely screamed three thirty. I wanted to collapse back into the oblivion of sleep. "I don't know what to tell you. I love you. I would not cheat on you. No one has been here."

He scowled, still standing frozen in anger. He had never frightened me before. He loved me. He would never hurt me. I knew that. But my internal organs were welded together so tightly I felt I might expel my stomach contents right there.

I knew he was drunk, but he wasn't slurring as he spewed accusation after accusation. Arguing how I had a non-existent man in his apartment. We had not argued since he found out Matt sent me a message so many months ago. I lay in bed, paralysed under his glare, voice hoarse from pleading.

It took well over an hour to calm him. Even then, he collapsed onto the bed out of exhaustion, still unconvinced. I had lain there with my heart beating fast, staring at the roof, mind spiralling out of control. Why couldn't I convince him? What had I done that made him so unsure about us?

Those questions still ran over and over in my head as I cradled my coffee on the balcony.

I heard the toilet flush and I tensed. I didn't turn around. I stared at the opportunistic seagulls milling about in hope a crab would show themselves whilst the tide was low.

His hand landed on my shoulder. I held my breath. But it was a gentle touch. He brushed my hair to one side and his lips grazed my neck. Soft, slow and tender.

I turned around and rested my head against his chest. My headache forgotten.

# *Autumn 2005*

The morning glow was barely hinting of the day ahead as we packed the last of our supplies onto the catamaran. Julian was relocating the boat for an old friend, which meant sailing up the coast for a couple of days before flying home. Julian wanted to make a fun trip of it, so invited Luke and his friend, Rachel. He told me all about Rachel beforehand, how Luke had harboured a secret crush on her since high school. He was hoping she might feel the same by the end of the weekend.

"This is the last and most precious of cargo." Luke grinned as he walked onto the deck balancing two cartons of beer.

I rolled my eyes at Rachel. We chatted, getting to know each other while Julian and Luke attended the final prep before we set sail.

"Okay ladies," Julian said, rubbing his hands together, "I think we're all set. If it's not on board now, it's not coming!"

"Well, if nothing else," Luke said, "we have forty-eight cans of beer. A diet of champions." He patted Rachel on her shoulder.

Julian came to my side and planted a kiss on my cheek. He whispered in my ear. "Are you ready to depart, lovely lady?" His thumb grazed the nape of my neck. He could still send shivers down my spine.

"Absolutely, Skipper." I kissed him and headed to the bow to untie the last of the cleats in readiness to depart. I unbound the rope in seconds; it was so familiar to me now. I smiled, remembering the first time Julian taught me how to tie onto a cleat. It was two and a half years ago. I had knelt, fumbling with the rope, before his hands landed over mine, sending that first warm flush through me. His strong hands had guided me through the figure eights with such gentleness. That first electric touch changed my life.

Even now, his touch still sent jolts through my body. I was more in love than ever before. Sure, we had had some small missteps from time to time, but every couple argues, and we always made up.

The sun teased its appearance on the horizon as we made it out of the river mouth. A light breeze took up the sails, and soon we were slicing through the smooth swell.

I joined Julian in the open-air cockpit and wiggled my hand into his back pocket. He leaned in and kissed my forehead.

We silently watched the first rays dance over the water, stealing the morning chill from our faces. Trillions of tiny diamonds shimmered over the ocean surface, so bright it hurt my eyes.

Two days later we were docked in a little bay behind Conjur Island on our last night aboard the boat. It was about twenty minutes from the marina where we would hand the boat over the following morning. It had been a wonderful trip. Luke was sweet to Rachel the entire time. Showing her around the boat. Offering her food and drinks. Teaching her how to steer the boat. He had whispered to me last night, "I'd rather stay her good friend than risk losing her if I put the hard word on." So, three of the four separate berths remained full.

"You're such a sweetheart Luke," I had said. "One day, you'll find a beautiful woman who loves you."

Now, Luke and I were lazing around the front deck while Julian prepared to barbeque the reef fish Luke caught earlier.

Julian was sipping a beer by the barbeque with Rachel at his side, laughing. My chest tightened a little at the sight. But I knew he was just being nice. He was nice to everyone. The jealous pang was only because I loved him so much.

A few hours later, everyone was having a good crack at finishing the last of the alcohol that we boarded with. But I was spent.

"I'm going to call it a night," I said and went over to kiss Julian.

"Night, sweetie. I'll be in soon." He took another swig of beer.

I laid in bed listening to the banter continue for a while. I must have dozed off because when I woke, there were no sounds from above. My watch showed it was two thirty in the morning.

Julian was not next to me. A sinking feeling came over me as I realised everyone except Julian must have gone to bed. It didn't sound like anyone else was up. My mind swirled at a million miles a second. Maybe he just fell asleep on deck. But what if he'd fallen overboard after too much to drink?

I scrambled out of bed and up the stairs to the galley. There were no lights on upstairs. No voices. No sign of him in the cockpit. I climbed onto his captain's chair and scanned the deck.

The moon cast a bloom of light onto the bow. I blinked, taken by the beauty of the moment. Under the stars, two figures were entwined, kissing with vigour.

I smiled, thinking Luke and Rachel were finally hooking up.

A split second later, my chest contracted. The figure was too short and stocky to be Luke.

"What the fuck?" I screamed.

They broke apart as if stung, eyes searching in my direction. I almost fell from the chair as I rushed to escape the situation. But we were on a boat. There was nowhere to go.

I darted back inside and bumped into Luke, who was running up the steps.

"Jess, what's happened? Are you alright?" He reached for me, and I pulled away shaking my head.

Overwhelmed with sudden nausea, I ran to the bathroom, locking the door. I collapsed over the toilet bowl, clasping its sides as if holding on for life. Nothing came out.

I panted, overcome with sweat and dehydration and nausea from whatever the hell I just witnessed.

Voices erupted in the galley.

"What's going on? What's happened to Jess?" Luke's voice was raised and urgent.

"Don't worry about it," Julian said.

"Rachel, what's wrong?"

The sound of hurried footsteps down the steps, followed by a slamming door.

"What the fuck?" Luke demanded. "What's happened?"

"Nothing!" Julian said. "Your friend down there tried to kiss me, and Jess saw. That's it."

For a while, there were no sounds. Then another set of heavy steps and another door slammed.

I leant back against the wall and tried to control my breathing. Each heartbeat slower and less bounding than the one before. Hollowed, I succumbed to the icy river winding through my veins. Numbed to my core, I hugged my knees to my chest.

Heavy footsteps thumped towards me.

"Jess, open the door. It's not what you think. She came onto me."

Julian knocked on the door and shook the handle. "Open the fucking door, Jess."

I couldn't speak. I could barely breathe.

He knocked on the door again and after a while, nothing.

I sat on the bathroom floor, crying. It could have been ten minutes. It could have been an hour. There were no sounds other than the gentle lap of water against the hull. When I finally returned to the bedroom, I slipped in, opening it without a sound. I expected to find a repentant Julian sitting on the end of the bed. Instead, he was splayed out and snoring.

I closed the door again and went to the spare berth, and cried until there was no water left in me.

≗

I got a text from Julian the following afternoon.

*Jess, this is all a big misunderstanding. I am in love with you and wouldn't do anything to jeopardise what we have together. I'm landing late tonight and can't wait to see you. You are my future, Jess. I love you. All my love, Julian xoox*

I had taken an early flight home, having escaped the boat as soon as it docked. Julian was expected to arrive in a few hours. I wallowed away the hours in self pity. The rain relentless against the window.

I was lying in bed when I heard Julian come home. I curled deeper into the covers, hoping he would ignore me, thinking I was asleep.

He entered the bedroom, and I felt a thump on the end of the bed as he sat. He patted my leg through the blanket.

"You can't ignore me forever, Jess."

I sat up and opened my eyes, meeting his for the first time in what felt like days. I did not know what I was hoping to see. Remorse? Guilt? Love? But his eyes revealed nothing.

"Look ... I had a lot to drink the other night." He looked away. "I don't even remember what happened."

I could only scowl.

"I love you, Jess. But you can't keep punishing me for something I don't remember. I don't even know what happened."

I shook my head, unable to find the words. Finally, I spat, "You were all over her. I saw you."

"Like I said, I don't remember. But I didn't mean any of it. I am in love with you. I wouldn't do anything to hurt you."

"Well, this hurts Julian. It hurts a lot." A tear escaped my still swollen eyes.

He moved towards me and placed both hands on my shoulders. His eyes pleading with mine. "I'll never let anything come between us. You are my future. I only want to be with you. I won't hurt you ever again."

My blurry eyes lingered on his. Searching. I wanted to believe him.

———

"Close your eyes." Julian called. He had just come home from work and found me flipping through a magazine at the kitchen bench. He disappeared out the front door again.

My hands covered my eyes. The last two weeks had been one loving gesture or surprise after the other. He left a note on my car one morning: *Have a wonderful day, my love*. On Friday, an enormous flower arrangement was delivered to my work. He even took me out for a surprise booking at Marshall's.

Julian was making a colossal effort to ensure I felt loved again. It was working.

Besides, I couldn't leave. I gave up so much to be with Julian. My entire life plan was turned on its head when I chose him. It was never my intention to lose almost all contact with my old school friends. It had happened gradually. I chose to spend more time at Rochford with Julian, ignoring their invitations to hang at the surf club. I barely even spoke to Rose anymore; our social lives just too different.

Luke was the other casualty of that fateful boat cruise. He had still shown up at the club; he couldn't let down the crew, but he didn't talk to Julian and I. He barely talked to anyone, just walked around in a sad daze, his usual exuberance gone. Thankfully, it hadn't lasted long. Julian wouldn't tell me exactly what happened, but they seemed thick as thieves again. Like it never happened.

It wasn't so easy for me. Julian had me questioning everything about our relationship. I even contemplated leaving him; eventually finding every excuse to stay. If Julian couldn't remember what he did, was it really cheating? He promised me he wasn't attracted to Rachel, that he must have been so drunk he lost all sense. I chose to believe him. I had to.

"Okay, are your eyes covered?" His voice an octave higher than usual.

"Yes, what are you doing?" I giggled, unable to contain the joy of anticipation.

I heard some jostling of what sounded like a carboard box in front of me. "Okay," he said, and my eyes flew open to see the most adorable black-and-white fluff ball I ever saw. I almost teared up as I reached for the kitten and snuggled it into my chest.

"Oh Julian, how adorable!" I cooed. "But I thought you hated cats?"

He shrugged. "I thought you might like her."

"She's a girl?"

"Yep." He watched me cuddle the kitten with his head tipped to one side. A warm smile lighting his face.

"Thank you so much, I love her already!" I leant over the bench and kissed him.

It was immediate. My brain flashed to an image of Julian near inhaling Rachel, causing my chest to tighten. Every time he tried to kiss me, I thought of that moment. The kitten meowed, and I forced my mind back to the happy moment.

"What are you going to call her?"

"I think I'll call her ... Buffy. What do you think?" It was my favourite show as a teen.

"I think it's pretty perfect. Like you." He walked to my side of the bench and kissed me again. I kissed him back, forcing Rachel out of my mind.

# Spring 2006

"Mum, did you see me?" Meghan cried.

"Yes, honey," Carrie said. "You've improved so much. I'm so proud of you. Did you have a good time?" She ran her hand over her daughter's damp hair.

We were on the balcony of the yacht club. Julian and I had just finished a junior training session. He had let me take the lead today, something he was doing more often these days, seeing how much I took to it. It was wonderful watching them all grow so much as sailors each week, but I was especially proud of Amelia and Meghan. They were unstoppable now, having mastered the junior dinghy to race solo in their age groups.

"Yep, it was fun! Mum, can I have a packet of chips?" The thirteen-year-old smiled sweetly. "Please."

"Sure sweetheart. We're going in a minute though." Carrie gave Meghan some coins.

"I'm going to head off in a minute as well," I said. "Are you looking forward to Saturday?" I couldn't wait for this year's Darvo River Classic; we'd been training so hard for it.

"Yes! I'm with Oliver and Bridget, so you better look out!"

I laughed.

We sat enjoying the sinking afternoon sun as Meghan crunched on her salt and vinegar chips. I never tired of this view. I had watched the sun set over this river hundreds of times and there was always something new to offer. Today, a small tinny was gallantly towing a much larger pontoon vessel along the river. The grateful looking day trippers on board were thanking their rescuer enthusiastically.

Light fingers swept my hair to the side and familiar lips brushed the back of my neck, bringing an instant smile to my face. I turned, putting my arm around Julian and smiled at Amelia, standing by his side.

"Mum, can I have chips too?" Amelia asked Carrie.

"You can share Meghan's, honey."

"But I don't like that flavour!"

"You did last week."

"Well, I don't *now*."

I smiled at the eleven-year-old's outburst. On the boat before, she was a picture of maturity, taking her sailing as seriously as any adult I trained with. Off the boat, she argued about junk food like any other kid.

"Well, next time you two can share a flavour of your choice, Amelia."

"Mum, I don't want to share," Meghan piped in.

Carrie inhaled deeply. "These two little darlings are both a bit tired, I think." She put a hand on each of her daughter's shoulders. "So I think it's time for us to go."

"Come with me, Amelia," Julian said.

Amelia's face lit up and she trotted away with him.

Julian returned with a self-satisfied looking Amelia, trailing behind and crunching on her own pack of chips.

Carrie pursed her lips. "Thanks, Julian, but it wasn't that I didn't want to buy her chips. I don't like to spoil them and give in to their every command. Come on, girls. Let's go."

"Whoops," he said with a shrug. "I guess it was me spoiling her though so you're off the hook."

Carrie shook her head, waved at me and led the girls away. Amelia grinned at Julian, who sent her a wink.

"Julian, I don't think you should have done that." I said when they were gone. "She might think you were undermining her parenting."

"Relax. It's no big deal. Now, I hope you're hungry. I'm taking you out tonight and you'll never guess where."

⁓

Luke paraded around the club room, holding our trophy up high. Our team had won the Darvo River Classic. Hours later, I was still buzzing.

I refilled my spritzer and joined Oliver, who stood at a bar table with Bridget, Sarah and Carrie. The room was the fullest I'd ever seen it; so many members had turned up to watch or join the race. Now, they milled about, celebrating or mourning their losses while music played loudly in the background.

"Hey Oliver, that was bad luck today," I said. His team got towed in straight after the race started.

"Yeah," Oliver muttered. "It's no fun competing when you lose steering."

"Do you know what caused it?"

"If you ask me," Bridget said, a twinkle in her eye, "it's because Carrie was on our crew."

64

"What?" Carrie cried.

"I've heard you're bad luck for the Classic, Carrie." Sarah smirked, balancing her exhausted three-year-old daughter, Emily, to her hip. "You have to face facts."

"It wasn't my fault we lost steering." Carrie threw her hand to her chest.

We all chuckled and the music stopped.

Julian stood on the stage tapping the microphone. "Can I have everyone's attention, please." A few final murmurs died off before Julian continued, thanking everyone involved in running and partaking in the event. He waited for the clapping to die down and said, "Unfortunately, there can only be one winner to take the trophy. It is my greatest pleasure to thank my amazing and talented crew for helping me take out that title again today. I would like all of my crew to join me on the stage."

I looked sideways at Carrie. She took my drink and pushed me towards the stage. I stepped up reluctantly, joining Julian, Luke, and the rest of the crew.

"Please, give a huge round of applause to my crew."

Applause filled the room again. I stood awkwardly, a little flushed, while Luke bowed with gusto. As the clapping died down, the crew stepped off the stage. I made to follow, but Julian grabbed my hand, pulling me to his side. I sent him a questioning look, but he was looking out at the crowd.

He cleared his throat. "I'm sure most of you know, Jess is not only an integral part of my race team, but is also the *absolute* love of my life." He squeezed my hand.

I let out a nervous giggle, feeling my face turn bright red.

The room was silent. He turned to face me. Staring into my

eyes, he lowered onto one knee. My hand flew to my open mouth. Tears already welling in my eyes. I recognised Carrie's squeal from amongst the crowd.

"Jessica Foster ..."

My lower lip trembled as Luke put a small box into Julian's hand and took a step back. I made brief eye contact with Luke, who smiled.

I gaped at Julian.

"Would you do me the honour of becoming my wife?" He put the microphone down and presented the open box to me.

Tears were spilling now. I struggled to find the words. I managed to get out a small "Yes", before he placed the ring on my finger.

He stood and kissed me.

The hoots and hollers must have been heard all the way to the river mouth.

§

Julian raised an eyebrow, seemingly in disbelief that his twenty-two-year-old bride-to-be already had a kitchen bench full of bridal magazines.

I shrugged and continued flipping through the pages of extravagant gowns. "When should we set a date?"

He pulled a chopping board from under the bench. "We probably should do some saving. Maybe about twelve months?"

"Yeah, I was thinking the same." I smiled at the thought of becoming Julian's wife in twelve months. "How many should we have in our bridal party?"

"I don't mind. Luke will be my best man, I'd rather keep it small." He started cutting a tomato on the board. "Did you get margarine when you went to the shops this morning?" He opened the fridge door.

"Yeah, it should be there." I continued flipping through the magazine. "What do you think of this style?" I held up the magazine, pointing at a mermaid gown, but he screwed his nose up.

"Where's the margarine?" He rustled through the shelves.

I left the magazine open and went to the fridge. I immediately spotted it and reached over his arm to grab it. "Here it is." I put it next to the bread he had ready for sandwiches.

I went back to the other side of the kitchen bench and returned my focus to the magazine.

"That's not my margarine."

"It was on special," I said, without looking up.

"But that's not the margarine I like."

I looked up. He was staring at me with his head slightly tipped back, looking down his nose at me.

I straightened my back, matching his stare. "It was cheaper."

His nostrils flared. "I don't give a shit how cheap it was. I like my margarine brand."

"It's all the same, isn't it?"

"No, it's not all the same. I like my brand." His hands gripped the edge of the bench.

"Okay. Sorry. Next time I'll buy the other brand." I shrugged, looking back at the magazine.

Julian banged his fists on the bench, making me jump. He snatched up his keys and stamped towards the front door.

"Where are you going?" I said in bewilderment.

"I'm not eating that crap." He slammed the front door.

It took me a few moments to realise he was being serious.

I'd eaten by the time he got back, and was sitting on the balcony, still flipping through bridal magazines with Buffy curled on my lap. I heard him bang around in the kitchen for a few minutes.

I tried to keep reading as he huffed about, knowing I had done nothing wrong. I waited for him to come apologise for his outburst, but he didn't speak to me for the rest of the day. He remained focused on the TV, watching the football, and ignored me throughout dinner.

The following morning, I stood in the kitchen with the guilty spread, waiting for my toast to pop up. I tensed when he came in, dressed for work. He flipped the switch on the kettle without a word and got some bread ready for himself to toast. I walked to the fridge and got his margarine out.

I wrapped my arms over his shoulders from behind, holding the spread in front of his face. "Julian, I'm sorry. You had mentioned you like this, and I just forgot. I'm sorry. I don't want to argue over margarine."

I felt his shoulders relax and he turned slowly towards me. His face back to normal. All traces of that former anger gone. He kissed me slowly at first, but we were entwined with mutual intensity within seconds.

§

"I can't wait for you to see it, Mum. It's perfect!" I said, turning right onto the esplanade. "The chapel is divine. It sits right on the cliff face. The glass panels open entirely if the weather allows."

"It sounds stunning," Carrie said.

I smiled at Carrie in my rear view mirror. "Mum?" I said, briefly turning to look at her in the seat next to me before returning my attention to the road. Her hands were folded in her lap, and she seemed to be intent on something out the window.

"Hmm?" Mum said. "It sounds very ... generous."

"Yeah, I know. But Lyn and Greg are insisting on paying for it. 'Only the best for our son'," I mimicked Lyn.

"That's nice," Mum said.

"What about the reception?" Carrie asked.

"Yeah, that too," I said, somewhat embarrassed. "She said to choose any menu we like. That she wants us to have the most wonderful day." I darted a glance at Mum. "It's pretty nice of them, huh?"

Mum didn't say anything until we pulled up at the store. At the sight of the dresses in the display window, her eyes lit up, our former conversation seemingly forgotten.

We had a booking, and the friendly staff met us at the door and showed me to a range they had prepared in my size. I was in awe; this was something I had waited for since I was a little girl.

I carefully stepped into the first gown, paranoid about tearing or marking it. I'd never worn a dress worth more than one hundred dollars. It was a figure-hugging chemise gown, with beads over the entire bodice. It felt heavy to wear and had a price tag to match.

I smiled at myself in the mirror, feeling like a princess. "Okay, are you ready?"

"Yes, hurry up!" Mum called, who was sitting outside with Carrie, eager for the show.

I stepped out slowly. Mum's hand flew to her mouth. "You look so beautiful darling." Her voice cracked.

69

I smiled at having brought Mum near tears.

"Carrie?" I turned in the dress.

"It's nice, but I'm not sure it's you. Do you know what I mean?"

I nodded and returned to the dressing room to try on the next dress. Mum and Carrie continued chatting.

Once changed, I pushed the curtain to one side, and stepped out with my head high and shoulders back. I walked forward with an imaginary bouquet and silly smirk on my face. I did a dramatic spin for them in the pearl-coloured chiffon, in another figure-hugging style.

Carrie made a face. "This is not the one, love."

"You look beautiful, though," Mum said, her voice still a bit croaky.

I tried on dress after dress and was losing hope of finding something I loved. I needed the right dress. The dresses I tried had all been beautiful, but something was off about each of them. Too many beads, not enough beads, too old, too modern, the wrong shade of white. I found reason after reason not to pick each dress and started to feel desperate. I didn't know why I needed the perfect dress. I grew up sold on the idea of 'happily ever after', and I felt like a failure for not getting this first step right.

I took my time stepping into the next gown. It was strapless with bunched gossamer waves at the bodice and spilled out from my hips, reminding me of a princess dress I used to put on my Barbie doll. I stared at my reflection for a long moment before quietly walking out of the change room.

I stood before them, face carefully neutral.

"Oh, beautiful, honey," Mum said, face aglow.

Carrie nodded. Wordless for once.

"This one's a bit pricey," I said, almost a whisper.

Mum got to her feet and walked towards me. She fiddled with the bodice from behind, looking at me over my shoulder in the mirror. "You're not going to tell me the in-laws can spare no expense and I can't even buy my daughter a nice dress!" In a softer voice, she said, "We are here to choose the right dress, not the cheapest."

I smiled, tears creeping into the corner of my eyes. "This is the one."

§

Julian and I pulled into my parent's drive half an hour earlier than we were expected. I wanted to arrive sooner, but it was hard enough to convince Julian to come earlier at all. He didn't understand what I was so worried about. "My parents will love the place," he had told me. "Trust me." I knew he was right and I wanted to believe him, but the anxiety only seemed to grow.

I opened the front door and was greeted by the aroma of roast lamb and rosemary. The smell sent my tastebuds into a frenzy and some of the anxiety faded. Whatever Lyn thought of the place, Mum would not fail with her cooking.

"Hello," Mum said, greeting us from the foyer. "You're here early."

"I thought I could help tidy up," I said.

Mum pursed her lips. "Can you clean the guest toilet then, please? I didn't get a chance to get to it yet."

My smile dropped but Mum looked delighted. She headed off towards the kitchen with Julian trailing.

I stomped to the laundry and snatched up the cleaning products before making my way to the guest bathroom, annoyed that she had left it so late, glad we arrived early enough for me to fix it. I opened the door and was met by gleaming tiles and toilet bowl. It smelled like a candle shop. Well played, Mum.

"Very funny." I grumbled, steeling a carrot baton as I joined them at the kitchen bench.

She raised her eyebrows. "We're not *animals*, Jess."

"I know," I said. "Sorry." But I couldn't help but compare it to the Rundells' perfect house. Mum had clearly gone above and beyond to make the house clean and tidy, but it was still full of clutter, and the only artworks on display were one's I'd made as a child or cheap prints. I had to remind myself I loved this place. It was my home. It told our story. It's the kind of house I wanted my future kids to have. But I'd been putting off this day for so long, I just couldn't think rationally. I lost count of the amount of times Mum had asked to have Julian's parents over for dinner. I always made some pathetic excuse, but Mum finally put her foot down now that the wedding was around the corner, and I was out of excuses.

Half an hour later, there was a knock at the door.

We all gathered in the foyer to welcome them in. There were polite kisses and handshakes all around. Lyn was in heels, gleaming with jewellery, while Greg was in his usual full suit and tie. I looked at Dad, dressed in jeans and a loose-fitting linen shirt, with Mum in a comfortable cotton dress.

Mum shook Greg's hand and I noticed Lyn giving her a quick once-over.

"I like your shoes, Eve," Lyn said, after a pause.

Mum beamed. "Oh, thank you, Lyn. Jess thinks they're a bit

plain." She shot me a smug look.

"Right, who'd like a drink then?" Dad held up the bottle of shiraz Greg had given him and ushered us down the hall.

Greg pointed at the bottle. "Should be a nice drop that one. Limited edition."

"This is just lovely." Lyn cooed at Mum as we went down the hall. She stopped in front of one of my artworks from Year 12, which Mum had framed. "Cute."

I screwed up my nose; I was so proud of that one.

"Oh and is this little Jess?" She pointed a bejewelled finger at a photo of me at the beach, grinning at the camera as I showed off my sandcastle. "Oh, you were a freckly one. I hope my grandkids don't get that gene." She laughed and moved on.

I exchanged a look with Mum.

Outside in the entertaining area, we pulled up chairs at the outdoor table as Dad wrestled with the wine cork. I excused myself when Mum called me to help bring out dishes of food from the kitchen. I was careful not to trip down the step carrying the lamb showstopper. We placed the dishes at the centre of the table.

"This looks great, Eve." Greg rubbed his hands together and everyone nodded in agreement. Mum smiled, puffing her chest with pride, and encouraged all to dish up.

"Did you say you chose your dress already, Jess?" Lyn asked, spooning peas to her plate.

"It's gorgeous," Mum said. "Wait till you see it, Lyn!"

Lyn smiled. "Are you sure you don't want to go to any of the designer stores in the city? I could go with you next week and pay the difference for one, if you like?"

I wasn't sure where to look. Mum coughed and reached for her water. She sipped, apologising for something going down the wrong way. Lyn didn't appear to notice, smiling with pursed lips as she awaited my response.

"Thanks Lyn." I looked at Julian, but he was too involved in his plate to notice the conversation. I glanced sideways at Mum, who looked affronted by my answer. I turned back to Lyn. "That's very generous. But I love the dress Mum got for me."

Lyn opened her mouth, head cocked, and nodded. "Of course." She leaned towards Mum. "This lamb is divine, Eve. So flavoursome." She put a small fork full into her mouth.

Mum flashed me an eyebrow raise when Lyn looked away.

Lyn fiddled with her large, heavy looking earrings as she chatted to Mum and me.

"Those are lovely," Mum said. "Where are they from?"

"Oh these? I got these in Manhattan, actually."

"We've never been," Mum said.

"Really? You absolutely must go."

"We're just more the camping types for holidays." Mum shrugged, shooting me another pointed look.

Lyn covered her mouth with her hand as she chewed and nodded slowly. She looked about to say something but seemed to think better of it.

"Have you done much camping Lyn?" Dad asked. He was always good at filling the awkward silences.

"Oh God no!" Lyn laughed. "I mean, I'm sure it's *lovely*. But it's just not for me."

Dad considered her with a bemused expression. Mum's stern eyes darted between mine and Dad's. I took it as a warning for us to zip our lips with anything offensive.

I squeezed Julian's thigh to encourage his involvement in the conversation.

Julian cleared his throat. "Mum and Dad would camp, I'm sure. If you can point them in the direction of a five-star tent looking over Central Park." He chuckled and returned to his plate.

Not the intervention I wanted. My eyes darted from one to the other around the table. Lyn threw daggers at Julian before returning focus to her plate. Mum and Dad looked on the verge of laughter, but looked pained trying to hold it in. Everyone making such an effort not to offend the in-laws-to-be. Except Greg. I did not know if Greg was even aware of anything beside his plate.

I cleared my throat. Keen to change the subject. "Lyn, you said you liked the yard. Mum actually designed all this. This is what she does for a living."

"Oh, that sounds fabulous, Eve."

We got through the rest of dinner unscathed, and after Mum's fabulous chocolate cake, Greg and Lyn headed home.

"Well," I said, "that went pretty well, I think."

Julian shrugged. "You worry too much."

I kissed him on the cheek. "I better help Mum with the dishes."

I found Mum in the kitchen.

"Thanks for dinner, Mum. It was delicious. It was a great night. Really."

"It was nothing," Mum said, shrugging. She lowered her voice, though it was only us in the kitchen. "Are you sure you don't want to go shopping with Lyn for a designer dress?"

I grinned at her. "No, of course not. I love the one you got me."

Mum smiled. She let her shoulders drop as if dumping a heavy burden. Even if I didn't love the dress, I would never do that to her, but I think she was second guessing. This whole evening had us all on edge and acting out of sorts. We could relax again now.

I grabbed the dish in her hands and loaded into the dishwasher. "Here, let me finish up. You deserve the night off."

Mum poured herself a glass of wine and joined Dad and Julian in the living room, leaving me to finish up cleaning.

Once alone, I sighed deeply, the anxiety falling from my shoulders at last.

# *Autumn 2007*

I leaned forward and kissed my *husband*.

It still felt unreal that he was my husband and I, his wife. He was the same person as before, but everything had changed. It felt like the beginning of the life I always dreamt of.

The ceremony had been everything I hoped it would be. It was like walking into a fairytale; the seaside chapel perched high on the cliff face, overlooking the sparkling ocean. The afternoon sun bathing everything in an incandescent glow. My white gossamer gown, every girl's dream, spilling out behind me. Dad walking me down the aisle, holding back tears. Julian, waiting for me at the end of the chapel, the man of my dreams.

Before I knew it, we both had said "I do", and Julian was lifting the veil over my face for our first kiss as husband and wife. We turned to face the crowd with our hands up and every guest stood to applaud.

Now, Julian and I were spinning around on the dance floor, surrounded by our friends and family.

"You look beautiful," Julian whispered, lips brushing at my ear lobe, *"Mrs Rundell"*.

Shivers ran up and down my body. Mrs Rundell. I could get used to that.

Julian spun me again before we walked hand in hand off the dance floor. We were pulled up by two of Julian's many cousins. There was no hope of remembering all their names.

"Welcome to the family," said the tall blonde.

His square-faced sidekick laughed. "I knew Julian would have to stick with one sooner or later."

"I'm not sure what you mean," I said, shaking my head.

"Yeah, how many girlfriends did you have to buy twenty-first presents for, Julian?" the tall blonde said, grinning widely.

Julian glared at the duo and steered me away with his arm around my shoulder. "A few of my cousins think they are comedians," he said, loud enough for them to hear.

We were curtailed by another of Julian's cousins. He leant in, planting a wet kiss on my cheek. I tried not to wipe it away immediately.

"I'm glad to finally meet you, Jess. I didn't believe you existed when I first got the invite." He laughed, standing too close for comfort. The stench of whiskey and cigarettes was strong.

I leant away, nodding and smiling, while Julian steered me away, sending another cousin yet another glare.

We passed the table where Mum and Dad sat with Lyn and Greg.

Lyn was chatting animatedly to Mum, her voice slightly slurred. "Oh these?" She fingered her earrings. "These are from a little local designer. He has a showroom but doesn't open to the public all the time. They are handmade, one of a kind."

"They are just beautiful," Mum said.

"Hey, how is everyone?" Julian asked as we joined the table.

"Great, how is our favourite couple?" Greg lifted a glass in cheers.

"I just met some interesting characters in Julian's cousins," I said.

Lyn gave Julian a questioning stare.

"Brad and Neville were being stupid," Julian said.

"Oh, pay them no mind Jess." Lyn hiccupped. "They have always been *shits*." She took a large sip of wine.

Mum and I shared surprised smirks. I'd never heard Lyn swear.

The MC announced desserts were being served and we made our way to the bridal table. I was looking forward to trying the lemon tart and managed to gobble a mouthful before Carrie dragged me back onto the dancefloor.

Carrie and I laughed when we spotted Julian spinning Amelia around, the twelve-year-old giggling with delight. Amelia and Meghan were the only children invited to the wedding; it wasn't even a question of them coming.

"Hello, Mrs Rundell," Luke said, grinning cheekily as he and his new girlfriend, Chloe, passed us by. He hadn't left her side all night.

"I like the sound of that!" I said.

"Congratulations," Chloe said with a warm smile. "It was a beautiful ceremony."

"Yeah, congratulations, Jess," Luke said in a silly voice.

I shook my head. "Hey, thanks for the great speech, by the way."

As the best man, Luke's speech was heartfelt, despite starting with his usual gutter humour. He had held the mic to his mouth and clutched the crumpled paper his speech was written on in his other hand. He'd cleared his throat loudly before beginning. "Now ... *fornication* ..." He paused as people looked at each other, cheerful bewilderment on most faces. "Sorry." He cleared his throat again. "For an occasion ... such as this ..." He was forced to pause as the room erupted with laughter. His face delighted.

"No worries, bud," Luke said. He held a hand to his heart, a playful expression on his face. "It came from the heart."

"It was lovely," I said.

"I could have easily gone the other way," Luke continued. "Plenty of material on your husband, but I chose the honourable route."

"I think you said plenty of embarrassing stories, anyway, Luke," I laughed.

"Ah but I didn't talk about the buck's night," he said, eyes twinkling.

My ears perked. "Oh? What happened?"

He fingered a large cross over his chest. "What goes on the mountain ..."

I put my hand up. "I know, I know ... stays on the mountain! You are no help, Luke."

He winked and twirled Chloe away.

"I wonder what happened," I said to Carrie, who had stopped dancing, watching Luke's retreating figure with a slight crease between her brows.

"Julian told you about the ..." Carrie let the word hang.

"Strippers?" I offered. "Yeah. He mentioned Luke wanted strippers before the night even happened. I'm okay with it. It's pretty normal for a buck's night."

Carrie nodded. "Jim got home at one thirty. It sounds like it was actually a pretty tame night. Luke's stirring things up."

I tried to hold my smile firm in place and nodded. "I'm getting another drink. Want anything?"

I walked towards the bar, mind reeling. I passed Julian, who was now spinning both Amelia and Meghan to a pop song I'd never heard of.

Julian had already told me there were strippers. But he didn't get home until four in the morning. If everyone else finished at one thirty, where was Julian?

My mind ran in circles. I couldn't stand it. The song ended and Julian came towards the bar. Marty from the club kept his pace and threw his arm over Julian's shoulder.

"Well, I hope your sex life was good while it existed buddy." Marty chuckled, patting Julian on the shoulder.

"Julian, I need to talk to you." My voice brisker from the sparkling wine. I scowled at Marty and pulled Julian away from him. His brow furrowed. "Where did you go after your buck's party?"

He looked affronted. "Jeez, Jess. I know we're married but just cool it with the ball and chain a bit. I was at Luke's."

"That's it? Just at Luke's?" My anxiety was replaced with instant guilt.

"Yeah of course."

"Shit, I'm sorry honey." I knew there must have been an innocent explanation. I drained my drink and dragged my husband back to the dancefloor.

How stupid to let something so silly almost spoil our day.

# Winter 2007

The latch on the front door clicked and I turned to see Julian coming in from work. His tie was already loosened, and he came straight to kiss my cheek at the dining table.

"Something smells good, Mrs Rundell," he said, making me grin wider. Nothing made me prouder than taking on the Rundell name.

"Thanks, there's a casserole in the slow cooker." I opened my purse, pulling out my new driver's licence. "Speaking of Mrs Rundell – look what I got today." I held out the licence confirming my changed surname.

"Well, have a look at that. It's official now, sweetie. No turning back." He kissed my lips before heading to the bedroom. I continued folding the washing on the table and smiled, reading the name on my licence again as it rested next to my purse. It was surreal to see the name in print. In a strange way, it felt more official than the actual marriage ceremony.

Julian returned after changing and headed to the fridge, grabbing a beer. He took a seat at the table as I continued folding, moving on to his socks and underwear.

"Oh," Julian said, "I've been meaning to show you a better way to do this." He did that a lot; liked to show me better ways of doing things. He grabbed the socks from my hands. "My socks are always folded like this." He unwound my simple ball up, taking time turning each sock inside out halfway up, before balling them together again.

I raised an eyebrow. "I don't get the point. It takes twice as long."

"Maybe. But look." He took the socks he had just bound and pulled one halfway up his foot before pulling the inside out part up to his ankle.

"It makes it much faster to put on." He grinned like he'd solved global warming.

I felt like saying, "I think you can fold your own damn socks." But I held my tongue. It was easier to do things his way. I didn't want to start an argument. Our honeymoon to Vietnam was months ago but I was still riding on the newlywed bliss like it was yesterday. Instead, I nodded and changed the subject. "So, looking forward to tonight?"

Rochford's annual general meeting was tonight and the President of over ten years advised he wouldn't be running again. It was the off season, and all the phones were still running hot around the club with rumours of who was in the running. Julian had put his name in the mix, and now was an official candidate to be President of the club.

"Yeah," he said. "Looks like everyone's going."

I parted my lips with a nervous grin. "Are you nervous?"

"Nah."

"You've got it in the bag. I know it."

He shrugged. He might have appeared nonchalant, but I knew how much he wanted the job. Rochford Sailing Club was his life. He'd given so much to the club. Everyone knew he deserved the job. I just hoped his age didn't get in the way. The retiring President was well in his sixties, and historically, most Presidents weren't as young as thirty-five.

"We'll see," he said, taking a swig of beer.

9

I woke to banging on the front door. Disorientated, I scrambled to pull on my dressing gown. The clock read three thirty am.

It was probably Julian. He must have forgotten his keys. He had kicked on in town with some guys after his landslide victory. He was now officially President of Rochford Sailing Club. I had headed home after the club shut, happy to let Julian celebrate to his heart's content with his mates. He deserved it.

The banging got louder. I fumbled for my slippers but quickly gave up, jogging barefoot towards the door. Torch lights shone through the windows.

I paused, looking through the peephole.

My jaw dropped. Two men in uniform. Julian in handcuffs.

I rushed to undo the chain and door latch.

"What's going on." I said, tongue heavy.

"Is this your husband?" one of the officers said.

"Yes," I choked. "What's happened?"

"It's just a misunderstanding, sweetie," Julian said. I tried to read his expression, but his head was bowed and the night hid his face in shadows.

I searched the officer's face instead. It was hard as stone. "We got a complaint from the people living in the apartment below you," the officer said. "They allegedly caught this gentleman breaking in

84

through their bedroom window."

"Oh my god!" I cried.

"I thought you locked me out. I was just on the wrong floor." Julian shrugged.

"We just wanted to see if he does in fact live here before we take him to the station."

I couldn't speak. I just stared at them, hugging my arms around my dressing gown. I nodded. The two young officers wished me a good night and told me I could collect Julian from the station some time the next day.

"I love you," Julian called over his shoulder as they led him down the steps.

I closed the door and let my full weight flop against it.

I couldn't find sleep again. I laid awake the rest of the night worrying about what conditions Julian was being held in. Concerned he might be cold or that he wouldn't have a mattress. Worried who he might share a cell with. As the hours drew on and night became day, my worry turned to anger. Who gets so drunk they actually break into someone else's house? I had never been that drunk. He should know better. He was not a stupid teenager anymore. He was thirty-five years old.

Several hours later and four coffees downed, I drove to the police station.

I entered the station and the constable behind the counter directed me to take a seat.

The officer led Julian through a barred door towards me. He looked about as well rested as I felt. His shirt untucked and wrinkled, face dark with stubble, and hair tufting off in all directions, due for a cut.

My jaw hurt from clenching my teeth so tight.

I led him silently towards the car. Once inside, I exploded, "My god, Julian, you're not a teenager! What were you thinking?"

He groaned. "Don't start."

"Are you kidding? I don't appreciate being woken by the police at three thirty in the bloody morning. I'm not going to 'give it a rest', Julian!"

He looked out the passenger window, avoiding my eyes. "Relax. They're not pressing charges."

"Who? The neighbours below us?"

"Yeah."

"Well, aren't you bloody lucky?"

"Get off your high horse, Jess. It's not like your fucking perfect."

My jaw dropped. How could he make this about me? I couldn't talk again. I would just say things I would regret. So I settled with glaring at him, letting my face do the talking.

He rested his head back on the seat and was asleep within minutes.

۰

# Spring 2007

The parrots woke me at daybreak. The racket, undampened through canvas, curving my lips into grin before even opening my eyelids. Lake Hemsworth was my favourite place to holiday; getting back in touch with nature and its rhythms, swapping alarm clocks for bird calls, mattresses for hard earth. No concern of folding socks correctly or buying the right brand of margarine. It had been a long road learning all his little idiosyncrasies. But I was glad to do those things if that's what made him happy. That's what love is. Small gestures and knowing your partners likes and dislikes. Here, Julian planned our campfire meals and cooked all the barbeque meats he desired. This was his happy place, and it was rare to hear him complain. The birds were a full orchestra now. I eyed Julian's sleeping figure next to me, as still as stone. He could sleep through a fire alarm.

Rustling and whispers came from the tent next to us. Probably Amelia and Meghan getting dressed. They were always early risers.

When I heard a zipper, I threw a hoodie over my flannelette pyjamas. I poked my head through the tent door and was greeted with a stunning sunrise across the lake. The gentle glow of the sun reflecting off the water brightened the weeping willows framing the campsite.

I stayed where I was for a few minutes, taking it all in, before crawling out of the tent. I mouthed a quiet good morning to the girls and Carrie.

Even out here, the day began with coffee. I put a pot of water to boil on the gas stove. I held up a coffee cup to Carrie and she nodded gratefully. When the coffee was made, we took our mugs to the fire pit and sat in the morning sun.

Amelia walked towards us with hair resembling a discarded bird's nest. She hated brushing it, so they had cut her long auburn locks to shoulder length to keep it manageable.

"You're going to end up with dreadlocks if you don't put a comb through that mop soon Amelia," I said.

She smiled. "What? There's nothing wrong with my hair." She stuffed a cap over it. "Is Julian awake yet?"

"Not yet."

"What would you like for breakfast, sweetheart?" Carrie asked.

Amelia was getting ash all over her fingers piling kindling into the burnt-out pit. The breeze picked up and blew the fine ash straight into my face. I coughed as it tickled at the back of my nose.

"Can I have a toasty with canned spaghetti in it?"

Carrie and I both turned our noses up at her answer.

"Yuck," Carrie said. "But alright. Can you get the fire going again, sweetie?"

Amelia nodded. She had always helped whoever was getting the fire lit. Often trailing after Julian and whatever activity he was involved in, as she was interested in all kinds of outdoor activities. Especially anything that involved dirt. Yesterday she joined Julian rigging fishing rods, baiting them and casting them into the lake at dusk. A little glow in the dark worm and bell clipped to the rod to alert them when a fish was on the line.

Julian was in his element out here, and I loved watching him

88

with the girls. It was easy to forget our little quibbles over the past few months. Newlyweds as we were, we still had our arguments, but seeing him be such a good mentor to these girls reminded me why I married him.

Last night, Julian had almost tripped as he darted across the camp, running towards the ringing bell and glow worm frantically jiggling. He'd shouted, "Someone get Amelia" as he headed towards the water, grabbing the rod to make sure he didn't lose the fish. Carrie went to fetch Amelia while we followed Julian to the lake.

"It's a good one," he said. He reeled in a little before letting it run out again.

In the glow of the fire, the half asleep twelve-year-old had stepped gingerly in her slippers towards us, rubbing her eyes.

"It's your fish Milly," Julian said, his smile open and encouraging. "Come on. Reel it in!"

She took the rod, looking dazed. She had been asleep for over two hours.

"That's it, Milly," Julian said.

A smile crept across Amelia's lips.

"Let it run a little now." Julian put his hands over hers for a second, guiding her, before standing back to watch. "That's it."

She looked at Julian for approval.

I couldn't stop smiling, imagining our future child looking up to Julian just as wide-eyed and trusting. Julian teaching them but not overbearing, guiding them but letting them figure things out on their own.

"Okay now," he said. "You've got it. Keep reeling."

Appearing more awake, Amelia's face filled with delight as the large fish thrashed in the shallows.

Julian walked forward and scooped the fish into the net and returned to her side.

"Check out this beast! Well done, Amelia. Do you want to remove the hook?"

She had screwed up her nose and shook her head. She might have been outdoorsy, but handling fish in your pyjamas was a big ask of anyone. However, she had more than happily posed for a photo next to Julian, proudly holding the fish in front of her. Both grinning ear to ear. One day, I hoped he would replicate the special moment with our own brood.

Now, Amelia appeared well-rested despite last night's disturbance. She stoked the fire, bringing it back to life.

"Are you going to cook the fish today?" I asked her.

Amelia's face lit up. "Yep! We're having it for dinner. When Julian gets up, he's showing me how to gut it."

I chuckled at her enthusiasm for the gory task.

"I'll wake him soon," I said.

I went back to the tent and found Julian, still deep in sleep. I put my hand on his shoulder. He stirred, opening his eyes, blinking at me. A frown passed over his face.

"Amelia's keen to gut the fish," I murmured, stroking his shoulder.

The frown vanished, replaced by a sleepy smile. "That girl. Tell her I'll be five minutes. Could you make me a coffee, sweetie?"

I nodded and left the tent. I grabbed his favourite camp mug and took care to spoon in the right amount of coffee and sugar. Twirling my hair in my fingers while I waited for the water to boil, I daydreamed of Julian as a father. There was simply no contest of a more perfect man to raise a family with.

# Summer 2008

"**D**o you think they are negotiable?" I asked the real estate agent, looking around the dated kitchen. The cream tiles, with stained grout, showed years of wear. But when I first saw them, I immediately thought of the original tiles in my parent's house when I was a kid. The house was in dire need of a renovation, but it felt like a home.

"Everything's negotiable," he said, throwing a salesman's grin.

I nodded and continued looking around, wearing my best poker face.

"Give us a few minutes," Julian said.

"Yes, of course." The agent exited through the front door.

"What do you think, hon?" I asked, leaning against the laminated counter.

His nose scrunched. "It's a good position. If I can't be on the river, I'll settle for being close to the club." His eyes showed disgust as they scanned around us. "At least you can see the river."

"The position is great. I know it's dated, but it's all cosmetic stuff."

He shoved his hands in his pockets and kicked at the edge of the kitchen bench. "Dated is an understatement."

"It's the best I've seen in our price range." I tilted my head, imploring.

He straightened. "But it doesn't have to be."

"We've talked about this," I said, taking his heavy hand in mine. "I want our first home to be *our* home. It was a very generous offer from Lyn, but can't we just do this ourselves?"

Another huff. "Okay. What if we put in an ultra-low offer and see how it goes? It's been on the market a few months. At least then we'd be able to afford to renovate quicker." He looked around the kitchen, his nose slightly upturned.

"Let's do it!" I squealed and kissed him.

I strolled through the house as Julian talked to the agent. My eyes were drawn to the kitchen's large breakfast bar. I pictured serving my children cereal at the bench someday. I could almost hear their toes tapping against the bench as they swung their feet impatiently on the stool.

Julian and the agent found me in the master bedroom where I was already picturing what colour linen I'd get, whether I'd stick with the floorboards or get new carpet, and where I'd put my vanity to catch the morning light.

"Let's go," Julian said, his face neutral.

Julian and I walked to my car. I made to go to the driver's side, but Julian took the keys from my hand and got into the driver's seat. He didn't have his car, as he had walked up from the club, and I met him straight from work.

I shrugged. Julian always drove, unless I was the only sober one. It didn't bother me and wasn't worth an argument.

As soon as he turned the key in the ignition, a pop song blared through the speakers. Julian reached forward and flicked the radio to the station he liked. He always did that. Never once had he asked. It irritated me, but I bit my tongue. Music, too, was not worth the drama of an argument.

"So, you put the offer in?" I asked.

"Yep. He'll let us know when he speaks to the vendor." He put my sedan in reverse and twisted to look over his shoulder.

"How exciting!" I clapped my hands staring at our potential home as we pulled away.

It was a long few days later, when Julian came home from work and plonked a bottle of champagne in front of me.

"Oh my god!" I squealed. "They accepted the offer?"

"We bought a house." Julian laughed and popped the cork.

I smiled, already daydreaming of bathing my little babies in the large bathtub. Barbeques in the yard with our friends. Julian always by my side.

。

I moved around our yard, full to the brim with our friends and family for our housewarming party. *Our* yard, of *our* first home. I'd been frantic the past few days making the house fit for company, but some things were still in boxes. Nobody seemed to notice, while Julian was putting the new barbeque to good use.

I approached Oliver and Nick, who were examining a water feature Mum helped me install.

"Mum designed that one," I said.

They nodded appreciatively.

"Having a good time?" I asked. They both nodded, the light strewn by the coloured party bulbs highlighting the rose on their cheeks.

"I'm empty, Jess," Oliver said, holding up his empty beer can. "I'll

93

be back. Great house by the way. Lots of potential!" Oliver left me with Nick.

"How are you liking the club so far, Nick?" He joined Rochford during the season.

"It's great!" Nick said. "I love how competitive it is and everyone is so welcoming."

"I'm sure it will feel like a second family to you before long. Where is it you're from again?"

"I went to school in Tawny and moved to the city for university, then to Darvo River last year."

"What did you study?"

"Marine biology."

"Cool. My friend, Rose, studied that." I sipped my drink and admired all the cheery faces a few hours into the boozy party.

"Rose Colley? She was in my year!"

"No way! What a small world." I slapped a hand lightly on his shoulder.

We were both giggling when Julian joined us and put his arm around my shoulders.

"Hey, Julian, you'll never guess. Nick studied with my friend Rose!"

"Is that right?" Julian raised his eyebrows, eyeing Nick. "Sweetie, did we have more chips to put out?" He was grinning at Nick.

"Yep, sure, I'll get some. Seriously, what a small world!" I smiled and left for the kitchen. I reached high in the pantry, grabbing a packet of corn chips and salt-and-vinegar chips.

I was pouring them in bowls when I heard shouts outside.

"Stop!"

"Get off him!"

A loud crack and something shattering.

"Stop!"

"You're hurting him!"

"Julian!"

I dropped the chips and ran outside.

I pushed through the crowd and saw him.

I screamed.

Julian's forearm was pressed against Nick's throat, pushing him up against the brick wall. Luke and Oliver were pulling at Julian's shirt, trying to talk him down. Julian's eyes glared up at Nick's. One side of his upper lip curled up in fury.

I grabbed at him, pulling with my full body weight. My efforts fruitless.

"Stay away from her, cunt," Julian snarled at Nick.

Nick's face had turned a dusky purple when Julian flung back his arm with such force I was hurled away, landing heavily on my backside. Still raging, Julian spun and pushed Luke to the ground before confronting Oliver, who put his hands in the air and backed away.

Julian panted, shooting menacing scowls all around, looking ready to fight anyone in his way. People backed further away. Finally, he leant forward and pulled me to my feet.

"I didn't mean to push you, are you alright?" His voice near normal again.

"What the fuck?" I pulled my hand away and turned to Nick. He was bent forward, clutching at his throat with a strange raggedy tune to his breath. "Oh my god ... Nick, I'm so sorry." I reached to see his neck. "Are you okay? Are you hurt?"

Nick rubbed at his neck and swallowed, wincing. The colour returning to his face.

I heard Julian muttering over my shoulder. I turned and saw Julian walking away, shoulders squared, led by Luke. Luke's placating tone drifting off as they rounded the side of the house.

With the party vibe lost, people started to leave. I apologised to each and received many sympathetic faces.

Eventually only Luke and his girlfriend, Chloe, were left. Julian was nowhere to be seen.

"Luke, what happened?" I asked.

"He says Nick said something about you that pissed him off."

"Really? That doesn't sound like Nick." I looked around. "Where is Julian?"

"He went inside." He put his hand on my shoulder. "Don't worry, bud, he'll be right as rain by morning."

I nodded without feeling very positive. "Poor Nick. Great welcome to the club. And my housewarming party ..."

"It was a great party, Jess." Chloe placed her hand on my shoulder.

"Yeah, we won't forget this one in a hurry!" Luke forced a chuckle.

I laughed a little, but tears welled in my eyes now the shock was wearing off.

"Hey, don't cry. Oh, come here." Luke pulled me into his chest. The top of my head barely reaching his shoulder. I let out a small sob.

The tears stopped, and I made Luke and Chloe leave, even though they offered to stay and help clean up. Suddenly sober, I went to work piling empty cans and bottles into the recycling bin. Buffy tailing me, making her first appearance of the night now that the guests were gone. Finally, when everything was tidied up, I went to the bedroom, exhausted, ready to collapse into bed. I couldn't face another confrontation, so I was relieved when I found Julian snoring.

The following morning, I spent time cleaning the remaining dishes I had left in the sink late last night, and disposed of the remnants of Mum's planter; the unwitting victim of last night. I let each piece drop from full height into the tall bin, leaving a gap between each bang.

Julian finally surfaced, looking dishevelled in his boxers.

I rounded on him in the kitchen. "What the hell happened last night?"

He huffed and turned on the kettle. "It was his fault. He ... said something about you."

"What?"

"You don't need to know."

What could Nick have said? He had always been friendly to me at the club.

"It's hard to believe anything he said would give you a reason to behave the way you did. You might have seriously hurt him."

"Yeah, well, he's fine, isn't he? He walked out of here."

"Julian ..."

"Fine, alright, maybe I shouldn't have pushed him that hard, but there is no excusing his behaviour."

"Which was?"

"No, I won't repeat it. He's a dipshit, Jess. Face it. He should have never come. Disrespecting the hosts of a party like that is unforgivable."

I looked at him suspiciously. Feeling tired again, I gave up. It was clear there would be no explanation. Julian would never do what he didn't want to do.

The following morning, I left early for work before he was up. I couldn't be bothered with him. Last night, he had been nice as pie, offering me hot chocolate and doing the dishes after dinner. I was not impressed.

In the evening, Julian came in from work holding a purple wrapped package. He held it out to me, eyes pleading. He didn't have to say sorry. I knew he was.

I took the gift from him and untied the bow.

His hand rested on my thigh. Something he rarely did since we were married.

I ripped open the wrapping paper. My jaw dropped.

"It's the latest model!" he said, grinning.

"Is this a new sim card too?" I asked, confused.

"Yep. You've got a new number. I've set you up on my business plan with the phone company, so you don't have to worry about anything."

"I have a new number?" I suddenly felt attached to my first ever mobile number. I forced a smile. I didn't want to seem ungrateful. This was a lovely thing for him to do. I didn't even want to think of the cost.

"Wait till you see the pictures you can take with this." He turned the phone over and showed me the lens.

I sat in awe of my larger, much flashier phone. I held my current phone up and it looked archaic. Maybe I did need a new phone.

I kissed him again. He put his arm around my shoulders, another thing he had rarely done since we married. I missed it.

# Winter 2009

Last night was the last straw. I walked into the living room and stood in front of Julian, blocking his view of the television.

He huffed as I grabbed the remote and lowered the volume.

"Look ..." I began. "We need to talk. This is happening more and more. I'm sick of being woken at five in the morning with you coming in drunk. I don't want to be married to a teenager. When are you going to grow up?" I lost a bit of composure as I waited for his response.

Without saying a word, he got off the couch and walked towards our kitchen. I followed.

"Julian, I'm serious. This has got to stop."

He poured himself a large glass red wine. Eyeing me, he took a mouthful. And another. He rubbed his stubble, his expression thoughtful.

"What about you, Jess?" His dark eyes reduced to slits. "When are you going to be perfect?"

My eyes matched his. "We're talking about you here, Julian, and your behaviour."

"You're not perfect, you know. You don't even put the lid on the toothpaste properly."

I squeezed my eyes shut. Hoping when I opened them, I would understand what he was going on about.

He went on, his voice louder. "You don't!" He pointed at me. "And it goes all crusty around the edge."

"*Really*? You want to make this about toothpaste? Should I get started on the fact you can't even be bothered picking your clothes off the floor to put in the laundry basket?"

He nodded and looked at the ceiling, a sinister grin forming on his lips. "You know ... this is exactly what everyone warned me about. You get married and she'll start whining about every ... little ... thing!" He jabbed his finger onto the bench with each word.

"No, it's not a little–"

He cut me off. "And they warned me marriage would be the end of our sex life!"

"What?" I crossed my arms.

"Exactly! We barely ever have sex anymore." He leant, defiant, against the bench, his face vicious.

"Julian ... we have sex all the time."

"Bullshit."

"I don't know what you're talking about. We have sex at *least* three or four times a week." My mind was reeling, feverishly searching for correct figures. I knew we had sex two nights ago, and the day before that. I thought hard. In the morning, yes, we had sex in the morning and the night before. That's four times just this past week.

"You need to get your head checked, Jess, because it's full of crap!" He stepped forward pointing at my head. "We never have it! I knew this would happen if I married you."

I pushed his hand away. "My god! It's like you're talking about a completely different relationship. We have sex all the time."

He kept going on. There was no stopping him. It was like winding up a toy that slapped cymbals together. You regretted it as soon as it started the horrible noise and this one seemed to have no end. An hour passed and he had chugged the bottle of red and was still going at me.

Two hours later, the entire neighbourhood was aware of our sexless marriage, how bad I was at cleaning the house, how little I worked and how I ruined his life buying this house. I was exhausted. Stunned and unable to make sense of any of it. Eventually, I could take no more and stormed off to the bedroom. It was Sunday night and I had to work the early shift in the morning. I needed rest. I switched off my bedside lamp when I heard him turn the door handle. I rolled onto my side, as far away from his side of the bed as possible, and pretended to be asleep. He made no effort to be quiet as he readied for bed.

When it was clear he had fallen asleep, I turned onto my back and stared at the ceiling. I was exhausted but couldn't sleep. My pulse; a garbled quiver. My brain confounded, searching for a way to avoid another tirade from him. I needed proof when he accused me of such things. He was so insistent, he could almost convince me of untruths. I decided to keep a diary of every time we had sex. He had me questioning not just my memory, but my whole self. I couldn't let that happen again.

The following morning, I left before he was up, so I didn't see him until late that evening. He ate his dinner on the couch with scarcely a grunt at me. After two more days of the silent treatment, I couldn't take any more. I approached him in the kitchen as he was rinsing a dish in the sink. I put my hand on the bench and faced him.

"Look, Julian, we can't go on like this. I feel like crap."

He nodded but gave nothing else.

"We both need to make more effort in our relationship," I said.

"Couples fight and argue. It's perfectly normal. It would be weird if we didn't."

I waited for his response. It was barely a sniff.

"I'm sorry that things got so out of hand." I searched his face. "And I'm sorry that I had a go at you. I would like us both to move forward and commit to being better. Better to each other."

He nodded again but stayed focused on his plate.

I shuffled forward and reached out to hug him. "I love you."

He sighed. "I love you, too."

As the words sunk in, my shoulders relaxed. The knots inside my gut resolved. Energy flowed the right way again. He still loved me.

# Spring 2009

Julian stopped to chat with Chloe when Luke pounced in protectively. Julian smirked and walked away towards our tent. Luke stared daggers at him.

The last time I saw that look on Luke's face was the morning after Julian had 'drunkenly' made out with Rachel, all those years ago. Just like that, I was plummeting back to the moonlit boat deck of the catamaran. Hands hungrily groping all over each other. Lips locked and moving with hurried enthusiasm.

"Jess?"

I blinked, turning my focus back to Meghan and Amelia who were toasting marshmallows on the fire. Each were snuggled into a camp chair wearing thick hoodies with hair still damp from sailing.

"Sorry, what did you say Meghan?" I said.

"She asked if you'll be up early to come out on the boats." Amelia blew out her flaming marshmallow and tentatively tapped at the charcoal skin before pulling it off and stuffing it in her mouth. Carrie and Jim were busy this weekend, but the girls were keen to come to the lake. They were never any fuss and their enthusiasm for sailing was infectious, so we offered to look after them.

"Oh, yeah, for sure." I smiled as Luke and Chloe approached the fire. Luke immediately started shoving potatoes into the hot coals.

All traces of his former glare gone.

Meghan took her time to get her marshmallow just the right shade of caramel and nibbled it from the end of her stick as Amelia extinguished another charred one. I couldn't help feeling a little off watching Luke. I thought this thing with Rachel was all in the past. But maybe Luke still struggled, as I did, when he thought of it. I pushed the images away.

"So, you're moving in then?" I asked Chloe as Julian joined the fire circle.

"Yep!" Her face beamed. "I know, it's been a long time coming but Luke and I are making it official."

"It's the beginning of the end." Julian laughed. "Next minute; marriage, then say goodbye to your sex life!"

Luke chuckled, probably only for Julian's sake.

"How are my two little champs going?" Julian smiled at Meghan and Amelia. "You both did awesome out there today. I reckon you're ready for nationals."

"Really?" Amelia said with a mouth full of marshmallow.

Julian nodded and cracked open his beer while the girls diverted their attention back to the diminishing packet of marshmallows.

Luke began massaging Chloe's shoulders. I shifted in my chair, struck with an unreasonable stab of envy. Julian would never massage my shoulders. He barely touched me nowadays. Except for sex.

"Oh you're the best," Chloe breathed. "Babe, that feels amazing."

"That's what she said last night too." Luke winked at me.

I contained an eye roll as Chloe slapped playfully at his hand. The tenderness he had for her was clear. Why did I feel so bitter about it? Just because Julian never touched me anymore, didn't mean I couldn't be happy for Luke. He deserved all the love and happiness in the world, especially after all he went through. I flashed again to Rachel and Julian entwined. Shuddering, I pushed my mind back to the present. Julian had never shown interest in Chloe. Luke had nothing to worry about. Neither did I.

# Summer 2009

"Yes! Meghan, well done!" Carrie cheered as Meghan brought her boat up to the sandy bank next to her sister's. Carrie trotted over and hugged her daughter, who had just won the cadets open class. She was red-faced and dripping wet, and beaming.

Amelia ran to her, and they embraced. Amelia was also soaked and exhausted, having won her race just prior to Meghan.

"Hey Jess, did you see our race this morning?"

I turned to see Catherine and Adele, an inseparable pair of bubbly eleven-year-old club juniors who I helped coach.

"I sure did, Cath," I said. "You only missed it by a whisker. Great work too, Adele. You made me so proud. All that practice we've done really payed off. How about next week I take you both out on the same course and you can nail that last tricky buoy?"

"That would be awesome. Thanks Jess!" Adele said, beaming, before the pair both ran to congratulate Meghan and Amelia. The girls all stood in the shallows, hugging and laughing and chatting excitedly about their races.

Julian jogged over to join the crowd that had gathered around the girls. "Great effort, you two. I couldn't be prouder." He high-fived them both.

As Julian turned away, Amelia kicked up water, sending it

splashing all over him. All the girls burst into fits of laughter as Julian's surprised face turned into a huge smile. He rounded on the girls. Darting forward in the ankle-deep water, he had Amelia and Meghan by the waist in a heartbeat, pushing them backwards into the deeper water. He dunked them both before walking out, chuckling and completely saturated.

Carrie and I laughed at the scene. I couldn't wait for him to share this kind of joy with our own kids. It had been two months since I stopped using contraceptives. If all went to plan, before too long, it could be our own children he was splashing with in the water.

"We'll need to head off soon," Carrie said. Jim and Carrie were heading up the coast to compete in a triathlon the next morning, and Julian and I had offered to look after the girls.

"Don't worry." Julian approached with Meghan and Amelia in a headlock. "We'll take good care of them."

Carrie smiled and kissed each of her now teenage girls on the forehead. "Be good, the both of you. And make sure you do what you're told and go to bed when you're asked. No phones after six pm, got it?"

Amelia rolled her eyes. "Okay, we got it."

A little later, Julian pulled his BMW into the President's allocated car space right outside the club and we headed upstairs to the restaurant. As we entered, we met Sarah and Tony, long time club members, who were on their way out with their six-year-old daughter, Emily.

Tony grabbed Julian's attention. "I'm glad I caught up with you, Julian. I wanted to talk to you about that stunt Frank pulled at the start of the race today."

The three girls ran off down the hall, giggling, and Sarah and

I stepped away while our husbands talked club politics. Julian had said being president sometimes felt like wrangling a bunch of eight-year-olds fighting over 'who's it' playing tag. He had a patient attitude to everyone's gripes and heard them out. I steered clear.

"Hey, Jess," Sarah said, her voice hushed, "do you remember that guy Nick, who left the club after just one season last year?"

I nodded. How could I forget Nick? I never saw him again after that night Julian assaulted him at our housewarming party. He threatened legal action on the club if we didn't return his membership fees. I put my hand on her shoulder and led her further away from Julian and Tony.

"Well, I ran into him at the shops the other day," Sarah went on.

"Oh wow. Long time no see. How is he doing?"

"He's getting married next year. To an old club member, actually. Kayla. He sounded thrilled. Didn't have anything nice to say about Julian, of course." She tipped her head to the side, raising her brows.

"No, well ... that's understandable." I rolled my eyes.

"Do you remember Kayla?"

"Yeah, I remember Kayla. She was nice." All I could muster was a half smile, flooded with a sudden memory of guilt. Julian broke up with Kayla to be with me.

"... anyway, Tony, if you want to put in a formal complaint, it's up to you." Julian walked towards us, his hand resting on Tony's shoulder. "The channels are open. I would just say that I think we can all work this out without it getting too out of control." He had his most calming, yet authoritarian, voice on.

We all said goodbye.

After dinner, we decided to walk home. It was such a nice night out. The girls were both hyperactive and giggly during

108

the short walk, offering piggy backs to one another and falling over laughing.

"You two are a bit too hyper," I said. "Must have been the milk-shakes Julian bought you." The girls' eyes had lit up with glee when Julian bought them giant glasses of chocolate milkshakes. He'd gone into the kitchen to make them himself, saying he didn't trust the staff to do it right.

I reached for Julian's hand. He didn't match my grip. Barely touching me at all. We didn't hold hands much anymore. Not like we used to.

We reached home, and as I opened the door, we were greeted by a meowing Buffy.

"Oops," I said. "I forgot to feed you."

Amelia picked her up. "Oh, you poor little kitty. Isn't she mean? Going out and eating before feeding you." She buried her head in the fur, giggling. "You gorgeous little fluff ball."

I shook my head at the girl. She was in the funniest mood.

"Amelia, Meghan, come and choose a soft drink from the fridge," Julian called from the kitchen.

The girls disappeared, returning a few minutes later with tall glasses of something red and bubbly. We sat outside and gossiped about the club for about an hour, Julian and I sipping on beers, and him frequently returning to the kitchen to refill their sugary drinks.

I yawned. "I don't mean to be a party pooper, but I'm going to hit the sack." I stood and turned to Amelia and Meghan. "I think you two can go to bed now, too."

"No, not yet," Amelia pleaded.

"We're not tired," Meghan said, smiling angelically.

I felt my disciplinary instinct waver. I would need to work on this whole parenting thing, before I had obstinate kids of my own to negotiate. "Fine." I put my hand on Julian's shoulder. "Make sure they don't stay up too late."

"Stop being the fun police for one minute, Jess, they're fine." Julian took another gulp from his can.

"Alright. Amelia and Meghan, you're all sorted, right? You've got PJs and know where everything is?"

They nodded.

"Okay, well make sure you both go to bed in the next half hour, okay?"

They both smiled sweetly.

It was very dark when I woke. I looked to the clock on my bedside table. Four in the morning. I rolled over, ready to close my eyes again before I noticed Julian was not in bed. I got up and shrugged into my dressing gown and slippers. I walked, soundless, down the dark hall, careful not to wake the girls.

I opened the door to the living room and noticed there were lights still on outside. I rushed over and pushed the blinds to the side, peering out. Amelia was sitting on the same chair as earlier and Julian stood behind her. Their heads spun towards me, surprise clear on their faces.

I pulled the sliding door open and went outside. Amelia's surprise waivered, turning into a smirk as I approached.

"What are you still doing up Amelia?" I hissed.

She rolled her eyes.

I blinked multiple times, taking in the rudeness of the fourteen-year-old. Julian sniggered and sipped on a drink.

I stared daggers at him and Amelia. "Get to bed. Right now!"

She huffed as she passed me and nearly lost her feet, stumbling over some crack in the ground. She regained her feet and slowly walked into the house, holding onto the door frame and then the kitchen bench, before disappearing down the hall.

When she was gone, I rounded on Julian. "What that hell? It's four am!"

He scowled. "Oh, calm down."

My lips pressed together, and I spun on my heels towards the bedroom. So frustrated with how irresponsible he was being, letting her stay up so late. I shouldn't always have to be the sensible one. I could become pregnant at any time, and he was still acting like a teenager. I was reminded of a comment Jim had made not long ago: "No one ever says, congratulations, you've got a teenager!" He was talking about Meghan and Amelia; I never thought it would apply to my husband.

# *Autumn 2010*

"So, Mum, we have some news," Julian said, cutting his steak.

"I knew it!" Lyn exclaimed, pointing at me with her fork. "As soon as you wanted soda water, I knew you were pregnant!"

I tried to smile. She'd taken the surprise right out of our surprise.

"Congratulations," Greg said. "I can't wait to be a grandpa."

"Greg, love," Lyn said, "would you get the bottle of champagne from the fridge? This calls for a celebration!"

Greg immediately got up and went to the fridge while Lyn continued to gush about being a grandmother. "Lyn?" Greg called from the fridge.

Lyn didn't bat an eyelid, looking straight at me. "So, do you have a due date yet?" I knew she heard him.

Greg looked, flustered, at the fridge door. He nodded at me, as if telling me it was okay to answer her. "It looks to be late spring," I said. "But I'll have a proper dating scan next week."

"Lyn!" Greg called.

"Oh, this is just so wonderful," Lyn said, stroking her earrings.

"Lynette Rundell!" Greg was red in the face now; as close to angry as I'd ever seen him.

Lyn calmly placed down her knife and fork. "Yes, Greg," she said finally. "What is it?"

"You asked me to get the champagne and I can't find it."

"It's in the fridge in the garage," she said, like he should have known.

He huffed, shutting the fridge door and went to the garage.

"So," Lyn continued, "are you going to find out the sex?"

"No," I said, at the same time Julian said, "Yes." We looked at each other. A shadow of a frown on his face.

"I think you two have some decisions to make." Lyn raised an eyebrow. "Of course, I think you absolutely should find out the sex, it makes perfect sense. You need to be prepared."

Greg reappeared with four glasses and a bottle of expensive looking champagne. He popped the cork and started pouring.

"I won't have any, thanks," I said.

"Oh nonsense," Lyn said. "It's fine to have a little dabble once in a while. I did when I was pregnant, and they all turned out fine. They want to wrap everything in cottonwool nowadays."

I grimaced. "Just a sip then, thanks Greg." I understood why Greg did whatever Lyn said. It was easier to keep her happy than try to win an unwinnable argument. Julian was just like her.

Lyn held up her glass. We followed suit. "To us becoming grandparents." We held our glasses in cheers, and as they drank, I pretended to sip and put the glass back on the table. Lyn didn't seem to notice, to my relief.

Lyn dabbed her mouth with a napkin. "I've wanted to talk to the two of you for a while about this. I have kept my mouth shut. I have bitten my tongue." She paused. "But surely the two of you don't intend on bringing a baby into your house in its current state?"

I gaped, unable to form a response. I looked at Julian, urging him with my eyes to defend our home.

"I mean," he said, "we have been trying to save for renovations, but you know." He shrugged. "It's hard paying a mortgage and saving ... and living."

I gritted my teeth. All I wanted to do was scream at him for not defending my home. But I would not let him, or Lyn, see my anger.

"Well, I'll hear no more of it," Lyn said, sawing at her steak. "Get some plans drawn up and I'll take care of it."

Julian's eyes lit up. "That'd be great, Mum. We'll pay you back."

"Excuse me." I stood. "I need to get some more water."

"Oh, Greg will get it," Lyn said.

"No, it's okay, thanks Greg." I waved at him to stay seated.

I walked to the fridge, taking my time, letting the cool air saturate my face and chest. I didn't realise how hot I had gotten. The open door blocked them from view, so I used the privacy to take a few deep, shaky breaths knowing it would look weird to linger too long.

The top shelf of their fridge caught my eye. Lined up in perfect order was the margarine I must buy, the cheese I must buy, and the sauce I must buy. She'd bought it his whole life and now he refused anything but. I felt a sudden urge to spit in their fridge. Instead, I snatched at the sparkling water and walked to the marble counter to fill my glass.

"Well, that's sorted out now, isn't it?" Lyn was beaming at me as I returned to my seat.

I nodded with the best smile I could manage.

In the car on the way home, I couldn't ignore it. "Julian, it makes me uncomfortable to take money from your parents. I thought we'd agreed to do this ourselves."

"We did. But it'd take forever for us to afford. Think about the baby, Jess. This way we can get it done before he comes." He turned the radio up.

I raised my voice. "He or *she*. And I would still rather save up ourselves."

He glared. "Well, we aren't managing to save much right now, are we?"

I returned the glare in force. "Well, maybe if you stop spending so much. Like the two thousand dollars you spent on that new bike. Which you have ridden once."

"Jesus, Jess, do I ever question your spending? I work hard and I like to once in a while buy something good. Is that such a bad thing?"

"No," I muttered.

"Look. Mum is doing something nice for us. You should be *grateful*."

"I *am* grateful. I just wanted us to do it ourselves."

"Well fuck, I can't win. You know, I never even wanted to buy a house there. I was pretty happy in my old apartment. But you wanted the house. I did it to make you happy." He whacked the steering wheel. "For fuck's sake! We have an opportunity to make it liveable now. We're taking it."

"Fine. Okay, sorry." I looked out my window. "But we *are* paying them back."

"Sure, whatever."

We didn't speak the rest of the way home.

———— ⚬ ————

I rolled over and looked at the alarm clock. Four thirty am. His side of the bed was cold. I took a deep breath, torn between wanting to

115

go find him and not wanting to move. If I moved too much, I'd vomit. That was my life right now – managing the best way not to vomit. I needed to go to the toilet anyway, so I forced myself up and headed to the bathroom.

No sooner had I flushed than I was retching, head buried in the bowl. When nothing more would come, I rinsed my mouth. I padded my way around the dark house, Buffy prowling at my side.

No sign of life. He must not be home yet.

I went back to the bedroom and picked up my phone to call him. No answer.

I texted him: *Where are you??*

I hurried to the toilet and vomited. Again. My stomach was empty, so nothing but a measly spoonful of bile came up, leaving my throat on fire. I brushed my teeth and went back to bed to call Julian. Again. Five more times and no answer. Two more text messages. Nothing.

I must have fallen back asleep because when I woke again, it was daylight, and Julian was fast asleep next to me. I didn't make it to the shower before vomiting bile again. This first trimester morning sickness was tougher than I thought. The energy for almost everything was sapped right out of me. I couldn't believe the first time I got morning sickness, I was thrilled. Another outward confirmation I really was pregnant. Now, it was getting old. I was ready for the baby to be born.

I stood in the shower for a few minutes, washed myself and was almost dry before I vomited again. When it had first started happening, Julian asked if there was anything he could do. But that didn't last long. Nowadays, he just looked at me like it was a hassle having to listen to my retching.

I made my way to the kitchen and quickly ate some toast. It was all about getting something down in the right window of time. Not fast enough, I would throw up. Too fast, I would throw up. If I was lucky and got the window right, I'd get some slight relief. For a time.

I left Julian asleep and headed over to Carrie's. We hadn't caught up in a while. I was so wrapped up in my pregnancy woes these past months, we barely kept contact. Carrie had been distant, too, dealing with a sick mother. I felt guilty for not being there for her, but knew I couldn't be of help when I could barely help myself. This catchup was long overdue.

We embraced at the door. "How are you feeling?" Carrie asked as I followed her to the kitchen.

I shrugged. "The same. How is your mum doing?"

"Not great."

Carrie flicked on the kettle and grabbed some teabags.

"Have they said anything about the future outlook?" I asked.

She looked down, nodding. "They don't think she has very long left." Her voice drifted off. She handed me a mug of tea while I tried to find the words. What should you say to someone who was losing their mum?

"Where are the girls?" I asked, hoping a change of subject would give me time to find the words of comfort my friend deserved.

"Meghan is staying over at a friend's and Amelia is still in bed, would you believe?"

"Yeah, so is Julian."

"Really?" She looked at her watch. "It's nearly midday ... teenagers need extra sleep, but I would have thought ... I mean, I can't sleep past six these days. What time did you guys go to bed?"

"I don't know what time he came to bed." I gripped my tea. "It was after four thirty."

Her eyes bulged. "God, four thirty! Does that happen a lot?"

I blinked, surprised she didn't know. We really had lost touch. "A fair bit. He likes to be the last man standing no matter where we are. He'll kick on with anyone or even just by himself."

She nodded wearily, looking as exhausted as I felt.

"I thought getting pregnant might force him to grow up a bit," I said. "That it might bring us closer together."

"I don't know what to tell you." Carrie stared at me like a lost cause.

I sat straighter, forcing a smile. "It's all good." I changed the subject again. We chatted for a while longer before I said, "I better get going." I drank the last mouthful of tea and stood. "Let me know how everything goes with your mum."

We hugged goodbye but it was lacklustre. We were both weary and drained. Me, from pregnancy, and she, from stress and pre-emptive grief.

ornament

# Winter 2010

I read the final chapter of my book, knowing I wouldn't have much more time, but I couldn't put it down. Julian was on the toilet. He had been there for at least half an hour. That was his bedtime routine, these days. He would take his phone to the toilet and sit there for ages. I prayed he would take his time tonight.

I hadn't always felt this way. It wasn't so long ago that I wished he would come to bed with me. Hold and love me. But I didn't feel his love anymore. There was no holding, no tender kisses, nothing. He had taken the love out of making love. It was just sex. Purely functional.

I now looked forward to the nights he didn't come home. At least I didn't have to have sex with him then. I had begun to loathe it.

My spare hand rested over my tummy, which had swelled significantly. My little darling sent butterflies around my uterus while I read. I couldn't feel it from the outside yet, but he or she was very active, particularly at bedtime.

The toilet flushed, and my reaction was immediate. I flicked my book shut and switched off the light in one swift movement.

I slowed my breathing and listened carefully. Hoping if he thought I was asleep, he wouldn't hassle me for sex. Some nights I got lucky.

He turned the handle and I inwardly grimaced. I had not heard the tap running, which meant he had not washed his hands, again. He never did. It disgusted me. A grown man using the toilet, wiping his bum and not washing his hands. I couldn't tell him though. That would be inviting a verbal tirade, where he would attack me with all the things I did wrong. Who knew what it would be this time? Maybe I didn't mop the floor right. Maybe I bought the wrong thing. Maybe I spent too much. Maybe I looked at a guy the wrong way, and suddenly, I was accused of having an affair.

I heard him clear his throat. I didn't move. He unbuckled his belt. I couldn't move, even though my body urged me to run. He let his clothes drop in a pile on the floor. I'd need to pick those up in the morning. He lifted the covers and slid into the bed.

His hand landed on my lower back. I tried not to tense. He moved it up and down. I regulated my breathing and focused on his hand. That disgusting, unwashed hand. His vile, unbrushed teeth breath on the back of my neck. He never brushed his teeth before coming to bed.

I had a decision to make. Did I go along with it again, or did I say I didn't feel like it tonight and wear the repercussions? It could just be the silent treatment. It could be an attack of everything I did wrong. But there *would* be repercussions.

I made the same decision I always did – the path of least resistance. I rolled onto my back, and he was on and in me in a heartbeat. Remembering he hadn't drunk too much tonight, I figured it shouldn't go too long. I laid there as he pumped away. After a while, a bead of his sweat landed near my mouth and I snapped it shut.

He kept going. I feigned enjoyment in the hope it would speed him up. It didn't. I couldn't remember the last time I enjoyed sex with him.

His filthy hands rubbed all over me. I wanted another shower. My chest was wet with his sweat now. He kept thrusting.

Finally, with a groan and some last, sharp thrusts, it was over, and he was off me. He leant and kissed me on the cheek before rolling over. He'd fall asleep in minutes, leaving me to lie awake with the memory of what just happened. We used to cuddle after sex. I couldn't remember the last time that happened.

I placed my hand on my stomach, the internal butterflies returned.

—§—

"Can you feel that?" I said to Catherine and Adele as I held their hands over my belly. I was sitting by the bar in the club room, sipping on sparkling water, glad the junior sailors were keeping me company. Since I got pregnant, I couldn't help train them much anymore, but I was trying to come to the club more often again, even though it was tiring. I felt cut off from the club, from my friends and students. All I had for company was Julian, and he was never around, even if I wanted him to be.

"Yes." Adele's eyes widened at the sensation of my baby's kicking foot.

"This is so weird," Catherine said, mouth open in awe.

"How did your training session with Julian go?" I asked.

"Great," Catherine said. "He says we're ready for the pre-season series." She cocked her head, her hand still on my belly. "I love babies

121

so much. Jess. Can I please babysit for you?"

"I want to babysit, too!" Adele said.

I laughed. "Of course. When my little munchkin is old enough. You both would be great babysitters."

I saw Luke enter the club room and my eyes bulged. He had a massive bruise surrounding a swollen shut eye. "Oh my gosh, Luke! What happened?"

His serious expression turned goofy in an instant. "This? This is nothing. You should see the other guy." He laughed and winced, putting his hand to his ribs.

I wanted to probe for more but was aware of the girls next to me, openly gaping at Luke. Luckily, I was saved by the sight of Catherine's mum entering the room to pick them up. They hurried away, waving.

"Luke, this looks really bad," I said when the girls were gone. "Did you go to a doctor?"

"Nah. I asked Chloe to slice my eyelid like Rocky Balboa had done in the movie. But she refused." He sniffed. "I'm thinking of trading her in."

I couldn't match his humour on the situation. "Who did this to you?"

Luke opened his mouth, but something caught his eye. I followed the direction of his gaze and saw Julian approaching us.

"Have you seen Luke's face?" I said.

"Yeah." Julian didn't sound surprised or concerned.

"I better run. See ya later, Jess," Luke said, avoiding my eyes as he walked away.

I shook my head at his retreating figure. I turned to Julian. "Do you know what happened?"

"Luke has mouthed off at the pub his whole life." He shrugged. "Not everyone thinks he's funny."

"But who would do that? It's terrible. He could press charges."

"Just leave it." He looked at his watch. "I'm late for a meeting. I'll see you at home later."

After he left, I finished my drink and headed out to my car, dialling Carrie on the way.

"Have you seen Luke?" I asked.

"Jess ... I'm sorry, I can't talk ..." Her voice quivered. "We lost Mum an hour ago."

"Oh god. I'm so sorry. Is there anything I can do?"

"No, I'm just spending some time with the family. I'll call you in the next few days."

"Okay, take care." I said goodbye and hung up. I took a moment, leaning against my car when I reached it. Poor Carrie. I lowered myself into the car and shut my eyes, exhausted all of a sudden. It was hard to gauge if it was more from my body, Carrie's devastating news or Luke's face. I wanted to be there for Carrie, but wasn't sure how. Luke wouldn't tell me who hurt him, but once, he would have told me everything. Pregnancy, whether direct or indirectly, had caused me to be out of the loop, out of touch with everyone. Even my husband.

I patted my belly and sighed. I thought pregnancy would bring us closer together.

───── ° ─────

# Spring 2010

Sleep eluded me. I was too distracted by the little wrapped bundle in the plastic tub next to me. Poppy Rundell. She didn't seem real. I couldn't stop staring at her, in awe that she came from my body. Created by us.

Julian lay behind me, his body curled against mine. His breath, slow and regular, on my neck. I couldn't remember the last time he cuddled me like this. Normally he only came near me when he wanted to have sex. Now, I felt the love radiating through his whole body.

Before Julian had fallen asleep, he held me tight and whispered in my ear, "I'm so proud of you, Jess. I love you so much." It took me by surprise; he had never said he was proud of me before. I snuggled closer against him.

It was the middle of the day but neither of us got any sleep last night. We were too busy bringing Poppy into the world. Labour was far worse than anything I could have ever imagined. Every time I closed my eyes, I relived the intense, painful event. But I forgot the pain whenever I saw our perfect little girl.

A while later, Julian woke.

"Sweetie," he said, "I'm going to head home and have a shower. I'll be back a bit later." He got out of bed and looked at Poppy, his expression soft.

"Why don't you have a shower here and stay the night?" I said. The maternity rooms were designed for the partner to stay overnight. That was part of why I chose to come here.

"I've got some things to do." He kissed me on the forehead. "Try to get some rest."

A little while later, a small knock at the door woke me, pulling me out of much needed sleep. My entire body was sore, like I'd been run over. But when I saw Carrie's face appear around the corner, my tiredness was forgotten. Meghan and Amelia were close behind, both beaming. They went to the tub, peering at my sleeping daughter.

"Jess, she's adorable." Carrie handed me a gift.

"I still can't believe she's here," I said.

They took turns cuddling with Poppy. I was glad they were here now. Meghan and Amelia seemed to have grown so much. Meghan was almost eighteen now, and Amelia was fifteen. A fluttering warmth erupted in my stomach as I imagined my own daughter, Poppy, as amazing teenagers like them.

My daughter. Would that ever get old to say?

Julian returned an hour later. He reached straight for Poppy; the sight of her lighting up his face like I hadn't seen in years. The smile that I loved returned at the sight of our daughter.

He sat next to me, cradling Poppy.

"Aren't you staying overnight?" I asked after noticing he had no bag with him.

"No. I have to go into work for a bit in the morning." His eyes didn't leave Poppy's, gently stroking her cheek with the tip of his finger.

"Oh, okay." I was too tired to be disappointed. "Carrie and the girls visited. They bought this for Poppy." I held up the onesie.

His eyes flashed something I couldn't read. "Cute."

He stayed an hour, eyes only for his newborn, and then left.

The following afternoon, Julian breezed back into the room. He kissed me on the forehead and scooped up Poppy, taking a seat next to me on the bed. I thought of that tender moment from yesterday as we cuddled, a moment that gave me so much hope that our connection had renewed with the birth of our daughter. It felt lost today.

"I thought you were planning on taking some time off work," I said.

"I was, but I had to go in for a few hours." Poppy looked so tiny in his huge arms. During my pregnancy, Julian had signed up for a gym, losing weight and bulking muscles, getting leaner and stronger while I got fatter. He was in the best shape of his life. I couldn't think about my flabby middle yet.

"Where's your bag? I thought you were going to stay tonight."

"I can't. The guys are coming over to 'wet the baby's head' and I need to get the cot together."

"Oh."

After he left again, I had a few more visitors while Poppy slept. She was up almost the entire night. I couldn't settle her. I gave up and rang the bell at four am. A midwife appeared and adopted a well-worn sympathetic grin when she saw me crying. First timers fall apart all the time, I heard.

I looked at her in desperation. "I don't know what to do. I've fed her, I've changed her, she just keeps crying." I paced next to the bed, swaying Poppy gently in my arms. "What am I doing wrong?"

She stepped forward, arms outstretched. "Nothing at all, love. She's just going to take some time to get used to our clock, that's all." The midwife leant forward and scooped Poppy from my arms. "I'll take her for a few hours. You need to rest."

My saviour.

I slept for a solid three hours for the first time in days and woke feeling almost human again.

Julian appeared late again the following day.

"I thought you would have been here earlier today," I grumbled as I wiped black sludge from Poppy's backside. "Did you have to work again?"

"No, but somebody had to get everything ready for this little dynamo to come home." He stroked Poppy's downy hair while I changed her nappy. He stunk of stale booze.

"Julian ..." I wanted to comment on the stench but left it. Too tired to argue.

He cradled her after she was clean and tucked into a onesie. "So, what time should I pick you up tomorrow?"

"What do you mean, are you not staying ... again?"

"No, I haven't finished her room yet."

I had to look away.

The following morning Julian arrived only just in time for our discharge. I had already fumbled Poppy's tiny legs and arms into her new jumpsuit from Carrie and packed my bags. Revived and ready to start my new life as a mum without being rescued by a midwife at the click of a button.

A midwife wheeled the bassinet to the car and left us to fuss over clicking in those enormous buckles to keep our little darling safe. Julian triple checked the buckles were secure. The car trip was short, and I couldn't wipe the smile from my face. Julian had spent a lot of time at home getting the house ready for her arrival. He had been a little evasive answering questions, so I expected a surprise.

Julian didn't do much of the housework except mowing the lawn. It was never really spoken about when we moved out of his apartment, I just automatically took on all the cleaning. But since he'd had some time off work, I imagined he had cleaned the place top to bottom.

"I can't wait to see her room," I said when we reached the front door.

As soon as he opened the front door, the stench of booze and stale smoke wafted over us.

"Julian, it smells like a bar." I pulled Poppy closer. I felt like shielding her from the odour.

"Yeah, I can't get rid of it. I've aired the place. One of the boys brought some cigars." He had my bag and walked towards our bedroom.

I stepped inside and my shoe stuck a little to the tiles, making a squelching sound as I lifted it. I looked closer. The tiles were disgusting; shiny and sticky from spilled drinks. No wonder the smell wouldn't go. He hadn't mopped. I headed down the corridor, eager to see Poppy's room.

Julian was waiting for me in her room. He smiled with pride as I walked in.

My eyes darted around the room. Jaw slowly dropping as I searched to see the effort and time gone into the room. Wanting desperately to put his lack of time at the hospital down to something good rather than the reality. He just didn't want to be there. I forced deep breaths through my nose to stay calm. But if I wasn't holding a sleeping newborn, I would have screamed. There was no surprise decorating. He hadn't even put the linen on her bed. The only thing he'd done was screw the cot and change table together.

I handed him Poppy and put the fitted sheet over her mattress. I placed the mat on the change table and swaddled Poppy firm. I lay her in the cot. She didn't make a sound.

I stalked past Julian into the hall.

"What?" he said, following me out. "What's wrong with you?"

I spun around. "Julian, the house is a mess." I threw my hands in the air. "I thought you might have decorated her room nicely and cleaned the house. All you did was screw the cot together. Something I asked you to do months ago!"

He crossed his arms. "It wouldn't matter what I did. You wouldn't be happy."

He stormed out to the yard as I stood dumbfounded, glaring after him.

I emptied my hospital bag and took my dirty clothes to the laundry. The basket was full. Of course, it was. I shook my head and shoved a load into the machine before filling the mop bucket and adding detergent. I had been instructed to rest. I was told a third degree tear needed time for the sutures to heal. Tears spilled down my face as I went to work mopping the entire kitchen, dining room and entryway. I began crying because of Julian, now I cried because the movement made my stitches burn.

I'd barely slept for four days. I thought we were doing this together.

Poppy couldn't possibly be hungry again. I hadn't even fallen back to sleep since I last fed her. Maybe she would resettle. She wailed louder. I needed sleep. Even just five minutes. I couldn't keep staying up all night and all day.

Julian was fast asleep. No point him getting up, he'd said. This was my job. It's not like he could feed her. I scowled in his direction and ducked out from under the covers. I didn't want to wake him. The last thing I needed was his complaints about not getting enough sleep either.

I walked down the hall to her room. I scooped her up and sat in the chair next to her cot. She was already rooting for my breast, flicking her head to the side, mouth open. When she didn't find it straight away, she stopped searching and squawked again. I pulled up my nightie and helped her attach.

"It's like you've been starved little one," I whispered. Small sounds escaped her throat as she gulped.

I winced. No one warned me this would be painful. That every time I fed in the first few days, I would get stomach cramps. I thought people were joking about cracked nipples. A nipple shield, they told me to get. What the hell was a nipple shield? This baby thing was a whole new world.

I breathed through another cramp, almost doubling over. Oh my god. All those laxatives the hospital gave me felt like they were working right now.

I let her feed as long as I could stand it. I couldn't handle her screaming and the pain of trying to get her to latch on again, but I had to get to the toilet. I stood and shuffled across the hall, ensuring she stayed attached. I could only take small steps because I was so swollen and the agony of the stitches pulling was worse at full stride. Since I mopped the floors a few days ago, the pain had been unbearable. I'd since tried every tip and trick people had given me. Frozen condoms in the undies. I'd looked sideways at the midwife until I tried it.

I got close to the toilet, but not close enough. I had no control. I fumbled around trying to pull the toilet seat down and lift my dressing gown out of the way at the same time. All with one hand. I swore silently at Julian for leaving the seat up again. I finally lowered onto the seat, but too late – it was everywhere. Clinging to Poppy, I surveyed the damage. I had soiled all over myself, my nighty and dressing gown. All caked with runny poo.

Tears dribbled down my cheeks. I was so drained. I sat frozen on the toilet for a long time, surrounded by the vulgar stench. Poppy kept suckling, completely unaware she was surrounded in shit. I was a terrible mother.

9

Julian hadn't hassled me for sex. I couldn't believe it. The eight weeks we were told to wait had come and gone, and still no hint of him wanting me. Maybe I shouldn't have been surprised. He barely looked at me most days. When he was home, his eyes were only for Poppy. And I knew I looked a mess. My appearance was the last thing on my mind as I nursed, wiped, washed and fed the seemingly forever hungry, forever crying newborn. I was lucky if I had time to shower most days. I guess I didn't have to worry about how to lose my pregnancy weight; I barely remembered to eat so consumed was I by Poppy.

I expected the stress of raising a newborn. What I didn't expect was Julian adding to it. Most days, I waited to see what mood he was in so I could adjust the mood I needed to be in. It was hard to decide what was more exhausting – a newborn or tiptoeing around Julian.

I looked up as the front door opened, unsure what to expect tonight. I watched his face as he headed towards the bedroom.

"Hi!" I said brightly.

He nodded. A small grunt escaped his mouth.

I followed him to the bedroom and approached him from behind, sliding my arms around his waist like I used to do. Like he used to do to me. I needed to make more of an effort. Maybe if he noticed these gestures to reconnect, he'd respond in kind.

He wiggled free with a huff. "Jess, I just got in the door."

I sat on the bed. Must have been a bad day at work. "How was work?" I asked, keeping my tone bright.

He shrugged, nothing else. Must have been a bad day all round. Or I could have done something to upset him. Maybe he had been waiting for me to approach him for sex and he was angry I hadn't. Three months ago, I would have done anything not to have to have sex. But at least then I knew after he finished, his mood would lift for a while. He'd be nicer to me. It's not that he was being mean now. Just indifferent.

"I've got ribs for dinner." That should have cheered him up, he loved ribs.

"Cool." He left the room.

I headed back to the kitchen to continue preparing dinner, unsure if I should keep trying to lift his mood. Julian was squat over Poppy's bouncer in the doorway. He wore the smile he used to give me. He was rubbing her tummy and pulling faces at her. She was full of smiles for him.

We ate on the couch while watching the television. No conversation, no acknowledgement of the meal, my presence. It was like I wasn't even in the room.

I went back over what I had done the last few days. Perhaps I'd made some small comment to upset him. Nothing stuck out.

His phone chimed. He read the message and smiled before replying. He spent a lot of time on his phone nowadays. I asked once who he was messaging and the glare he shot me was appalling. I wouldn't ask again.

After dinner I bathed Poppy and settled her with ease into her cot. At least one person in this house was being easy.

I returned to the living room and we watched television for a while longer.

"I'm going to watch the end in bed," he said in the ad break, flicking the television off.

So he did know I was there.

I agreed and headed towards our walk-in closet to get changed for bed. I looked at myself in the mirror, turning to the side, trying to suck my tummy in. I had lost a lot of weight since giving birth. But my body still didn't look like mine. I lifted a stretchy lace negligee over my head. It was snug but I couldn't have worn it at all a few weeks ago, so I felt good about myself. Maybe he would see me now.

I walked into our bedroom and stood next to the bed until his gaze shifted from the television. He looked me up and down before his attention returned to the screen.

"That's a little small for you, isn't it?" he said, straight faced.

I looked at my protruding stomach, firm under the satin material.

He was right. I was disgusting. I walked back to the robe and pulled it off, changing into the oversized t-shirt I had worn like a uniform for months.

Maybe he was not attracted to me anymore. What if he didn't love me anymore? I had to fix our relationship. I couldn't keep going with him barely acknowledging my existence. I still loved him and wanted our future together, but I needed to feel loved. I'd never forgive myself if I didn't try everything. As much as sex had become a chore and certain habits of his appalled me, I was willing to do whatever it took to feel his love again.

I got into bed and scooted over close to him. My body flush against his. He was on his back, chin to chest, eyes only for the television on the wall. I put my arm across his chest and kissed him on the cheek. My hand caressed under the sheet through his chest hair, along his lean stomach and down to where he used to encourage my hands. My mouth wandered down his neck and I ran my tongue along his jawline before leaning over and kissing his mouth.

No response.

I pulled back and glanced at his hand, his firm grasp of the remote unfettered. I stared into his unmoved eyes, hunting for a whisper of emotion. Nothing.

I sat back and leaned against my pillows.

"Is there someone else?" I said before thinking it through.

"*Jesus Christ*, I'm just watching the television."

"You haven't touched me lately."

"Because I've been letting you get over ..." He gestured up and down my body with his hand. "... *all this*." His face full of revulsion.

It stung and I turned over. "Sorry," I got out in a meek voice.

I laid for a few seconds, tears filling my eyes, before his hand reached for my shoulder and lowered me onto my back. He leant over me and kissed my mouth. Not tenderly. It was impatient, his tongue firm and invading. His full weight over the top of me, I tried to slow the pace, but he was running this show.

His penis hard against my leg. His hands rubbed over me. No delicacy or care. His fingers entered me. Hard, fast and rough. I recoiled from the pain. My stitches were fully healed but I was by no means *normal*. I had a new normal I needed to discover now.

He pulled his fingers out and replaced them with his penis in a second. He was looking forward. Not at me but at the bedhead. He thrust hard and fast as I lay under him in shock. I stared, disbelieving, as his chin moved forwards and back over my forehead. Was he going to look at me at all? It seemed to go on and on. When he was finally done, he lay onto his back and refocused on the television.

Supine, I stared at the ceiling. A discarded piece of trash.

# *Summer* 2010

I wish I hadn't come here. We were in the middle of a heatwave. Not any old heatwave, but the type you read in the papers where the very young and very old or frail perished. Despite my hesitation, Julian assured me the cool change would hit the following day and insisted we go on a weekend away to Rushworth for their annual regatta. Now I was holed up in the cabin, clueless to why I ever agreed to come.

If I left the air-conditioned cabin, I met an oppressive wall of stifling heat that did not let up. It was impossible to function. I wouldn't have cared if I didn't have Poppy. It was too hot to take her outside, so I stayed with her all day in the cabin. But even inside with the air conditioner on high, she could only wear a nappy and felt slick with sweat in my arms.

It had just been me and Poppy in the cabin all day. Julian popped in every now and then to check on us, but never stayed long before heading back to the water. Carrie, Jim and the girls were around, so were Bridget and Oliver, but they, too, only popped into say hi. Amelia had stayed for a moment to gush over Poppy, but naturally, everyone preferred to be by the water, watching the races and socialising, not cooped up inside with me and a three-month-old.

Night arrived, and I was still alone. Julian had gone drinking with some friends by the water. There was nothing to do except eat, watch television, and sleep. So I went to bed. I drifted in and out of sleep; Poppy needing to be fed more frequently. I worried she was dehydrated from perspiration.

I woke to her stirring in her cot at almost one in the morning.

There were voices on our deck. Probably Julian and some club friends. I ignored them, too exhausted to care. I fed, changed and settled Poppy again.

No sooner had I settled her and drifted off to sleep, than I awoke. I checked the clock. Four am.

I rolled off my damp sheets. Still no sign of Julian. I fed and resettled Poppy. There were no more voices. I peered out the window onto the front deck. Julian was asleep on the wooden deck. I shook my head, fed up with his behaviour. He did next to nothing to help with Poppy today. Nor did he care I was stuck in the cabin all day, losing my mind from heat and boredom while he drank and had fun. It was like I didn't exist anymore.

I went outside. I was shocked by how warm it still was. Pre-dawn usually offered more reprieve.

There was a sheen on his open-mouthed face.

"Julian," I hissed.

"Wha?"

"Julian. Get. Up. Come inside."

He grunted.

"Julian, get up," I pleaded. I didn't want other people to see my husband asleep outside.

He rolled onto his side and pushed himself from all fours to standing. Scowling at me when he met my glare. As he passed, I caught a whiff of his breath. I wished he would brush his teeth. In a moment, we'd be in bed, and I knew he'd lay there, breathing out of his mouth, his foul breath wafting all over me. I almost regretted telling him to come inside.

I had barely shut my eyes when I woke again. Six thirty am. Poppy was already awake.

The cabin was barely a comfortable temperature, despite the air conditioner being on all night. I carried Poppy out onto the front deck to feed her, but it was already too hot. Thirsty leaves hung limp to the many trees bordering the park, and the morning sun caused sounds of a cackle as it woke them from their night of mercy. I headed back inside.

It seemed we were in for another day stuck inside. This was not what I had in mind for my first weekend away with my baby.

I woke Julian in time for him to grab a lift with Oliver to the foreshore. With my plans for the day limited again to the cabin, I wasn't sure what to do. I turned on the television and flicked until I found an old film. The air conditioner was noisy running at full capacity, and I was still sweating at rest.

By late morning, cabin fever got to me. I opened the front door during Poppy's morning nap and was overwhelmed by heat. I stepped outside and shut the door quickly to keep the cooler air in. The tourist park was bordered by vast parklands, thick with undergrowth. The wind had picked up now, and it was unnerving watching the treetops thrash about with the strong gusts.

It seemed hotter today. I didn't think it was possible. Breathing hurt; like the hot air was burning the fragile mucosa lining my airways.

I couldn't bear it for long and hurried back inside. Poppy was screaming. I unwrapped her; she was bright red and shiny. I took her to the couch, and she latched on like she had never had a drink. After feeding her, I filled the sink with cool water and sat her naked body in the water. She couldn't sit up on her own yet.

My eyes wandered back to the little air conditioner roaring its hardest. It wasn't even lunchtime. There was meant to be a cool change coming; I could only pray it came soon.

"Knock, knock." Bridget poked her head through the door.

I perked up with the visitor. "Hi. You've finished up early."

"Yeah, they've cancelled the rest of the races today. They'll run them tomorrow morning."

I gazed out the window. "I thought the wind looked a bit hectic."

"It got dangerous, so they pulled the pin. I wanted to come and see how this little darling is doing in the heat." She tickled Poppy on the tummy. "But you're doing just fine aren't you, little one, because your mummy has made you a little private pool."

I smiled. "So, everything is finished up?"

"Yep, they should all be trickling back to the park soon." Bridget let Poppy grab hold of her finger; she was trying to force it into her mouth. "Have you seen the news?"

"No, I've had the movie channel on."

"They're reporting the cool change is not hitting here until tomorrow afternoon."

My jaw dropped.

"It's still forecast to hit home later today. Anywhere south of the ranges, it should still cool down." Bridget swapped her finger to the teething ring by the sink. Poppy shoved it into her mouth as she did anything she got hold of.

"Oh no." I chewed my lower lip.

"Oliver and I are packing up and heading home. It's ridiculous out there, Sarah even fainted on the foreshore." She spooned the now tepid water over Poppy's head.

"That's awful. Is she alright?"

She nodded.

"Hopefully I can talk Julian into leaving today too." I wiped the sweat from my brow. "It's just too hot for Poppy."

Bridget said goodbye and I stood by the kitchen sink, waiting for Julian's return. Carrie also dropped by to say her family were staying. But they were in the main building, not a cabin, and it was cooler in their brick-walled rooms.

Two hours passed and no word from Julian. The event had been cancelled for the day, so what could he possibly be doing? He had a three-month-old baby roasting in a tin cabin in a record heatwave. He should at least call to check how she was doing.

I stared at Poppy on the play rug. Her fingers and toes flew about without coordination. When she caught hold of her toe, she shoved it in her mouth like a prized lollypop. She was adorable and blissfully unaware of the danger outside.

I needed to get her out of this heat. She looked content sucking her toes, so I started packing our things into the car. I kept the car running with the aircon on to cool it so she wouldn't burn on the seat buckles.

When packing her cot into the car, Julian finally appeared. He was red and beaded with sweat. "What's going on?"

I slammed the trunk. I wanted to scream at him but couldn't delay getting out of the sun. I could almost see my trigger cells producing brown pigment within seconds of exposure. Sunburn would soon follow. I had to keep going.

"We're leaving," I grunted. "It's too hot. It's not safe for Poppy."

He just nodded at me.

I wanted to ask where he'd been. What could possibly have been more important than us. Poppy's safety. But Poppy was my priority now, so I stalked into the cabin and scooped her off the floor. I threw my handbag over my shoulder and headed back to the car.

He followed, watching as I buckled her in. I waited for him to beg me to wait, to tell me he'd pack his stuff and come with us. He didn't. Nor did he ask us to stay. He leaned in and kissed Poppy's forehead, checking her belt buckles before closing her door.

I slammed the car door and clicked my belt harder than necessary. Over two hours of driving ahead of me, and I was already wearied. I pulled the car away, and through the rear view mirror, saw Julian enter the cabin.

I shook with anger, gripping at the wheel. I drove along the main highway. Light debris blew all around, the wind a constant whistle above the radio.

I got to the turnoff where I needed to head south, but a police car blocked it. I wound my window down and the heat immediately invaded the comfortable car. My face frying in the sun as I squinted at the officer.

"Was there an accident or something?" I asked the officer.

He shook his head, wiping the sweat from his upper lip. "Fires." He looked at Poppy in the back seat. "Where are you headed?"

"Darvo River."

"Right." He looked down the road. "You need to head through Mitchelton. It'll add a fair bit. But much safer today." He looked to the sky, and I followed his gaze to the hazy orange glow in the south.

I pulled away in the direction he instructed, the fierce winds flattening the long grass of the paddocks to my right. Treetops thrashed about wildly and savage gusts made me grasp tightly to the wheel to keep it under control.

An hour and a half in, and Poppy was screaming bloody murder. I pulled over but dared not shut the engine off. I hadn't seen another car for over twenty minutes; we were so remote. I didn't even know where we were. Somewhere on a road to Mitchelton. No phone service. It was late afternoon, but the sky was so dark a red, it could be confused for night. The wind unrelenting. How long could a tiny baby last in these elements? If the car broke down or a fire came, we wouldn't stand a chance in these apocalyptic conditions.

I could not risk heat coming into our cool car, so instead of opening the door I climbed onto the back seat over the centre console, unclipped the red-faced Poppy and carefully pulled her to my chest. An expert now, she latched on in no time. I swallowed hard, looking out the window. Should I turn back? I couldn't decide on the safer option. I trembled as she fed. I'd never prayed so hard. Please God ... please let me get my baby home safely. *Please.*

She finished and I did my best to change her into a fresh nappy in the cramped space. She screamed when I buckled her into the seat again.

"Sorry, my darling," I hushed. "I don't have a choice. I need to get you somewhere safe."

I contorted back over the centre console and put the car into drive, hoping the movement would placate her. It didn't. I tried to concentrate on driving, but it was intolerable to listen to my baby in such distress.

It was dark and blustery; debris flying everywhere. We could have been on mars. I couldn't see much; smoke blocked where I'd come from and where I was headed.

Poppy picked up the volume.

Hot tears streamed down my cheeks. "Shh, Poppy ... Mummy's here, honey."

Her howling reached a new level.

"Shh, baby, you're okay, we'll be okay. Shh."

Half an hour later and I thought I might start wailing louder than her. She coughed and spluttered but finally, she succumbed to exhaustion with a few gasping breaths. My heart rate tachycardic and bounding, I felt every urgent beat. Despite the silence, there was no relaxing. I was in flight mode.

When I finally reached the outskirts of Darvo River, I cried tears of relief.

We drove up our driveway and with trepidation, I opened the car door. Cool air drenched my face. The wind, though ferocious, had changed direction. Despite smelling of smoke, I inhaled deeply. We were safe.

I glanced at my phone now we were back in service. No missed calls or messages from Julian. Just a message from Mum asking how Poppy was coping in the heat.

Once settled inside, I put Poppy on her playmat. She lay kicking and waving her arms about, smiling broadly with her gums on show. It was as if the prolonged tantrum in the car never happened.

I turned on the television to the news broadcast. They were running a story. Our state had been ravaged by wildfires. They still didn't know the human toll. They showed helicopter footage of a road where a fierce fire had crossed. Everything blackened or gone. The remnants of a car in a ditch completely burnt out, no sign of even a tyre.

My head collapsed into my shaking palms.

That could have been us.

9

"Oh Jess, I don't like the sound of that."

I held my phone to my ear, balancing Poppy who was having a feed. "Mum, it was fine," I lied. "There were police out directing where it was safe. We were never in harm's way."

"Why didn't Julian go with you?"

I sighed. "You know he has commitments at the club. He couldn't just drop what he was doing because I wanted to go early."

"Still, you'd think he would have insisted. He could have asked someone else to help or something. He has other priorities than just that club now." Her voice grew higher. "Poppy is only three months old."

I heard the front door unlock. "Mum, honestly, I told him he should stay on," I said quickly. "It's fine. Anyway, I have to get going and change Poppy."

"Alright, well, I'm relieved you two are safe."

I hung up as the door opened, and Julian stepped in. I'd had two days to fester while he stayed at Rushworth. Carrie had told me all the racing had been cancelled and he'd stayed on anyway.

I gritted my teeth at the sight of him. I might lie to Mum about Julian, but I was done lying to myself about how badly he treated me.

I confronted him immediately. "I can't do this anymore. I want you to move out."

He raised one eyebrow. "Fine."

I went to Poppy's room and changed her, waiting for him to pack

144

up and go. My heart rate up again. I waited for a while, listening for a door to slam, a suitcase wheeling. Nothing. I went back out to the living area, and he was sitting on the balcony with a beer in hand.

"I thought you were going," I spat.

"I don't have anywhere to go. I'll sleep on the couch." He put his beer on the table and came towards me. "Let me hold my daughter."

He smiled at Poppy as I handed her over. His eyes lighting up and hers matching. He sat back in the seat with eyes only for Poppy.

I stormed off.

True to his word, he stayed on the couch. Two weeks went by and still, he slept on the couch. I had no clue why he didn't leave. I didn't want him here and I knew he didn't want to be here. But I did not bring it up again. He didn't even pretend to comprehend that anything he had done was wrong. Who would leave their wife and newborn to drive home by themselves in those dangerous conditions? I was outraged he didn't care more.

We barely spoke. He would go to work each morning and come home, paying no interest to me, not acknowledging I was even there. He still cuddled and cooed over Poppy, throwing her the smiles and grins I fell in love with so many years ago. But I could have been a cockroach in a corner.

I just wanted to go back to what we were. What he promised we would be. The feelings he gave me at the start. I craved his love. That's all I wanted. I could cope with anything else so long as I felt his love again. Where had it gone wrong? Maybe I should have tried harder. Done more. Kept the house tidier. Paid more attention to my appearance so he would still be attracted to me. I'd lost most of the pregnancy weight, but appearance had not been a priority. I was lucky if I ran a comb through my hair most days.

I had given him his out. Why wasn't he taking it?

I didn't need much; I just wanted him to be nice to me. I had gotten used to the lack of affection, but I could no longer tolerate feeling about as useful as a chewed-up chicken bone.

I couldn't wait anymore. He hadn't spoken to me in two weeks. He wasn't leaving, but he was not in our marriage. He was constantly on his phone, doing God knows what. Texting, social media; I had no idea. I wouldn't dare ask.

I stomped in front of the television. Poppy was bouncing on his lap while he watched.

"Julian." I waited until he looked at me. He took his time. "Either you choose to be in this marriage ..." I gulped "... or I leave." My mouth felt sticky getting the words out. "But I refuse to live like this a day longer."

I stared at him, waiting. He stared back, expression unreadable. Poppy gripping at his chest while he mechanically bounced her up and down.

"Jess, I still love you."

My shoulders caved forwards. I was drained. Physically and emotionally spent. "Julian, I love you, too." I slumped next to him. "But I can't live like this. You're living here, but you're not here. We're not speaking." I shook my head, my eyes pleading. "I love you so much. All I want is to be with you, but we both need to do better. We both have to put more into our relationship for it to work."

"Yep." He put his hand on my leg as I brushed over Poppy's soft hair with my palm.

And that was enough for now.

# *Winter 2012*

I had crawled out of hiding.

I was sleeping better, had regained energy and muscle tone, and now that I had returned to work and a social life, I was feeling human again.

Tonight we were at the club, giving farewell to Amelia, who was moving away to study. Almost everyone from the club had turned up. She would be missed. It was the first time I'd been at a club party in forever. Now that I was no longer breastfeeding, I was ready to make a night of it.

Rhonda had other plans. She had me cornered, while I searched for Carrie in the crowded alfresco, begging to be rescued. It's not that I didn't like Rhonda. She just couldn't get through a sentence without putting her foot in her mouth. She had no filter for offence and as one of the biggest cash contributors to the club, felt it bought her the right to know and comment on everyone's business. An enormous gossip.

"Can you believe Amelia is almost eighteen?" Rhonda said, sipping from her glass. "What a hoot! It's so sad she's moving away." Her smile faded. "My Paige adores her."

"How old is Paige now?" I asked. I'd lost track of time in my baby haze.

"She's thirteen ... going on twenty-eight, I might add." Her full smile recovered. "Did you hear what course Amelia got into? Journalism, would you believe?" She shook her head. "I don't think I would let my girls move interstate at seventeen. What do you think about it?"

I shrugged. "Amelia's always been a pretty switched-on kid. I think she will be just fine."

Five minutes was enough to be stuck alone with Rhonda. A wave of nausea hit me and I thanked God for the excuse to leave. "Excuse me, Rhonda, I need to head to the bathroom. I'm feeling a bit nauseous all of a sudden."

Rhonda raised her eyebrows sceptically, but I ignored it, happy in the knowledge I wasn't lying to get away from her. I *was* nauseous. It made no sense. I'd only had two drinks, but it felt like I was hungover. Maybe a gastro bug?

I was heading down the hall to the bathroom when I heard Julian's voice. Following the sound, I turned left at the end of the hall.

"Come on, Milly, it doesn't have to be like that." I heard him pleading as I rounded the turn.

"I'm serious." Amelia's voice firm.

"What doesn't have to be like what?" I asked, approaching Julian from behind and putting my arm over his shoulder, partly to steady myself from another wave of nausea.

He took a step back, appearing surprised to see me. His face quickly composed back to a blank expression.

"She's just worried she won't be able to sail as much as she wants to, that's all." Julian put his arm around my waist. A rare display of affection.

Amelia nodded smiling. "Yeah, I'm going to miss being so close to the water."

It was the end of an era. I put my arm around her.

"Honey," I said, "the water and everyone will always be here. You have dreams to chase." I squeezed her and she smiled.

"That's right," Julian said. "You can come anytime, and we'll take you out on the water."

"Amelia, we're going to get going if you don't mind. I'm not feeling so good. But we'll pop by and see you before you leave, okay?"

Amelia kissed my cheek and walked back towards her party. I turned to Julian.

"Everything okay?" he said, his voice cool.

"No. I think I might have gastro. Can you take me home?"

Julian dropped me off and returned to the party. I only just made it home and to the toilet before vomiting. I sat back against the wall, wiping my mouth with toilet paper. But as fast as it had come on, it was gone again, leaving me famished.

Suddenly ravenous, I cooked some toast and had one slice. I felt good. For about one minute. I ran to the bathroom and vomited again.

This wasn't right. I hadn't felt like this since ... since ... oh no. Shit. Shit. Shit.

I rummaged around the back corner of our vanity where I had a left-over test from nearly two years ago. The use-by said it was still fine.

As I peed on the stick, I couldn't help thinking of the last time I took one of these. Back then, I was praying for two lines. Now I needed one line. Julian had made it abundantly clear that his once large family plans had changed since having Poppy. He didn't want more children. He'd told everyone. He constantly made jokes to anyone who would listen about how shit his life was now he was married with a kid.

I looked at the clock. It had already been five minutes. I didn't want to look.

I flipped the plastic over.

Fuck.

I didn't know how to tell Julian. I was scared he would tell me to get an abortion. As I lay in bed trying to fall asleep, I had to consider all the options. But I couldn't fathom destroying something growing in me. This couldn't be for nothing.

I fell asleep, torn between what to do.

It took all of the next day to summon the courage to tell Julian.

I approached him while he was fiddling with a new speaker system he'd recently bought.

"Julian." My voice weak. "I need to talk to you."

"Yeah, what?" He kept his focus on the speaker.

"I'm pregnant." I burst into tears. "I'm so sorry."

I waited until his lungs fully expelled. It took time. Controlled and loud from his nostrils. Was he going to explode?

"I didn't mean for this to happen, I'm sorry." My face wet from tears and snot.

He inhaled again. He blinked at the ceiling, eyes wide.

"I'm sorry."

He lowered his eyes. "God, Jess. Come here." He pulled me into his arms.

He wasn't mad.

My vessels expanded and blood flowed again. I closed my eyes, burying my head in his chest.

"Thank you so much for this." I welcomed Lyn inside the house.

"Not at all. I love spending time with Poppy." Lyn strode in and placed a large basket on the bench.

"What's that you've got there?" I pointed to the basket.

"Oh." She smiled. "This is just some cereal for her breakfast."

"Poppy already had breakfast."

"I also made her a sandwich for lunch and cut up some fruit she likes. She adores strawberries, you know." Her bright pink lips spread broad.

Of course, I knew. She was my daughter. I tried to force a smile. "You know, we have plenty of food for her here. You didn't have to go to so much trouble."

"Well, I wasn't sure, you know. You've looked so tired lately. It was no trouble." Her hand rubbed along her necklace. Her eyes sympathetic.

I wanted to say, 'Maybe if your son helped a bit more around the house, I wouldn't look so tired.' But I held my tongue.

"Well, I need to get to work," I said. "You can call me if you need anything."

"Do you need me to do any housework or organise dinner?"

There were a million jobs I needed done, but I didn't want her help. I wanted my husband's help. He did nothing around here. I needed him more now I was pregnant again, but if anything, he was lazier than ever. He stepped over toys. I doubted he even knew how to turn the washing machine on. He wouldn't even change a toilet roll.

"No thanks," I said. "I have a day off tomorrow to catch up on cleaning. Just enjoy some time with Poppy."

I left them to it and headed off to work. The day was long and hectic. Quite a few emergencies to deal with. When I arrived home, it was with a satisfied exhaustion of a good day's work, but I was glad it was over.

As I opened the front door, I was hit by the strong smell of bleach and air freshener. Poppy's beaming face charged to greet me, and I crouched low to cuddle her. It was not easy to pick her up now with my belly seeming to grow inches each day.

I found Lyn in the kitchen unpacking grocery bags.

"Oh hello. How was work, Jess?"

"Good, thanks," I said slowly. "What's all this?"

"Dinner is in the oven. It is a casserole from Met's Meats. They're delicious."

"You didn't have to do that." Didn't we have this conversation?

"All the washing is on the line. It's not dry yet, but you'll need to bring it in because it's forecast to rain."

She hadn't listened to a word I said. I didn't want her help. I wanted Julian's help. Not even his help, I just wanted him to do slightly more than nothing. Even just put his clothes in the basket, rather than leave them in a big pile by the bed. I wanted him to hang some washing for once. I would do back flips if only he folded some.

"Lyn, I thought I said don't worry about the washing," I said, working hard to keep my tone friendly.

"Well, there was a huge pile in the laundry and some on the floor of your room."

What was she doing in our bedroom?

She went on. "Anyway, whilst I was out, I picked up a new kettle. Yours was looking tatty." She held it next to her beaming face.

I stared at her, straight faced. I was not even trying to smile now; I was trying not to explode. "Our kettle works fine."

"This one is better. It's the same one I have." She batted her eyelids and patted the top of the box. "Julian said he liked it when he last came over."

I huffed. "Right. How was Poppy?"

"A dream. She watched cartoons while I got the housework done."

"I really thought you might have just enjoyed some time to play with her."

"Well, who could possibly relax in such a mess?"

I almost stumbled back. It felt like a punch to the chest.

"Right ... well, I need to get changed."

Lyn smiled and, getting the message, went to say goodbye to Poppy. They hugged at the front door before Poppy turned and wrapped her arm around my leg, stuffing her thumb into her mouth. I shut the door with a thud. Poppy ran off in the direction of her room as I leant against the door, staring at the ceiling. Deep breaths.

I stomped to the washing line. There was way too much for me to bring into the house. I had nowhere to put it all to dry it. Rain drops spattered my forehead as I was pondering. I swore, and left it.

I went about putting the groceries that Lyn had bought away. The cereal she liked. The spreads she liked. The cheese she liked. Julian would be thrilled.

I walked into the bedroom. The pile of clothes next to Julian's bed was gone. I had been leaving it there in silent protest.

All the things on our bedside tables were rearranged. I opened my bedside drawers. My hand flew to my mouth. What on earth? She had neatly arranged everything inside. All of my personal things. She had gone through everything.

Shaking, I walked into the bathroom. She had hung fresh towels; identical and straight. A new air freshener on the wall. A new bottle of hand soap; the same brand I'd seen in her own home.

I looked inside Poppy's bedroom. The floor had been thick with toys when I left. I hadn't had the energy to put them away before work. Now it was spotless.

I sat on the edge of Poppy's bed, head in my hands.

It was clear. Julian was not the problem.

I was.

§

"There's a bottle in the fridge if she wakes, but I'm almost certain she won't stir," I said to Julian, who was stretched out on the couch.

"Is she asleep?" He kept his eyes on the television.

"Almost, I think she will settle. She's had dinner and a bath and I've put her to bed." I looked at my watch. "I'm going to be really late if I don't go now."

"What time will you be home?" He finally looked at me.

"I don't know, it depends how long dinner takes."

"What's this for again?" His eyes slanted.

"I told you, there is a new vet starting at the hospital and we are having a staff dinner to welcome him."

"Him?"

"Yes."

"What time will you be back?"

"Julian ... I will be back after dinner."

"Who's going?"

I took a deep breath. I almost never went anywhere without him. The least he could do was say have a good time and don't hurry home. Enjoy yourself.

"The entire staff is going," I said. "We were told in no uncertain terms to please attend."

He nodded and looked back at the television.

"Okay, well, I'm going." I leant and kissed his cheek.

He grunted in response.

My cheeks were hot by the time I walked into the private room at the restaurant work had booked. People looked to be finishing their entrees.

"Oh Jess, I was worried you might have been ill or something." Our practice manager, Gayle, stood to welcome me.

"I'm so sorry. Poppy had a bit of a meltdown." More like I was doing everything to avoid Julian having a meltdown.

I'd learnt from experience it wasn't worth going out without him. His mood was not worth it. His interrogation. I would never enjoy myself while I was out, too distracted by what I would be going home to. I had no choice tonight. Work had made that clear. But I wish I could have skipped the formalities of meeting my new colleague and just stayed home.

Gayle took me over to meet my new colleague, a fit looking middle-aged man.

"This is Jessica Foster," Gayle said. "She's one of our most experienced nurses. Jess, meet Patrick Thomas."

A warm smile filled his face. "Pleased to meet you, Jessica." He stood, extending his hand.

"Call me Jess." I shook his hand, before we both sat.

Even with Julian plaguing my thoughts, I enjoyed the meal. It was nice to be served, once in a while. Julian rarely made dinner or cleaned up or helped in any way. It was a welcome change.

When a waitress came to the table to take coffee orders, I stood.

"I actually need to be going," I said, reaching for my jacket.

"You only just finished your meal," Gayle said.

"Yeah, sorry. Will I see you tomorrow morning Patrick?"

He smiled; a smile that reached his eyes and never faded throughout dinner. I couldn't help smiling, too; it was infectious. "Yes, that's right," he said. "I'm starting in the morning and looking forward to finding my way around."

"Don't worry, we're all here to help." I stepped back. "Sorry Gayle, I really have to go. I'll see you tomorrow."

It was nice to be out, but it wasn't worth prolonging the inevitable. I drove home and hurried in the door, walking straight to the living room. Julian saw me and looked at his watch. He raised his eyebrows. Maybe that's all it would be.

"How was Poppy?"

"She eventually fell asleep."

I nodded. "What are you watching?"

"It will be over before I can fill you in on the details."

"Oh."

I went to the kitchen to make myself a cup of herbal tea before bed. I flicked the kettle on and almost jumped when I turned around to see Julian had followed me. I hadn't heard him coming.

"You scared me," I said, my hand on my swelling belly.

He stood there, staring, tapping his foot. I waited for him to speak but he didn't, so I reached for the tea bag, taking time to gauge the tension growing in the room. It was so familiar now. Like static electricity or the change in air pressure right before it pours. It was coming. Was it just that I went out? It could be something else. I scanned over the last few days and could think of nothing I did wrong. The pressure too much, I decided to just get it over with.

156

"Is something wrong?" I said.

He flicked his eyes to mine and almost smiled. Did he enjoy this? "How long have you been in touch with Matt?"

My shoulders bent forwards a little. I took a deep breath. "Look Julian, he just messaged to see what I was up to. His wife is pregnant with their third child. He was happy to hear I'm pregnant."

He nodded furiously. Like he had caught me in the act. In the act of what? Seeing that my ex-boyfriend was alive and well. That he had children.

"This is no big deal. We are not regularly in contact. It was just a few messages."

He crossed his arms, nostrils flaring. Still saying nothing.

Tired of apologising for not doing anything wrong, I had a sudden rush of courage; "You can't tell me who I can and can't contact."

"I know. Just like I can't say who you can and can't fuck, right?" A drop of spit flew from his lips.

"Oh god, Julian. I'm pregnant with your second child. I'm not fucking anybody else."

"Well, who would know?" He threw his hands up. "You're certainly not fucking me."

That wasn't true. I still kept a diary.

"Julian, I'm sorry, I don't want to upset you. Honestly, it was just a few messages filling each other in on family life. We are not back in regular contact."

His lips were pressed firm in defiance.

"I'm serious. I don't want Matt. We were just saying what we've been doing."

The circle continued. The revolving door of accusations, fury, dishonesty and loathing. It went on and on until I was exhausted.

The clock ticked. It was late.

"Julian, I have to get up early for work." My voice drained. "I need to go to bed. I promise, I am not having any affairs."

He spun on his heels and stormed back to the living room while I headed to the bedroom. I ran my hands over my face, squeezing my eyelids firm. I changed into pyjamas and brushed my teeth, leaning heavy on the vanity with my spare hand.

I climbed into bed and placed my hand automatically to my bulging tummy. The nudges bringing a small grin to my lips. I waited for my heart rate to fall, enjoying the sensations of my backflipping foetus. I let the irregular little prods distract me as I tried to settle my mind enough to bring sleep.

As I lay there, one thing played on my mind. How on earth had he accessed my private messages?

_

# Spring 2013

I closed my eyes and breathed in the ocean. It was exhilarating to feel the wind in my hair, the salt glaze to my lips. I had missed this. Being out on the ocean brought a clarity of mind and spirit that I could never find elsewhere.

Since having Ricky six months ago, I'd barely seen the ocean, let alone sailed across it. My days were spent feeding, cleaning, wiping bums. It had been a tough time. Since day one, I was alone. Even during labour. Julian's parents had come into the hospital, and Julian wanted them to come in. Between vomiting and leaking amniotic fluid, I said no. I didn't think it was too much to ask for a bit of privacy with my body preparing to expel a human in all its goriness. So he took them to a café and I was almost glad he wasn't there at my side, watching me ride contractions, puffing on the gas. His face of revulsion was not wanted. Like last time, he did not stay a single night in the double suite. But unlike last time, I hadn't asked him to. Better to be alone than be disappointed.

Six months had passed of me doing everything to raise Ricky. Sure, Julian was a great father, but only when he was around. And that wasn't often. So it was a relief to finally be out on the ocean doing something just for me. For my pleasure. To not have to worry about nappies and feeding constantly. Just a couple of hours out here and already I felt revitalised. Content.

After we docked, I hopped off the boat, unable to wipe the smile from my face. "That was so invigorating." I said to Meghan, who had joined our crew today. "How's uni been going?"

"It's great!" Meghan said. "Not too long and I'll be a fully qualified physiotherapist."

I patted her shoulder and she beamed with pride. Carrie's face matched. It was good to see Meghan again; I'd known both of Carrie's daughters since they were kids. It was strange not seeing them anymore, both having gone away to study.

We headed towards the club as a group.

"Meghan, are you staying around to help with the junior training session?" Julian asked.

"Yeah, of course," she said smiling.

"How is Amelia doing?" I asked Carrie.

"She's looking forward to visiting over the holidays and meeting baby Ricky," Carrie said.

"Liking the course?" Julian asked.

"Loving it! And she's made a nice little group of friends from the campus. She even has a boyfriend." Meghan smiled over her shoulder at me.

"Oh!" I exclaimed. Meghan had dated boys through high school, but it only occurred to me now that I had no memory of Amelia ever having a boyfriend.

Julian walked ahead to the equipment shed without another word.

"Her first boyfriend ... remember those days?" I nudged Carrie.

"Yeah, all too well."

I put my hand around Carrie's shoulder. "Oh my goodness! I just realised, Amelia is going to be the same age I was when I started dating Julian! Can you believe it?"

Carrie's eyes grew. "Has it really been so long?"

"Yes! I know. I was such a baby. I don't know what he saw in me. Gosh. And now I have babies of my own."

Carrie continued to the club and I went to see how the junior classes were going with Meghan. We walked into the boat storage area where all the under eighteens were getting their boats prepped.

Catherine, Adele and Emily hurried over when they spotted me. They all hugged me in turn.

"Where's Poppy and bubba Ricky?" Catherine gushed, looking around.

"They're having a day with my mum and dad."

They all looked a bit disappointed.

"Hey Jess, can you help with my boat?" Emily said, her upper lip screwed in frustration. "I'm struggling with a knot. I think I've done it wrong again."

"Sure Em, I'd love to help."

Emily caught me up on all the good things in her life while we prepped her boat together. I felt a similar wave of contentment as I helped her. Different to being out on the water, but just as fulfilling. With every movement, I was returning to myself, to who I was before having kids. Not a mother, not a wife. Just Jess.

I waved them all off as they hit the water, Julian leading them out on a tinny. One day, he would be leading Poppy and Ricky out into the ocean, too. There were few sports where an entire family could be involved in one club. That's what I loved about sailing. It seemed to nestle itself under one's skin and was passed down like a gene inherited.

But it was more than that. Carrie, Jim and the girls, all the juniors we coached, Bridget, Oliver, Sarah and Tony – they were all family. A found family, brought together by sail and water.

# Autumn 2014

"Where are you?" Julian asked, no smile in tone through the phone line.

"I told you, I am at an education session for work." I covered the mouthpiece as I spoke, turning from the others so they couldn't hear what I was saying. "Anyway, we are finishing up soon, so I will be home in about half an hour."

"Yeah, but *where* are you exactly?"

I froze. I hadn't told him the education session was being held at a restaurant. I hadn't even thought to.

"It's at that restaurant on the corner of Parkyn Parade."

"Right. I thought you were meant to be at work?"

I lowered my voice to a whisper. "I told you it was a work education night. Not that it was held at the hospital." Frustration edged in my tone.

"Right," he said dryly and hung up.

I needed to get home. I made my excuses and left earlier than everyone else who was enjoying the opportunity to socialise after the talk. I needed to be ready to handle him tonight. Probably just apologise that I didn't give him the correct information and say it wouldn't happen again. My stomach was heavy. It wasn't only because of the confrontation I was hurrying home to negate. How on earth did he know I wasn't at the hospital? I stopped at the traffic lights and picked up my phone, turning it over in my hands. Was he tracking me?

He already had access to my private messages. I'd surmised long ago he knew my passwords to all my social media accounts. When I'd confronted him, he'd gotten angry, changed the subject and accused me of flirting with someone at the club. I knew better than to bring it up again. But the possibility he was tracking me was new. And disturbing.

I pulled up the drive and hurried to the door. The sooner I got through this, the sooner I could get some sleep.

I walked to the living room. "I'm home!" I announced brightly, hoping my tone would placate him. "How are the kids?"

He took his time to answer, and when he did, he didn't look at me. "I gave Ricky a bottle twenty minutes ago."

"Great, thanks."

He grunted. Twice in one year I had been out in the evening without him. Only twice. Normally, if anyone asked me to catch up in the evening, I declined, using the children as an excuse. But as much as I tried, I couldn't get out of work events. He refused to understand this.

I stared at him, waiting for him to have a go at me or show he was not speaking to me. I figured the latter, so I turned to head towards the bedroom.

"Why didn't you tell me it wasn't at the hospital?" His voice boomed and he was on his feet, red faced.

So, we were going to do this.

"Julian, I'm sorry. I didn't realise I didn't tell you."

"Well, you didn't!"

"I'm sorry."

"Who was there?"

"Almost everyone from work."

He nodded with his nostrils wide. "Right." He scowled. "You know I know what's going on right?"

"What do you mean?" I frowned. "I was at an education dinner."

"Oh, now it's an education dinner, is it?"

I let out a sigh. "Well, not really a dinner, more like finger food while we got a talk from a company that wants us to buy their products."

"Sure. Right. *Educational*."

My shoulders slumped, there was no point arguing with him. "Julian, I'm tired, I just want to go to bed."

"You know I'll know if you bring someone here. I'll know." He stepped towards me, chin high.

"Julian, do you really think I'm going to bring someone here with two little kids?" I stamped my foot. "I'm not having an affair!"

He glared at me, smug and hostile. "Just know, I'm watching, Jess. I see everything."

"I'm really tired. I'm going to bed." I hurried away, my shoulders low, fortitude stolen.

I opened my phone as soon I got into bed. I searched rental properties in the area to gauge how much money I needed if I ever needed to leave in a hurry. I had five thousand dollars saved in a separate account. I didn't love him anymore. Our life together was miserable. We showed happy faces around the club all the time, but they were masks. We were nothing like that at home. I didn't exist unless I had done something wrong, like broken one of his unspoken rules, or if he wanted sex. I had to ask permission to do normal things I knew other people would do without a thought. It was a constant mental battle to read and manage his moods. It was like I was a temperature gauge with a faulty thermometer. I was constantly reading and measuring him, but I couldn't handle his moods anymore. The exhaustion overwhelmed me.

But even though I wanted to leave, I knew in my core, staying was easier.

I heard his footsteps in the hall. I hurriedly deleted my search history, hid my phone away, and flipped open my book.

He entered the bedroom and went to the toilet, never once looking at me. As soon as he shut the toilet door, I grabbed my phone again and searched: *Is my husband controlling*? I was led to a twenty-question survey. I read through each question one at a time, swallowing hard; I could tick almost every box.

How did I get here?

The toilet flushed. I deleted my search history again and shut the phone off. When he came out, I pretended to be asleep.

Ricky woke me the following morning, rattling the side of his cot. I stood and walked to his doorway. He beamed his widest grin when he spotted me; it never failed to warm my heart. I picked him up and carried him straight to his highchair. Poppy stirred as we passed her room and met us in the kitchen, dragging her stuffed rabbit along the floor.

Julian was late out of bed, and I had the children dressed and fed before he came out to the living room.

"Hey sport!" Julian scooped his son off the ground and held him high above his head. He giggled in response. "Daddy has to go to work now." Julian said and popped Ricky down, kneeling next to Poppy. She threw her arms around him.

166

"Do you have to go, Daddy?" She said with puppy eyes. "Can't you stay and play with us all day?"

"Poppy, you have preschool today anyway." I said, drying a dish in the doorway.

Julian didn't acknowledge me but held a sweet expression for his children. "Sorry, my little champs. I would love not to have to work. I'd rather spend all my time with you." He matched their disappointed faces. "I have to get going. I'm already late." He hugged them again and left without a glance at me.

# Spring 2014

"**A**re you positive this is okay?" I looked out the passenger window of Carrie's SUV as we drove south through the ranges. I couldn't stop scratching at my index finger with my thumb nail. This felt wrong.

"Of course, it is," Carrie said from the driver's seat. "He knows all about it. He even helped me pack your bag."

"This just sounds so unlike him."

"Yes, well," Bridget said from the back seat, "sometimes even a toad can behave like a prince. Isn't that how the story goes?"

I forced a laugh. "Something like that." I turned in my chair, looking at both women. "Are you really certain this is okay with him?"

"Yes!" they cried in unison. Their exasperation clear.

"You can relax." Carrie patted my leg. "He has the children under control, and we have everything else under control."

I breathed a sigh of relief. I had never been on a holiday without Julian. For the girls to surprise me with a weekend away for my birthday was more than exciting – it was terrifying. In a thrilling sort of way. Like I was doing something I shouldn't. Knowing that Julian was okay with it, I gave myself permission to enjoy it. It still worried me that he said it was fine to them. I knew better. Just because he told them it was okay, didn't mean it was. There would be consequences.

Well, I was here. There was no going back. I could either worry the whole time or enjoy myself. I decided on the latter.

We arrived in the lakeside town of Doncurry and checked in at the resort. The surprises kept coming as the girls popped a bottle of bubbles on arrival. We changed in time for our dinner booking at the restaurant attached to the resort. We devoured the degustation with matching wines over four hours before collapsing in blissful fullness at midnight.

The surprises continued through Saturday. The morning was filled with a decadent spa session that involved me getting pasted in green muck from head to toe and wrapped up like a sous vide sausage. I lay across from my friends in the shared treatment room and while they threw jokes around about what we must look like, I nearly teared up, suddenly overwhelmed by their care and love, which had never faded over the years.

We spent the afternoon sunning by the pool, sipping cocktails. The revelry of being away from daily monotony was clear on all our faces. I didn't have to think of anyone but myself. It was the most free I'd felt for ten years. I hadn't realised how heavy a burden it was tiptoeing around Julian until I was away from him. This mini escape was like coming up for air.

I was onto my third fruity concoction of the afternoon, laughing with Carrie and Bridget, when my phone vibrated. Julian.

"Hey, how are you?" I said, walking out of earshot.

"Good," Julian said, sounding like he meant it. "How's your holiday?"

"It's been amazing! We'll all have to come one day. Thank you

169

so much." I ran my fingers through my hair, still soft from the spa treatment. "How are the kids? What did you get up to with them yesterday?"

"Actually, we were home. I wanted to get stuff done in the shed, so I got Catherine over to babysit."

I paused. "Really? You didn't even go out?"

"Nah, but I got what I wanted done."

"Right. Okay." My bliss marred in one minute of conversation. He went on to ask me to transfer some money into our joint account.

I spoke to the children for a few minutes before returning to the girls to finish my cocktail.

"That was really strange," I said. "I mean, I shouldn't be mad because he let me come on this trip but ..." I wasn't sure if I wanted to tell the girls this; I didn't want to bring down the mood with my domestic worries. But they were all looking at me expectantly, so I continued. "But he has never looked after the children for a weekend by himself. I'm only gone two nights and last night he got Catherine over to babysit."

Carrie raised an eyebrow. "Where did he go?"

"He said he was working in the shed."

"You mean he was home?" Carrie said, bemused.

"Yeah. It makes no sense why he'd get a babysitter. I guess he's just lazy." I sighed. "Or doesn't care."

"I was right," Bridget said. "That man is a toad. Why don't you leave him?"

"I wouldn't know where to start," I said in a small voice.

"Come on, Jess. Julian isn't here. We still have another fifteen hours here and we are not wasting any more of them on him."

Bridget stood and reached for my hand. "We're getting another round."

Her infectious smile was impossible to resist. She was right. This was my break from Julian. Who knew when I would get another?

———

# Winter 2015

Ricky ran from the living room when he heard the key in the door. His little legs almost tripped in his uncoordinated hustle. I followed him, grinning.

I pulled open the door as Julian pushed inwards and I gave him a wide smile. He didn't return it.

"Daddy!" Ricky squealed.

"Hello sport," he said in a dull voice, picking him up but lacking his usual enthusiasm.

"You're home early." I took Ricky from him.

"Yep."

Something was wrong. It was not unusual for him to ignore me, but he would normally give more attention to the children.

I followed him to the kitchen, where he headed straight for the fridge, got a beer bottle and cracked open the top. He leant against the counter and slugged the neck. His shoulders slumped.

"Julian, what's happened?"

He took another long swig of the beer and cast his eyes down.

"What is it?" I pushed.

He took another swig, the bottle near empty. "I was made redundant today."

"Oh my god." I made to reach for him but held back when his

172

shoulders tensed. "What happened?"

"They're downsizing management." He stared at the floor.

"Shit, what are we going to do?" I hesitantly squeezed his shoulder. He didn't shake me off.

"I don't know." He rubbed his brow. "I need some time to think."

He grabbed a six pack and headed out the front door.

I didn't see him until the following morning when I woke, and he was beside me, snoring. I got Poppy ready and took her to preschool. Julian surfaced near lunchtime and shuffled into the kitchen in his boxers. He stood there, staring at the floor.

"Where did you go last night?"

"Luke's."

"I called him at ten thirty. He said you weren't there." I flipped the coffee machine on for him. I knew he would need coffee.

"For fuck's sake, Jess," he warned. "I don't need your shit right now. Okay?"

"Fine, okay, sorry."

"I went to the pub with Marty, alright? Satisfied?" He glared at me.

I nodded and went about making lunch for Ricky. Julian made himself a coffee and headed to the balcony. After I finished making lunch, I followed him.

"Do you want something to eat?" I asked gingerly.

"No," he grunted.

I nodded and sat next to him.

He turned to me, his hair sticking up to the left and plastered flat on the right. "Sweetie, I was thinking. This may not be such a bad thing." His sour expression softened. "I mean, I'm getting a big payout. Something like a hundred k."

"Oh, wow!"

"Yeah. So if we are smart about this, we'll end up better off. If I get a job fast enough, we'll be able to finally sell this place and maybe afford something on the waterfront."

"Oh my god, that would be amazing. You're right. This could mean a fresh start for us."

He'd always made such a big deal about never wanting to live here and how marriage ruined his life. Maybe if he lived in the house of his dreams, he could be happy again. *We* could be happy again. Perhaps we could rediscover that relationship from so many years ago.

We could be fixed.

# *Autumn 2016*

Poppy encouraged her three-year-old brother to sit between her legs at the top of the big slide. I smiled, remembering doing that with her a few years ago to coax her down. Eventually I'd promised her a milkshake if she was a brave girl and gave it a go. After going once, I couldn't keep her off that slide.

Ricky was the opposite; he had no qualms going down the big slide. I was sure he was humouring Poppy's motherly, protective nature. He didn't need encouragement, rather, strict supervision to make sure he was not doing anything dangerous.

These sweet interactions made my heart melt.

"Mummy, are you watching?" Poppy called. I nodded and laughed at their squeals as they descended in tandem.

"Time to get going, you two!" I stood and drained the last of my coffee. It was almost six pm.

"Mummy, please, one more, please." Ricky cried, his hands in prayer position before taking off; not waiting for an answer.

"Only once, okay!" I called.

"Hey Jess, how are you?"

I turned towards the familiar voice and smiled. "Hi Chloe!"

Chloe stopped on the path with her pram. I leant in towards her six-week-old girl. "How are you little angel?" I cooed before looking back to Chloe. "How are you going with it all?"

"I feel like we're getting there," she said, sounding tired. "I had no idea what it was going to be like. I mean, I know what you and others told me I might expect, but honestly ... who really believes that's what's going to happen, right?"

My smile broadened. "I don't think anything that anyone says can properly prepare you for motherhood. Is Luke being helpful?"

"I don't know what I would have done without him. I don't think I would have gotten through the last six weeks. He's been amazing. So supportive. He gets up and brings her to the bed for me to feed her when I'm exhausted and then changes and settles her again. I mean, I'm sure it's just the norm, right? Julian would have done that stuff, I'm sure."

I forced a nod. "Oh yeah. Of course, that's normal." It just wasn't my normal.

"Anyway, he's getting dinner ready while I get a bit of fresh air. I feel bad. I've been home all day and he's the one organising dinner after a long day at work." She fussed over the muslin swaddling her baby. "He's done almost all the housework, too."

My thumbnail was wearing down the skin on my index finger. "Well. You *are* in this together." I shrugged and glanced back towards my children.

"Great to see you, Jess. We'll catch up soon, yeah? I feel like we've been in hibernation or something." She smiled, waving as she walked away.

I wondered what fabulous dinner Julian had arranged after being home all day. I turned back to the children, wearing my sternest face, and told them it was time to go home.

On the walk home, I couldn't help growing a jealous rage towards

Chloe. She had everything. A family and a great guy who adored her. Once upon a time I would have been happy for a friend in that scenario. Not now, I hated her for it. I didn't recognise the resentful, awful person I had become. I compared my unemployed husband to Luke. It had been six months since the redundancy, and there was no sign of him getting work. We were almost out of money.

I had no idea what he did while I was at work. He sure wasn't applying for jobs. Nor was he looking after the children or doing housework. Even on the days the kids didn't have daycare or school, he organised to drop them to my mum. He was in bed every morning when I left to drop them at school or daycare. Granted, he did a load of washing the other day – and expected a medal for it. Other than doing the dishes a few times, he did nothing else to help. He still stepped over toys and wouldn't change a toilet roll. My shoulders were slumped as I headed up our drive with the children in tow. I waved to Julian's friend, Marty, as he was pulling out of our drive.

"Daddy!" Poppy squealed and bolted towards Julian, who stood at the top of the drive. Ricky hot on her tail.

"Hello, my little princess!" He threw her high in the air before landing her on his hip and scooped up Ricky to his other hip.

"How was your day?" I asked, hoping to hear he had an interview. Something. Anything.

He shrugged. "It was busy. I was working on my resume."

I nodded and walked into the house. As I passed him, I smelled the stench of beer on his breath. Six months unemployed and he was still working on his resume. I tidied the lounge and carried the toys to their toy box. I passed the dining room table, and it was overflowing with laundry.

"And tell me exactly how many times you jumped from the top of the slide?" Julian asked Ricky, tickling his tummy.

"At least sixty-six times," Ricky proudly explained through his adorable lisp.

I smiled as Julian placed Ricky down and both kids scampered towards their rooms.

"I did the washing." Julian pointed at the pile of laundry on the table.

You mean you brought it in off the line and dumped it all on the dining room table. I couldn't be bothered dealing with all that on a Friday night.

"Thanks." I feigned gratitude. Any hint of sarcasm would bring a fight. I couldn't handle another one. I headed down the hall and passed a new feature of the hallway; a hole in the plaster of the wall. When he'd told me the payout was already spent, I'd cried, "How could you do this to us?" and he punched the wall near my head. I should have known better. There were always consequences if I lost my temper.

Now we were living off my wage. It broke me when I started diving into my escape kitty for day-to-day expenses. He'd promised a house on the water, and now, I was losing hope we could even afford to keep living here.

He followed me into Ricky's room. "Do you want pizza for dinner?" he asked.

"That sounds great, thanks." I said.

"I'm going to head over to Marty's later to catch the game, so I'll get dinner now. Cool?"

"Yeah, no worries." With any luck I wouldn't see him until tomorrow. He normally stayed out most of the night when he headed over there. I smiled at the irony of looking back at the days when I used to worry if he didn't come home. Now I looked forward to it.

"Okay, I'll be back soon." He tapped his hand on the door jamb, before heading down the hall.

Tears rolled down my face as the front door shut. Now I was alone, I was free to feel.

# *Winter 2016*

I handed over my card at the end of dinner. My stomach sunk, knowing that was the last dollar left of my escape money. It was a club dinner he insisted we had to be at. I didn't want to come and pretend to save face. God forbid anyone at the club knew the truth – we were broke. I watched Julian laughing with his friends around the table. The almighty president had been unemployed for over ten months.

"Thank you," I said to the waitress and stuffed the now useless ATM card back in my bag.

My eyes darted to Julian as more laughter erupted around him. Always conducting the room. My tongue furled around an uncomfortable metallic taste in my mouth, watching the façade.

"Hey, Jess, is everything alright?" Carrie's hand landed on my shoulder.

"Oh yeah. 'Course. I'm just tired, that's all. I'm going to head off." I threw my friend the cheerful face I had mastered and hugged her.

No one knew more about my troubles at home than Carrie. But even she didn't know the half of it. Most of it, I barely admitted to myself. I walked over to Julian and pretended to laugh along with whatever they were talking about.

"Hey, I'm heading home."

He looked at me, smiling. "Okay, give me a second and I'll come too."

I forced another smile. "Okay, great." Not great at all. I didn't want to have sex with him. I watched him drain his beer and everyone said good night.

"Making the most of the kids away, huh, Julian?" Marty smirked and nudged the guy to his right; the table erupting in laughter again.

I smiled along. How entertaining for them all. Julian looked smugly over his shoulder and threw his arm around me as we walked away.

I got ready for bed as soon as we got home. Exhausted. Annoyed. Frustrated at his lack of enthusiasm for a job hunt. And now I would have to climb into bed and wait for him to come and fuck me.

I escaped; delving deep into my novel. A love story so unlike my own. After all these years, I'd lost hope of a happily ever after. This was not who I fell in love with. I did not love this man. What he promised our life would be had disappeared; a dream carried away in a stiff offshore breeze. How stupid to believe I could catch it. To believe it was ever real.

The toilet flushed and I flicked the light off and pretended to sleep. His steps were heavy down the hall. How much did he drink? That same routine. No brushing teeth, no washing hands after he crapped. I regulated my breath. In and out. In and out. Heavy exhalations. Cold air slapped at my back as he lifted the covers to get into bed. The room was dark except for some bluish shapes on the wall cast by invading moonlight. They shifted in the breeze of the open window. I swallowed. In and out. My breath moderated. I stiffened as his hand landed on my back. He lazily rubbed it up and down; the foreplay ritual. My eyes flew open as his body came flush against mine. I needed to fight all my instincts not to squirm away from him. I wanted to scream, 'Don't fucking touch me!'. I couldn't. I knew what I needed to do. Just go along, find somewhere pleasant in my head to go and wait it out. But that was getting harder. There weren't many places in my head left; I'd lost all hope. I'd stopped googling rental houses in the middle of the night. It was no use. I was broke. I couldn't leave.

His lips landed on the back of my neck, and I tensed again. Just relax. Go along with it. It would be over soon. Before long, he was in me from behind. His hand gripping my hip, he started thrusting. I watched the shape of our dark blue shadows on the wall, gaining momentum. My jaw clenched. His hand reached for my breast, and I slapped my elbow firm against my side to block him. It was involuntary. My body knew what to do, but it was working against me. He thrust and I tensed, rigid as death. I told myself to stop. Calm down.

I couldn't take it anymore. His foul breath on the back of my neck. His disgusting unwashed hands on me. I couldn't stand him in me anymore. I spasmed with every thrust. My lower jaw felt ready to crack. He thrust again and I stiffened. Every muscle of my being contracted painfully.

He pushed my hip away and recoiled. I panted. Nostrils flaring. He flicked on the light, and it illuminated him, standing over the bed.

"What the fuck is wrong with you?" he spat, red faced, pulling up his dirty jeans.

I moved my jaw slowly and jostled my tongue around in my mouth. I'd never felt this type of rage. I took a second and lifted my back towards the headboard. Pulling the covers with me over my knees now at my chest. I hugged them there. I could do this. My saliva so viscous, each word demanding great concentration. He glared down at me. I needed to do this now.

"Julian ..." My tongue was not working properly. I swallowed again. "I think we should go our separate ways."

His face looked about to explode. He stepped back.

I gathered strength. I had always been scared to leave, scared of what he might do. I had no fear in this moment. My children were safe with my parents, and I was done being treated like this. Never again. A warmth spread through my chest as I sat up and stared back, jaw set.

His stare threatened a deadly storm as he stalked around the bed. I didn't move, silently watching him leave the room.

He slammed some cupboards in the kitchen before the heavy footsteps headed back towards me. He reappeared, still shirtless, carrying a bottle of whiskey and a glass. He slammed the tumbler on the dresser and poured a large shot, downing it. He composed his face.

"*Who* is he?" Such venom in his voice.

I didn't move. "There is nobody else."

"Yeah, right!" His aggression rising.

I remained calm. Heart rate normal. "Julian, neither of us are happy." A statement. No pleading in my tone. I would not console him. I would not calm him. I was in total control for the first time since I could remember.

He took a moment, sizing me up. "I knew it! I knew there was someone else! I knew you would do this to me." He chugged another shot and slammed the glass.

I didn't jump. I didn't react at all, only continued looking at him flatly. I would not back down. His anger didn't scare me anymore.

All my nerves and internals stripped long ago. There was nothing left to hurt.

"There is no one else," I said evenly. "I think we would both be happier if we weren't together anymore."

"Bullshit!" Another shot downed.

"There is no one else. I am not happy living with you anymore."

"You know ... I'm the *smartest* man you know!" He pushed his thumb to his chest. I gave him nothing. He looked at the floor. I watched him think. His eyes shot back at me. "I'll take the kids then!"

"No. You won't."

"How could you do this to them?"

"They are not going to grow up happy with two unhappy parents."

His nose screwed up and he looked down at me, his chin high. "You know, I took our marriage vow seriously!" Hand to heart. Beating.

"So did I." My voice completely level. Unmoved. I was done.

He continued for a while. More shots of whiskey. He looked so confused at my lack of reaction. The usual cycle wasn't going to plan; I was not giving in, and would not be worn down this time.

His face contorted, near purple now, and his eyes searched the ceiling. He threw his hand over his mouth. A muffled sob escaped. His shoulders collapsed forward, and he wept. For the first time, I was seeing him weep. I watched, unmoved. It was about time someone else shed some tears around here.

His hand shot to a notebook resting on the dresser and grabbed the pen next to it, ripping the lid off. He leaned over and commenced scrawling feverishly on the page. I sat quietly. Waiting. He sobbed again. How long would this last?

"What are you doing?" I asked.

"I'm writing a note to my children."

"Why?"

"Because I love you guys, Jess." He spun to me, eyes beseeching. "You and the children are all I have." He paused and sobbed. "I'm going to drive my car off the cliff and ..." Another sob. "I want my children to know I love them."

I took a deep breath, not moving. He was not being serious. He scribbled away, wiping tears with the back of his hand and sniffing hard. But he looked genuine. I'd never seen him like this.

I gritted my teeth. He was bluffing. I had never stood up to him before. I would not back down now.

But it looked so real. He couldn't fake tears. I kept watching. Sympathy creeping into my eyes.

He finished and slapped the paper down. "Make sure they get that." His voice cracked and his face was in his palms again. His eyes glimpsed mine as he stepped into the doorway before pausing. "I love you, Jess." Another loud sob.

Fuck, what if this was real?

I got out of the bed as he stepped into the hall and pulled my nightie down to full length. I stood next to the bed as he took a few steps down the hall. "Wait ... stop! Let's talk about this."

His tears dried.

— ⁕ —

I let the shutter slam on the letter box. Another day, more bills. More final warnings. The phones had already been shut off a few

185

times. I was relieved we could pay the electricity before that was cancelled too.

On top of the pile of bills was a curious business card. I balanced my bag of groceries and walked up to the house, flipping the card over.

*Julian Rundell, please contact Detective Laura Keen.*

A landline number was listed. Surely the police didn't get involved with late bills.

I looked at my watch and rushed inside. Poppy finished school in ten minutes and would be worried if I wasn't there on time.

I dropped the business card and bills on the bench. I had hoped to have time to change out of my smelly work scrubs.

"Julian are you home?" I called. No response. Weird. He was normally here on a Tuesday. I texted him as I trotted to the car.

*Where are you?*

He responded fast.

*Just at the club, home soon. I'll cook tonight xxx*

I smiled at my phone and got in the car. He might still be unemployed, but he had been attentive and kind over the last few weeks since I threatened to leave. He promised he would drink less, help more and get a job. So far, he was doing as he promised. All I needed to do was stand up to him to see a change. Perhaps if I had been tougher years ago, he would have treated me better. Nothing was a fast fix, but he was working hard at it. Maybe now we could move forward.

After dinner, while Julian was doing the dishes, I remembered the card from the detective.

"Hey, did you see that card from the police I left on the counter?"

"Oh yeah." He didn't miss a beat.

"Do you know what it's about?"

Lifting his lower lip, he shrugged. "No idea, I'll give them a call tomorrow."

My stomach knotted a little, remembering the time the police knocked on my door with Julian in handcuffs. I pushed the memory away and went to bath the children.

The following afternoon, I was exhausted. We were short-staffed at work, and it was only me and my boss Patrick for most of the day. Not that it was all bad. I loved working with him; we got along great and he was so kind to pets and families. But we needed the extra hand. By the time I got home with the kids, I was dreaming of sleep, praying Julian was home to help out with dinner so I could go rest.

"Julian?" I called.

No sound. No lights on.

I walked to the kitchen and stared into the fridge, waiting for inspiration. I closed the door, remembering the police card. I reached for my phone and dialled Julian's number. It went to message bank. I texted him.

*Hey, we're home, just organising dinner. What time will you be home? xo*

Nothing.

I threw together some fried rice for the children. While I cooked, I couldn't stop glancing at my phone, but nothing. It was Wednesday. It was strange for him to disappear midweek. Three hours later, after the children were in bed, I texted him again. No response. Should I start calling around?

As I was tossing up who I should call, it rang. Finally.

"Hey, I've been worried, where are you?"

"I'm at Marty's." His voice gravelly.

"Is something wrong?"

"I got interviewed by the police today."

My hand went to my forehead. "What do you mean, interviewed? Why? What about?"

"That detective ... *Laura*." His sour tone dirtying her name. "That fucking bitch of a detective interviewed *me* about messages I'd sent to Emily."

My mind raced. "Emily? Do you mean Emily Robinson from the club?"

"Yeah." His voice unwavering.

My brows came together. "Tony and Sarah's daughter?"

"Yeah."

I paused. "Julian, I don't get it. Why would you have sent messages to Emily?"

He was quick to reply. "It's nothing. They were completely innocent messages. But that bitch of a detective was going on about me using a carriage service to cause offence ... or some bullshit. Apparently, there's an investigation into me!"

This didn't make sense. "What was offensive?"

"It's nothing. It's just some jokes about her hurting her butt in training one day."

"What was offensive?" I pressed.

"Nothing. It's all just stupid. It was all said in jest. It was nothing." His most reassuring tone.

I shook my head. "Why were you messaging her at all?"

"Because I'm her fucking coach, Jess. I thought she looked a bit disheartened one day at training, so I've been encouraging her to stay interested in sailing. It's all about her confidence. I was trying to do something nice!"

I recoiled from his sudden aggression. "Julian, this sounds bad." I deliberately used a placating tone.

"Trust me, it's not. It's all club politics. Tony is just being vengeful because I supported his disqualification a month back." His aggression nudged more at frustration now.

"Really?" It didn't feel right, but I was drawn to my automatic instinct to calm Julian.

"Yeah, it's those fucking Robinsons being spiteful."

"Okay." I swallowed and let the silence be for a moment. "Well, what's going to happen now?"

"I can't do anything until the investigation is complete." His tone back to normal. "Look, I just had to clear my head at Marty's. I'm staying for a drink. I'll be back later."

"Right, okay. Bye."

"I love you."

"You, too."

I stared at my phone for a long time.

—·—

I pretended to watch the television but I didn't even know what was on. Julian's voice drifted through the balcony doors. For the first time ever, it appeared he was not the one doing the most talking. I'd just made us both a coffee when Oliver phoned. Word about the investigation was getting around the club.

I sipped on my coffee, hearing strained for any word I could make out. I watched him through the sheer blinds, pacing back and forth. It didn't look like good news.

He hung up the phone and spent a few moments staring and swiping on his screen before coming back through the glass doorway. He sat next to me, reached for the remote and started flicking.

"What did Oliver say?" I asked.

"He said that Tony has sent a transcript of the messages to the committee to read."

"What does he think you should do?"

"Well." He kept flicking through the channels, pausing on one. "The AGM is this Saturday and I'm going to step down as president."

I stared at him. "What? Just for now?"

He shrugged but didn't look at me. He returned to flicking through the channels.

"Julian, what do you mean?"

He slammed the remote on his knee and glared at me. "I *mean*, I have to step down from the club because I'm being investigated by the fucking police."

"What, the whole club?"

"Yeah!"

I blinked and contemplated the enormity of that. Julian had lived and breathed that club since well before I'd known him. This seemed cruel. All of his spare time was spent there. In a way, he was more married to that club than he ever was to me.

"There has to be another way."

He sighed. "It'll be fine Jess, don't worry about it." His voice controlled again. He patted my leg and returned attention to the remote.

"Really?"

"Really." He nodded. "Hey, I was thinking we should see if your parents will babysit and we should head away next weekend. Just the two of us."

My eyes lit up at the prospect of a holiday. We had not been away by ourselves since our honeymoon nine years ago. He really was changing. At least, he was trying to. That had to be worth something.

"I'd love that," I said.

―――― 。 ――――

We arrived at the club and went straight to the club room, where long tables had been joined to form a makeshift conference table. A few rows of chairs had been added in case we got a good turnout for our annual general meeting.

Julian spoke to Luke in hushed tones in the corner. I'd never seen Julian so forlorn. Defeated. It was unlike him. The Robinsons were not there but I was so furious with them for what they had done, I could burst.

Luke looked down, shaking his head every now and then. He reached and patted his best friend on the shoulder. Julian was lucky to have such a great friend. No matter what Julian had done over the years, Luke always stood by his side. Defending him when he'd been too aggressive. Counselling him. Forgiving him when he kissed his crush.

Carrie had taken on the role of secretary for the club the last twelve months. She opened her laptop near the head of the table and gestured to Julian and Oliver she was ready to start the minutes. Everyone moved to take seats around the table. I sat next to Carrie.

"Can we have everyone seated and quiet now, thank you" Oliver announced and sat.

Julian stood at the head of the table. "Thank you all for attending the Rochford Sailing Club annual general meeting." He cleared his throat. "Today I am formally stepping down as the president of this wonderful club." His voice fractured. "It pains me to say, as I'm sure most of you are aware, that there is a current investigation by the police into me. Until this matter is resolved, I have decided it is in the best interests of the club if I cease my involvement with Rochford."

I looked around the table. Most heads were bowed. Poppy and Ricky in the corner, completely absorbed by a movie on their tablet. My whole body was tense. The silence unbearable. This was wrong. Julian was the heart and soul of this club.

Julian nodded to Oliver and walked away, out onto the deck, not sitting in for the rest of the meeting.

Oliver cleared his throat, breaking the silence. "Okay, with that concluded, I think we should move forward—"

"Sorry?" I interrupted. "I'm sorry, Oliver, but is anyone go to say how ridiculous all this is?"

"Look, Jess, I—"

I raised my voice. "No. I'm sorry, but I want it in the minutes right now that Julian can step back into his previous roles within the club as soon as he is cleared of any wrongdoing." I couldn't stop feeling the need to defend him. He was showing signs he could change. I couldn't stomach the idea of these false accusations making all of this for nothing. "And I want to have the entire Robinson family banned from Rochford for life, for their slander."

He nodded, his expression kind, but his voice was firm. "Jess, I think we should certainly discuss this later in the meeting. For now, I would like to continue with the agenda items and vote in our new committee for next season."

I nodded, searching the room for signs of support. A wink, a twitch – even eye contact. The table and floor appeared all consuming to the quorum.

I said nothing as the meeting continued. No one else brought up the elephant on the deck who was necking his fourth beer, staring out towards the river mouth. Oliver announced a brief break while the votes were counted. Bridget handed Carrie a stapled document with a too-serious face.

"What's that?" I asked.

"It's the transcript of the messages between Julian and Emily," Bridget said. "What did you think of them?"

"I haven't read them."

Her eyebrows hit the ceiling.

"I mean, Julian explained what was in them. It's all a misunderstanding. It was all said in jest. I haven't asked him to read them." Bridget's surprised look turned to pity. She patted my shoulder and walked back to her seat.

Carrie curled her lips slightly and focused on the paper. Curiosity enticed my eyes to the page. I read over her shoulder.

*It would be great to take the day off and hit the water* 😉 *hot weather, hot girl. Only thing that would make it better would be naked. Ha ha.*

I blinked fast. I must have read it wrong. Emily was thirteen. He couldn't have written those things to her. I leant in closer as Carrie turned the page. My hand flew to my mouth. A slight effort to hold in whatever deluge was ready to spew for his words.

Emily's responses were so awkward, I could cry for her.

*Ha ha. I have to go to school. Seeya* 😊

His response:

*I wish I was back at school chasing after little hotties like you.* 😊
*haha*

Blood drained from my skull, circling down my blood vessels like a bath plug gurgling. There were muted voices around the room but all I could hear was my own harsh swallow. Carrie finished reading and handed the pages to me. I put the document in between my elbows and held my head, heavy in both hands.

I read on.

Julian:

*You did awesome training the other day.* 😊

Emily:

*Thanks, it was fun. I need to be more careful though, when I slipped, I bruised my butt. Haha*

Julian:

*Hahaha that happens sometimes. You must have been trying super hard. I can massage that butt for you. Haha*

Emily:

*I'll be more careful next time* 😊

Julian:

*I'll be able to help you next time. As long as I'm the one who gets to massage your butt. Hahaha* 😊

This can't have been Julian; it didn't sound anything like him. What was with all the hahas and smiley faces? Who was this guy?

I finished the last page and needed to talk my jaw into closing. Every breath a forced command. My guts, so full and twisted. I was scared to move, I would burst.

My ears ringing, voices took time to return. I was still in a room full of people. I gulped again. My breath coming faster and faster. My face flushing.

"Jess?" Carrie's voice a whisper.

"I have to leave." I couldn't meet her eye.

"Okay, I'll help you."

I couldn't talk anymore, I'd lose it. I managed a nod, rose from the table and almost stumbled to the corner of the room.

"Poppy, Ricky." I motioned for them to take their headphones off. "Time to go. Gather your things." I tried to smile. I didn't do a good job.

Bodies moved to the side as I stepped forward through the crowded room, eyes on the door. Carrie grabbed my shoulders and forced my eyes to hers. "I'll finish up here and come straight over."

I told my head to nod; I was not sure if it did.

I walked down the stairs, the children following behind, chattering something I couldn't hear. I got to the door, unlocking my car parked in the president's spot. Hot tears filled my eyes. Stepping was challenging, as though trudging through hot tar. I struggled forward. The kids ran ahead and dived into the car as the door to the club shut behind me.

"Jess!" Julian's voice called urgently.

I spun on my heal and glared at him. "Don't you come home!" My voice was rigid, demanding.

"Jess I can exp—"

I threw my hand up in his face. "You sound like a fucking paedophile!" I pivoted on my heel as the torrent ran free. I swiped my eyes with the back of my hand as I reached the car door. I willed control. With a long breath, I threw myself into the car and started it instantly.

"Wait, Mummy, isn't Daddy coming?" Poppy's brow furrowed in the mirror.

"No, honey." I adjusted the mirror so she couldn't see my face.

"But Mummy," Ricky said, "Daddy said he'd go on the trampoline with me when we get home."

"Sorry honey, not today."

I reversed the car and Julian's face filled my periphery.

"Bye Daddy." They sung and waved with enthusiasm.

I shifted the car into drive and accelerated, glancing in the rear view as he stepped forward. A broken looking man. The man I felt sorry for only minutes ago. He'd never looked sorrier than his slumped figure in the rear view getting smaller by the second.

The kids' whining ceased when I promised them ice-cream. I drove on autopilot, pressing the heavy tears into my cheeks with my palm. We pulled into the driveway, and I blinked slowly, having no recollection of steering the car there. I parked and the kids dove out of their seats, sprinting for the yard. The weathered springs of the trampoline strained and screamed with every bounce before I'd even closed the driver door.

I walked into the house, pushing my cumbersome feet forward and collapsed onto the couch. My bag slipped from my shoulder and spilled open. I didn't bother to pick it up.

He lied. And I had believed his bullshit. I always believed him. What else had he lied about? I couldn't understand why he sent those things to a child. He told me he was being nice. Encouraging her, he'd said. Helping her confidence. Those texts didn't sound like him. Not at all like my husband. He never sent me a smiley face in a text. Pages and pages riddled with ha ha has and smiley face after smiley face. The deluge hit again, and I let it take me. I sobbed.

My brain was frazzled, but I pushed myself to function for the children. I ran a bath and called them in. They would play for hours in the bath if I let them. With them entertained, I went to the kitchen and opened a bottle of red wine. I filled a glass and took long sips leaning against the counter. Another deep breath. I needed to feed my children.

Laughter exploded down the hall and a large splosh. I ignored the water war, filling my arms with whatever was available in the fridge. I couldn't manage making a meal. I chopped carrots into sticks. *I'd love to be back at school chasing hotties like you.* I drained some more wine and forked some gherkins onto the platter. *I want to be the one to massage your butt.* I sliced some cheese. *Hahaha.* I threw crackers on to the plate.

"C'mon you two, dinner's ready." Another long sip. I refilled my glass, wiped the residue from the corner of my lips and headed down the hallway.

The children were in great spirits. I helped them change into pyjamas and set them up with the platter on the coffee table in front of cartoons. I walked back to the kitchen and reached again for the stem. Another slug.

Who the fuck did I marry?

∘

A knock at the door distracted my scrambled brain. Anxiety flooded me. I was scared to face Julian. When I saw Carrie through the peep hole, I untensed. As I pulled the door open, she tilted her head, sympathy clear in her eyes. She pulled me into a strong embrace.

"Come in." My voice husky.

She held a bottle of wine and followed me into the kitchen.

"Where are the kids?" she asked, grabbing herself a glass from the cupboard. I poured hers and topped up mine.

"On the couch. I'll put them to bed soon."

She nodded and followed me through to the sitting room.

"Hey!" Carrie smiled widely, her arms outstretched. "There's my two favourite little munchkins."

"Carrie!" Poppy jumped from the couch and Ricky tripped on the corner of the rug following her. They hugged Carrie and were immediately drawn back to the television as an attack was launched on the main cartoon character.

Carrie followed me onto the balcony. The afternoon breeze had dropped off. It was still and quiet, but for some distant sounds of life continuing as normal around the neighbourhood. Cars on streets, kids laughing down the road. The overcast sky grew dimmer by the moment. No beautiful sunset tonight. Even the elements were downcast today.

We sat next to each other, facing the view, and I threw a plush blanket over our legs. The stem of my glass gripped firm with both hands on my lap. I sipped slowly.

"This is enough to leave him ... right?"

Carrie's hand landed just above my knee. "Yes." Her voice barely above a whisper.

The kids laughed hysterically at cartoons through the glass door. Carrie's hand was firm; my cherished constant for so many years. I took another sip. The cool dusk air waking my senses. Pulling me up a degree from complete numbness.

"How could he write those things?" I asked, blinking my heavy, swollen lids.

Carrie squeezed my knee again. Her eyes searching the distant river.

"I mean, it's bad right?" I said.

Another squeeze. Her gaze was thoughtful. She nodded slowly, "Those messages made me feel sick."

"He's going to make it so hard to leave him. Do you know that?"

She looked at me, face determined. "Jess, we're here for you. We'll help you through this."

We sat in silence, watching a swarm of teenagers race past on bikes on the street below.

"I wonder if he's ever told me the whole truth about anything."

Her brows rose. "Probably not."

"I wonder if everything he ever told me was just half-truths. He's always so pushy in his rightness all the time. If I ever bring anything up about how he treats me, he turns it around on me. I can't let him do that now."

"I'll help you."

"I just can't believe he could write those things." My chin dropped and tears flowed. With the children distracted, I let them fall freely. Carrie's arm wrapped around my shoulder, and she tugged me nearer.

After some time, we moved inside and Carrie helped me get the children to bed. The night chill had beaten us. She sat with me for a long time before saying that she had to go. We both stood and moved to the front door.

"Jess, call me at any hour if you need anything at all." Her hands firm on my shoulders.

I nodded and tried to smile at her.

"Love you," she said.

"You too."

We embraced and I waved her out the front door.

I shut the door and my chest constricted. Gripped by a sudden and overwhelming fear the instant I was alone. My brain swirled. I'd been frightened to leave for years. I had seen him angry. Witnessed him punch people and near choke them. He had never hurt me or the children physically. But his aggression had always been present, like lava in his veins, sitting dormant for periods and erupting without warning. The hole in the wall a constant reminder.

Where was Julian's head at now? What if he had reached his lowest and decided to do the worst? Realised I was done this time and turned on me? Would he come for me overnight? I never thought he could write messages to a child like that, so I couldn't know what he was capable of. I looked around the house, my head frantic with what ifs. He had keys. He could come home any time.

I went to every window and made sure they were locked tight. I jammed the laundry and front doors with broom and mop sticks in the hope they might be enough to stop him. At least slow him, so I had warning.

I got into bed late and full of wine. I tossed throughout the night, somewhere between sleep and delirium. Each time I woke, fear stabbed in my chest at the thought of him next to me. My hand reached to his side of the bed and a wave of relief swept through me when I confirmed he was not there.

The following morning, I woke early. My mouth sticky and dry. I skulled the water from my bedside table and breathed shakily. The first night was over.

—♀—

I made the children breakfast, trying to decide when to call Lyn. Sooner was best. She needed to hear this from me, not Julian. He wouldn't tell her the truth.

I left Poppy and Ricky at the kitchen bench with their cereal and went into my bedroom, closing the door behind me, and made the call.

"Hello?"

"Lyn, it's Jess."

"Jess, is everything alright?"

"No, not really. I need to tell you. I'm leaving Julian."

She gasped. "Jess ... no ..."

"Yes. You need to hear me out. Julian is under investigation from the police for some indecent messages he sent to a thirteen-year-old girl at the club."

"What? There has to be some mistake. He would never ..."

"I read them. They're bad." My voice cracked.

"No."

"Yes. Besides, I haven't been happy for a long time." I sniffed, and a sob escaped. Tears crept out the corner of my eyes. "Lyn, he's been controlling for years."

"No."

"Yes." I was properly crying now.

"Jess, where is he?"

"I don't know. I assume at Marty's. I told him not to come home. It's over, Lyn."

"Jess, I need to call you back."

"Yep." I hung up the phone. Unsurprised.

Throughout the day she sent me multiple messages. Lyn had tried to contact Julian but wasn't getting any response. I told her I hadn't

201

heard from him, but she didn't seem to believe me.

My skin prickled knowing a confrontation was coming. In the past, he was always able to convince me of his truth. I knew he would try to convince me this was not true. I couldn't let him break me again.

All day I was on edge. Nothing from Julian.

Finally, a knock on the door. It was almost a relief to get it over with.

My chest caved to see two uniformed police officers in the doorway.

"Hello, Mrs Rundell?"

I nodded, gulping.

"We've had a call from Mrs Lynette Rundell. She's concerned for her son, Julian Rundell. Can we come in for a moment?"

I stepped back, opening the door wider. The children's attention was locked on the television, and I led the officers through to the dining room. No one sat.

"I left him yesterday," I blurted. The tears stinging again as I rehashed the investigation, the messages and our marriage. How controlling he was. That I was worried what he might do. I didn't know what he was capable of. It all flowed out as a desperate purge.

Sympathetic nods from the officers came as I hurried through the convoluted story. One of them was taking notes.

"Ma'am, has your husband ever threatened harm to you or the children?"

My face contorted as tears continued to spill. "Not harm so much, I mean, he scares me, but he's never hurt me or the children. I tried to leave him about a month or so ago and he threatened then that he would take the children if I left him." I sniffed and reached for another tissue.

"Has he ever threatened to self-harm?"

"Umm, yes well, that same night. When I tried to leave him, he said he was going to drive the car off the cliff. He even wrote good-bye letters to the children. That's why I stayed." I wiped under my eyes with the tissue, working hard for composure.

"Well, I am going to leave you with my card, okay? Can you give us a call if you hear from him at all?"

I nodded. "If you find him, can you make sure he doesn't come here? I can't face him. Please don't let him come here." I felt like grabbing his lapels to instil my desperation.

"We'll let you know if we find him."

I saw the policemen to the door.

The rest of the day disappeared in a blur of the activities of daily life that I had to attend to. When I put the children to bed, I poured myself another glass of red. A warmth swirled through my head, and I realised I couldn't remember when I last ate. Since the meeting, I had just had red wine, coffee and water.

I put the television on after doing my new night-time safety checks, wedging doors and locking windows. My phone finally rang. A private number.

"Jess Rundell," I spilled, urgent for news.

"Hello Jess, this is Officer Matrix from earlier today."

"Right, yes, hello."

"Ma'am, we have located your husband. He was at a bar in town. I have taken him to the hospital for a psychiatric review."

"So what happens now?"

"They will assess him and if he is deemed to be no risk to himself, he will be free to leave later tonight."

"Does he know he can't come here? I don't know what he'll do.

Please don't let him come here." I begged.

"Ma'am, I will pass on your concerns."

Two hours later the phone rang again.

"Jess Rundell."

"Hello Mrs Rundell, I'm a nurse at Darvo Hospital and have your husband here this evening."

"Okay, what's happening?"

"We are letting him go tonight. He has been assessed and found not to be a risk to himself."

"Make sure you don't let him come here." My voice shook.

"Are you concerned for your safety?" she asked in a professional tone.

"He's never hurt us," I choked through sobs. "He threatened to take the children once."

I was shaking all over, consumed with uncertainty. Freezing cold in the warm room.

"Please, don't let him come here," I begged again.

"I will tell him to make other arrangements for tonight."

"Thank you," I breathed.

Two hours later, I was still frozen on the couch. Pulled back to the moment as my phone rang. Another private number.

"Hello, Mrs Rundell, my name is Mason Love and I'm calling from child protective services."

I looked at my watch. It was nearing midnight.

"I've had a report someone has raised concerns about the safety of your children."

"I think the children are safe," I said. "I just want to make sure my husband doesn't come here."

"Can you fill me in on all the details?"

I swallowed at the concerned voice and rallied energy before going through the whole story again. He wanted to know all about our relationship, the investigation, everything.

It was over half an hour later when he finally hung up. My eyes were shutting involuntarily. I tidied the kitchen and walked down the hall after double checking the doors were wedged shut. I kissed the children, calmed by the presence of their regular breaths in sleep.

I woke before sunup. My chest tightened automatically, followed by an overwhelming sweep of relief when I realised, again, he was not next to me. I sent a text message to my boss, Patrick.

*I'm so sorry, I can't come in, I'm sick.*

I didn't know where to find the energy to get out of bed. I laid there for a long time, staring at the ceiling. A little thud came from the next room, followed by hurried steps in my direction. Ricky paused in the doorway, assessing the room, saw I was awake, and launched towards me.

"Mummy." The warmth and glee of my toddler helped sooth my soul. We snuggled for a while; every second gaining strength enough to lift my body from the bed and get about the tasks that I must attend to. I got Poppy ready for school despite the fog in my head. We forgot her homework and her lunch the first time we tried to leave, but we got back on track.

"Is Daddy coming home today?" Poppy asked from the back seat of the car.

"No, honey, I'm sorry, not today."

Simultaneous 'humphs' from the rear.

I changed the subject. "How about you two choose what we have for dinner tonight?"

I pulled up at the school, leaning over to kiss Poppy before she dived from the car after spotting a friend. A few minutes later, Ricky and I were parked at the supermarket. After checking the bank balance on my phone, I lifted Ricky into the trolley seat and thought about what would be the easiest to manage this week within my meagre budget. Steering the trolley towards the electric doors, I caught a glimpse of my dishevelled hair. When did I last brush it? I looked like a zombie and didn't feel much better.

"Don't touch that." I stopped Ricky from pushing his finger through the film over a watermelon quarter. Halfway through the fruit and veg section, my phone rang.

Another police officer. I immediately forgot his name.

"Ma'am," he said, "we have been advised that you may feel at risk from your husband, Mr Julian Rundell."

I reached for one of the 'free for kids' pieces of fruit, and Ricky's eyes lit up, grabbing the banana.

"Well, it's all happened very suddenly. I'm really not sure if there is a risk."

"Has your husband ever been physical with you or the children in the past?"

"No, not physical."

"I need to advise, if you are feeling frightened for either yourself or the children, you can take out a restraining order."

"How does that work?" I asked as I walked through the aisles, grabbing anything on special that caught my eye. Ricky was making a mess with the banana, but he was entertained. I left him to it.

"I can lodge it for you with the report I have received."

"What happens if he comes?"

"You need to call the police."

"What if I don't take the order out. Can he come whenever he wants?"

"Ma'am, being your house, you can legally change the locks. But given it is also his house, he can enter that house at this stage, and it is not illegal."

"Well, this all happened a couple days ago, and he hasn't turned up yet."

"Okay."

"I'm concerned, I mean, I'm scared that an order would only aggravate or provoke him. He might do something *worse*."

"Sometimes it can cause upset, yes."

"And essentially, a piece of paper isn't going to protect me if he comes in a rage."

"The decision is up to you Mrs Rundell."

Pushing or threatening Julian had never done any good. He only ever escalated when stood up to. I was too scared to provoke him.

"Thank you, but I will leave it."

—§—

By Friday, I needed to get back to work. I couldn't keep making excuses. Patrick found me in the staff room of the animal hospital, pouring my third cup of coffee for the day.

"Oh good, Jess, you're back," Patrick said.

I smiled as best as I could. "Yeah."

He studied me. "Are you well enough to work? You look dreadful."

A diet of coffee and wine for a few solid days may do that to a person. The multiple breakdowns as soon as the children were out of earshot didn't help either. The last – on the drive here. A valve had released like an overfull dam as I waved Ricky off to daycare.

Flooded with so much hurt, I struggled to contain the deluge of tears. I managed to control myself as I pulled into the work carpark.

Now I couldn't pretend. I tried to keep my voice steady. "Actually, my marriage ended last weekend."

He stepped forward and reached for my shoulder. "I'm so sorry."

I nodded and thanked him. I couldn't find my smile though.

"Let me know if you need anything okay? If there's problems picking kids up or anything. We can be flexible."

"Thank you so much." The school drop offs and pickups were almost all done by me, anyway. It was an anomaly the few times Julian ever helped logistically. In fact, it had been easier so far with him not around. One less person to pick up after and less washing.

I stumbled through my morning. A feisty moggy landed a scratch on my arm. I normally would have avoided it. My brain was not coping with anything slightly challenging, but luckily, I was confident in my job and able to function as if by muscle memory.

At lunchtime, my phone vibrated with a message from Carrie. *Jess, can you come over before you collect the kids today? I need to talk to you.*

We both finished at lunchtime on Fridays and often tried to catch up for lunch. Not today. I thought that's what she might have been contacting me for. But something about the tone of her text was off.

Carrie greeted me at her door before I could ring the bell. We hugged but there were no smiles from her. A tension lingering around her eyes stood out, so unlike her normally laid-back demeanour.

She led the way to her kitchen bench, where we had shared so many good times over the years. The morning brunches when her girls were young and laughing at cartoons while we sipped on coffee.

There was no noise today. Not even the radio.

"Coffee?" Her tone was formal.

"Yes please, thanks." I took a seat on a bar stool as she prepared the coffee. She was oddly quiet. "Nice fern, is that new?" The pressure of the silence too much for me.

"What?" She followed my pointed finger to a planter in the corner. "Oh, yeah, a few weeks ago." She poured the coffee and handed mine over. I wrapped my hands around the almost too hot mug, bringing it to my nose.

Carrie's nails were tapping on the bench as she stared out her kitchen window. She had barely looked at me since I arrived.

She stopped, and swung her head to face me. I put my coffee down.

"Jess, I need to tell you something."

I sat a bit straighter.

She cleared her throat. "When I read those messages the other day, I was appalled, and not just for Emily."

I nodded, my red eyes as wide as I could manage.

She went on. "Back when Amelia was fifteen, I got an odd anonymous message warning me that I shouldn't trust Julian with her."

"What?" I exclaimed.

"Please Jess, this is very difficult for me. I need you just to listen." I'd never heard my friend so severe. I nodded and watched her nails rapping again at the bench top. She gave up and paced her side of the bench.

"Jess, I had no idea what to think. I asked Amelia if Julian had ever done anything to make her uncomfortable or anything he shouldn't be doing. Her face was so grossed out, she promised me no, he would never do that."

My chest tightened. A vice squeezing so hard I could burst.

"I decided to get hold of her phone records to see if there was anything on there. I couldn't get details of the messages back then, but Jess ..." She paused, pacing and glared at me, hands firm on the bench. "There were literally hundreds of text exchanges between Julian and Amelia."

"Oh my god!"

She returned to pacing, eyes to the floor, rushing her words as if there was a time limit. "Obviously, I was concerned about that. I wanted to know more. I called the phone company, and they couldn't help. I ended up phoning the police." She gushed all this with barely a breath, her hands flailing wildly in front of her.

"You never told me any of this." My eyes blinking faster until I could focus on her. "What did the police say?"

She nodded and continued, her hands busy gesturing while she paced. "The officer I spoke to said that they could investigate if I wanted to. But Jess – they also said that it was very *normal* for a coach to exchange messages with an athlete in their experience. It doesn't mean anything is wrong."

"You never told me." I barely registered what I had said. I was frozen, staring at my closest friend.

She swallowed, brow furrowed and waved my comment away. "I was worried what was in those messages. I asked Amelia again and she promised me there was nothing wrong with the messages, it was all about the club and stuff. She assured me again and again, I warned her I might get the police involved and she begged me not to. She loved everything about the club. It was such an integral part of her existence at the time. She didn't want that to change."

I had nothing to say, I just stared into my cup, unable to comprehend.

"Jess, do you remember Julian telling you he was coming to a meeting at my house when you were pregnant with Poppy? It was right before Luke was beaten up."

"No."

"Well, one day, I called him and said I wanted a meeting. I got Luke to come as well so Julian didn't feel ganged up on."

"No one ever told me any of this." My head shook side to side.

"Jess, we all sat at this very bench when my children were at sleepovers, and I confronted him with my evidence of the messages. I asked him why he would be sending my fifteen-year-old hundreds of messages." Her voice cracked.

"What did he say?"

"He got on the defensive straight away. He swore he'd never done anything wrong, had done nothing but go out of his way to encourage the juniors. Build their confidence and love of the sport. He said he was just being a good coach." She looked at the ceiling. "I could scream, remembering that conversation."

I stared at her, my coffee untouched.

"At one stage, he said something odd. About things not being great at home with you." She looked away, as if afraid to meet my eye. "He said he was getting marital advice. From Amelia." She frowned. "It was such a strange thing to say. Even Luke said, 'You were asking a fifteen-year-old for marital advice?'" She shook her head. "I remember it so clearly, Julian's head swung around and I thought he ... he looked like he might deck Luke." She met my eyes again. I couldn't look away. "It was all so tense. Jim could barely speak. He was so angry. I've never seen him like that. The thought of Julian doing ... And Julian went on and on. Trying to defend himself. It wasn't good enough. The whole thing – the night, it ended badly. I told him I was going to go to the police. To ask them to investigate. Jess, you should have seen him. I've never ... Well, he left in a huff. He didn't say another word to any of us. God ..." Her eyes pitched to the ceiling again. "My god ... You don't know how much I wish I had gone to the police. After reading those messages to Emily, I knew ... I just knew ..." Her eyes glistened.

My chest puffed with shallow, rapid breaths. Not enough room in my lungs for oxygen. Carrie kept going, never meeting my eye.

"So, the following morning I prepared to call the police to investigate. But before I did, really early, Julian called me. He was hysterical. In tears. Really blubbering. He begged me not to. He promised nothing bad had happened. He was *really* convincing. He said that it was all just stupid, innocent messages. I asked Amelia again and she said the same. They both promised."

I stared at her with one brow raised.

"You have to understand Jess, my mum was dying. And my god, he had sent me so many beautiful emails and messages during that time. He was a great friend." Her voice cracked again. "You were pregnant. Life was full on, and they both promised me. God, I wish I could go back and push further now."

"You never told me any of this," I murmured.

"I couldn't tell you. Don't you understand? I couldn't. You were carrying *his baby*. I had no proof, and everyone denied there was anything wrong. You would have believed him anyway. You were so in love with him."

I nodded, taking a moment to absorb.

"The only sure thing out of any of this is if I told you, it would have been the end of our friendship." Her strung shoulders dropped.

She was right. I knew she was. I would have never questioned my husband. I sat for a while in the quiet. Drained. I reached for my coffee and took a small sip, hoping it would help open my chest so I could breathe. A realisation flashed at me.

"My god, Carrie – look at what was in those messages to Emily."

She closed her eyes. "I know, I'm so scared." She opened her eyes again. They were properly wet now.

"I have to go and get Poppy." I lied. I had another half hour free. I got up and hugged her before showing myself to the door.

I didn't want to hang around. I needed to take all this in, and I couldn't help but feel a bit betrayed. Everyone had been lying to me. I forced autopilot back on and picked up my children. Poppy flew to the car, her lips spread wide, ponytail flying out behind. A half smile reached my lips as she dove into the back seat. Would I ever get my smile back? What hope was there if my children could not even make me muster a full grin?

It was the same when I got to Ricky's daycare. The carer delved into an enthusiastic rehash of Ricky's day. I nodded along, filled in the appropriate oohs and ahs, but was none the wiser to what Ricky got up to. I was present only physically. I glanced to the floor as she tattled on and was taken by a sudden urge to be in the foetal position. And stay there.

"Time to go, buddy." I ruffled Ricky's hair as he curled his arms around my thigh. "Thank you," I said to the carer, whose name had left me.

When we got home, I shoved a store-bought lasagne in the oven and collapsed on the couch. The kids were busy dragging toys from their rooms to the living room and I stared at the blank television.

My chest crushed with that relentless vice. I pictured Julian winding the lever tighter. All those years he had lied. I had no idea how much he was keeping from me. Now we knew about two teenage girls. How many more were there?

My phone vibrated, tearing me from my rabid thoughts. A blocked number.

"Hello?"

"Jessica Rundell?"

"Yes, hello."

"My name is Lara Thicket. I'm calling from child protection. We have had a report about your children and are required to make an appointment in your home to assess their safety."

"What do you mean. Who made a report?"

"That's confidential."

"Right okay, well the children are safe but I'm happy to meet with you." I rubbed my hand over my sandpaper eyelids.

"Great, how about Monday at four?"

"Sure."

I stewed on this for a while. Why would child protection need to investigate my children?

My phone vibrated again. It was Carrie.

"Hi," I said, not sure if I could speak yet.

"I'm not on speaker, am I?" Urgency in her voice.

"No." I got off the couch and headed to the kitchen, away from the playing children.

"Good." Was she panting? "Julian molested Meghan."

I gasped. The only sounds were Carrie's shattered breaths. Eventually I needed to let the air out. I slowly exhaled, searching for words.

"My god ... I'm so sorry." I clawed at my forehead.

We stayed on the line, only breathing through the phone. The

214

rhythmic in-and-out of our autonomic nervous systems at work.

Carrie finally said, "Meghan just called to tell me. I had to tell you straight away. Jess, she's speaking to the police."

"Good, my god." I rubbed at my temple. "When did it happen?"

"She said it happened at your house before you were pregnant with Poppy. It was one night they stayed over."

I was shaking.

"She says she got messages from him too."

I was drowning. Could barely breathe. I lifted my chin to coax more air into my lungs. It didn't work. My breath rapid. I wanted to vomit.

Ricky squealed and ran between my legs with Poppy chasing him. He had hold of her doll and was poking his tongue out.

"Cut it out," I snapped, harsher than I meant.

"But he stole my doll," Poppy whined.

I ripped it from Ricky's hand and gave it Poppy. Taking off to my bedroom and letting the door slam behind me.

"Sorry," I said. "What can I do, Carrie? Should I come over?"

She sniffed. "No that's okay. I'm here with Jim. We're just trying to process all this. Jim is so angry."

"Yeah, I don't blame him. This is unbelievable."

"I'll talk to you soon." Her voice low and flat.

"Bye love." I could only match.

My feet protested holding my weight. I collapsed on the bed, brain spiralling. I tried to tell myself this couldn't be true. How could he hurt Meghan? But I knew it must be. Hundreds of moments flashed of Julian with Meghan over the years. I searched for signs and found none. Tears flowed hot and thick. I never saw it. That scum. A guttural howl escaped my chest as I punched at my pillow. How had I not seen it? I hugged my stomach tight and wept.

9

I opened the front door. Outside were two women in their thirties, dressed casually but neatly. One had a laptop bag over her shoulder, the other held a notepad. The one with the notepad introduced herself as Lara Thicket. Her smile was warm, and I welcomed them into the dining room.

"Are the children home?" Lara asked.

"Yes, they're watching cartoons."

"Great, we'll meet them in a little while if that is okay. But while they are entertained, we might ask you some questions."

I bristled at the thought of my children being questioned by child protection. It felt intrusive. I had done nothing wrong. I pushed it aside as I needed these people to help me. The accusations against Julian kept adding more questions. I didn't know if he was safe around my children. I had been wrestling for the answers.

The other lady opened her laptop.

Lara sat and readied her notepad. She cleared her throat. "Is your husband home?"

"No, I left him just over a week ago."

"Can you tell me about that?"

I gave her the whole story. The keys tapping feverishly on the laptop from the accomplished typist. I finished the story and gnawed on the dead skin on the side of my thumb.

"Jess, I've told you that child protection is currently investigating the safety of your children. I have decided that given the nature of

216

the accusations and the police investigation into your husband–"

"Ex-husband," I interrupted. "Well, will be as soon as I can make it legal."

She nodded and continued. "Right. Your ex-husband. At this stage, we are going to have to insist that the only contact he has with your children is to be supervised within line of sight and hearing. Are you able to supervise this contact?"

I snorted, screwing my face up. "No."

"Do you have anyone in mind who would be able to supervise?" Her professionalism unwavering.

"His mother." As much as I didn't get along with her, I trusted her with my children.

"Okay, we will gather her details and organise that. Until we have met with her, I am going to have to insist on no contact with any of the paternal family. Jess, this is very serious. If you do allow contact, particularly unsupervised, with the father, you will be deemed by the department to be an unprotective parent."

I frowned. The suggestion was insulting. I always protected my children. I would die for them.

After meeting the children and showing them to their bedrooms, a requirement of the investigation, I showed them to the front door. Bothered by the intrusion into my life, but lighter. One less thing to worry about.

———— ⌀ ————

*Come over.*

Another text message from Carrie.

I didn't want to go. This couldn't be good news. Carrie was never that blunt. I organised for Mum and Dad to have the children overnight. When I arrived to drop them at their house, Dad said nothing. He just embraced me, almost too firm for comfort. My parents had not taken the news well. They had loved Julian. It broke their hearts to learn the horrid truth about the father of their grandchildren.

I thanked Dad and drove to Carrie's. When I parked, I was in no hurry to leave the car. I needed to sit for a while. I took deep breaths, almost to light-headedness. I closed my eyes tight, took one last big breath, and willed myself out of the car.

Jim answered the door. His face dropped and empty, as if someone had died. I hugged him. His eyes stayed on the floor as he pointed me to their lounge. It was dusk and they had no lights on yet. The usual warmth of their home gone. Nothing cooking on the stovetop. No radio. I almost shivered.

Carrie sat motionless on the couch, her expression empty. Her two hands were clasped around a wine glass in her lap. Shoulders slumped.

"Hey Carrie, you alright?" I sat next to her.

Her eyes were wet and puffy. Something looked broken in her.

Jim put a glass of wine on the coffee table in front of me. I thanked him. He said nothing and left the room.

"Carrie?" I whispered.

Her eyes closed for a long time, and I watched her chest rise only a whisker. That was the first sign of life. Finally, she opened her eyes to meet mine. Her lids hung half closed.

"Amelia called." Her voice was raspy.

I nodded and squeezed her knee. She lingered in tortured silence.

Giving me nothing, only an assured foreboding. I waited. Forced patience whilst searching her face. Finally, her eyes darted to mine.

"Julian sexually assaulted Amelia multiple times when she was a teenager," she said flatly.

An odd groan escaped my chest. I didn't know I could make a sound like that. It came from deep in my belly. Solid. Moving up. Threatening to choke me.

Carrie stared straight ahead. Her face contorted with immeasurable pain.

"I'm so sorry," I managed, holding her knee firm. I couldn't think of what more to say.

"That fucking cunt sexually assaulted my teenage daughters." Her lips almost too tight to let the vicious words out. I'd never heard my friend use such language. I squeezed her tighter as she took a long sip of wine. I didn't know how I had any tears left but they spilled freely down my cheeks. My head collapsing into my hands, I sobbed.

—— ჽ ——

I didn't know how I got home. I must have driven. It couldn't have been legal. I didn't remember getting into bed. Julian's red face, fierce with anger, was chasing me down the hall. His arms outstretched, reaching for my dressing gown flowing behind me. I tried to scream but there was no sound. I woke as he caught me, beaded in sweat, lifting myself onto my elbows. I looked to my left – no Julian, thank god. I was panting. It was three am. Buffy was forced to reposition after my start disturbed her. I laid staring at the dark shapes on the ceiling, ears strained, listening for any sound out of place. Gripped with fear and revulsion, I didn't sleep again.

The sun eventually rose, and I got myself into the shower. I stood under near scalding water, running over my back. Eyes closed. Hand to tiles. I needed to get ready for work. I don't know how I managed. I shoved a load of washing in the machine and turned the dishwasher on. I tried to force my eyelids open all the way, testing my capabilities.

My face was blank as I closed the car door and drove to work. Tears spilled the moment I pulled out of the drive. I merged onto the highway, towards the animal hospital, swiping at tears as they came. I rubbed them on my pants, the wheel slippery. I pulled into a carpark under a magnolia tree, spluttering. I tried to pull myself together. I needed to stop crying. I couldn't. I had to start my shift, but my legs wouldn't work. I slapped the sun visor down and looked at the mirror to fix my face. It couldn't be repaired. I cried harder, unable to catch my breath. Rubbing hard at my face did nothing. I couldn't stop.

I fished around in my bag. Locating my phone, I called Patrick.

"Hello Jess." His voice buoyant.

"I can't get out of the car," I choked.

"Where are you?"

"In the car park."

"Stay there, don't drive anywhere, I'm coming."

Moments later, Patrick's concerned face appeared by my window. He opened the car door and sat in the passenger seat.

"Jess, what's wrong?"

"He's a paedophile!" I wailed.

He recoiled, at first, before reaching for me, encircling his arms around me, letting my head flop to his shoulder. No concern that I was smothering him in tears and snot. He rubbed the top of my back. His hands warm and strong.

"Stay here, I have to go back in and move some things around. I will take care of it. Wait here."

My shoulders shook. I could barely nod.

He was back in minutes. "Come on." Patrick ushered me from the car. He led me to his car, and I sat heavily into his passenger seat. The car was immaculate and smelled of his gentle, almost chocolatey cologne.

A few minutes later, we pulled into the beach carpark. It was deserted, being midweek and winter. I stepped out of the car and took a few steps to the beach path. The frigid, salty air clearing some brain fog. Patrick's arm landed over my shoulder, and I hugged my jacket tight around my waist. Colder than almost ever before, we stepped onto the beach and strolled north.

He asked questions and listened patiently as I purged the story of my relationship with Julian. I told him everything about the sexual assaults, the messages, the police investigation. I didn't stop there, I expelled all the hidden truths I'd held inside for so many years. For the first time, I told someone the full truth of living with Julian. He nodded and listened. Never once talking over me as Julian would have done. He squeezed me into him, holding me up, like it was the most natural thing on earth.

I fell silent when I was done. He stopped walking, the waves crashing meters away. We were completely alone for miles of pristine white sandy beach. Patrick turned to face me and hugged me firm to his chest. An embrace so foreign after all these years. He was taller than me by a head at least, and my cheek was warm against his chest.

I didn't want to let go, needing to cling to his warmth. I barely knew this man outside of work. Yet here he was at my lowest, holding me up, warm and caring. It was a long embrace as my stuttered breaths regulated. He leant back, lifting my chin and looked into my eyes.

"Jess, this is a lot to deal with."

I could only nod and wipe at left over snot with a tissue.

"With so much out of your control, I think it's probably good to start by just taking control of one thing. I think you should do it today. Let's head to the shops, I'll buy you a coffee and we can get you a new phone plan that he doesn't have any control or access to. He shouldn't be reading your messages and tracking who you call, whether you have something to hide or not. That's *not* okay."

"Okay." I couldn't explain my gratitude.

Within in an hour, I was stood outside the phone shop, smiling from ear to ear. For the first time in years, I had control over my own phone, and Julian couldn't see who I was calling or texting. A weight gone from my shoulders. This had not even been on my short list of things I needed to get done after leaving Julian. But it felt like a talon of his had been ripped from my back.

"I'm going back to work. You should take the rest of the day." Patrick embraced me again.

I searched to explain how much this morning had meant to me. I couldn't verbalise it, so I just squeezed him a little tighter.

With one last clutch to the top of my arms, Patrick smiled, and I followed him to his car.

Reinvigorated, I spent the afternoon not crying for a change. Inspired to be proactive, I sent out multiple messages to people, giving them my new phone number. My very own private number. I revelled in the freedom of that. To know I could text who I liked, when I liked and not have to wait for the inevitable repercussions if I contacted someone on my banned list.

My mind drifted. We knew of three girls affected within the club. I couldn't live with not knowing if there were others. I needed them all to know that I was not supportive of Julian.

I thought back over the years. The dozens of teenage girls and families involved in our club. Had any quit the club because of Julian?

With Buffy curled on my lap, I typed a message to all the girls in the club.

*Hello lovelies, I want you all to know that I am aware of some of the accusations of sexual assault and inappropriate messages against Julian. I believe every one of them. I want you to know that I left him as soon as I read the messages. I am horrified he could write those things to young girls. I stand firmly with you all and want justice to be done. It is so important to me that anyone who has been either messaged inappropriately or otherwise harmed by Julian should speak to the police. People like Julian rely on the shame of the people they are hurting to keep their secrets and silence. It is not the victim's shame – this is his shame to carry. Silence only helps perpetrators. I don't want him to ever be able to hurt anyone again. The truth is the only way to make sure of that. I hope the whole truth can be told and he sees consequences for his actions. He must be stopped from doing this again. I love you all and stand with you.*

Barely a minute passed and I had messages flooding back.

From Meghan:

*Statement booked in. I would have said something years ago, but I didn't want to hurt you Jess. And I thought I was the only one. If I'd known he was doing this to anyone else, I would have come forward years ago – love you Jess.*

From Adele:

*Oh Jess, you writing this means so much to me. I mean, I was so embarrassed and so young when I started getting messages from Julian, I honestly didn't know what to do. I couldn't even tell my family. He stopped sending them when I called him a 'pedo' in response to something dirty he wrote when I was 14. We all love and look up to you so much, we never wanted you to get hurt. I didn't want the club to suffer either. I mean ... he is the 'president', I didn't think anyone would be on my side. Love you!*

From Amelia:

*I love you.*

They kept coming.

I read on and started responding with how sorry I was. How heartbroken I was that he hurt them. My guilt grew. All those times he was smirking as he typed on his phone, but I was too scared to question him. I should have checked. My gut had told me, and I ignored it. Pushed it away with the fear of his anger. I could have stopped all this years ago if only I opened my eyes wider and wasn't so chicken. I should have found a way to check his phone.

I sat sullen in blame, my legs curled under me on the couch and the children spread on the carpet, eyes glued to the television. My phone rang.

"Luke?" I answered, surprised. Scrambling to my feet, I walked away from the children.

"Jess, did you send all the girls a message telling them to talk to the police?"

"How did you find out about that?" I shut my bedroom door behind me.

"Frank showed it to Julian. Said Paige showed him and Rhonda."

"Jesus Christ!" I slapped my hand to my forehead. "They showed it to Julian?"

"Jess ..." He let out a long sigh. "What did you expect? They've been friends with Julian for over twenty years."

"I expect them to do the right fucking thing!" I spat and shoved my thumb to the red button, missing the old phones you could really slam.

Betrayal cut at my insides. I stood in rageful disbelief, letting the sharpness fade, leaving a smouldering burn I couldn't abate.

Julian had not come for me so far. All he'd known was that I left him. Now he knew I was actively encouraging others to come forward. I felt exposed. Didn't they understand the danger I was in? The danger we were all in speaking out against Julian.

I was furious with Luke. I had not heard from him in weeks. Figuring he had sided with his best friend, I had not contacted him. But then for him to ring and shove it in my face that Julian knew I had betrayed him. There was nothing funny about that. He'd seen what Julian had done. He knew the danger. It was not a game.

I wanted to scream but knew I couldn't. My children needed me strong and in control. So I went through the motions of dinner, bath and bed for the children, before laying on my bed for a long time.

I tried to read my book but read through the same paragraph at the top of the page three times and still had no idea what was happening. I gave up and stared at the roof. I don't know when I dozed off.

I woke from the same nightmare. Julian chasing me. I couldn't scream. This time he caught me, and I was wrestling on the ground under him. His wild black eyes boring into mine as he snarled.

Again, I was sweating. Heart bounding, threatening my sternum. I reached for my phone for distraction. I got on messenger and spotted Carrie active.

I wrote:

*Hey, can't you sleep either?*

Her reply was quick.

*No. I don't know if I'll ever sleep again.*

I replied:

*Me neither. Carrie, we can get through this ... we have to.*

I watched the three dots move and stop. She started again.

*I don't know if I can.*

My throat felt tight.

*I'm so sorry I haven't been there for you as much as I should be Carrie. I really am. I don't want to lose our friendship.*

The dots disappeared. She was not replying. How could she stay friends with someone who let her girls be abused right under her nose? Finally, the dots reappeared.

*Come to the Lake this weekend, we have a cabin booked. Stay with Jim and I.*

I thought about it for a few minutes.

*Are you sure you don't want to go, just the two of you?*

A few minutes for her response.

*No, come along. Some of Jim's friends are staying up there too. This way, I won't be alone when they are hanging out.*

I breathed a sigh of relief.

*That would be lovely. Child protection gave the go ahead for the children be supervised with Lyn, so they are staying there this weekend.*

She responded:

*Great, we'll shoot past and pick you up in the morning.*

I smiled through a yawn.

*Okay great, try to sleep. Xx*

*You too. Xo*

9

"Are you two all set?" I helped Ricky pull the backpack over his shoulder as we made our way to the door. I opened it, relieved to see Greg rather than Lyn to collect the children. I hadn't spoken to Lyn since that one phone call the day after I left Julian. All the communication I had with those two was with Greg via text.

"Grandpa!" they squealed and threw themselves around his legs.

"Hello!" He ruffled each of their heads and looked to me. I couldn't read his expression, somewhere between sympathy and discomfort. "Jess ... alright?"

I nodded, squeezing my lips into a taught half smile. "Thanks for picking them up."

"I'll drop them back Sunday ... just after five?"

"Great, thanks." I bent over and kissed both the children. "Have a great time."

They waved goodbye as they walked away with their grandad.

I paused, taking in the solitude for a moment. It was a welcome respite to let my face drop to its desired position. Acting happy for the children grew tiresome.

I got about packing and was wheeling my bag to the front door as Carrie walked up the drive.

"Hey." I smiled at her. There was a question in there, too, the recent awkwardness between us had caused me to toss and turn, unsure if our friendship could survive this.

She hugged me firmly. Tears prickled my eyes. I kept them at bay. Her hug gave me hope I wouldn't be losing another vital relationship.

I let Carrie and Jim guide the conversation during the drive to the lake. The topics stayed on work and upcoming events at the club. Julian didn't come up once. It was refreshing. Neither quite seemed themselves, but they might never be again.

Late that afternoon, Carrie and I sat on the deck of the cabin, overlooking the holiday park. Jim had left for a run around the lake. Kids raced their bikes passed the cabin, calling out in holiday glee. I looked at Carrie. She stared out at nothing, her face looking lost in torture. I assumed where her head was and put my hand to her thigh. I knew it came in waves. One minute you could almost convince yourself nothing even happened, the next, you were inconsolable.

"I don't know how to live with this." Carrie's face solemn, voice flat. "I don't want to live with this."

"No don't talk like that," I said. "We are all going to get through this."

"I *trusted* him." Her lips curled and flattened.

I winced. "I know."

"All that time we spent together."

"I know."

We were still in our silence, stewing over our grief and betrayal.

The only noise the pack of pre-teens riding past with constant yabbering and laughter.

"I didn't protect my babies." Carrie grimaced and tears flowed, creating glistening paths down her cheeks. She didn't bother wiping them.

I grabbed hold of her hand. "That's not true. You did everything you could." My eyes pleading with hers. Desperate to console her. How do you console someone whose two children were abused by a loved and trusted family friend? The betrayal was infinite.

"Jim can't even talk about it. He listens and hugs me, but he can't face it yet. It's breaking him."

I kept firm to her hand.

She kept going. "You know, he manipulated us all. Like little pawns on a chess board. Moved us all around for his entertainment. Made himself look so ... trusting. Such a great family friend. He'd say to me, 'Don't worry, I'll look after your girls.'" She'd animated the way Julian speaks. Held her chin high and patted me on the shoulder with a deep voice. "He manipulated all of us."

Julian was the most trusted club member. No one would think twice trusting him with their children. I visualised Carrie's chessboard metaphor and saw all of us as pieces on his board. Julian looking down, rubbing his chin, smirking. I thought of that night when I tried to leave him, and he threatened to kill himself. He'd smugly stated that he was the smartest man I knew. That was probably what he was talking about – what he got away with for so many years. The 'smartest' man I knew delighting over his ability to destroy more lives. I felt sick.

Carrie's tears stopped flowing, an angry expression taking their place. "He needed us for access to children." Her nostrils flared. "He needed you most of all, Jess." Her face whipped to mine. "Without you ... he had no veil of decency. Who would ever suspect a married man with children of his own? Your presence ensured trustworthiness to everyone."

I leant forward, rubbing at my eyes. They were raw and irritated, puffy from weeks of tears and lack of sleep.

"My god," I said. "You're right. I made him look so ... so respectable." I visualised him standing over the chessboard and using me, his unsuspecting queen. The one with the ability to wipe another piece from the board like they were nothing. Guilt swelled in me, sickened by the realisation of the role I played in his evil games. This wasn't something you could expel.

Carrie scoffed. "You know, I even reassured some people at events and things, 'Don't worry, Julian will be there, he'll take good care of your child.'" She shook her head.

"Carrie, I'm so sorry."

"This isn't your fault, Jess. I know you had no idea." Her eyes flashed to mine with reassurance.

"Thank you." I felt lighter. At least a little.

"I just can't get over him ... doing that to my babies." She clapped her hand to her mouth, and her eyes melted into grief. Her pain palpable. I could do nothing but hug her. The squeals from the biking kids rose and fell in another lap. We sat in silence for a long time.

The rest of the weekend went by with nice company, normal conversation and even some laughs with other friends of Carrie and Jim's at the park. I felt slightly renewed.

I arrived back home and was unpacking when I heard the door open. I followed the noise and found Greg with the kids. He had Ricky slumped over his shoulder, fast asleep, and Poppy was gripping

Greg's hand loosely. She barely smiled at me, and all three looked exhausted. I didn't invite him in and didn't prolong the awkward conversation.

The children sparked up with a hot meal and by the time I had them in the bath, they seemed their normal chipper selves.

"Guess what, Mummy?" Ricky didn't wait for me to guess. "We went to a dairy farm and even saw cows being milked."

"Yeah, Mum," Poppy piped in, "I got chosen out the crowd to milk the cow, but I couldn't do it. It felt gross." Poppy screwed her nose. She was almost six and still scared of most new things.

"I would have done it, Mummy!" Ricky proclaimed.

"I know," I said smiling, squeezing shampoo into his hair.

"And Daddy bought us donuts at lunch," Poppy chimed.

"Ooh, aren't you two lucky?" I smiled broadly for their sake.

"Yeah, and then he took us on the nature walk."

"What did Grandma and Grandpa think of the nature walk?"

"They didn't come." Ricky's hands were busy filling a squirt toy underwater.

"Where were they?" I kept my voice light and face straight.

"They were tired and waited for us in the car."

I looked away, biting my lip. I turned back to face them, throwing a cup of water over Ricky's head to rinse the soap. "Sounds like you two had a great time!" I plastered a smile.

Ricky shot Poppy with the squirt toy, making her squeal and splash him back.

"Okay, time to get out." I lifted Ricky out, got him dry and dressed into his favourite dinosaur pyjamas. I took my time with their bedtime routine.

"Mummy, are you going to let Daddy come home soon?" Poppy

asked in her sweet voice.

I was taken aback. "Oh honey, I'm sorry ... but Daddy won't be able to come home." My voice trailed off.

"That's not what he said, Mummy, he said you wouldn't let him come home."

"Did he really say that?" I searched her eyes. Of course, he would have said that. Why would she make that up?

"Yes, I'm not lying." Poppy raised her voice.

I rubbed her back. "Oh, sweetie." I lifted her onto my knee as we sat on the reading chair in her room. "I believe you."

She smiled and shoved the book she had chosen towards my face. I tried to listen as she read, but my mind kept drifting. I forced sweetness into my voice when I helped her sound out some of the words. Determined not to let my daughter see the gall within.

After kissing them both goodnight and leaving them to settle in each of their rooms, I went to the living room, making sure to close the hall door. I didn't want them to hear this conversation.

I pressed the call button on my phone.

"Greg. It's Jess."

"Jess, what can I do for you?"

"Did you leave the children alone with Julian today?"

Silence. He sighed into the phone. "Jess, it was at the end of a very long day out. We were tired. It was only for a very short time." His voice exasperated.

"Greg, there's more." I needed to be careful what I said. "There's more than just messages."

"I'm not sure what you mean."

"I've heard that Julian ..." I swallowed. "That he physically assaulted girls."

232

Silence and another long sigh. "I'm a facts man Jess. When all this is investigated, I'll know the facts."

"Yes, Greg." My voice growing in frustration. "But in the meantime, you need to supervise my children properly."

"We were, but it was hard."

"You need to do better." I'd never spoken to Greg so forcefully. Or anyone for that matter.

"Jess, we don't believe all this. We think this supervision is completely over the top. Julian would never hurt his children."

"It doesn't matter what you think, Greg. Child protection says you need to supervise properly. If it happens again, I will call them!"

"Okay Jess, I'm tired. I'm heading to bed."

"Bye." I hung up before he could respond. I was shaking, unaccustomed to being so rude.

I sat heavy in my frustration. All that talk over the weekend of Carrie feeling powerless to protect her children. Now here I was, helpless too.

# Spring 2016

arrie sat across the café table wearing rounded, oversized sunglasses. An armour we almost never left home without nowadays. Puffy eyes seemed constant. We lent in close so we wouldn't be overheard in the busy café.

Since Carrie had been contacted by Laura Keen, the detective who was investigating Julian, she had kept me up to date with any information she was allowed to share. Carrie was going to give a statement and said the most important thing was to not discuss hers or other people's evidence. The detective said this could be a very big case and wanted to make sure it was handled properly. We spoke almost daily, not just to hold each other up, but also to keep each other up to date on the case.

"So how did it go?" I asked.

"There were a lot of members there." Carrie had agreed at the request of Detective Laura Keen to organise a meeting with the entire club present.

"What did Laura say?

"She made it clear that she thinks Julian Rundell is a very dangerous man."

My eyebrows shot up.

"I told you when she interviewed him that first time back before the AGM, Laura said he made her skin crawl." Carrie spooned the froth from her coffee. "Anyway, so after Laura introduced herself, Meghan stepped forward. She was so brave, Jess. I wish you saw her."

We decided it wasn't a good idea for me to go along to the meeting. Some people hadn't come forward earlier because they didn't want to hurt my relationship with Julian. We wanted everyone to have an opportunity speak freely, without fear of hurting me.

Carrie continued. "Meghan said in front of the whole club that Julian assaulted her when she was a teenager and has given her statement to the police. She encouraged anyone else to give any information they had and to speak to the police if Julian had done anything to them."

"She's extraordinary." I shook my head in pride.

"I know. I am so proud of her." She smiled. "I spoke to a few people. But get this – Rhonda told me that Paige had shown her messages on her phone from Julian."

"Oh my god. Not Paige too?"

"But wait ... Rhonda said she won't pass them onto the police."

I screwed my face. "*What*?"

Carrie's face darkened. "She's so frustrating. Her words were, 'I don't want to get anyone into trouble'."

Gobsmacked, I leant back. "Unbelievable. But we're not talking here about petty misbehaviours to earn a slap on the wrist." I lowered my voice to a near whisper. "We're talking about child abuse."

"I know." She rubbed her forehead. "Anyway, there were quite a few of the junior cohort there as well. Some were teary. Poor girls. They mingled together but I didn't see anyone speak to the police." Carrie sipped her coffee, eyes distant. "Marty made his stance clear. He shouted, 'This is all fucking bullshit!' and stormed out."

"What about Luke and Chloe?"

"They were no shows."

She continued and I shook my head as she reeled off the names of other people who seemed to be sticking by Julian. I never thought child abuse could be so divisive. How wrong I was to assume the victims would be believed and supported. My skin crawled with the reality, there were people I called friends backing an accused child abuser. The hardest was Luke and Chloe. They were close to Carrie and Jim, too. How could Luke rationalise sticking by a man accused of abusing his friends' daughters?

The investigator had told Carrie that the burden of proof fell to the prosecution. The victim needed to prove it, whilst the perpetrator sits pretty with the comfort of reasonable doubt. Three girls reported Julian either messaged them indecently or had physically assaulted them. There was no possible gain for them to be making it up. It was only making their lives harder. How could some people not understand this?

"I really thought those people were my friends," I said, disheartened.

"So did I. I think it's pretty clear though. We can't underestimate the power Julian still has."

We finished our lunch and I mulled it all over on the drive home. I pulled into the drive, frustrated with people like Rhonda that kept quiet out of loyalty to Julian. But even more hurt by Luke and Chloe, people I thought were my good friends, remaining loyal to Julian. Loyalty to an accused child abuser was nonsensical.

As soon as I entered my quiet home, Buffy hassled me for food. Rubbing herself against my ankles in figure eights. I gave my now greying cat a scratch behind the ears. It seemed like an eternity ago that Julian had gifted me Buffy. I shook my head, pushing away what was once a happy memory.

Walking through the kitchen, I noticed the flashing light of the answering machine. I frowned. No one rang on the home phone anymore.

I pressed the button and kept walking.

A sinister deep voice stopped me in an instant.

"I'm coming for you, Julian. I know what you did. You're gonna die, you fucking cunt." Beep.

I could not move. Every muscle fibre tensed. I didn't recognise the voice. Everyone I knew was aware I'd kicked Julian out. What if this guy thought I was still with Julian? What if they came when the children were here? Terror took me, and I had no clue what to do. I had to pick up the children in an hour. I couldn't bring them home.

I reached for my phone.

"Hi, darling," Mum answered.

My voice shook. "Mum ... there's a death threat on our answering machine."

~

We moved out in an hour. When Poppy asked why we were leaving home, I struggled to find an answer. How could I tell her she was unsafe? In a panic, I told her there were snakes in our house and we had to leave to stay with my parents.

Now safe at my parents' house, the shock and terror had passed. In its place was a cold numbness.

This was not how I thought my life would turn out. Moving

237

back in with my parents in my thirties. It felt like failing in life. I couldn't fathom how to climb out of this mess. I walked my bag to my bedroom in quiet disdain for my life choices.

I plonked on my bed, gazing around my childhood bedroom. The aubergine feature wall – I was thirteen when I begged to have it painted. Dad had spent hours taping it out properly to ensure it didn't bleed into the white. Back in a time when my biggest concern was an aesthetic bedroom. Now look at me. Rooted out of my home, afraid for my children's safety, with an accused child abuser for a husband. Not to mention broke and with a divorce settlement to organise. This was not what teenage Jess had in mind for her future.

At least I had my parents to help with a roof over my head. I would have nowhere to go if not for them. When I arrived today with my children in tow, Mum had drawn me into a tight hug and whispered, "Honey, you're all welcome here as long as you need."

Tears stung at my eyes, but I blinked them away. I rose from the bed and unpacked my things. I had a feeling I'd be here for a while.

I opened the wardrobe and couldn't help but smile. A worn Pearl Jam poster hung on the inside of the wardrobe door. I had taped it there years ago, when I was going out with Matt in high school. We both loved Pearl Jam. We used to chill out in this room after school, listening to music. I'd sing their songs at the top of my lungs and Matt would beg me to stop through fits of laughter. I longed for the simplicity of what my life used to be. I had a wonderful boyfriend and great friends. Everything was ahead of us. But I gave them all up for the promise of one man. A man who opened me up and gorged away all my good bits. All that remained were systemic functions mandatory for survival. The richness and warmth of the old Jess was gone, I was just an empty vessel going through the motions of daily life.

I sat back on the bed, grabbing my phone. I could not sit idle. I dialled the number for Detective Laura Keen that Carrie gave me. Carrie said that Laura was reserved about speaking to me because I was Julian's wife, and wives normally side with their husbands.

She needed to know where I stood.

"Laura Keen," she answered.

"Hello, my name is Jess Rundell."

A slow intake of breath. "How can I help you, Jess?" Her voice was controlled, professional.

"Laura ... I know Carrie said you don't want to hear from me, but I have to tell you, I have definitely left Julian."

"Right." She sounded sceptical.

"I have," I implored. "I left him the minute I read those messages. They disgusted me. You have to understand."

"Uh huh ... Mrs Rundell, in most circumstances, a wife will stick by her husband."

Tears were flowing now. "Well not this circumstance! You have to understand. I love those girls. I am appalled by what he did. I want to help."

"Jess, it's still early days in the investigation," she said, her voice softening. "Him finding out about these more serious accusations at this point can only hinder an investigation."

"I cut contact. I only message through his dad. I won't tell them anything. I want to help."

"Would you be willing to give a statement?"

"Absolutely!"

"Even if that means giving evidence in a courtroom in front of him?"

"Yes."

"Great, well, I will get your email and contact you with further details."

"Thank you." I hung up the phone. It felt good to be proactive. To be of some potential help.

The following morning, the kids woke early and I led them quietly out to the living room. I grabbed the remote and settled onto the couch in between them. They both snuggled into my side, and I switched on the cartoons. Ricky pointed and laughed as a character tripped and stumbled down a grassy slope. I stared through heavy lids, barely paying attention.

The hall door opened and Dad shuffled out in his slippers and dressing gown. He stopped short as he spotted us snuggled on the couch. He smiled, but when his eyes met mine, it faded. He looked like he wanted to say something. He dipped his head in sympathy, remaining silent. What could a parent say in this situation? This was not something they prepared you for.

I hugged my children closer.

◦

Moving house was taking longer than it should have. We couldn't possibly take all the toys to the one room Poppy and Ricky shared at Mum and Dad's. I'd had to cull. But instead of sorting through what we needed, I got stuck reminiscing over every little item. Memories flooded back in unwanted waves.

Now I was going through their baby toys. I picked up Poppy's first blocks, remembering the moment I'd first built her a block tower. She was just a baby, barely able to sit up on her own. The look on her face when she saw it. Her shock when she slapped at them and they toppled to the ground in a bang. She squealed for joy. I'd called Julian into the room to watch and we laughed at Poppy's delighted face. At the time, it was one of those family moments that felt so special. One that gave me hope our connection would grow again.

A rush of guilt flooded me as I enjoyed a time with a man so heinous. Another happy memory lost, tainted by the present. I would gladly rid him from my brain entirely, but how could I wipe the good times I shared with my children and friends? I feared he would have to forever remain a scourge to my past.

I looked inside the spare bedroom's wardrobe and my shoulders sagged.

My wedding dress hung in a plastic protective sheath. Underneath were piles of boxes with all our old photos that didn't make the albums. I reached for the box at the back containing photos from high school, accidentally knocking over the box in front. It tumbled to the floor, losing its lid. Photos scattered over the carpet.

I spotted a photo of Julian with his arms around teenage Meghan and Amelia. The girls were each proudly holding a trophy.

I retched. It almost doubled me over.

I snatched the photo and ripped it down the middle.

More photos kept appearing. One with his smiling face in between Carrie's and mine. That smile I fell for all those years ago. I never noticed it didn't quit reach his eyes. A salesman's smile. I fell in love with his smile. It was the first thing I noticed about him. But there was coldness behind his dark eyes.

Angry tears dropped as I furiously tore at the photos. Each with more desperation, not content until his face was torn and unrecognisable. My whole life had revolved around him. How could I look at any memory now with happiness?

I ripped apart every photo with him in it. Pausing at the last – one of the two of us at our wedding. He was looking at something over my shoulder, while I looked up at him with adoring eyes. Even on my wedding day, I was like a little puppy dog, wagging my tail eager to please, searching for pats and attention and there he was – looking right past me.

I tore and tore until the pieces were too small to make out anything.

My face mangled and wet, I looked up at the wedding gown and wrenched it from the hanger. I grabbed the boxes of my high school memories and stormed from the room.

This was the last weekend I had to grab our things before Julian would come and do his part.

He could deal with a mess I made for once.

# Summer 2016

Poppy ran into the kitchen in a state of over-excitement. Ricky was quick to follow. They had both just returned from a weekend with their father, under Lyn and Greg's supervision. Even now, after a few months of weekly visits, I remained on edge all weekend until they returned home.

"Did you have five hundred Mars bars?" I asked as Poppy hugged me.

"No," Poppy said. "Only chocolate mousse and a thick shake at lunch. We went out to lunch after the circus."

"The circus! Aren't you lucky?"

Poppy didn't bother answering. She took off down the hall with Ricky at her heels.

I went to the bathroom and filled the bathtub. I helped Poppy and Ricky take their clothes off as the tub filled. They both jumped in at ankle depth and I gathered up their dirty clothes.

"Mummy," Poppy piped, "why are you trying to take the house and all Daddy's money?" She looked at me like I had let her down.

I dropped their dirty clothes and squatted next to the tub. "Honey, I am not trying to take all of Daddy's money or the house."

"When can we all go home?" Her face eager.

I sighed, using a careful tone. "We won't all be living together again, and we are not going back to our old house."

"But Mummy," Ricky said, "Daddy said he got rid of the snakes ... so we can!" His face lit up as he spoke of Julian. His dad; his hero.

"Sorry sweetheart, it's not that simple." I looked at my fingers, noticing I'd been rubbing holes in my skin with my nails.

"But why can't we live together anymore?" Poppy asked, face dropped.

"Well, let me explain it this way. When you do something bad or naughty, what happens?"

"You send us to timeout."

"Right. There are consequences to our actions, and the choices we make. Your daddy's done some bad things, and as a consequence we can't live together anymore."

"He says he didn't," Poppy said, spite in her eyes.

"I'm sorry, honey, that's just not true."

I watched her face carefully. The slightest raise of one eyebrow and curling of her lips. She didn't believe me. I took a deep breath, unsure how to navigate.

Ricky saved me the trouble of thinking of a response. He said, "And Daddy took us to the oval to kick the footy. And he got us an ice-cream."

"An ice-cream too?" I feigned a smile. "Yum. Did Grandpa have a kick too?"

"No, they weren't there."

"Not Grandma or Grandpa?"

"They stayed in the car."

I looked for calm at the ceiling but I wanted to scream. Lyn and Greg had simple instructions. When Julian was with the children, they must be there to watch and listen. It was infuriating.

Ricky dove into another monologue about the weekend and chatted about everything they were allowed to do at Grandma's but not with me. The things they got at Grandma's. Daddy bought them a new game. Daddy took them to restaurants I couldn't afford. Daddy took them to the circus. He didn't have a job; Lyn and Greg must have been funding all the frivolity.

Maybe if Daddy paid some child support, Mummy could do some fun things with them, too. Not just the school runs and after school sport.

After they were bathed, changed and amusing themselves with toys, I took the opportunity to duck out to the yard to call Lyn. It had been a long time since I'd had a discussion with her. All my interactions had been with Greg. I was not looking forward to it.

I walked along one of the stone paths and sat on a garden seat bathed in the evening sun. Insects danced around a flowering shrub next to me, glowing in the sun stream. All seemed normal in the arthropod world. I prayed I would get a normal again.

I dialled Lyn.

It took several rings before she picked up. "Jess. What can I do for you?" Lyn's voice tight, careful.

"Hi Lyn." I cleared my throat. "The kids have told me that they were alone with their dad at the oval today. Is that true?" I kept my voice level. I didn't want to argue, I just wanted my children supervised.

She sighed loudly. "Look, Jess." A long pause. "They were in my line of sight the *entire* time. We were at the café up the hill."

"But Lyn, I really need you to take this supervision more seriously. I will have to tell child services if you aren't supervising."

"Look Jess, it's no secret you don't like me. After everything I've done for you, I can't understand why, but you have pushed me away for years."

"What has any of that got to do with it?" I screwed my face, glad she couldn't see me.

Another loud sigh and long pause. No qualms keeping people waiting. "We are both hoping for different outcomes from this investigation." She said it like it was a sour taste in her mouth. "I have no doubt that all this will be over soon, and when it is, he will be able to spend more time with his children. The way he's meant to – without Greg and I watching over him. It's not natural."

"He's had opportunities to spend time with his children for years. He's never been into Poppy's school to volunteer or Ricky's day care. Even in all that time he was unemployed. He has never wanted to play with them more than he does now."

She sniffed. "I think we are all just hoping for different outcomes and until this is all over, we all are just doing our best."

I shook my head. I'd had enough. "Lyn, you need to supervise my children properly with him. If you don't, I will call child protection."

"You do whatever you think you need to do." Her voice was quiet, curt; a poster for passive aggression.

I hung up. I couldn't say goodbye to that woman. She was just as frustrating as Julian. I felt like throwing my phone at a tree. Instead, I phoned Carrie. My constant.

⚘

It was a battle to stay focused at work since leaving Julian. I wasn't close to anyone at work. I was never really allowed to be. When they

246

all went for after-work drinks, I used to say no. After a while, the invitations stopped. Most staff tiptoed around me now like I might break. Except for Patrick and a few I'd worked with for years. They gave me tasks to do, calling me out if I was not focusing, even just talking to me like I was a human being. Some seemed afraid to ask me how my weekend was or what I was up to. Perhaps afraid of the answer they might hear. I could hardly blame them.

"Hey Jess, do you need to head straight off?" Patrick was in the tearoom doorway as I gathered my bag.

"Um actually, no I don't," I said. Mum was taking Poppy shopping after school and Dad was taking Ricky to watch him play football. "What did you have in mind?"

"Give me five and we'll duck to the esplanade for a drink?"

"Sounds good." A little buzz ran through me. Six months ago, I wouldn't have been able to grab a drink with any work colleagues. Not without Julian's permission. Even then, it wouldn't be worth it. Now, it was like a weight had gone. As hard as life was right now, the freedom was exhilarating.

I met Patrick on the esplanade and we walked to a bar. I sat at a table outside and Patrick left to order me a gin and tonic. On the stage next to me sat a heavily tattooed guitarist in a floral dress and doc martins, strumming and singing an acoustic cover. I watched, mesmerised.

"I've been wanting to catch up with you for a while." Patrick returned, placing a glass in front of me. He had ordered himself a fruity cocktail.

I looked at his kind face and couldn't help but smile.

"How is everything going?" he said.

I took a long breath. Where to start? "I told you I moved into Mum and Dad's, right? Well, I got a lawyer for the family court stuff.

He's been trying to organise a financial settlement out of court for me."

His eyes shifted, looking at the beach. "I have all that ahead, too." He winced a little.

It dawned on me I knew very little about him. "Really?"

"It's nothing as complicated as what you're dealing with. I'm not after sympathy." A small grin reached his eyes. "But I'll take some anyway." He chuckled. "Honestly, this has been a long time coming."

"Patrick, I'm sorry."

His eyes met mine and we sat in silence until we both ended up smiling again.

"I don't really want to talk about that anyway," he said, eyes twinkling.

"I'm here if you want to talk about it."

He sipped on his drink, holding my gaze. He had lovely eyes. "Thanks, Jess."

It was a beautiful evening, the sun low, casting long shadows out to sea. We chatted for hours. The conversation flowed; no awkwardness or searching for topics. It was the most fun I'd had for a long time. I couldn't remember the last time I had a night that wasn't consumed by thoughts of Julian, his alleged crimes and the uncertain future.

When we got back to our cars, he hugged me goodbye. It was long and firm.

"My god Jess, there's nothing of you."

I shrugged. "The divorce diet works, I guess," I said dryly.

He smiled, again. It was hard not to smile back. I fought an urge to dive back into his arms and cosy my cheek into his soft linen shirt. To eat in his scent. He always smelled great. But I stopped myself. The night was already perfect as it was.

Our gazes locked for one last smile, eyes lingering for a second before we each opened our car doors. The smile didn't fade as I drove home. I'd been wearing a fake smile for so long, I almost forgot what it felt like to smile genuinely.

That night, for the first time in months, I didn't dream of Julian chasing me down the corridor. I didn't dream of anything. I awoke fuelled. Ready for whatever came.

The after-work drinks with Patrick became a weekly occurrence. We tended to visit the same bar and if the weather allowed, took the same outdoor table. I found myself looking forward to it each week. It was nice to chat to someone going through something similar. The logistics of separation were emotionally draining, and it was a relief to be able to vent about it.

The more I got to know Patrick, the more I wanted to spend time with him. His body language told me it was reciprocated.

Tonight at the bar, the acoustic songstress was back playing an Adele cover. Patrick was drinking another cocktail while I sipped on my gin and tonic.

"What's that on your hand?" he asked, concerned. He gently took my hand into his own. His fingers encircled mine and my breath caught. A warmth ran up my arm, right through my frozen organs. My eyes lifted to his.

"I burnt myself on the iron the other day," I said.

His eyes stayed on my hand, and he gently stroked his thumb along mine, each nerve end firing shots of warmth through me. I was shocked when my cheeks flushed. How long had it been since a man made my cheeks flush?

His eyes met mine and I looked away, at the singer. I pulled my hand away, clearing my throat. "She's great, isn't she?"

I wanted to slap myself for pulling away. To lose the feeling of his hand around mine. But this feeling frightened me. I had been celebrating for months that I no longer had to have sex with Julian. I thought I could happily live the rest of my life without having sex with anyone ever again.

Something stirred deep inside when Patrick moved his thumb over mine. I thought that part of me was dead. It scared me it was returning. I was not looking for physical attraction. Those feelings led me to the mess I was in now. I couldn't face that hurt again. To be with a man who never gave me what he promised. The vows of love and trust, like flour through a sieve.

But Patrick was not Julian. There was nothing about these two men that was alike.

It didn't take long to fall back into our easy rhythm of conversation and my reaction to his touch was all but forgotten. He was interested in what I had to say. He asked questions and waited for the answer. I accepted the bare minimum from Julian for so long, talking to Patrick felt like a marvel. But this was how conversation should be – listening, showing interest. Julian had only listened to my conversation in the early days or if it suited his needs.

I looked at my phone, surprised how late it was. "I'm going to have to make a move." I took the last sip of my drink.

"Wow, time flew." Patrick said, smiling.

We wandered into the now dark car park. Patrick walked me to my car and enveloped me in a hug, as was now a custom. This was what I looked forward to the most each week. My face rested against his chest as he squeezed just the right amount. I didn't want to stop hugging him. That same stir ran through me, and my heart rate climbed. His breath landed soft on the top of my head, tickling at the stray strands. He pulled back gently and cupped my cheeks. He looked at me with a question in his eyes. I gave a small nod. His lips brushed against mine and, despite telling myself I didn't want this, my lips matched his and pressed firmer. We moved together in a natural rhythm as though we had kissed a thousand times.

For a moment, I was intoxicated. My breath becoming ragged, I pulled away, shaking my head.

"I'm so sorry," I murmured, my brows twisting together. "I don't know if I want this. I mean ... I want this ... you know ..." My voice trailed off and I stared at his face.

He was smiling and I wanted to kiss him again. "Jess, it's completely understandable. There's no hurry. I love our time together just the way it is." His hands landed on my shoulders. "I will never pressure you to do anything you don't want to." His eyes stayed on mine.

My brow unfurled and I stood on my toes and kissed him on the cheek. We hugged again for a long time before we said goodbye.

9

I looked at the dark clouds hanging low over Rochford. It gave me a heavy heart just pulling into the carpark. Julian left some kind of force over the building. There was so much of him still here, it felt smothering to be in its vicinity.

I spotted Bridget waiting by the front door. She walked towards me, smiling. We hugged. "I just went inside," she said. "It's all clear. No one's there."

She handed me the keys. Bridget and Oliver were some of the

few that I still trusted from the club. They had made it very clear how disgusted they were in Julian. Too many others were either clearly sticking up for Julian or on the fence. Not good enough for me. Their silence just further supported Julian. Nobody should be indifferent towards child abuse.

Bridget had to hurry off. She blew me a kiss and got in her car.

I stood by the front door of Rochford, chewing on my fingernails. I felt exposed here, like he had eyes on me. I couldn't escape the feeling of wanting to run for cover.

I was relieved when I saw Detective Laura Keen pull up in an unmarked police car.

We had just finished signing off my statement at the police station. She had asked if she could come to my old house and the club to take photos. I was more than willing to oblige, despite my apprehension of being in either space now.

She climbed out of the car in her dark pantsuit and sensible heeled shoes. She adjusted the camera strap hanging over her neck. One eyebrow seemed to naturally sit higher than the other, drawing my eye as she spoke. A perpetual look of inquiry on her face – a born detective.

We had spoken over the phone a lot, but I had been hesitant to meet her in person. But her smile was full and genuine when she welcomed me to the police station this morning. I liked her immediately. It was tough going through such sensitive and personal topics like my sex life with a stranger, but she somehow made it okay.

I opened the door to the club, wincing as I stepped over the threshold. I didn't belong here anymore.

I showed Laura through to the members bar, and so many amazing memories came flooding back. The stage in the corner looked more scuffed than I remembered, but it still brought back memories of Julian. It was the spot he promised to love me forever when he asked for my hand in marriage. Once a treasured memory, now unwanted.

I pressed my lips together and turned away, looking out at the river while Laura walked around, the beep and click of her camera the only sounds.

The river didn't help. There were even more memories in that boatyard and marina. There was no escaping. My mind whirled trying to stop them coming and I shook my head, walking to the hall. I waited for Laura outside, staring at my new sandals. No memories of him there.

"I'm all done in there," Laura said, coming out of the members room. "Do you mind showing me the equipment shed? I've heard it's under the building."

"Sure. Why do you need to see that?"

"I can't tell you that." But her face said I already knew the answer. I gulped, thinking of the hours he had spent with the juniors down there.

There were still so many secrets.

# *Autumn 2017*

It was just after seven in the morning when I pulled into Carrie's drive. She had agreed to come to support me in the Family Court today for my first hearing.

My mind wandered back to that summer afternoon when I was served the papers from Julian's lawyer. The best in town, I was told. He had ignored my offers of a fair financial split and instead decided to take me to court. I cried when I got the papers. I was already thousands in debt to my lawyer; he said it could come out of my settlement. But I had to come up with the two thousand dollar fee to pay a barrister today to represent me today.

Carrie hurried out her front door to my car.

"Hey, love," she said, climbing into the passenger seat. She leaned in to kiss my cheek. "It'll be good to check out the court district in town. I have a feeling we might be spending a fair bit of time around there."

I gulped. Nerves were getting the better of me. We stopped at the bakery to order coffees and agreed to split a toasted sandwich. Better to go with some fuel, even though I had lost my appetite in anticipation of the hearing.

"So, you got your statement all signed off?" Carrie asked, sipping on her coffee.

"Yeah, it was pretty emotional," I said. "But I'm glad it's all done. Anything to push the process along. What can possibly be taking so long?" I rolled my eyes.

"Laura says it's a big case. Apparently, there are something like twenty witnesses on the list."

My eyes popped. "Twenty! That's so many. Do we know the total number of victims?"

"Unsure. She can't tell me. I know there is one eyewitness, though. I get the feeling that a lot is riding on that witness."

"Who could it be?"

She shrugged as I turned onto the highway.

With our coffees long since drained, we drove into the court district and found a carpark. We were on the footpath within a few blocks of the Family Court when I froze. Julian was crossing the street ahead of us, flanked by Lyn and Greg. Julian wore a business suit with the jacket undone. His chin high and hand stuffed leisurely into his pant pocket. My heart bounded against enormous pressure.

"Jess ... what?" Carrie followed my eyes and grabbed my hand firmly when she spotted them. "That *fucker*."

Ice had taken my chest and the air was trapped again, sharp and jagged. I hadn't laid eyes on Julian for six months.

"I don't think I can do this." I pushed the words out through raspy breaths.

Carrie's eyes were full of hatred towards the trio. She squeezed my hand. "Yes, you can." She steered me forwards.

As we rounded the corner at the rise, Julian and his crew had disappeared. I could take a little more air in. We continued along the bustling city street and came across the glass fronted, multi-level building. The 'Family Court' title plastered along the second level.

Large, automated doors opened, and I took a last, full breath, as if I was a freshwater species deep diving into the ocean.

We lined up at the security checkpoint. The smooth security system operated seamlessly and quickly. The unsmiling security guard instructed me what to do and showed me through the scanner.

When we were through, Carrie and I searched the enormous foyer for my barrister, though we had no idea what he was supposed to look like. In the end, he found us. A short, older man, he introduced himself before leading us through to a stark room. A table and a couple of chairs the only inhabitants. I was comfortable in this little haven, away from anywhere Julian might be.

My two-thousand-dollar-a-day speaker spent the first hour leaning back lazily in his chair, one ankle crossed over his knee and fingertips pressed together. He gave me a run through of how our little Family Court routine was going to play out. Carrie and I nodded along patiently, waiting for him to get to the bit where I got to stand up in court and ask for a fair settlement after telling my story. Everyone would understand that I wanted and needed to get on with my life as soon as possible. This back and forth through lawyers was already months old and thousands of dollars deep.

I looked at my watch and wondered when he would show me to the courtroom. He disappeared a few times for chit chats with the other side. Carrie and I stayed in that little room the entire morning. Was this how they normally got results in family court? By wearing people down with boredom? The hours ticked by. I left the safety of our private room for a toilet break and scowled when I saw my barrister laughing with the lawyer representing Julian. It looked like an 'old boys' club meeting.

Hours passed before we finally got to enter a courtroom. I spotted the dreaded trio sitting behind their legal representatives and I headed to the other side of the room. I sat on the seat furthest away from them and kept my gaze forwards. Nothing to gain looking at him.

Finally, our case was mentioned.

Then it was over.

What the hell? I thought I was going to get a settlement. All we got were what was called interim orders that the children's visitation was to stay the same, the children would get appointed a lawyer, and a mediation conference would be scheduled for later in the year. We were adjourned for another mention hearing in a month.

As soon as we were dismissed, Carrie and I were quick out the large glass doors.

"I thought courts were for decisions," I said.

"That felt like a colossal waste of time!" Carrie spat out.

"That was nothing like what I thought it would be. That guy, my two-thousand-dollar speaker, didn't even *speak*. He just stood and nodded for the two seconds that the judge spoke." I shook my head. How could this be a system where things got done?

Carrie and I walked to the car, both drained by the joke that was the family court system.

"God, another month," I said, unlocking my car. I thought I would only move in with Mum and Dad for one month. It had been over four months already. As if I didn't feel enough of a failure. Now I couldn't see an end.

"Don't worry love, it could be worse."

We plonked into the car.

"How?" I exclaimed.

"You could still be with him."

—◦—

# *Winter 2017*

I spotted Poppy through the swarm of uniformed children. She waved when she saw me, and sprinted to the car. She was barely in the car before she was running me down on her fabulous day.

"Oh guess what Mummy?" she said breathlessly.

"Tell me." I turned at the roundabout and headed back up the crowded street. I drove slow, with so many young kids darting home.

"Daddy came in and did a reading in class today!"

My head snapped to her delighted face, and I worked hard not to scream out 'What?'. I composed my face and said, "Oh wow, honey. You must have loved that." I struggled to keep my voice level.

"It was the best! He hasn't seen my classroom before."

"Yeah, I know." I forced a half smile.

There was a very good reason he had not been in her classroom. I had her move schools at the start of the year. A school where no one would know who her dad was. I was terrified if word got out about the allegations against him, it could have terrible effects on her.

"Was Grandma there with him?" I asked.

"Yep!" She exclaimed with pride. "And she was reading to kids, too."

Every morning the younger levels had parents come in and volunteer reading. A parent would take each child individually to a quiet nook in the back of the classroom and read with them. I had only managed to get in a few times with work.

My eyes widened when the realisation dawned on me. "Hang on. Was Daddy just reading to you? Or other kids too?"

"Others too!" Her face lit up.

I turned into the street towards Ricky's day care. I was furious. How could he? It was only last month I got a call from Laura Keen. She wanted to make sure my children wouldn't be with him when she charged him the following day. I'd nearly dropped the phone. The investigation had taken months and I almost felt that day may never come. But on that sunny spring morning, Julian was taken to the station. They charged him with a number of indictable offences and Laura promised many more would follow in her full brief of evidence. He was released on strict bail conditions. I thought those conditions meant he couldn't be alone with any female under sixteen.

My car hit the parking curb harder than I meant to and Poppy's head jolted forward.

"Whoa, Mum!"

"Sorry, honey." I cut the engine and we walked towards the front door of the day care.

My anger peaking, I paid no attention to my surrounds. As I approached, a man came out the front door carrying his little girl. It took me a second to realise it was Luke.

Poppy dropped my hand and ran forward.

"Uncle Luke!" She threw her arms around his hips.

His eyes met my scowl, and his smile dropped before correcting it for Poppy.

"Hey, there little nugget! What's up?"

259

"We're getting Ricky." Poppy squished Luke's daughter's cheeks, making her laugh.

Luke cleared his throat. "Jess, I've been meaning to–"

"Actually, we're in a hurry." I pushed past him, grabbing Poppy's hand on the way. This was all I needed. A run-in with a Julian sympathiser.

I rushed to collect Ricky and take them both home. As soon as they were set with an afternoon snack, I hurried to the rear of the yard, dialling as I went.

"Laura, it's Jess."

"Is everything okay?" Laura asked.

"No! Is there anything in Julian's bail conditions that makes it illegal for him to enter a school?"

She kept her cool when I was anything but. "Not specifically. But he can't be alone with any female under sixteen. And he has to abide by the family court orders in regard to contact with your children. Jess, tell me what's happened."

"He went into Poppy's class today and read with children. Not just Poppy. I mean like ... reading with other people's children!"

"What? By himself?" There was a spark in her tone.

"His mum was with him but apparently, they were each reading alone to other peoples' children. Surely this is a bail violation?"

I waited for her to shout that she was leaving now to lock him up. I waited. Nothing.

"Laura?"

"I'm sorry, Jess." The spark gone. "The law is an arse. If his mum was there ... technically he was not breaking bail."

"So, you're saying that if he walked in there alone, he could be arrested, but because his mother escorted him into the school, an

260

alleged child sex offender is allowed in that school?"

"I'm sorry to tell you Jess but yes, that's right." Her voice kind but professional.

"Well, fuck!" I took a moment to calm myself. "So, there is nothing you can do?"

"I'm really sorry. Maybe the school can do something?" She sounded disheartened by her own institution.

I had to thank her and hang up the phone.

Two hours later, I was sat next to Patrick on his couch, drinking a glass of wine. I spent a lot of spare time here now. We were becoming inseparable.

"That's outrageous!" Patrick shook his head. "What did the school say?"

"I spoke to the head and they said their hands were tied. They don't require police checks on people volunteering in the school with the children."

"*What?*"

"I know. Apparently, there are current recommendations from the board of education that they should get police checks but it's up to each individual school to implement the recommendations."

"So, you're saying a person charged with child sex offences can be sitting next to anyone's little kid in a private corner of a classroom reading with them? Independently?"

"That's exactly right." I slugged my wine.

"What about child protection? Can they stop this?"

"No, his mother was there." I grimaced. "No one can help me. So, the only choice I have is to actually tell parents and wait for the uproar! And that's not an option. We'd be a news story, and that was the whole purpose of me moving her to a new school. So that no

261

one knew who her dad was. Now he's waltzing into her classroom like he's fucking father of the year!"

"What are you going to do?"

"Mum's going to plead for Lyn to see sense, in hope she won't take him in again."

I didn't resist as Patrick guided me against him. I leaned the full weight of my life into him, and he pulled me closer, kissing the top of my head.

9

Mum was rapping her fingernails on the kitchen bench when I walked in. A mug of tea next to her, abandoned. Her face barely managed a smile when she saw me.

"Hey Mum," I said. "Where are the kids?"

She glared at me. "They are digging in the garden. Covered head to toe in dirt."

I frowned. "Is something wrong?"

"Jess ... that woman!" She threw a look over her shoulder to make sure the kids hadn't come inside.

"What woman?"

"Lyn Rundell," she said darkly. "She's more brazen than a monkey. I'm wild at her."

"I thought you were okay with her going?" It was grandparents' day at Poppy's school today, and Lyn had told Mum that she and Greg were going. Mum had seemed okay with it, or so I thought.

"Of course. They have every right to. In fact, I was feeling sorry for them. They don't deserve the mess that he's caused. It must be

262

awful for his relatives. I felt bad for them." Her eyes bolted to mine. "Until today, that is."

My eyes widened and I took the stool opposite her. She flicked another glance over her shoulder.

"How dare she!" Venom on her lips. "She brought him to grandparents' day! Of all days. He was in the classroom on *grandparents'* day."

"Jesus Christ! Mum, I'm sorry."

"Don't blaspheme." She lifted her tea and sipped.

"Sorry." I felt my lungs deflate again. I was not surprised. They seemed to have no shame.

"It was awful. The poor teacher. She looked at me so awkwardly." Mum's lips pressed together so firmly they were barely visible.

I thought if the school knew, they could stop him entering. Instead, everyone was expected to act normally. It's only child sex offences he's accused of. Don't worry though, because his mummy was there supervising him. No matter that the police, child protection and the school couldn't stop him.

"I've had enough of being pleasant to that family," Mum said. "Trying to keep the peace for the sake of the children. I went to Greg and said, 'Greg ... he shouldn't be here!'"

"What did he say?"

"He said something about him being the father and that we all have to get used to still seeing him."

"What did you do?"

Mum lifted her chin. "I said, 'No I do not have to see him, Greg!'"

"Gosh Ma, I'm proud of you!" She was one of the most nonconfrontational people ever.

"Then I went up to her. I walked to Lyn, and I said very

unapologetically ... I said, 'He shouldn't be here!'"

My eyes grew wider and I couldn't help but to smile. My mum taking on the Rundells. "What happened?"

"She took a long breath – you know how she is. Making everyone wait like she's the most important woman in the world."

"Well ... Mum, to be fair, she did breed the 'smartest' man I know." My sarcasm almost drawing a smile to Mum's raging face.

"Anyway, she had the nerve to spit back at me, 'He has every right to be here!'"

"No way! She's unbelievable."

"I know. I just blustered and said, 'No Lyn, he doesn't – it's *grand-parents'* day!'"

I burst out laughing. Mum joined in the belly laughs for a few moments before we both shook our heads and fell into silence again.

"How are we going to stop this?" I asked.

"I have no idea. We have to make them realise that just because Poppy likes him there, it's not in her best interests. We'd be plastered all over the TV or something if it came out in public. Then, none of us could show our faces in the community again."

The shame of association with an accused sex offender.

# Spring 2017

I looked at my ring finger resting on the steering wheel. The once perpetual tan line from my wedding and engagement rings had long faded. My body smoothing the skin tone, a natural rejuvenation helping wipe the memory of him. It'd been over a year since I wore them, the bond long broken, but he still had a hold over me. My hopes rested on today.

I parked the car. Carrie and I downed the last of our coffees and walked the familiar path to the family courthouse in the city.

"Today is the day," I said, as much to myself as Carrie. Rallying enthusiasm had become a chore.

"Absolutely," Carrie said. "Positive thoughts. Today is your day!" She almost stamped as she marched the city path.

We sat in another little conference room. My two-thousand-dollar-a-day barrister, who I had to borrow money from my parents to pay for, sat relaxed opposite us. The morning started as any other family court day. I had now experienced a few. Sitting and waiting.

My barrister cracked annoying dad jokes as we waited. His attempt at lightening the mood. For two thousand dollars, I expected a full comedy gala.

After a time, a squat woman entered the room and introduced herself as the senior registrar mediating our financial settlement.

She had a no bullshit tone and I instantly respected her. We chatted about the options for financial settlement before she left to talk to the other side.

We sat quietly with the comedian out of jokes. I thought back to my other times in family court. Those other hearings had been an emotional roller coaster and an enormous waste of time. There was an expectation that everyone would sit in a room together, no matter the trauma. My chest collapsed each time I laid eyes on Julian. I didn't know what was worse – being forced to sit in a room with him, or the lack of movement and some future plan forward. Every time a hearing ended, it was to learn nothing was concrete and I must do it again in a few months. There was no urgency. Didn't they understand I was still under his control until I could sell the house? I couldn't provide a stable and comfortable home for my children and nobody seemed to care.

The hearing where I met the children's lawyer was the most emotionally draining of all. I had been so eager to meet him.

"I am here to represent the needs of the children, and *only* the children," the lawyer had said.

I thought great, he'd help me keep that scum bag out of Poppy's school. I explained my concerns that Lyn and Greg weren't supervising properly. That Julian was telling Poppy lies about how I was trying to take everything from him, and I was concerned he was trying to turn the children against me. All under the apparent watchful eye of his mother.

The lawyer listened intently. He explained he had a history in criminal law, so he was well equipped to deal with these matters. He turned to me, straight-faced, and said, "You know, there is some evidence to suggest that just because he has abused other people's kids doesn't mean he would abuse his own children."

My jaw dropped. I glared at him, waiting for him to say something about understanding my concerns. But he just sat staring at me, unmoved.

"Well I bet I could show you some evidence to suggest that he could," I nearly yelled, blinking back angry tears.

My barrister yawned loudly bringing me back to the present. I continued to sit, rolling my phone in my hands as my lips flickered a smile thinking of the time I got a letter from Julian's lawyer stating how inappropriate it was that I had Carrie in open court as my support person, given that she was involved in his criminal matters. I was a witness involved in his criminal matters, too. Did that mean I couldn't attend my own family court hearings either? It was comical they were upset by her presence.

Carrie nudged me, pulling my attention to the senior registrar re-entering the room. I sat up in my chair, ready for good news. An offer.

She sat heavily. "I'm sorry, Jess. They are not meeting your offer. Not even close."

My face dropped.

"Look Jess, I have to tell you. What they are offering is far below what I think you should settle for. I've looked at the charges he is facing. It is highly likely, in my opinion, he will get a lengthy jail sentence if he is found guilty."

My ears perked. I once loved this man. It was strange to think I now wanted him imprisoned. I chewed my lip – was that what I wanted? I wished for justice, sure, but did I wish for suffering? I'd heard Jim talk of what they did to 'rock spiders' in prison. Could I wish that on anyone, even a perpetrator? The only thing I knew was

I never wanted Julian to be able to hurt anyone else. That meant jail.

The registrar continued. "If that happens, you are the one left raising the children. You are going to be entitled to much more. And you will need it."

I searched her face and found only professional sympathy. "I would happily leave with nothing if it meant I never had to have anything to do with any of them ever again," I said.

She gave a solemn nod.

Carrie turned to me. "Jess, don't take what they're offering. You will run out of money paying all the ongoing legal fees. You're right, they are not going away. They will continue to fight for as long as they can."

I nodded, my lips pressed firmly together.

"Jess," the registrar said, "I see here that you have filed paperwork for the divorce."

"That's right," I said. "I have another hearing to finalise it next month."

Her eyes softened. "Let me see if we can take care of that today. Save you another trip."

My eyes lit up. "*Really*?"

She smiled with her whole face. "Really." She stood and left the room again.

She returned a while later, smiling broadly, holding a document. She said nothing but rested it on the bench in front of me and pointed to the signature I recognised instantly.

My jaw dropped. "He signed?"

She nodded. "Now we just need you to sign here, and you are divorced."

Thirty minutes later, Carrie and I were toasting a glass of bubbles at a bar across the road.

"I actually feel lighter, would you believe?" I said.

"Of course, you would," Carrie said. "I knew he wasn't a great partner, but I had no idea the extent of it. All that phone tracking stuff – it's creepy."

"I can't believe it. Divorced!" My eyes were wide; hope restored. Something finally happened after months in family court. Even though there would be no financial settlement any time soon, the children and I would live with my parents indefinitely, and the conciliation conference was a complete disaster – I couldn't wipe the smile off my face.

I took a long sip. Lyn and Greg seemed content bankrolling the family court proceedings for their unemployed son at whatever cost. Their bill must be in the thousands. Mine certainly was. But I couldn't stop smiling. It had been more than twelve months since I read those torrid messages and revolted from the fellowship of Julian. Now, I was officially free of the Rundell name. I was back to being Jess Foster.

"So, enough about that brute!" Carrie said. "Tell me about the holiday to Thailand."

"Oh my god! I'm so excited. Patrick is taking the kids and I to Phuket for ten nights."

"So ... everything is great with Patrick, I presume?" Carrie glowed with a cheeky smile.

"More than great. He's nothing like anything I'm used to at all. He's genuinely nice. I mean, he makes me feel good about myself."

She grinned. "That's what a relationship is meant to feel like, Jess."

I couldn't contain a smile thinking about Patrick. I'd found a comfort in his ease. He was a wonderful support and distraction from all that was difficult. He made me remember there was good in the world. I thought back to the first time he met the children at the food and wine festival. He was sweet to them without being awkward. We had spent more and more spare time together over the past few months.

"I know," I said. "Sometimes I have to pinch myself. He's been great with the kids too."

"That's all sounding good then. I'm really excited for your holiday." She downed the last of her glass.

"Me too. Except for one problem." My face screwed.

"What's that?"

"I have to get permission from Julian to take the children overseas."

Carrie winced. "Oh."

ء

*It is clear to me that you do not have the best interests or rights of the children as a priority. I have asked for your response regarding makeup time because the children will miss valuable time with their father and with your lack of appropriate response I can only assume that you are not committed to upholding their rights and therefore, I am left with no choice other than to place the children on the DO NOT FLY list tomorrow. Regards, Greg.*

The text was clearly from Julian. Perhaps a little shorter than his usual garble. But they were his words no doubt. It didn't seem to matter how much I begged Greg not to forward his messages. I couldn't get him to understand my inner turmoil at receiving them.

Patrick discarded the six of hearts, smirking as he laid his winning hand down. His smile faded when his eyes landed on my face. "Everything okay?"

"What the hell is a 'Do Not Fly' list?"

"I don't know. I've never heard of it. It doesn't sound like something you want you or the kids on with an overseas trip planned though."

"No." I started googling as Patrick rounded the kitchen bench. He flipped the kettle on and slipped his hands around my waist in one smooth movement. My head flopped back into his chest as he landed soft kisses along my shoulder line. His phone pinged, spoiling our moment and he rounded the bench again to pick it up.

He chuckled at the message he received and grinned as he typed a response. My throat closed, overcome with paranoia. It wasn't something I could control. Who was he texting? Who was making him smile like that?

"Do you want to play another hand?" His smile turned quizzical when he saw my twisted expression. I felt like scratching his face. That's all it took. One unexplained text message and I was sent spiralling into a jealous rage. I no longer recognised myself. This happened all the time, particularly when he smiled and laughed with someone else. My brain spun in furious circles as I watched his animated conversations. So deeply terrified of being played the fool again. My past betrayal overwhelmed. Would a nice man, who treated me well, ever be able to earn a comfort in his actions from me?

I shook the thought away. "Sure." I forced a friendly expression on my face.

He reached over the bench and kissed me. "Don't stress. We'll get legal advice and sort it out."

He always seemed to know the right thing to say.

Four weeks later, I sat in the passenger seat of Patrick's car, bound for the international airport. I looked at him and he smiled as he placed his hand over my fingers, rapping on my thigh. Ricky and Poppy argued about the centre back rest being up or down.

"Cut it out, the both of you," I snapped.

A few weeks ago, I had to have another expensive meeting with my lawyer who advised he didn't think Julian could put the children on the 'Do Not Fly' list, and we decided to go on the trip, as planned.

"Oh look, there's a plane taking off!" Poppy squealed. This would be my kids' first time on a plane.

I hoped we could take off. My worried eyes flashed to Patrick's again. He had paid for this whole holiday. If we couldn't get on the plane, it would all be lost. He didn't seem worried at all. His outward persona the complete opposite of mine.

We found a carpark and went through the check in and security. I was properly sweating as we lined up at the customs counter.

"Oh my god," I said. "I must look so guilty." I clawed at Patrick's arm.

"Just relax. What's the worst that can happen?" He shrugged.

"I can be accused of illegally trying to flee the country with my children," I whispered so Ricky and Poppy couldn't hear.

Patrick rubbed my back. "Don't worry. Soon we will be laying by a pool, cocktail in hand and all our stressors left behind us."

I tried hard to control my breathing.

"It will be fine. You watch." He squeezed my hand and ushered me forward with Ricky when it was our turn. The customs officer took his time looking at our departure cards and passports. I was convinced he was about to call security.

I waited with my heart pumping out of my chest. A single trail of sweat snaked down my spine. I shifted uncomfortably. His steely glare could see straight through me; he knew I was hiding something. I watched him reach for his phone. This was actually happening. I was going to be corralled by the federal police. I went to say something, to explain everything, and just as a croaky mangled word formed on my lips, he waved us through. I almost skipped all the way through duty free.

"I hope you never do anything illegal." Patrick laughed. "Because your face looked so guilty back there." He threw his arm over my shoulder, and I could finally smile.

I lazed in my tropical respite for the entire trip. Phone turned off.

9

I heard a car in the driveway and moments later, Poppy ran into the kitchen, Ricky at her heels. I checked my watch. It was their first supervised visit with their dad since we'd returned from our holiday a week ago. Already it seemed a distant memory. We were back to reality.

"Mummy!" Poppy squealed. "Guess what?"

"What?" I said.

"Grandma and I made invitations for my birthday party!"

"Really? But Poppy, we already talked about you not having a party this year. Remember, we are going to take some friends from school to the movies?"

"Yes, but Grandma said that I can have a pool party at her house

273

and that way, Dad can come too!"

"Where are the invitations?" My eyes darted to her bag.

"Grandma said she will hand them out in class tomorrow." Poppy's face was ecstatic.

My nostrils flared. That woman was driving me nuts. Did she really plan to invite a bunch of eight-year-old girls, in bathers, to a pool party where an alleged child sex offender was present? He knew some of his victims from that early age. Lyn should know better. Besides, he had a hearing booked next month to decide if his case would go on to trial. Any rational person would wait until after that.

It was with considerable effort I found a level voice. "Poppy, honey, I'm really sorry but that party is just not possible."

Disappointment flooded her face. "What? But why? They said ..."

"I'm sorry, Poppy. I'll let them know you can't have a party there and we have already made plans."

Her disappointment fled and a black rage took her eyes. "That's not fair!"

"I'm sorry Poppy, I–"

"You never let me have any fun! It's not fair!" Her torn face grew redder with her outburst. "It's all your fault! I hate you!" With a final stamp of her foot, she spun and ran towards her room.

I closed my eyes, burying my face in my palms. Her attack seemed to have been brewing for a while. A distant storm making a slow encroachment, threatening savage damage. Each time Poppy returned from spending time with them, she was a little more distant, angry, and cried easily. Outbursts, misbehaving, and talking back were more frequent. It was a constant battle how best to deal with her. Should I give in to her bad behaviour? Walking on eggshells so as not to disturb the fragile structure of her emotional state. I walked on eggshells around her dad for years and it only enabled his bad behaviour. The only thing worse than being with Julian would be to raise children who acted like him. So I forced myself to hold her accountable.

"Ricky," I said, "why don't you find Pa and tell him all about your weekend."

He sped off, unfettered by the drama.

I heard Ricky chatting away to my dad in the living room. I walked out towards the yard, his voice trailing behind. Ricky was saying Poppy got one hundred dollars from the tooth fairy at Grandma's. I shook my head. One hundred dollars from the tooth fairy. If only the tooth fairy would pay some bloody child support.

I stalked to the back garden. My fingers shook with anger as I tapped the call button on my phone. I hadn't spoken to her in months, but she left me no choice. This party could not happen.

"Hello." Lyn's voice was careful.

"Lyn, it's Jess." I did not bother wasting time with pleasantries. "Poppy told me you're planning a pool party for her birthday. Is this true?"

"That's right, Jess. She—"

"Do you really think it's a good idea to hold a pool party for an eight-year-old with an alleged child sex offender present?"

An audible gasp. "He is guilty of nothing more than an ongoing relationship with a lady."

"A lady?" I scoffed.

"Yes, and I've heard you were up to the same things, Jess."

"What?" I struggled not to yell. "I never cheated on him."

Lyn huffed.

"I was never unfaithful to him," I said through gritted teeth.

"Ever. And not because he was a good husband or he didn't deserve it. Lyn, I was terrified of your son!"

"Jess, I–"

"He is a predator!" I couldn't stop from yelling now. "He did not 'have relationships' with teenage girls. He abused children!"

"Well ..." She took a long breath and paused. "I guess the evidence will speak for itself."

"Look." I made an effort to calm my voice. "I just want you to cancel this party. Don't hand out the invitations to Poppy's friends. They don't know what he's accused of. Imagine if it got out. Are you going to field questions from angry parents wondering why you invited their kids to a pool party with an alleged child abuser?"

I waited. No response. "I'm serious, Lyn. This is not in Poppy's best interests. Surely you know that."

I looked at my phone. She hadn't hung up. I strained my ears and could faintly hear her breathing.

"Lyn, if you go ahead with this, I'm calling child protection."

A click. Gone.

I gripped my phone. I was always left wanting to throw it at a brick wall after speaking to her.

My anger didn't dissolve overnight, and I decided to call child protection.

I dialled the number and got another person I had never spoken to. I needed to rehash the entire story to the new lady, who at least seemed understanding. I got to the part about the party.

"How is she going to supervise a pool party and keep him within line of sight and hearing the entire time? It seems impossible."

"You're right," the lady said. "It is quite unbelievable that she would ever think any of this would be okay."

276

"So, what can we do about it?"

"Unfortunately, if the party doesn't actually go ahead, they haven't technically done anything wrong."

"Okay." It was fruitless. "Thank you for your help."

—◦—

# Summer 2017

Carrie and I waited patiently in the bakery for our coffees and toasted sandwich. It was a familiar routine that brought some comfort to our court days. And there had been many of them. But none like today.

"My legs are shaking," I said to Carrie, who was standing near the door.

Carrie's eyes shifted to me. "Mine too." She glanced around the busy bakery, looking perplexed. "Actually ... all of me is shaking. I can't wait until this is all over."

"I read my statement over five times when I got home last night. I'm so nervous. I don't want to get confused on the stand."

"Me too, but Laura said not to stress too much. It's all just part of the process."

"I don't get why we all have to go through this twice."

"I guess it's so they don't book trials for cases without enough evidence. That's how Laura explained it. It's just to see if there is sufficient evidence to go to trial."

They called our name and we took our coffees to the car and drove the familiar route to the District Court.

"Dinner was nice last night," I said, trying to distract myself. "It was great to see the girls. Thanks for inviting us."

I hadn't seen Amelia since all this came out. I had seen Meghan a fair bit as she lived in the city and often came up to visit. But Amelia remained interstate most of the time. Neither Amelia nor I knew what to say to each other last night. We just hugged, at first. It was strong and reassuring. I tried to communicate a lot in that hug. I wanted her to know how guilty I felt for not seeing it. Not stopping it.

After the hug, it was like nothing had changed between us. Dinner reminded me of the old days. All of us seeming to push the negativity away and focus on the love for a while. The girls jumped on the trampoline with Poppy and Ricky. My kids squealed in rapture at being double bounced by the older girls, who seemed to relish in the chance to be one of the kids again. They were so grown up now, but there were still traces of the girls they used to be. Before they were plunged into the world of deceit. Before their innocence was stolen, their childhoods fractured.

"Yeah," Carrie said, "the girls were tired after testifying but both really wanted to see you and the kids."

"I'm glad. They seemed to like Patrick too."

"He's a great guy, Jess. They are happy to see you happy."

I smiled sadly. A fresh wave of guilt flooded me. The girls hadn't spoken out about their abuse in part because they didn't want to ruin my relationship with Julian. Because they wanted me to be happy. Would the guilt ever go away?

Nerves took us both to our own quiet concern for the rest of the drive. Neither able to relieve the other, our presence alone must suffice. I finally parked the car, squeezing Carrie's hand before we walked to the courthouse.

We headed to the fifth floor of the district court and it wasn't long before Laura's friendly face rounded the corner. We had been in regular contact for over a year now. Today, it felt like seeing an old friend. Certainly, she had the reassurance of one. Like a younger mother hen, protecting her brood of witnesses. She gave us both a tight embrace.

"Follow me." Laura led us to yet another insipid conference room, where we would wait until called to the witness stand. No pictures lined the dull cream walls. The only décor was the table and chairs, both worn with age. I doubt the furniture had ever left the room. It unsettled me to know that for decades, this room had hosted people like me, waiting nervously to go to court to hear their fate. A musty smell from lack of air flow added to the sense of foreboding.

We assumed our positions, pulling up chairs around the table, knowing full well we could be here for hours.

Carrie and I stared at the walls. My thumb nail scraping incessantly on my now calloused index finger. My lungs didn't want to fill; respirations shallow and faster than normal.

Laura appeared again after a time. "Carrie, it's your turn."

Carrie gulped and stood awkwardly. She hesitated and went to pick up her bag. "Should I take this?" The protocol so foreign.

"Sure, you can put it at your feet. Phones off though, ladies."

I stood to hug my friend. "Good luck." It was a stupid thing to say. The right words were missing.

Laura smiled at me as she put her arm around Carrie's shoulders and led her away.

I sat waiting, sweating. Elbows firm on the table, looking at my watch, my phone, the unmoving door. Tapping, scratching, thumbing, reminding myself to breathe. Breathe. I was not the one accused of a crime.

How exhausting the last few months had been. Hearing after hearing. Family and district courts. The first time we went to one of Julian's criminal hearings, we expected big things. Eager to see some form of justice prevailing. Instead, it seemed just like the family court. There were multiple hearings where the case was literally just mentioned, that's it. All that travel for a day, wasted. No action.

I had watched the barristers, solicitors, police and prosecutors all file into courtrooms for two-minute hearings before returning to their day. Carrie and I tried to make a game of it. We tried guessing who was there for what crime. It was usually easy to spot the crim amongst the suited lawyers and barristers. Some even showed up in their tracksuits. Others tried to look presentable, like Julian, always in a dark suit and tie. Maybe in the hope he looked too respectable to be accused of such horrific crimes.

"What do you think that guy's done?" Carrie had whispered in between hearings, pointing at a neatly presented guy in his early thirties.

I summed him up quickly. "My money's on traffic offence."

Carrie cocked her head. "I'm going with tax evasion."

I nodded and we waited patiently for the case. A courtroom, I had long decided, was where wasted hours went to die. Finally, the neat looking guy walked with his legal representation to the front of room. The judge announced the case and read the charges. His crime was photographing his penis on a six-year-old's face. Both our jaws dropped.

We should have known better than to trust our judgement.

The door opened, and I was pulled back to the present. Carrie walked in, her face pale. Laura followed her in.

"How did you go?" I said, hugging Carrie. "Are you alright?"

"Sorry Jess," Laura said, "but it's time for you to come through now." Laura ushered me towards the open door.

I grabbed my bag and hugged Carrie again on the way.

"It's not that bad," Carrie said, her voice unnaturally high. "You'll be fine."

Laura placed her arm over my shoulder and led me down the hall. "Now, Jess, inside the courtroom is a judge up the front, the lawyer and barrister for the prosecution are at the bar table. They are sitting nearest to you. On the other end of the table is the defence team. Julian is seated behind them, and his mother is also in the gallery."

"That's it?"

"Uh huh. It's a closed hearing." She squeezed my shoulder. "Don't stress. Just answer every question honestly. Stick to your truth."

"Okay." I swallowed, my mouth dry.

Laura pushed open the courtroom door. I froze. Her eyes urged me forward. As I passed her, she whispered, "Don't forget to bow to the judge."

I stepped forward.

I tried to stare straight ahead at the elevated judge's bench, ignoring the shape of Julian in my periphery. From the bench, a small, middle-aged woman looked over her glasses at me. I made eye contact, gulped, and bowed my head. Laura bowed and pointed to the witness box. I cursed my shoe choice as they squeaked with each step in the otherwise silent space.

I reached my chair, behind a small wooden counter. My lips drier than ever, I felt Julian's eyes boring into me, trying to tear my feet from under me with a look. I refused to meet his eye.

I stood in the boxed area allocated to me. It was higher than the rest of the room but for the judge. I couldn't understand why the witness box was an actual box, but was grateful for the comfort it gave. There were people in this room I never wanted to see again and the little box was like a shield. A welcome barrier.

"You can take a seat, Ms Foster." The judge had a surprisingly kind voice.

"Thank you," I murmured.

I sat, taking stock of my side of the room. The judge, the prosecutor and barrister, with Laura behind in the gallery. All safe places for my eyes to land. It was far easier imagining Julian was not here. I did a double take as I noticed an invasion on our side of the room. Lyn Rundell was sitting, scribbling onto a notepad on the prosecution side of the room, rather than sitting behind her son. She must have felt my eyes on her and looked up. I looked away. Why had she chosen to sit there? Was she distancing herself from her son? It felt intimidating to have her that close.

The judge asked me a few questions about my divorce status in a patient tone. She then invited Lisa Edwards to address the court. From the bar table, a petite woman wearing a figure-hugging dress suit stood.

"Jessica Foster, I am the barrister for the prosecution."

She had the type of voice that made people sit up and pay attention. She asked me a few simple questions that I couldn't get wrong. Like my name and profession. I nodded when she asked if I had been married to Mr Rundell.

"You need to answer yes or no, Ms Foster, because this is being recorded and will be transcribed later."

"Sorry." My voice small. I tried to swallow again.

She confirmed my written statement and tendered it for the court. She handed me to the defence. That concluded the matters for the prosecution for that hearing.

A man with perfectly coiffed hair stood and cleared his throat. His skin was clear and almost shiny. He appeared to have a better skincare regime than me. His voice was soft as he asked me easy questions about the history of my relationship with the accused. I answered every question, never letting my eyes fall to the creep behind him. The questions kept coming. Asking me about particular nights or days that I remembered. I was not sure of their relevance, but I answered each honestly.

I didn't know how long I sat there answering his questions. My thighs grew slick with sweat. I hoped it wasn't pooling on the seat. I worked hard at controlling my shaky voice. In time, I found it easier to speak. The room, which was so confronting on entering, felt less hostile now. I was not too outnumbered and managed to block Julian and his mum from my mind.

"Now, I believe you and Carrie Walsh are good friends?" He looked to his sheets of paper and only glanced at me when it was my turn to speak.

"Best friends," I responded.

"*Best friends.*" He looked back at his papers. "How long would you say, roughly, have you been best friends with Mrs Walsh?"

"Um ... probably fifteen or sixteen years."

"Did your best friend, Carrie, tell you when she had a meeting with your husband in relation to concerning phone records involving her daughter Amelia Walsh?"

"No."

"Did she discuss ever having concerns about your husband and her daughter with you?"

"No."

284

"Your Honour, I have no further questions."

Lisa Edwards stood and looked at the judge. "Just one point to re-examine on, Your Honour."

"Okay, go ahead." The judge said.

Lisa Edwards cleared her throat. "Ms Foster, did Julian ... did your husband ever tell you that he was confronted by Carrie with concerns about him and her daughter, Amelia Walsh?"

"No."

"No further questions."

The judge thanked and excused me from my chair. I pitied the person taking the sweaty chair after me. I stood and threw a quick glance, almost by accident, at Julian. His legs were stretched out as he leaned back in his chair. His fingers interlaced over his bulbous gut. His facial expression, so unconcerned, like he could be relaxing on the couch watching a car race.

Smug bastard.

◊

Giving evidence left me frazzled. The moment Carrie and I were both cleared to go, we hurried out of the courthouse. Ready to grab a drink, our post-court ritual.

On the way out, I spotted a familiar face. He stared back at me, eyes wide in recognition. The last time I saw his face, it was squashed against my brick wall, Julian's forearm pressed against his windpipe. We all hesitated; there was no avoiding each other.

"Nick ... what are you doing here?" Probably an impolite question to ask someone going into a courthouse, but my manners had left me. My brain mangled from emotional exhaustion.

"I'm giving evidence," he said.

"What? In Julian's case?"

He nodded, staring at the ground.

"But you only knew him such a short time," Carrie said. "You couldn't have known ..." Her voice trailed off to a near whisper. "You didn't know, did you?"

Nick looked nervous. Clearly taken aback by our unexpected drilling. "No. I knew nothing at all back then. My evidence is all related to Kayla. I only found out what he did to Kayla once we were well into our relationship." He set his jaw, frowning at the both of us. "I'm corroborating what she told me."

Carrie and I exchanged questioning glances.

"Kayla?" I said. "You mean Kayla who was at the club when I joined ... she was Julian's girlfriend?"

"My god, is she involved? Nick, I had no idea." Carrie's voice was apologetic.

"Yep. Sure did a number on her. I'm not allowed to discuss this though." He looked at his hands before raising his eyes to meet Carrie's. "Carrie ... I'm really sorry about what happened to your girls. Please believe ... I mean, I want you to know ... if I had've seen or heard anything, I would have said something."

Carrie's eyes turned glassy. "I believe you. Thank you."

"I better go. I have to meet Laura."

"Wait! Can I have Kayla's number?" I blurted without thinking if it was appropriate.

"Um, ok."

We hurriedly did the exchange, and we wished him luck. He left towards the courthouse and we made our way out, utterly drained.

Two days later, I sat outside a café, basking in the late afternoon sun. My foot tapped on its own accord under the table. At first, I was surprised Kayla responded to my text message. Blown away that she agreed to meet with me. I had assumed all these years that she must have hated me for breaking up her relationship with Julian when he left her to be with me.

I sipped on my coffee, wishing it was wine.

I looked at my watch. Five minutes late. Maybe she changed her mind.

From between two parked cars, Kayla emerged. When I last saw her, she was a beautiful twenty-two-year-old, and while she had obviously aged since, she appeared more vibrant than ever. Her face was sheepish when she spotted me. I stood as she got close. Before I could find words, she threw her arms around me. I hugged her back. Hopeful my embrace would express as much as I got from hers.

Our pleasantries were short. When she ordered a wine, I did too. She told me how she met Nick after he had left the club. They were married now and had three children. It was a relief to see her so happy and content.

I turned the glass in my hands, watching the traffic idle past on the busy street. "Kayla ..." I paused, choosing my next words carefully. "I really want you to know how sorry I am for everything that played out back then. I never wanted you to get hurt."

"Don't apologise," she said. "You practically saved me."

I frowned. "I don't understand."

"Look, Jess, I know you're a witness for the prosecution too. That's the only reason I'm speaking to you at all."

"I know we have to be careful what we say. We can't talk about our evidence."

"All my evidence is from before you came along anyway, so I'm fairly sure we can't be accused of collusion. But I will be careful what I say regardless. I can speak more freely when it's over. And believe me, I intend on standing from the highest mountain and screaming what that asshole did."

I smiled at her bravado. Maybe years away from him made you stronger. I couldn't even be in the same room as him without melting into a puddle of shameful weakness. Exactly how he wanted me.

"Kayla, I hope you don't mind me asking. How are you involved in this case?"

She threw her head back with a wicked smile. Like she was relishing telling a horror story to a child. "You don't know? I assume Julian never told you when we got together?"

I shook my head. "No. I mean, I knew you were twenty-two when I joined the club, and everyone said you had been together a couple of years."

"Try almost eight years."

"Fuck – *what*?" I almost spat.

Her smile looked plastered. I couldn't read it. Was it to mask disgust? Regret? Shame? She sipped her wine before continuing. "It started with little notes he left in my training bag. He was twenty-two at the time and good looking. Super talented sailor. Everyone loved him around the club. Fuck. Even my parents loved him then."

"My god, Kayla, I had no idea."

Kayla sat in thoughtful silence for a moment. "I thought he was wonderful. The notes started innocently enough, just encouraging things like 'great job today' or 'great tack, angel face'. Simple stuff, but he made me feel special in those notes. Wrote that I was his favourite and thought I had the most talent of any of the juniors. I felt like the chosen one or something."

"He was so much older."

"But not when he was with me. He giggled and we made jokes and I lost myself in him. That sort of slow flirtatious build-up went for a long time. He would walk past and deliberately brush against me. He made excuses to be alone with me." She looked at her fingers, gliding up and down the wine glass stem. "Then on my fourteenth birthday, that was the first time he kissed me. He took me out on the boat, offered me some one-on-one practice ... like it was a birthday treat. Made me feel so special. He had been flirting for months and brushing his hands lightly over my bum all the time. It gave me goosebumps."

I stared, transfixed. Unable to say anything. Not sure if there was anything to say.

Kayla continued. "At first ... you know ... I was really uncomfortable. I mean. I had never kissed anyone or even held a boy's hand. I was so nervous and confused. I was a fucking child." She took another large sip and glanced around. Nobody in the café was paying us any attention.

I gulped and nodded. Trying to show my understanding but not wanting to interrupt.

"Anyway, in time, the butterflies of fear and discomfort changed. I grew to love him. He made me feel so special. We waited until I was fifteen to have sex."

My hand flew to my mouth. *Waited* until she was fifteen. Like it was a joint decision. He made her feel like it was her choice. I could do nothing but shake my head. My voice was shaky. "My god, Kayla, you must have been so confused."

"Oh god yeah! I was still a child. I mean, I thought I was all grown up and in some kind of fun and secret relationship with a wonderful man. He promised me the world. When I was old enough, we were going to marry."

"I'm so sorry Kayla."

She shrugged. "It's funny, you know, looking back. Seeing what he was able to accomplish all this time in secret. He snuck me a mobile phone in my training bag because Mum wouldn't let me have one. That was back when almost everyone started carrying them."

His insipid infiltration so covert under the radar of loving parents.

"You have to understand, Jess ... I never knew any better. It's like I was a puppy being trained or something. Like a loyal little border collie. And he couldn't get enough of me. I would tell Mum I was catching the bus home from school, but really, it was Julian who picked me up and would drive me out to somewhere secluded to have sex. I can't even remember how often that happened."

"Did no one ask any questions?" I asked. "No one realised what was going on?"

"No. Because he always had a 'proper' girlfriend. A legitimate one above eighteen, so he looked respectable. Scumbag."

I put my hand on hers and squeezed. "I'm so sorry."

"Don't be sorry. It was my own damn fault. I made all those decisions. By then I was completely besotted with the man. He was my little secret. I loved him. I would have done anything for him." She paused, sipping her wine. "And I did, you know? I did things I didn't want to do. For him. Like, he got me to pose for photos. Naked photos. I felt so uncomfortable, but I wanted to please him." She looked disgusted.

"No. Not one bit of any of this is your fault."

She looked away as tears welled. She gave small, hurried nods.

I'm not sure if they were meant for me or herself. This all happened twenty years ago. Surely, by her age, she had reconciled that it wasn't her fault? But it didn't seem that way. She looked like a broken woman in that moment. Did people ever recover from this? The physical abuse was one thing. The mind games were what appeared to torture her the most. The control, coercion, fear, shame, confusion, secrets. All that rolled into a ball for one lonely teenage brain to compute and manage, completely alone. Of course it was still with her.

"I bet he still has those photos." She shook her head, looking revolted. "He's held those over me for all these years. He never threatened directly to share them, but the inference was always there. If his little 'puppy' didn't do as she was told, there would be punishment."

"Leverage."

"Exactly!"

We sat in silence, taking it all in.

"You know, it's funny," I said. "I've looked back over the years, and I see now that Julian stole my twenties from me. Like, those years were wasted on the promise of a wonderful future if I behaved, like you say, the way he expected."

Kayla's eyes held mine, nodding. Understanding.

"Kayla ... he stole your teens."

Tears that threatened earlier now fell down her cheeks. She sat still, ignoring them. How many tears had she shed because of him? How many had I? Had all the others? I'd wager Julian's count was zero. We could fill a swimming pool while he sat dry-eyed.

Kayla's phone alerted. She checked it and grinned.

"He did steal my teens," she said, "but he's going to pay the price.

He's going to have a full criminal trial next spring. It's booked to run for three weeks." She showed me the email from Sally Teale, the prosecutor.

I matched her smile. So, the hearing was a success. Enough evidence for a full trial.

"What a relief," I finally said. My heart lifted before dropping in recognition of the timeline. Next spring – another year away.

"You know, Jess, you coming along ... it was the best thing that ever happened to me. I was finally able to have a normal life, and eventually I met Nick. He's wonderful. It took me years to tell him the truth about Julian. He hated him anyway, of course."

"Yeah, with good reason," I said.

"Do you even know what happened that night? The night he attacked Nick? Knowing Julian, I doubt he told you the truth."

"He said that Nick said something awful about me." My phone alerted. It was an email from the prosecutor.

Kayla laughed. "All Nick said was that he thought Julian was batting above his average to have you. Like as a joke. And then Julian threw him into the wall."

I rubbed my hands over my face, right to the back of my neck. "Of course ... it wasn't something nasty about me. He offended Julian's ego."

"And we know what ego and power mean to Julian."

I didn't say anything. My stomach churned learning yet another truth about Julian.

"You know my biggest regret?" Kayla asked.

"That you ever met him?"

"Nah. Not even that. It's shaped me, you know? That's why I work with teenagers now. I know the importance of self-esteem and emotional wellbeing. I work hard to give teens tools to recognise unhealthy relationships."

"What amazing work." I smiled with earnest. "So what *is* your biggest regret?"

"Not saying anything back then." Her face dropped back to sadness. "I could have put him in jail and no one else would have been hurt."

"Honestly, I don't know what to say. None of this is your fault. You are not to blame for his actions towards you or anyone else." I reached forward and squeezed her hand again. Her eyes looked tired now.

"I really thought I was the only one." She held my gaze.

"I believe you."

—◦—

"No Ricky, that's not right!" Poppy slapped her palms on the dinner table. "Grandma was there!" She threw Ricky a threatening glance.

"Oh right," Ricky said. "Yes, Grandma was at the pool too."

I looked at Patrick across the dining table, raising my eyebrows. He echoed my expression.

"The important thing is that you all had a good time," I said, eager to relieve the tension.

"Mummy, I don't like onion." Poppy held her fork with a limp sliver of red onion hanging off it.

"Well, everyone else likes it, Poppy. Just eat around it." I shook my head and continued eating.

She put her fork down and picked through the chicken salad with her nose screwed up. We were at Patrick's house, the kids having spent the day with their father, under supervision. We were all used to staying with Patrick now. He even bought bunks for the kids.

"Ricky got his uniform for school today," I said in a bright tone. "Two more weeks until his first day. And a whole new life for me with only one school drop off and pickup now they're at the same school."

"Yes, I bet," Patrick said. "That will be fantastic."

My eyes shifted to Poppy, who looked even more disgusted now she had gathered at least five pieces of onion to the side of her plate.

"Poppy, get on with it. You're not having dessert if you don't eat your dinner." I threw her a stern look.

Her head flew up at me. "Well, I can't eat it, can I? Because it's full of onion!" She shouted, angry tears spilling down her cheeks. Poppy slammed her fork onto her plate and stormed from the table.

Even Ricky's eyebrows were raised as we sat in the wake of her fury.

"Sorry, Patrick, I don't know what to do with her lately. She's so angry all the time."

"Don't worry about it. I'm sure it's just a phase she's going through."

I sighed. "It better be over fast."

I put Ricky and Poppy to bed after she calmed and apologised. When I was done, I collapsed into Patrick's side on the couch in front of the television. He pulled me in close, his hand resting on my hip.

"Poppy's been seeing a counsellor for months," I said. "I don't know what more I can do. She's so angry and upset when Greg drops her home. She's so unlike her normal self."

"She's probably just confused by everything," he said.

"No, it's more ... she's *really* angry. Defensive. I don't ask about the supervision but if Ricky says anything, she explodes that 'Grandma was there'. Like she's been told to say that or something. Maybe it's just a feeling. I'm not sure."

"Just keep doing what you're doing. Talk when she wants to talk and be there for her. But don't pander to her every whim to avoid an explosion. That won't work." He hugged me in close.

"Yeah, you're right," I said.

"Tell me more about today."

"I told you most of it on the phone, but I'm pretty relieved I'm going to get a settlement."

"A huge relief. It means you can finally get on with your life a bit. So, did it all get signed off in court today?"

"That's the part I don't understand. They said they didn't want to sell the house, so his parents are going to pay me out of it in a lump sum. They could have done this a year and a half ago and saved me a lot of nightmares and lawyers' fees."

Patrick squeezed me again and kissed the top of my head. "It doesn't seem fair."

"I know. It's like the system is designed for the cashed-up bullies to win. Like they can wear down the broke person. It's not fair. And I was expecting that we would agree on an amount, and they would transfer the money over, right? A simple transaction. But no. Apparently they have another five months before they have to pay."

I stared forward, not seeing what was on the television. Each time I went to court I came home feeling run over. Combinations of frustration and turmoil wore me down. Add on a few Poppy induced anxiety explosions, and by the time I could sit in calm, I was a dead weight with nothing more to offer.

"That's outrageous," Patrick said. "How does anyone struggling without family support ever survive this system?"

"I'm sure some don't." I snuggled my cheek against his chest. His scent soothing. My body relaxed into his arms as I never had with Julian. Patrick enjoyed affection as much as I did. I felt completely calm in his presence. I could truly be myself, no longer living on a crumbling path that could fall away at any moment.

"Another five months is ridiculous," Patrick said, hugging me tighter.

"Tell me about it," I said through heavy blinks.

# Autumn 2018

I sat flicking through my phone absentmindedly in the waiting room while Poppy was in her counselling session. I remembered gawking at the recommendation child protection had long ago written in a report, suggesting that Poppy attend counselling for the purposes of learning self-protective behaviours. Spending time with an alleged child sex offender hustled the system to invest money into teaching children to protect themselves rather than cancelling contact. It was sickening.

I checked the time. I needed to get Poppy and Ricky to swim class. It was a juggling act with the two now at school.

Poppy appeared, smiling, from the corridor, followed close behind by her counsellor, Simone. She was my height, with a lyrical tone to her voice. Importantly, she was warm, kind and she made Poppy laugh.

Poppy wrapped her arms around my waist.

"Have you got a few minutes, Jess?" Simone asked.

I looked at my watch. I didn't have one minute. "We're meant to be at swimming."

"It's important. Poppy, can you please stay here? You can play with the toys."

Poppy's eyes lit up as she ran towards the abundance of toys in the child-focused facility.

I followed Simone down the hall. Her usual joyous face turned serious when she stopped. "I have to be a bit delicate here, Jess." She looked around to ensure we were alone. "I need to tell you ... Poppy has disclosed some things to me that I ..." She paused, appearing to search for words. "Well, some things that I feel I need to discuss with child protection."

My heart rate went up. "What do you mean? What kinds of things?"

"I think it's best for now that I discuss that with child protection first. But out of courtesy, I wanted to let you know you might expect a call from them."

"Should I be worried?"

"You're doing all the right things, Jess. Just keep doing what you're doing." She patted me on the shoulder.

"Okay." I said, feeling anything but reassured.

Poppy was bubbly and perky on the way home, and I didn't want to bring anything up that would break her mood. Besides, what she spoke of to her counsellor should be confidential.

I found myself watching my phone the next few days before finally, a blocked number called. I was at my parents' house, where there were too many people around for privacy. I answered the phone as I hurried outside, pulling the sliding door shut behind me.

"Am I speaking with Jessica Foster?" a young woman's voice asked.

"Yes, call me Jess," I said, walking down the garden path, as far out of earshot and line of sight as possible.

"Jess, my name is Kirsten Rogers. I'm calling from child protection."

"Uh huh." I hurried along the pleasantries.

"There have been some safety concerns raised about your children, Poppy and Ricky."

298

"What kind of concerns?"

"Unfortunately, at this time, I cannot disclose that information to you. I need you to understand that I am running a full investigation into this matter and until that investigation is complete, your children are to have no contact with the paternal family at all."

"Right, okay. They're meant to collect them in the morning." My voice a little desperate.

"I will give them a call," she stated.

"Okay."

I hung up the phone and decided not to mention anything to the children yet.

Two hours later, my phone rang with another blocked number.

It was Kirsten again, and I headed out to the yard.

"That mother-in-law of yours is a piece of work!" Her exasperation clear.

"Yes, well, that sounds like my ex-mother-in-law," I said, taking whatever humour I could. "The stories I could tell you."

I followed the garden path to the same secluded place. The sun, not reaching my little nook by this time of the afternoon, and the autumn air, suddenly frigid.

"Look Jess, they are saying they have family court orders stating that they can pick the children up in the morning. She even called my superior to complain. She didn't get far. But she tried."

I rolled my eyes. "Brazen is on the list of her known behaviours."

She chuckled as I wrapped my arms around my chest, balancing the phone between my ear and shoulder. Wishing for a cardigan.

"Our solicitor says that if the family court orders are by consent and you agree to alter them, we can intervene in the meantime. Are you okay with that?"

"Yes, of course."

"Okay. Well, I will give them another call and let them know they are not to try to contact the children, at all, until they hear from me again."

"Good luck with that," I said with a smirk.

"Thanks," she said dryly. "I also need to meet you and both the children early next week. And it might not be a bad idea if you have somewhere else to stay for the weekend. Just to avoid a confrontation in case they try to come and pick them up anyway."

"Sure. I can stay with my boyfriend."

I said goodbye to Kirsten after we arranged a time for her to interview the children. I walked to the house. My brain doing tumble turns with the change of events. I watched the kids, busy digging for potatoes in a garden bed. I opened the door and heard Mum's stern voice.

"It was not Jess. I'm telling you, Lyn, it wasn't her."

There was silence while I assumed Lyn was giving mum an earful. I stalked down the hall in her direction.

"No! I'm telling you it wasn't. And we don't even know what's happened." Mum spotted me from her seated position on the end of her bed. She rolled her eyes. "And we are all very concerned why this is happening."

I'd heard enough. "Mum, just hang up the phone. There's only one person to blame for all this. Hang up. You don't need to listen to her crap!" My volume grew with each word.

Mum waved me down. "Look, I'm telling you. It was not Jess who called child protection."

I raised my voice in hope Lyn could hear. "But if I was concerned about the safety of my kids, I would not hesitate to!"

Mum gestured with her hand to indicate Lyn was rambling. She held the phone shaking her head.

"Just hang up." My voice level again.

"Lyn, I have to go," Mum said.

Another pause.

"Goodbye, Lyn."

Mum hung up and let her shoulders drop. "That woman!" She cursed.

<br>

———○———

<br>

Three days later, I was waiting in the long line of cars to collect the children from school. Already further back than I needed to be, I had raced from work after a busy day. I tapped impatiently at the wheel. I didn't want to be late to meet with the investigator from child protection.

Rain started smattering the windshield from a dark cloud that had been threatening since I left work.

I glanced again at the clock as I finally reached the front of the line. Poppy and Ricky spotted me and dawdled towards the car under their umbrellas. I waved for them to hurry. Any other day, they would run. Typical. When you needed to be somewhere, they moved in slow motion.

"Hi, how was your day?" I said quickly, taking off before belts fully clicked.

"Good."

"Good."

"What did you learn today?"

"Nothing."

"Nothing."

"Great." I accelerated up the street with the windscreen wipers at full speed. I weaved through the traffic on the packed streets. The traffic lights ahead turned red and I slammed on the brakes in time to stop from crashing into the car in front.

Whack! We all shot forwards in our belts.

"Mummy, what was that?" Poppy cried.

I spun in my seat. "Are you two okay?"

They gave synchronised nods.

"Good," I said. "Wait here. I'll be right back. Stay in your seats."

"Mummy, what's happening?"

I shut my car door and jogged to the back of the car, inspecting the damage from the SUV that rear-ended me.

"I'm sorry. I'm really sorry. Are you okay?" A flustered woman hovered near me. The owner of the SUV.

I squinted through the rain. I couldn't see much damage. Her car seemed to bear the brunt of it. She watched me, concerned. I looked at my watch.

"I have to go." I spun on my heels.

"Don't you want to swap details?" She trailed after me. Cars continued queuing behind us. I ignored it all, opening my car door and throwing myself into my seat, turning the ignition on before I'd even buckled up. I made it through the green light as it turned to amber. My rear view showed a confused, sodden woman standing between her flashing hazard lights staring after me.

"What happened, Mummy?" Poppy said.

"That was fun! Can we do that again?" Ricky chimed.

"No, it's nothing to worry about," I said. "Just a little accident.

No one is hurt. It's fine."

We were five minutes late when I pulled into a car park. Was that enough to be viewed as a bad parent? I hustled them from the car, holding the umbrella over them. I didn't bother holding it over myself. I was already soaked through.

"Now, I told you that you are going to meet a nice lady, right? She's going to ask you some questions today. It's nothing to worry about at all. Just answer all her questions honestly, okay?"

"Kay kay," Poppy sang.

"Okay," Ricky said. Already bored.

I pulled open the door leading to a small, concrete stairwell. It was badly lit and unwelcoming. We followed the sign up the stairs, and the receptionist's smile made up for the tired building. She directed us to the waiting area. There were toys everywhere and the kids didn't miss a beat. I sat, uncomfortable, on the plastic chair, avoiding the fabric couch in my sodden clothing.

A twenty-something woman with a sparkling nose ring walked towards us. She wore a welcoming smile and introduced herself as Kirsten, the woman I'd spoken to on the phone.

"I'm going to have a little chat with all of you today," Kirsten said to the kids. "Does that sound okay?"

The kids both nodded and smiled. They loved an opportunity for a monologue.

"Right. I'm going to chat to you first, Mum. Are you two happy playing here?"

Twenty kids could be happy playing there for hours, the toys were so plentiful. They both nodded with enthusiasm, and I followed Kirsten down the hall to a small room.

Kirsten wanted a rundown of all my concerns. I gave it. The

criminal matters, the concerns about what Julian was saying to the children. The worries that their grandparents weren't supervising. I told her about them going into Poppy's school and trying to plan a pool party. Everything. The tapping at the keyboard and understanding nods came throughout. It was all over in about twenty minutes, and she led me back to the children.

After she had spoken to the children, she asked me to follow her once again.

"Jess, both the children have confirmed, independently, the same disclosures. We are filing an urgent application in the children's court tomorrow to stop the current contact with their father."

My face screwed up. Not more court. I was meant to be on a court hiatus until the criminal trial. That was seven months away.

"No but ..." I shook my head. "Why do you have to take it to court? You're child protection. Can't you just change it?"

"I'm sorry. It doesn't work like that. We all have processes."

"Well, do I have to go? I need to work. I have missed so much with all these court hearings."

Her face was sympathetic. "I understand. Look, it's really important you attend. These current arrangements for supervised visitation are in place by consent. That means you agree to them. That also means, at this moment, you are not acting as a protective parent."

"*What*?" I cried. "But I tried to change those orders. I tried." I couldn't keep the desperation from my voice. "No one would help me. Not the children's lawyer. Not you guys. I called child protection months ago saying I don't think they are safe. No one would help me!"

She blinked, unrattled by my outburst. I guessed she saw distraught parents all the time. She still looked understanding. "Jess, we are going to help now."

I looked at the blank wall and interlaced my fingers so tightly they changed colour.

Fuck. Not more court.

9

Dad was at my side in the district court waiting area while we waited to be called into children's court. I'd grown so used to waiting; my mind would go into an anesthetised state as it tried to calm and prepare for what was to come. It made it easy to lose track of time. I did not know how long we'd waited when I felt a nudge. I stirred, blinking. Dad pointed at Kirsten, who came bustling over to us, balancing a pile of heavy folders in her arms.

I sat straight.

Kirsten handed me a document. "These are the orders we are asking to override the family court orders. We view the grandmother as an unfit supervisor. We are requesting no contact with the paternal family except the father, who can visit once a week, supervised at our centre."

"Can't we go for no contact at all?" I asked. It seemed a no brainer to me.

"You can ask for whatever you like. You are representing your own interests. Tell your lawyer that when they arrive." She put the folders on a spare chair and sat next to me. Her face softening. "I need to tell you, Jess, so you don't get a shock in court. Both the children disclosed that they have spent several nights sleeping in a bed with their father."

I burst into tears. Dad put his arm around my shoulder.

305

So many scenarios ran over in my mind. They were all bad. I could hardly breathe at the enormity of the thought. A man charged with multiple sex crimes against several child victims, and now reports of his own daughter sleeping in a bed next to him.

Kirsten's face was sympathetic. "They did not disclose anything else, but given the charges against him, well, we all know how inappropriate that is."

I could only nod.

"I have to get going. But listen out for his surname when the case is called."

"Thanks," I blubbered.

I pondered the potential horrors, crying as Dad murmured 'shh' and 'come now' into my ear. I couldn't focus. My mind spinning into appalling unknowns. I tried to force myself to focus on the knowns. All his other alleged victims were older than Poppy. I clung to the hope he would not hurt his own daughter. Of course, my mind went there; she was the only one he had legal access to for months now. I cursed the system. I sobbed before growing conscious of the many eyes upon me. There were dozens of people biding time in the court waiting area for their own hearings. After a while, I composed myself, and like most other court days, we sat, and we waited. I focused on the fact that I had child protection on my side, fighting to make sure it couldn't happen again.

When I met with the lawyer allocated to me, I did as advised and asked for no contact with any of Julian's family. After another wait, we were called into a courtroom.

The hearing was short, sharp and typical. I did not have high expectations. Julian and Lyn wanted to contest the orders. They wanted Lyn to continue to supervise. The court adjourned over lunch, and we were told to reconvene after. The judge would decide then if there would be a contest hearing.

Dad coaxed me to a local café for a sandwich. I picked and nibbled at the edges as Dad filled Mum in on the morning's non-event.

We headed back to the near-empty waiting area after lunch. My lawyer spotted us and took us to the same little room as earlier. Her lips were pulled into a smirk as she held the door for us. She told us that Detective Laura Keen showed up during the lunch break and Julian had been arrested for breaking bail. He was on his way to County Court for an urgent bail hearing. Dad and I couldn't contain our amusement at our court hearing being adjourned for his arrest.

Carrie laughed over the phone as I rehashed the events of the day.

"A sleepover, is that what she said?"

"Yes," I said. "When Kirsten called me, she said the bail hearing is to be held tomorrow. Her words were, 'he will be having a sleepover in custody'."

"Well, I hope he gets comfortable." Carrie chuckled.

The following day, Kirsten told me that Julian had been released because the court was satisfied that under the children's court orders, he could not break bail in the same way again.

Another children's court hearing was scheduled for the next month.

The waiting game continued.

The kids loved the train ride into the city. They were all grins and wide eyes. It was worth it to see their faces. They were delighted with their day off school and adventure into the city. They didn't get to visit very often.

The last day in children's court had been adjourned because the children's new lawyer for these hearings had not had a chance to meet them. I made my displeasure clear over the phone when he told me only the day before the hearing. I huffed when he said I still needed to attend court, knowing nothing would happen. I had to ask for another day off to show up for an adjournment.

We got off the train and went up the escalators to street level. I took a second to get my bearings. I looked up the address the new lawyer gave me on my phone. It was not too far. We should just make it in time.

I hustled the kids along the street faster than their wide eyes could take everything in. I tried to picture it through their young eyes. The tooting horns, traffic noise and crowds of people overwhelming the senses. Smells of aged bitumen and bagels intermingling. I wished little things like walking a city street could bring me as much joy as it did a child.

We reached the skyscraper and looked up. The kids dropped their jaws.

"We're going up there?" Poppy's eyes were eager.

"Uh huh," I said. "The twenty-eighth floor."

We waited on our level until a young lawyer in a three-piece suit approached us.

"Hello, you must be Jess, Ricky and Poppy." He smiled at us each in turn. "My name is Andrew Cummings. Follow me."

We followed him to the nicest conference room I'd ever seen.

Artwork lined the walls, a far cry from the barren, white walls I was used to at court. The windows overlooked the city below, and the furniture seemed to be of this decade. Ricky pulled out one of the high-backed swivel chairs and immediately started spinning in three sixties. Poppy followed suit with verve.

Embarrassed by their behaviour, I said, "That's enough you two. Sit still. This is not a playground."

Andrew smiled. "It's okay to play a little, but we are going to have a chat first if that's alright with you all." The children stopped spinning, looking at him. "Okay. Like I said, my name is Andrew, and I am your lawyer for the proceedings in children's court."

Well, shit.

Both the kids stared at me. Dumbfounded. I had never spoken about court or anything to do with court with the children. Why on earth would an eight- and five-year-old ever need to know anything about court? I had told them we were coming to the city to meet with someone who had their best interests at heart, and they would be asked a few questions. That's it.

I threw Andrew an angry look. He did a double take, dropping his smile before returning his attention to the confused children.

"So," he said, "what that means is, I will take your wishes to the court."

I continued to glare at him.

He pushed on. "So, how are the visits with your dad at the special centre going?"

The children went once a week for a two-hour visit with their dad at the child protection building, supervised by a case worker. I had to drive them after school to the dank building where I first met Kirsten.

"Great!" Poppy offered quickly. "But I want to see him more."

"Me too!" Ricky parroted.

"Okay," Andrew said, "well I can certainly take those wishes to the judge."

I squeezed my arm rests and gritted my teeth. Had this guy even read our file?

"Look," I said. "I know the children both want that. But kids want a lot of things that aren't in their best interests." I gestured to Ricky. "Ricky wants to drive a car. And Poppy would eat lollies for dinner every night. But I don't allow either of those things because it's not good for them. Right?"

Andrew nodded and cleared his throat. "Yes, it is sometimes tricky to find a balance."

A balance. Julian had been accused of abusing multiple teenagers. He was facing dozens of charges in a criminal trial in less than six months. If found guilty, he would go to jail for a long time. Nothing good could come from increasing contact with the children. Surely that was setting them up for a bigger fall. When my kids were adults, would they look back at these times and think, 'Boy, I'm so pleased there were all those important, professional people in positions of power that ensured I maintained a relationship with a child abuser'? I raged at the thought.

"Look, Mr Cummings, I'm a single working mum." I leant towards him, not happy having this conversation in front of the children but feeling forced. "It's up to me to ferry them to school, activities and all these visitations. Plus, someone needs to make sure they keep up with schoolwork, learn to read and maintain some semblance of a normal life. But for Ju–" I gritted my teeth. I refused to say his name. "For him, it's two hours of pure playtime. When is it my turn to get two hours to sit down and play with my kids? All this talk of him bringing age-appropriate toys and lollies each visit. Spoiling them rotten. Of course, they want to go more." I threw my hands in the air.

He sat back in his chair, looking like he was taking it all in. "Ms Foster, I will endeavour to keep all that in mind, but please understand that I am here to represent just the children."

"So am I!" I pounded my chest.

The meeting ended soon after. A whole morning wasted.

I decided to take the children to a bustling Vietnamese restaurant called City Pho that we spotted on the way back to the train station. We ordered spring rolls and a wonton noodle soup. The kids spent time wrapping their spring rolls in lettuce leaves like I showed them. They dipped them in the sauce and tasted with trepidation. Their eyes widened as they devoured the new flavours, and they downed a full plate in no time. Both seemed unperturbed by my outburst in the conference room. To them, it was just a fun day out in the city.

◦

I tapped the lid of a jar of pasta sauce on top of the bench, putting my full strength into twisting it open. It wouldn't budge. I eyed Patrick, who stood on the opposite side of his kitchen bench, sipping on a beer.

"So, when is this contest hearing?" Patrick asked, seemingly oblivious to my struggle.

"In two months," I grunted, twisting again. "And it's booked for two days. So, I'll need another two days off work." I looked at him with hopeful eyes.

He smirked. "Lucky you have a good boss."

I laughed as I continued to wrestle with the jar of pasta sauce.

"Do you want some help?" he said.

"No. I can do it." I tapped the jar lid again on the table.

"And this hearing will decide if his mum can supervise again?"

"Yeah. She's saying she did nothing wrong. That none of them have done anything wrong. This is all my fault. Don't you know that by now?"

Now he laughed. "Come on. Let me help with the jar."

"No, I don't need your help." I snapped. I instantly felt bad. "I'm sorry ... I'm just so frustrated." Frustrated with the rollercoaster of wasted court dates where nothing happened. I shouldn't take it out on him.

"I know." His eyes met mine, soft and understanding.

"As if the visits at the child protection centre haven't been hellish enough. The thought of her caring for them again makes my skin crawl." I made a disgusted face.

"I thought you were meeting the case worker in the alley way now, so you don't have to run into him?"

"I am." It was a dark and dingy laneway I would never usually go in, but like everything else, I had no choice. It was either face the unknown lurking in a dodgy alleyway or risk running into who I knew would be out the front.

The first visit had been traumatising. It was such a close call not to run into Julian in that dark concrete foyer of the child protection building. Julian and Lyn were crossing the street towards me just as I got out of the front door. After that, I had asked to change the contact time by dropping the kids in earlier. Their only solution was to meet the case worker in the alley at the back of the building.

Patrick met my eyes with sympathy. "This will all have an ending, Jess. Just keep in your head ... this is not what forever looks like."

He rounded the bench and weaved his arms around my waist. I felt my shoulders drop. His soft lips landed on the side of my cheek. Nothing but reassuring affection. I put the jar on the bench, closed my eyes and relaxed into his strong arms.

"Thank you," I breathed. "I know I get wound up."

"You are going through extraordinary circumstances."

He gave another squeeze before returning to the other side of the bench. I reached for the jar. I twisted it again and finally freed the lid.

We both smiled.

# *Winter 2018*

Those familiar sweaty, anxious nerves had taken me again. I sat in the waiting area of the children's court tapping my foot. Rubbing my thumbnail. Shuffling my folder of documents. A cycle of waiting, worrying; rinse, repeat. Groundhog days that left me withered and hopeless. Thinking I would not see an end to them, that my life would never be normal, that justice would never be served.

"Stop tapping your foot. It'll be fine." Dad looked nervous too.

"Sorry," I muttered, and stopped tapping. "I know."

My eyes lit up as I saw a familiar face striding in my direction. Her face grinning broad when she met my eye.

"What are you doing here?" I said to Detective Laura Keen, and we embraced like old friends. I supposed we were, in a strange way. In the last eighteen months, I'd spoken to Laura on the phone more than most of my friends. In normal circumstances, she was exactly the type of person I would be friends with. I felt at ease with her. Maybe a lot of it had to do with her hearing about such personal aspects of my life.

"I'm giving evidence in your hearing," Laura said with a smile.

She squeezed my shoulder and excused herself to chat to Kirsten. I looked at the two women, feeling my confidence grow. I had the police and child protection on my side. It was comforting.

We didn't have to wait for much longer before we were allowed into the courtroom. Our hearing was called much earlier than any other court day because it had been booked for two days.

I gazed around the room. It was certainly fuller than usual; the bar table was at capacity with lawyers and barristers. A quiet buzz of excitement filled the room. My least favourite trio sat behind their legal teams. I gave them nothing.

"All rise." A court staffer called, and we all followed the order.

The judge entered and took her seat. She wore a stern face and shuffled through some papers, calling out our names. Eyeing each character in this debacle.

"I think I would like to take some time to read more about this criminal complaint before we move forward with any contest," the judge stated, looking to the bar table.

And in the blink of an eye, we all stood for her to exit again.

I didn't understand. Why couldn't this have happened *before* everyone was called into court to start a two day hearing? But who was I to question the system?

I spent the break chatting to Laura in the waiting area. Our case was announced over the loudspeaker again and we all filed back into the room.

The same routine continued. Once the judge took her seat, I sat tall and waited to see what would happen next.

The judge cleared her throat. "After reading part of the brief of evidence, I have decided to take the road of extreme caution in this matter. I will not be hearing any contest today." I almost clapped. Lyn was to keep her title of unfit supervisor and Julian could only see them once a week at the child protection centre until after his criminal trial.

Relief flooded me, cooling my vessels from the raw burn of anxiety. What a rollercoaster.

# Spring 2018

"This has just been ridiculous!" I said to Patrick. "I can't believe he did that to the kids."

Who was I kidding. I shouldn't be surprised by anything that man was capable of any more. I thought that for every horrid thing he had done, he at least still cared about his own children. But no. He was finally showing his true colours to them, too.

He didn't tell the children about the trial, forcing me to take them to a visitation I knew he wouldn't be at. It had been left up to me to explain to them why they would no longer be seeing their dad for their normal weekly visits at the child protection centre. On his last visit with them, before the trial started, I had braced for the children to be upset when I picked them up, convinced he would have said goodbye.

Over that week I made call after call to child protection. I told them his trial was starting so we needed to formally cancel the visits, at least for those weeks. But every time they told me I couldn't cancel them. It had to be done by Julian, and if I didn't show up, it would reflect badly on me.

His trial began and I still had to make the drive to child protection and sit out back for over half an hour before the case worker confirmed we could leave. The children burst into tears when they found out their dad wasn't coming.

317

I scowled at Patrick as he typed something into his phone. My blood boiled. "Patrick are you even listening to me?"

He tapped another button and put the phone back down. "Sorry, what were you saying?"

Who was he texting? What secrets was he keeping? I shook my head, knowing I was being irrational, but I could not stop the questions from forming in my head. I let out an angry sigh. "I was talking about him not telling the children about the trial. About me being forced to take them to a visitation that I knew he wouldn't be at!"

"Jess, sorry, that really sucks." He put his hand over my clenched fist.

I softened slightly at his touch. "They were both in tears and it was completely avoidable. It wasn't fair on them."

His phone pinged with another message. I tensed again. I had eyes of fire as he smiled at his phone. I wanted to slap him. Who was making him smile like that? I felt sick and full of rage. He typed a message, his smile not fading. But his face was tilted away from me. Hiding it from me. This was too much. All those times I watched Julian on his phone, too scared to question who he was messaging. I couldn't live through that again.

He tapped the send button and put his phone down. He looked at me, still wearing that same smile.

"What's so funny?" My voice had a sting.

"Sorry, that was my mum. She wanted my shirt size."

"What?" My anger faded.

"She wants to buy me a shirt for my birthday, and I told her my shirt size. Look at her response." He showed me his phone.

*My ... haven't you been in a good paddock!*

I had to laugh. Patrick was anything but overweight.

Patrick chuckled. "I had to remind her that she hasn't bought me a shirt since I was a teenager, so that would explain the larger size!"

I apologised for being so testy. He put his arms around me. "I understand." He lifted my chin. "This will all be over soon."

I rested my head against his chest. Overcome by guilt for my jealous aggression. Would I ever be able to trust again?

૭

Carrie and I sat in the waiting area of the Office of Public Prosecutions. Julian's criminal trial started over a week ago and today, it was her turn to take the witness stand. This was it. All the evidence from the victims had concluded for the prosecution's case. Her girls gave their evidence days ago. Now, it was time for corroborating evidence.

It would be me tomorrow. I had to distract myself to stop feeling sick. But I couldn't help being excited too. A macabre eagerness to see how it would all work out. Like watching the footage of a horrific event. Stunned, horrified and unable to look away.

It wasn't long before Detective Laura Keen strode in with the prosecutor, Sally Teale, and the barrister for the prosecution, Lisa Edwards.

Carrie and I stood. We both hugged Laura and shook hands with the other women. I was instantly buoyed by this powerhouse of intelligent women. They led Carrie away to a meeting room to prepare her for court.

With Carrie gone, I spent time reading over my statement again. I'd lost count of how many times I'd read it, hoping that by the time I was cross examined on it, my nerves would be gone and I could speak with grace and calm.

I scanned the wall of pamphlets and plucked one offering hints for being a witness in criminal court. One tip – visit a courtroom before the court date. Tick.

The pamphlet encouraged exercise and having a bubble bath. Reminded me that I was not on trial. Told me I didn't have to look at the accused. Talked of breathing and visualising.

I visualised the slap of a gavel and a judge calling guilty. That would feel good. Worthwhile. It had been hard to see a future. It had been almost two and a half years since I read those text messages, and since then, my life had been an endless cycle of shitty court dates and a host of unknowns in front of me. It felt like I was finally at the beginning of the end. I prayed for the ending we needed. The victims needed justice and I needed freedom. A not guilty verdict was unfathomable.

While I waited, I drank three cups of tea. Fiddled with my handbag. Scrolled on my phone. Blocked more people on social media I used to call my friends. It had become a ritual; every time I opened a social media app, I would block yet more so-called friends. I had been putting it off for so long, hoping people would see sense. Many hadn't. These events had divided so many. They were either against Julian or I would no longer call them friends. I could not tolerate indecision or sitting on fences.

I'd had enough of that depressing task and flicked through a trashy magazine, scowling at the paparrazzi photos of celebrities with their children. No smiling faces. Clearly not wanting to be photographed. Their rights disregarded just because they were in the public eye. It didn't feel right. I threw it back to the coffee table.

Just like my rights were disregarded when I married badly. I saw it so clearly in hindsight. How did I let it happen? It was a slow encroachment on my autonomy. If he had started our relationship with jealous rages, tracking me, reading my messages and treating me with indifference until he wanted sex, we never would have been together. If he put me down or made comments about how poorly I cleaned the house or how little I worked at the start, we never would have been together. It was a slow and steady drip of rules and personality shots. A gradual sapping of energy that came with the corrosion of my self-worth until I had so little, I had no energy to fight or even argue what was right or wrong. All I could do was follow the path of least resistance to survive each day. That path was whatever made him happy. Now here I was, out of my confusing haze. Ready to tell my truth. To do what's right.

I needed to forgive myself for those choices but feared I would never be able to.

My head shot up with the sound of the door opening and Carrie appeared in the doorway, her head dropped, pallid again. I stood and embraced her.

"I have to go back after lunch," Carrie got out in a small voice.

We decided on City Pho for lunch, a new favourite since taking my kids there, and the walk seemed to do her good.

"Was he rude to you?" I asked as we took our table.

"The defence barrister? No actually, not at all. Mr Doveton was very softly spoken and polite."

Two steaming bowls of soup were delivered to our table. Carrie breathed in the master stock.

"What's the jury like?" I said, blowing on a spoonful.

"A lot of them seem older. It's a mixture of men and women. I couldn't read their faces. Lisa said the jury liked me though."

I smiled and had another spoonful. "Did you see *him*?"

Carrie grimaced. "He's at the back of the room, behind a barrier, with a security guard at his side. He looked normal. Smug."

"Were many other people there?"

"A few. He had a cast and crew taking up most of the gallery. I assumed they were family. They were sitting around Lyn and Greg. I recognised some of the cousins from the wedding and Rhonda and Frank were front and centre."

"Were Luke and Chloe there?"

"No, and that surprised me. I was expecting Luke there in his support."

I finished my soup. Carrie's was half full. Funny how nerves shrunk your stomach.

Later that afternoon, with her evidence complete, we met at the OPP and walked to the car.

The trip home was quiet. She was exhausted and nerves had stolen my voice now I was one step closer to landing in that chair.

"Jessica Foster," a male voice boomed down the corridor.

I gulped, stood and adjusted my dress. I stepped forward into view of the man in uniform. He waved for me to hurry. We turned into a small alcove, and he pulled open a wooden door, motioning for me to walk through. The courtroom was full, and all eyes were on me. The last time I entered a crowded room of people waiting for my arrival was my wedding day. I stood frozen in the entrance, unsure where I was meant to go. I remembered to bow my head to the judge and the uniformed man led me forward. I walked down the centre of the gallery, past prying eyes.

I looked towards the judge. Determined to hold my head up. I wanted to look strong, and for Julian to know I was better without him. I knew he was at the back of the room in a fenced off area and felt his eyes burning into the back of my skull. Perhaps eager for me to turn, I knew better, if I didn't engage, his power over was void. My hairs stood on end but I was ready for him to see me today. I'd had my hair recently cut and blow waved into a nice bounce. I picked out a figure-hugging, flattering dress. Not showy or revealing, just complimentary to my shape. My makeup done with care. It was important I looked my best in front of the jury. I wanted them to see me and think, 'He had no reason to be looking elsewhere. This wasn't about infidelity. It was predation.'

I wanted him to see me and think, 'How could I destroy us?'

I stepped up to witness box and swore on the bible to tell the truth.

I scanned the jury. Just as Carrie had said, they were mostly older and a mixture of men and women. Their faces were all on me. Some looked away as my eyes landed on theirs. It was a strange kind of meeting. I must talk to them but will never be introduced. Face to face, seven metres apart, the bar table between us. Foreign and uncomfortable surrounds.

I was instructed to sit. I made sure I sat tall. I had nothing to hide.

Judge Cunningham said some official pleasantries and invited the prosecution barrister, Lisa Edwards, to commence. Her tone was strong and professional. She was small in stature, but I noticed a ferocity in her. A 'don't mess with me' demeanour.

I flicked a glance to the gallery. Laura had perched herself between Lyn and me, blocking Lyn's face. A gesture I would not forget. Julian's cousins and distant family friends were dotted around her and Greg.

Lisa confirmed my name, profession, and questioned how I met Julian. I gave the details of our courtship when I was nineteen. I explained how I met Carrie and the friendship I had developed with her and her daughters.

I got on a roll. Looking at Lisa and to the jury and judge when answering. Drawing on my drama studies from high school, making sure I projected my voice and concentrated on diction. I wanted them to know I was not scared of him now. I forced my nerves at bay, refusing to shrink away. Today was my turn to speak out. To corroborate the truth.

For the first time in fifteen years I was unfettered, articulate and unwavering in Julian's presence. Maybe it was the railing between him and the rest of the room. Maybe it was his position in the rear of the room. Like he wasn't allowed to bear witness to the truth with the rest of us. Knowing he couldn't talk over me. For the first time in his life, he was relegated to the back blocks, rather than pushing himself to be the centre of attention.

Question after question, I was able to answer with clarity. She asked me if I had ever felt uncomfortable about Julian and Amelia or Meghan.

"There was this one night back before I was pregnant," I said. "Meghan and Amelia were staying overnight, and I got up at four am and Julian wasn't in bed yet. I looked for him. I walked out to the back deck, and he was standing behind the chair Amelia was sitting in."

"Do you remember when that was?" she asked in a gentle tone.

"I only remember that it was four am and Amelia was fourteen at the time."

"Fourteen?"

"Yes, I remember being mad at the both of them. Because I had told her to go to bed when her sister did. She had ignored me and he ... he kind of sniggered at me. It made me uncomfortable. But then I talked myself out of any worry because he would stay up on his own all the time."

"And, just to be clear, you are dating this before you had a baby?"

"Yes."

"How would you describe your relationship with Amelia and Meghan?" She tipped her head to the side.

"I've been close friends with Carrie since they were little. I love those girls."

"You babysat them and took them on multiple camping holidays with you?"

"Yes."

"What would you and Mr Rundell do for them when they came away with you?"

"We looked after them. We did everything that parents would do." As I spoke, I looked at the jury. The audience that counted.

"Describe some of those duties."

"We cooked for them, help set up their tents and beds. Supervised them. Coached them in sailing."

"So, was Mr Rundell their coach?"

"Absolutely. Always."

She nodded and moved on, asking me to talk about Catherine's involvement in the club and how she babysat for us.

"Was there a specific time that you recall learning Mr Rundell engaged Catherine to babysit when you were away?"

"Yes, I clearly remember that, when Ricky was one, I was away for the weekend. I remember being mad when Julian told me he had got her over to babysit. He only had to look after the children that one weekend. It annoyed me that he hired a babysitter, and he hadn't even gone out."

"Can you confirm that Mr Rundell was a coach for the Rochford Sailing Club?"

"Absolutely. The whole time."

"Thank you, Ms Foster." She turned towards the judge. "They are the matters for Ms Foster, Your Honour."

The judge nodded and looked over his glasses at the bar table below. He directed a morning tea break.

I was so wound up. Electricity rushed through my deepest dermal layers with each step towards the little waiting area. When I got there, I stood with my arms wrapped around my middle, looking out the window at the uninspiring view. The sun remained absent. My heart rate was up and thready. I sipped on water, talking my mouth into swallowing. Adrenaline on high, my body rejected the idea of food.

I didn't know how much time passed before that booming voice was calling for me again down the empty corridor.

I was led back to the chair. Everyone else already in position. Laura's head was back in place, blocking my view of Lyn. The corner of my lips lifted as I met Laura's eye and she gave an encouraging smile.

My attention shifted as Mr Doveton was invited to commence his cross examination. He stood holding a document and cleared his throat.

"Ms Forster ... is that how I pronounce your name?" he asked.

"Foster," I said stiffly. He knew very well how to pronounce my name.

He cleared his throat again. "Right ... sorry, Ms Foster?"

"That's right." I nodded politely.

"One of the first things that you noticed and liked about Mr Rundell was his talent as a sailor?" He looked at me with raised eyebrows.

I gave a small nod. "That's right."

"And certainly, a personality brimming with confidence. Would you agree with that?" He lifted his dewy chin in my direction.

"Yes, he's definitely a leader." I shifted in my seat, uncomfortable praising Julian.

"And he was popular amongst other club members?" He was speaking fast, it felt like a quickfire round.

"Yes."

"And from what you could see, he stood out to others, and stood out to you as an accomplished sailor?"

"Yes." I'm sure Julian was loving hearing how great I thought he was.

Mr Doveton went on for a while about the club and Julian's wonderful nature before changing the subject to my pregnancy with Poppy.

"As I understand it, during that pregnancy, you suffered quite severely from morning sickness, is that right?"

"Yes."

"Struggling so much so that it was difficult for you to work as a veterinary nurse?" He snapped the paperwork by his hip.

"Yes, it was difficult. I remember going home early a few times

327

and having some sick days, but I kept on working." Was he trying to paint me as weak?

"Would you say it impacted on the amount of work you engaged in, and you were spending more time at home?" He looked down his nose at me.

"I had been doing regular overtime until then, so I stopped doing that, but I still kept my permanent shifts." Was my pregnancy on trial?

Mr Doveton asked me about one of the previously tendered documents. I confirmed Julian was listed as the President and the Coach in that document. He asked about other people's involvement, and committee members of the Rochford Sailing Club.

"It was a group effort," I said. "Everyone was welcome to contribute, but there was still a clear structure of decision makers, and Julian was at the top." I shifted again in my seat.

"There was structure and a team of coaches in place within the club, would you agree with that description?"

"Yes."

"There were a number of people involved in that capacity?"

"Yes."

"Would you agree that it was a requirement of the national governing body of clubs that coaches have a certain level of qualification?"

"Yes."

"I will direct you to the document previously examined that lists Mr Rundell as a qualified coach."

"Alright, yes." The document was passed to me by the tipstaff.

"If I suggested to you that he was accredited purely to satisfy the structure of the club, would that be a fair comment?" He waved the papers around in the air in a dramatic fashion when saying 'satisfy'.

Losing me in his theatre, I said, "I'm sorry, can you repeat that?"

"Sorry, I will reword. The accreditation referred to in that document does not mean Mr Rundell was actually coaching."

I looked at the document. "It specifically states: 'Your qualified coach is Julian Rundell'."

"Can I suggest to you though, Ms Foster, that he was not a coach of Rochford Sailing Club, but merely qualified as one." His emotionless eyes bored into mine.

"He was *always* a coach," I said firmly, my brows furrowed.

Mr Doveton kept going and asked me what Julian's role was in relation to each complainant. My answer was always the same – he coached them. Readied them for regattas. All around great guy.

Mr Doveton abruptly changed the subject to a trip to Lake Hemsworth when Poppy was a few months old. "I suggest to you that your relationship was in trouble at that stage?" Once again, he managed to look down his nose at me despite my elevated position in the room. That took skill.

"We'd had a fight a few months earlier, but he'd promised things would change and we were working it out."

"You had an argument, and you asked him to move out?"

"Yes. But he only moved into the living room."

"And after that you both decided to stay together and planned that trip with Amelia and Meghan to Lake Hemsworth?" It sounded odd laid out like that.

"But we were fine by then ... or I thought we were."

"I understand Meghan was eighteen at that time and Amelia was sixteen, is that correct?"

"That sounds right."

"Did Carrie approach you and ask you for a lift for her daughters to Lake Hemsworth?"

"No, we were going, and we invited the girls to come with us. Just like any other time in the past."

"You arranged to give them a lift, would you agree?" His upturned palm thrown in my direction.

"When they said they wanted to come, there was no question that they would come in our car with us."

"The arrangements for Amelia and Meghan were organised between yourself and Carrie, is that correct? It did not involve Mr Rundell?"

My brows knitted tight together. "It always involved Julian."

"I'm suggesting that on this particular occasion Mr Rundell had no involvement in organising the girls to attend. This was organised between yourself and your good friend Carrie?" His hands flapped about with each word. It was distracting.

"That's not true." I squirmed in my seat, uncomfortable with confrontation.

"It may have been the case when the girls were younger that you jointly arranged to look after the girls on similar trips, but on this occasion, can I suggest to you that there was no arrangement for Mr Rundell to be involved in the care of Amelia and Meghan?"

"There absolutely was an arrangement for them to be in our joint care." My voice rose in protest.

"Would it be a fair summation that by that time, Amelia was a very independent sixteen-year-old?"

"She was a normal sixteen-year-old. She still required supervision and looking after." I felt my face screw up. Was he really suggesting the maturity of a sixteen-year-old mattered when talking about sex offences?

"And this trip to Lake Hemsworth was not a Rochford Sailing Club event?"

"No."

"It was more about celebrating your birthday and social activities, camping as a group. Is that a fair comment?"

"And sailing."

"Was the situation that those activities were undertaken in an informal manner?" Both edges of his mouth shifted down in question.

"We were practicing for future regattas and Julian was coaching the girls in race tactics."

"Would it be a fair comment to suggest this was just a group of people engaging in their hobby?"

"We were training. Julian was coaching." My voice had gone stiff. Mechanical. My mind trying to figure out where his line of questioning led.

"Wasn't it the case that Mr Rundell was simply imparting his knowledge of a skill?"

I tilted my head, trying to comprehend his words. "That's coaching ... isn't it?"

"Mr Rundell was not coaching in any formal capacity on that trip, was that the situation?"

I frowned. That was the same question. "Well, given that he was their coach, we just took it that he was coaching them."

"Well, can I put it to you that this was an unofficial case of Mr Rundell imparting knowledge, not coaching."

"He was their coach. He had been since they were little girls."

"There was no coaching happening at Lake Hemsworth, was there? This was just a case of friends casually helping people and enjoying an activity socially. Would you agree with that?"

How many ways could he ask the same bloody question?

"No!" I tried to keep my voice from rising. "Julian set the times we would practice, what they were each working on and what were the next steps. I don't know how else to describe it. He was coaching."

"Ms Foster, you undoubtedly would have been mortified to read the accusations about your husband, Mr Rundell." He paused before continuing again, his hands reached out in understanding. "You would have been horrified." Another pause. "Would that be a fair statement?" He awaited my answer with pursed, plump lips.

I blinked. Taken aback by the change in pace and line of questioning. "Yeah ... Yes."

"Can I suggest to you that you felt an enormous amount of betrayal for his breach of marital trust?"

My eyes flicked towards the jury and back to Mr Doveton.

"Yes." My voice very small now.

"You sent a message to the girls in the sailing club after learning of some of the accusations?" His voice was even softer.

"Yes."

"Encouraging the girls to come forward if they themselves had any accusations against Mr Rundell. Is that a fair statement?" He gestured his flat palm out to me when it was my turn to speak.

"Yes. I felt guilty that some of the girls would not come forward because they wanted to protect my marriage."

"Can I suggest to you, Ms Foster, that at that time your feelings towards Mr Rundell were extremely negative?"

"Yes." I suppressed rolling my eyes. "Yeah."

"I would ask you to have a think about that, Ms Foster." He took the opportunity to pace a couple steps back and forth behind the bar table with his index fingers against his lips. "Because of the extremely negative feelings you have for Mr Rundell, you might well be exaggerating the role your ex-husband was playing at the Rochford Sailing Club?"

"How can I exaggerate the role of a coach and the President?" I couldn't keep the edge from my voice now.

"You have very significant negative feelings about Mr Rundell?" He gestured again to the back of the courtroom. I didn't follow his hand. I knew who was back there and had zero intentions of meeting his gaze.

I felt my cheeks flush at this understatement and could scarcely get out, "Yes." My eyes fell to my lap as I willed myself to control my emotions. My earlier bravado gone, drained from his emotional line of questioning. This felt an unfair tactic, having me talk of feelings.

The confidence my hair and outfit had given me was ripped away. I felt like a silly little girl playing dress ups. It had all been an act. I was broken. I couldn't hide it.

He kept going, almost yelling. "I put it to you that you are inflating and misrepresenting Mr Rundell's role within the sailing club?"

My eyes shot up to meet his hostile glare. A trace of that fire still burned inside me. "I'm not!" My voice was firm and full of conviction.

Mr Doveton held my gaze as my face distorted and hot tears spilled down my cheek. At that, he paid me no further attention and turned towards Judge Cunningham.

"No further questions, Your Honour." He sat and rearranged the multiple folders surrounding him.

The tipstaff held out a tissue box. I took one gratefully and dabbed under my wet eyes.

Judge Cunningham excused me, and I stood in a daze. I stepped down from the box and headed back along the aisle of onlookers, eyes only for the carpet. I collected myself with each step. I couldn't let it end like that. A crushed looking, tearful woman. I forced myself to look up. To regain some of that earlier bravado. I raised my eyes and looked straight at him. He was chuckling to the police guard by his side. His smirk remained as he met my eye. I rallied to hold his stare. To not look away. My eyes were wet, not because I was fragile, but because I was accused of lying. I lifted my head higher, holding his stare.

I mouthed under my breath, "Now I see you."

His smile faltered and he looked away.

I'd won.

<br>

The drive to court was typical. Carrie and I ate and chatted, sipping on coffee. Perhaps there was an extra lightness to our voices now. Relief that the hardest part was over. As witnesses, this was the first time we were allowed in the courtroom to watch proceedings. We were at the pointy end of the trial. Closing statements were about to commence.

We walked to the court with Sally from the OPP, through security and broke step only just before entering the courtroom. We knew we would be outnumbered by Julian's supporters today. We braced for it. I collected myself as Sally opened the door. Hushed tones evaporated as we entered. The court was not yet in session. How very different it felt from the last time I entered this room, the jury box empty, no judge at the helm.

As expected, Julian's family filled the majority of the central gallery seats. Carrie and I walked past. We went to the front row, nearest to where Lisa and Sally sat. Right in front of the jury. Lisa was already at the bar table and greeted us both warmly. Carrie twisted in her chair, scanning the room.

"He's not in here yet," she said, "He must come in just before the session starts."

"I didn't spot Luke on the way in either," I said.

"No. He's not here. Bastard."

My feelings had long turned on Luke and Chloe. Luke's one phone call to me did nothing but confirm his loyalty to Julian. I was surprised he was not here next to Lyn.

Judge Cunningham took his seat and invited the jury in. I watched them file forward and take the same seats they had occupied daily for over two weeks.

Lisa stood when invited and commenced the prosecution's closing arguments. Her voice was clear, articulate and strong as she explained how Julian sent messages to multiple girls in note form and through text. The messages started innocently, focused on complimenting their sailing, before turning flirtatious. He did this time after time to multiple girls, some as young as eleven. Eventually, the texts led to touching and physical assaults of multiple victims. Then she presented the evidence from the complainants.

It started with how Julian met Kayla when she was twelve years old as a junior member of the Rochford Sailing Club. She stated that Julian was a talented and trusted senior sailor. Lisa talked of the notes of encouragement Julian left in Kayla's training bag.

"When Kayla was fourteen years of age, whilst attending an end of season awards dinner at the Rochford Sailing Club, Mr Rundell got Kayla alone in the storage sheds underneath the club under the

335

guise of showing her something 'cool'. Once alone he said to her, something along the lines of: 'You shouldn't be allowed to wear that dress in front of me'. He then walked behind Kayla and massaged her shoulders before leaning down and kissing her on the neck.

"He went on to tell Kayla something along the lines of, 'There's nothing to worry about, it's just a bit of fun'. Mr Rundell turned her around and asked her to hug him. In her evidence, she states that she was nervous, scared and frozen, unsure as to what she should do. Mr Rundell then kissed her on the lips.

"Mr Rundell went to significant efforts over the next year to be alone with the fourteen-year-old Kayla many more times. Each time kissing and touching, which lead to him one day, after training, in the storage shed under the club, inserting his fingers into her vagina.

"When Kayla was fifteen years of age, Mr Rundell encouraged Kayla to skip a day from school. He picked her up from where her bus was supposed to collect her and made a phone call to the school to say that she would not be attending due to illness that day. He took her to his place of residence in Darvo River and had sexual intercourse with her, whereby Mr Rundell performed oral sex on her before he inserted his penis into her vagina."

I squirmed at the details.

"So skilled a manipulator was he, he convinced Kayla it was true love that she was feeling and she entered into a secret relationship with him."

I gulped hearing it laid bare. Raw in all the atrocity of the truth for the jury.

"Members of the jury, I will take you back to the evidence and sworn testimony of Mr Luke Yardley," Lisa announced.

My jaw dropped. Luke's testimony? I met Carrie's eyes. They

were as wide as mine. I looked back at Lisa, incredulous. It made no sense.

"Ladies and gentlemen of the jury, you heard Luke Yardley confirm he had knowledge of the relationship between Mr Rundell and Kayla from the time she was fifteen years of age. The defendant even gloated, in Luke's words, about 'popping her cherry'. Luke also corroborated evidence that Kayla had been talked into posing for nude and sexually explicit photographs for the defendant at the age of fifteen. Luke gave testimony of being shown many of those photos over the years that Kayla and the defendant kept a secret relationship."

"Oh my God," I whispered to Carrie.

"I had no idea," she whispered, shaking her head.

"Luke Yardley described walking in on the defendant at his apartment in Darvo River and seeing Mr Rundell and Kayla engaged in sexual intercourse when she was the age of sixteen, whereby Kayla was performing oral sex on Mr Rundell."

I felt sick. It had been bad enough listening to the truth from Kayla, but the story resonated even more hearing the nitty gritty truth through the prosecutor. It sounded harsher and out of place when announced for an audience. I rubbed at my forehead.

"You heard in Kayla's testimony, confirmed by Luke," she held up her index finger, "that the secret affair went on between the defendant and Kayla until she reached eighteen. That entire time, the defendant maintained public relationships with other women who were not under the legal age of consent." Lisa paced behind the bar table as she spoke, occasionally pausing to look at the jury to ensure they were engaged. Who wouldn't be?

"And when Kayla turned eighteen, they decided to go public. The defendant almost twenty-seven at that stage. The relationship now legal in Mr Rundell's eyes, and although questioned by Kayla's parents, accepted by club members on a whole."

Lisa continued explaining that Julian ended that relationship and went on to marry me. He always looked decent in the club.

She moved on to tell how Julian met me, Carrie, Jim, Amelia and Meghan.

Lisa detailed how one evening, before I was pregnant with Poppy, when Meghan and Amelia stayed overnight; "Mr Rundell's wife went to bed and left the two teenage girls in Mr Rundell's care. It was in the evidence of both Meghan and Amelia that Mr Rundell bought them milkshakes with alcohol as a secret at dinner that evening. He snuck both the girls more alcohol when he returned to his house, disguising it in the soft drink he let them each choose.

"Both Meghan and Amelia gave evidence that Meghan went to bed, leaving Mr Rundell up alone with Amelia. It was during this time alone on the back deck that Mr Rundell massaged Amelia's shoulders before leaning in and kissing the fourteen-year-old on the neck.

"It was in her evidence that her head was cloudy, but she remembered feeling uncomfortable with the physical contact."

Lisa described his assault of Meghan that same night.

"She froze and rolled over, away from Mr Rundell and he left the room."

She went into more detail before moving onto Catherine's evidence. "Mr Rundell was coaching Catherine when he started sending her messages via Facebook Messenger when she was thirteen years of age. In time, she became a regular babysitter for his daughter, Poppy, and then his son, Ricky, after he was born."

"It is Catherine's evidence, corroborated by Jessica Foster, the defendant's then wife, that she babysat for Mr Rundell in the spring of 2014 whilst his wife was away. In her evidence, Catherine explained that she was not aware Mr Rundell's wife, Jessica, was not home when she agreed to babysit. He did not go out. He bought her alcoholic beverages in the form of flavoured vodka in a glass bottle. He got her to put his children to bed before encouraging her to sit next to him on the couch. He lent in and kissed her on the neck before moving and kissing her on the lips. She told him she had a boyfriend and did not want to have sex with him. He kept going.

I near doubled over at the thought of me, devouring a degustation and matching wines with my best friends, while this was happening to poor young Catherine on my couch while my children slept down the hall.

"It is her evidence that she remained frozen for a time while Mr Rundell sexually assaulted her, before telling him to stop. Mr Rundell then said something along the lines of 'cock tease' to her before she ran outside and called her mother to collect her."

No wonder Julian seemed okay with me going away for that weekend. I knew it couldn't have been about me having a good birthday. He leapt at the opportunity. He probably planned all along to get Catherine over and trap her. Talk about walking into the wolf's den.

She described that when Catherine returned to Rochford some months later, Julian publicly berated her in front of club members for her absences and lack of dedication. I remember that day. I thought it was disciplinary action at the time but now see something much more distressing. He was showing her he was in charge.

I turned back to see Lyn, sitting in front of her son. Surely no one could listen to all this evidence, all the pre-planning, the secret notes, the testing of compliance he did. Surely, no one could see this as any fault of the girls. Her face was hard to read. But her chin was still elevated.

As she read on, it finally made perfect sense why Julian lost his job. A lot of his offending had occurred while I was at work, and he *should* have been at work.

The story continued and Ms Edwards made note that a number of victims mainly kept quiet about their experiences 'out of concern for their friend and mentor, Jessica Foster'. They were also concerned how it would affect the club.

As his stature climbed in the club, his offending became more brazen. The junior club members a constant supply source. Messages sent to girls between eleven and thirteen. Touching and kissing them at fourteen. Escalation in physical assaults at fifteen or sixteen.

Lisa confirmed he was in a position of power and trust to all of the victims. Sometimes as a babysitter, a coach, or as an employer while we were paying them to babysit. The many years of secrets and lies spilled open like a body splayed for autopsy. The gruesome truth naked and gory for all to see.

I glanced back at Lyn again. Her face didn't shift to meet mine. Defiance in her eyes.

The whole case and torrid jigsaw puzzle complete, Lisa finished her closing statements confirming to the jury that the prosecution had proved guilt beyond reasonable doubt.

Carrie and I looked at each other. We had tears in our eyes and sat in shocked silence. We had both taken in a lot. Much more than what we each knew about his offending and just how far his tentacles reached.

Judge Cunningham adjourned for lunch before Mr Doveton would take to the stage.

Carrie and I took solace in our favourite Vietnamese restaurant, City Pho. The familiarity provided warmth and respite from the shock of court. After lunch, we headed back to the courtroom and took our seats close to jury. Away from the accused.

Mr Doveton gave his closing arguments with theatrical vigour. His pauses felt rehearsed. At times, I near gasped at the elevation in his tone. If we were to believe Mr Doveton's version of events, the defendant was an official coach, but did not coach in the capacity of coaching. He never babysat any girls, rather, it was described that they were in my care. His other defence was that he was not paying a babysitter, and it was organised by me. Mr Doveton never once could say none of it happened. The evidence was too strong to the contrary.

At one stage he even explained some of Julian's more sexualised messages to a fourteen-year-old by throwing his hands in the air and announcing, "Maybe he was trying to prove he wasn't gay."

Both Carrie and I let out audible chuckles at that. Julian would be horrified by that defence. That anyone would ever question his sexuality.

He ended his speech after repeating the words 'reasonable doubt' again and again through the dialogue. I knew he was just doing his job, but I felt like slapping him. Apparently, Mr Doveton was one of the top barristers in town. Certainly, costing a pretty penny. But how to defend the indefensible? Deny, attack, flip the roles. Play with titles. Obfuscation. Reasonable doubt and of course – he was only trying to prove he wasn't *gay*.

"And with that, ladies and gentlemen, I put to you, the jury, that the prosecution has not proven their case beyond a reasonable doubt. The defence rests, Your Honour."

At the end of the speech, Judge Cunningham released the jury to break. He explained The Charge would be read the following day and adjourned until the following morning.

Carrie and I followed Sally, Lisa and Laura back down the street to the OPP.

"What happens now?" Carrie asked with eagerness.

"The judge will discuss with the jury the points of law that they need to refer to when deliberating," Sally said. "It's called 'The Charge'. You are welcome to attend, but I would suggest taking the day off tomorrow. It's quite dry and we know there won't be a verdict tomorrow."

"So, after the points of law, after The Charge, do the jury start deliberations?"

Lisa interjected, smiling. "Yes. And before you ask, we have no idea how long that will take."

I met Carrie's eye and said, "Well, we want to be there for the verdict."

"Unfortunately, we can't give you any notice. We all have to stay within close proximity of the court. Once they decide, we only get about fifteen minutes notice to get up there from our offices."

Sally said she would advise us when they started deliberating. We said goodbye and thanked the three women for all their great work. I wanted to feel confident we had the better case, but it was hard to judge knowing that the defence got the final word.

My guts twisted with worry.

<hr/>

I woke relieved to see Patrick and wriggled into his warmth. For so many years, I lived without a loving touch in bed. There was next to no touching unless Julian wanted to have sex. I hated when my mind went back there, especially when I was with Patrick. Patrick had once made me jump when he touched the small of my back one morning while I slept. I woke in terror. Now, he knew not to reach for that spot on my back. My body didn't forget. Years later, it still flooded fast with memories of Julian.

Would there ever be a time when I felt a particular touch and didn't flinch? Patrick was tolerant and understanding. I snuggled into the comfort of him.

Patrick enveloped me in response. "Good morning, lovely." His lips brushed my earlobe with each syllable and came to rest on my neck. I was acutely aware now of how broken my farce of a marriage was. Sure, Julian had said kind words, and there were small gestures of love in the early days. But I looked back now at those empty words often written on a card. The empty 'I love you' before bed. With Patrick, it was different. Patrick showed those things.

I always longed for a closer connection with Julian, but the only thing I longed for with Patrick was more time. I had fallen hard. I was at times on edge, and I still felt sick when he got text messages. I would never naturally trust again. I had to accept I was a work in progress.

"Good morning." I rolled onto my side to face him and nuzzle in again. Nose to toes; a connection.

"Do we have to get up yet?" he asked with his eyes still closed.

"Not yet."

"You're coming to work today, right?"

"Yes, I will grace you with my presence today," I said with a sleepy smile.

Patrick's eyes opened and a soft grin spread across his lips. He kissed my lips gently at first. Our hands navigated our now known curves and crevasses. Our breath growing heavy as we moulded against each other, moving in a synchronised rhythm.

The alarm blared and Patrick spun to slap it off before rolling back towards me.

"Now, where were we?" He brushed each word against my lips with his.

I pushed him away playfully. "We have to get ready for work."

"We might be a few minutes late this morning." His hands worked their way around my body.

"Okay, you've convinced me," I breathed, picking up our rhythm again. We lost ourselves in each other making love until we were forced to leave our warm bed for work.

It was after lunch when my phone alerted with a message. I snatched it and read the message from Sally.

*Jury have commenced deliberations.*

My heart skipped. This was the real pointy end now. The closer he was to incarceration, the closer I was to freedom.

The next day, I met up with Carrie. We started our day with the usual bakery and coffee routine. Our drive into the city was full of expectant nervous chatter. It was different than any other day we had come in to the courts. Today we had no plan, nowhere to be. We were only there in case a verdict was reached. Otherwise, we had free time to kill. We parked the car and looked at one another.

"I don't think there is much chance of a verdict this morning," Carrie said. "Shall we do some shopping?" She asked.

I shrugged. "Sure. I'm not sure what else to do."

We wandered the shopping centre closest to the court district. It was within a fifteen-minute walk, so we were safe if we got the call for a verdict. I tried on a few shirts. Bought a small bag for Poppy and a t-shirt for Ricky. I usually loved shopping, but the joy was sapped today. We each checked our phones every couple of minutes to make sure we hadn't missed the message.

By four o'clock, we knew that we wouldn't be getting a verdict today. We walked with our heads bowed to the car. I had not realised how draining waiting could be. I thought I would enjoy a nice day out with my best friend and an early verdict would be a bonus. But we found ourselves obsessing over our phones, eager not to miss the call from Sally.

"It feels like the longest day of my life," I said.

"I know," Carrie said. "And now we get to do it all again tomorrow."

9

It was Groundhog Day. We arrived in the city and pulled into the exact car spot as the day before. I looked at Carrie. A notable dark tinge under her eyes. I was the same. No amount of concealer seemed to help. We were noticeably worn down, our faces unable to hide the cracks. I imagined what damage of prolonged elevated cortisol levels could have on the human body. If it was showing on the outside, what was the inside toll? My hopes rested on a verdict today.

We walked around the court district in the morning. Aimlessly strolling the pavement. Neither of us talked much. Nothing more to say. We had long had the discussions about how realistically, sex offences were hard to get a conviction. Lengthy jail sentences came even harder.

"I was feeling confident after Lisa's closing statement but now I'm not so sure." I let my doubts fumble from my lips. They were tearing at my insides; I needed to speak.

"I know," Carrie said. "It makes me think they're second guessing. I feel like the longer it drags to get a verdict, the more likely it won't be the one we want."

"Let's get a coffee." I spotted a coffee shop we hadn't tried and started towards it. Within two steps, I was turning on my heels as I spotted Julian and his parents outside. I turned and took a second glance. Julian was lounged back, staring at his phone, ignoring them both. A privilege he may not have much longer.

"Shit, not there," I said, walking away.

Carrie looked at what disturbed my path, before jogging to catch up to me.

"Nope, we're definitely not going there," she said.

The morning dragged. As did lunchtime, and by late afternoon we were near convinced – it was all bad news.

"At what point do they believe there is reasonable doubt?" I said.

"I don't know." Carrie rubbed at her scalp. Exhaustion clear.

I took a long breath. It was so difficult to muster energy for positivity. It was easier to give in to the worst case scenario.

Carrie's phone rang. Both our eyes lit up when we saw it was Sally.

Carrie quickly answered. "Hi Sally." Her voice hopeful. "Yes, okay. We'll be right there."

My eyes were near popping out of my head. Not since waiting to go into labour had I been so impatient and expectant of anything. Energy gushed to my extremities and we started at a jog back in the direction of the court.

"It's not a verdict," Carrie said.

My heart dropped.

"Apparently the jury have a question for the judge," Carrie continued. "All the legal teams have been told to attend. Sally's hopeful it might be something small and we may have a verdict soon after."

We scurried through security as fast as they allowed and raced to the court. Sally stood outside the courtroom.

"Hello ladies," she said in a warm tone. "Why don't you two come and wait in here." She showed us through to another crappy little conference room. This one at least had a window.

We each took a seat but neither spoke, eyes glued to our phones. Waiting for a ping. My heart was in the back of my throat, bounding. Expectant. Desperate for the verdict to be 'guilty'.

"My Fitbit says I'm stressed." Carrie half smiled.

I smiled back. "Smart watch."

"Yep."

The lightened mood didn't last long. We sat quietly and time passed in sloth steps. I let my mind wander to dark thoughts. Doubt so ingrained in my head about reasonable doubt, I couldn't push them away. I thought about what a 'not guilty' verdict would mean for me and my family. The price would be astronomical. Julian would be free to fight me for unsupervised visits with the children, and he would get it. I would be stuck in a legal battle with him until my children were of legal age. He would be free. The gravity of it all fell heavy.

My jaw shook. I would have to let him take my daughter for sleepovers. He would have free access to other girls. The damage inconceivable. The consequences so utterly all consuming.

My mind spiralled in the distraught resolutions of life without a guilty verdict.

The door opened, tearing me from despair. I bolted upright in anticipation.

"Sorry ladies, there won't be any verdict today." Lisa said it almost casually, with no clue of my internal turmoil.

I burst into tears and collapsed back into my seat. Really ugly crying.

"Hey, hey, hey." Laura rushed to my side and pulled the chair next to me. "This is not bad news." She put her hand on my shoulder.

"He'll do it again," I blurted. "He isn't going to stop."

Laura drew me into a hug. "Come on, ladies. This is not bad news."

Carrie sat silent, staring forward.

I stuttered through my tears. "We thought that the longer the jury take, the more likely they are questioning bits of law and whether there is reasonable doubt."

Laura sighed. "Look. You can both shove your negative thoughts right where they belong. This does not mean, not even a little bit, that they are considering the worst. It just means they are being really thorough and doing their job well."

Carrie and I nodded and tried to take her words in. She hugged me firmly. I sniffed like a small child after an outburst most of the way home. When we parted, there was no more to say except, "See you tomorrow."

<hr />

"All rise," the tipstaff called.

I didn't think my heart could race any faster. It had reached a level where there were no distinguishable beats, rather a flourish of intermingled thready sprays shooting through my arteries. I stood and gulped. A line of sweat beaded my upper lip. Would I pass out before I heard a verdict? I forced a deep breath and was relieved when Judge Cunningham wasted no time taking his position and I could sit again. He invited the jury in. It was only an hour ago I got the call from Sally as Carrie and I sat in a restaurant.

"We have a verdict!" Sally had exclaimed.

I nodded to Carry and ripped my jacket from the back of my chair, ready to make a run for it.

"But wait, there's no need to hurry," Sally had said quickly. She must have sensed our frenzy through the phone. "They want to read it after lunch. It's one of the jurors' birthdays and one of them brought in a cake."

"They want to eat cake?" I had asked in disbelief.

Now, an hour later, we watched the jury file in. Their faces straight, giving nothing away. It was hard to imagine just moments earlier they were merrily singing 'Happy Birthday' and cutting cake. No sign of that frivolity now. They avoided the eyes of the eager gallery and took their seats.

Business commenced quickly. The judge's associate stood and directed her questions at the foreperson on the jury.

"Have you agreed upon a verdict?"

A man who looked in his sixties stood and cleared his throat. "Yes."

"How say you on Charge One – of 'Indecent act with a child under sixteen', do you find Julian Rundell guilty or not guilty?"

"Guilty," he said in a clear voice.

Carrie and I were gripping each other's thighs. We turned to each other, a whisker of a smile on both our faces. One down.

"How say you on Charge Two – of 'Sexual Penetration of a child under sixteen, under your care or supervision'. Do you find Julian Rundell guilty or not guilty?"

"Guilty."

"How say you on Charge Three – of 'Rape'. Do you find Julian Rundell guilty or not guilty?"

"Guilty."

Carrie's shoulders shook. Tears rolling down one after another as her lips quivered. I remembered watching my wedding video years ago, before any of Julian's accusations came to light. I'd laughed when the camera panned to Carrie, who led the bridesmaids down the aisle. She was trying to smile through her tears and her shoulders shook back and forth, like they did now. She had cried out of love for her friends, overwhelmed with emotion for our future lives together. If only she had known what sort of future that would be. Perhaps she would have cried for different reasons.

Carrie's shoulders shook again and tears filled my own eyes. All the people in the gallery supporting Julian were at that very wedding. No one could have seen this coming. Except perhaps Julian. But then, he was the 'smartest' man I knew and never would have envisaged getting caught. Now here we were – guilty.

The associate and foreperson continued to read. There were more than twenty charges.

All guilty.

Convicted.

It was all over in about five minutes. For over two years, I had waited to hear a jury of Julian's peers see him for what he was. Today, a jury had found him guilty on multiple counts. Justice felt just today. All the victims were heard and believed.

He was no longer an alleged child sex offender. He was a convicted child rapist.

Judge Cunningham thanked the jury for their service, and they were excused. Their job done. He set a date for the next hearing for two months away. He revoked Julian's bail and ordered he be remanded until his sentencing.

"Bailiff, please remove the prisoner."

It was jarring. In a good way. I watched him stand. His normally composed face was the darkest shade of red. Just before purple. I'd only seen him that red in his explosive rages years earlier. He was led from his nook at the back of the room and exited through a special door; not allowed to use the door of the general public. He was now a prisoner.

I locked eyes with Carrie and said a million unspoken words before we embraced for a long time. Most of the gallery was gone when I looked up. Julian's supporters exited the field fast in defeat.

Lisa and Sally were all smiles as they gathered their belongings on the bar table. They led us through to that same conference room I had my meltdown twenty-four hours prior.

How much five minutes could change a mindset. I was smiling so wide it almost hurt. A smile of hope. Tears of relief spilled down. I threw myself at Laura and sobbed again into her arms repeating, "Thank you," over and over.

I hugged Sally next; she couldn't look happier. Finally, I came to Lisa, her composure still intact. Unflappable. She wore a controlled smile, maintaining her strait-laced professionalism. I was not sure whether to hug her at first, but abandoned any question and wrapped my arms around her small frame. It was a fast embrace. She pulled back, squeezing my shoulders as she held my eye. Her normally serious face upturned in a smile. She winked and said, "We got the motherfucker!"

# Summer 2018

Patrick's hand rested on my hip as I lay in the sun, keeping one eye on the children. He had booked us a beach summer holiday straight after the trial, thinking whether the result was good or bad, we could do with time away. He was right. The moment we arrived, my energy sapped, and all I wanted to do was lie on the beach and rest. For the past two years, my body had been running on fumes. Anxiety was high, stress the baseline, and upon seeing the sandy shores, it entered into recovery mode. As relieved as I was that Julian was now a convicted man, I needed this holiday for restoration. I wasn't sure if I could find normal again.

Ricky and Poppy looked cute in their matching rash shirts. Their hair wet and tangled from playing in the waves. Skin golden and slick with sunscreen. They piled another load onto their sand project. Not so much a castle, rather an empire for crabs. They were decorating each peak with seaweed and shells. It was a precise game for Poppy, more haphazard and 'wherever things land' for Ricky.

I didn't want this holiday to end. The last few years had been so out of control and hectic. Now, I finally felt like my life was back in my control. Sitting on this beach, on the other side of the country, I realised I wanted a new life, a new everything. I needed to purge my life of Julian completely. I couldn't drive along any street at home without having a memory of him there. Almost all of my clothes, even my swimsuit, contained memories of where I wore it with Julian. I could take a thousand showers and never wipe the scourge of him from my body.

But maybe a new ocean could.

I rolled over and scooted closer to Patrick, who was reading a book. "I think I want to move here."

He put the book down and frowned slightly. "What? Are you serious?"

"Yeah. I mean, what's really in Darvo for us?"

"My practice, for one."

"But we could start a new practice."

His eyebrows went up, but he was not looking at me like I was crazy. He was taking me seriously, his mind seeming to whir as he thought about it.

I waited, hopeful.

"Yeah, I guess it's possible," he said finally. "I've always loved this part of the country."

I gave him a grateful smile and lay back on the sand. I closed my eyes, letting the warmth of the sun penetrate every pore. And for the first time in what felt like a lifetime, I felt peace.

# *Winter 2019*

I leant back in the private booth of the busy café, my body and soul weary. This was all meant to be over. I should be happy. And I had been. When Judge Cunningham handed down Julian's jail sentence five months ago that peace my body had dared to feel was validated. I was free.

"To clarify, Mr Rundell, I am sentencing you to fifteen years and three months total term imprisonment. You will be eligible for parole after a period served of twelve years. You will also be placed on the sex offenders register, for life."

I could breathe. Oh god, I could breathe again.

My children would be adults by the time Julian was released into the community. I had to fight the temptation to jump the bench and embrace Judge Cunningham.

After that, all the matters in the children's court were closed because Julian was incarcerated, and I had that coveted 'Protective Parent' title back. It was all going to plan. Until my final day in family court.

I had gone alone, treating the day as a mere checkbox formality. Instead, I was ambushed. Lyn and Greg, with Julian's lawyer, standing up and stuttering in front of the registrar that Julian was appealing his conviction and wanted visitation with the children at the prison. Lyn and Greg applying to intervene in our proceedings for their own visitation every second weekend and on school holidays. My brain had frozen. I actually giggled under my breath. My sense of humour so sick now. That was before I cried.

It wasn't over.

I had left the courtroom in a daze, escaping to the bathroom. I took a long time running my hands under the cool water in the sink. I stared at my reflection. Any trace of my former vibrancy was gone; I looked haggard, sallow. Older than my thirty-five years. I had thought this was as far as I would have to push myself. Instead, I felt I had spent years ascending a mountain only to now see the true peak was out of sight. And now the trail looked even more jagged and treacherous.

The door behind me had opened. I stared at Lyn in the bathroom mirror. My nostrils flared and I spun to face her.

"Look, Jess–" Lyn had begun.

"How dare you speak to me!" I thrust my index finger towards her face. "You want my children to visit a prison full of paedophiles? You disgust me!" I shoved the door open, resisting the urge to slap her upturned chin.

I'd huffed on the other side of the door. I never used to be an angry person. Now I burst with rage. I wanted to kick, slap and break something. In my haste to leave and escape Lyn, I'd almost barrelled straight into Greg. He was cradling Lyn's pink Prada handbag.

"Sorry," he'd said in a small voice.

"What for, Greg?" I'd cried, voice echoing down the empty corridor. "Are you sorry for paying to fight me in family court? Or are you sorry for not supervising my children properly with a child rapist?"

His eyes were downcast, like the answer was in her bag.

"Which is it, Greg?" I spat, arms crossed.

"I'm ... I just want to see my grandchildren," he said in a sad tone. His face matched.

I shook, incensed. "Well, fucking grow a pair then! Stand up to your wife and that son of yours and you can have a wonderful relationship with your grandchildren. Do the *right* thing. Stop supporting his court battles." My rage had faltered, my voice softening. "Please leave this out of court. I beg you. I'm exhausted." My whole face screwed up as I'd waited for his response.

"I'm sorry." He'd lowered his head.

It was no use.

Now here I was. Over six months later. Waiting in a nearby café while the family consultant interviewed my children. She had to present a report to the court for our trial. *Another* trial. She had already spent five hours interviewing me yesterday. I had been straight on the defensive, sure Lyn and Greg had already convinced her. I gave a long-winded rant about why my children were better off without the Rundell family. Probably sounding hysterical as I spilled out everything, wanting her to believe the truth and feeling rushed against the clock. I had the impression my mothering and relationship choices were on trial.

Resigned that I had failed, I felt stuck in a system I never knew could be so cumbersome to the soul. I thought the family court was there to solve family disputes, but it seemed to favour contact and upholding relationships at whatever cost.

I rubbed my tired eyes. I clutched at my coffee, eyeing the complimentary cookie on my saucer. I wondered if I would ever get my appetite back. Coffee probably only made the perpetual anxiety worse, but it got me through most days. I sipped again shaking my head. It seemed crazy that one woman's report could dictate my future. My children's future. I could only hope what they were saying to her did not sow any seeds of doubt into her mind about Julian being a fit father, being someone safe for my children to visit in jail. The whole thing was absurd.

Julian was a convicted child rapist, and he was still able to control my life. What sort of system allowed that? So much was still out of my control. That freedom I let myself revel in at the sentencing hearing was all just a fantastical mirage. It didn't seem fair. I couldn't move on until we had an outcome and that was still months away. How many hours had I spent preparing documents for all the different hearings the past few years? I thought after the criminal trial was over, I would be free. But child sex offenders still had rights to their own children. It made no sense.

I looked around the café. People chatting with wide smiles and animated hands. I barely had the energy to lift the cup of coffee to my lips. I couldn't recognise the person I was now. So weak. Like a dead branch just waiting for a stiff breeze to let me tumble to my resting place. I was tired of holding on. So tired.

I sipped until my cup was empty. Watching the people chat and relax. Trying to remember the last time I'd been able to do that.

I walked slowly back to The Office of Judgement and met Clara, the family consultant, waiting with Poppy and Ricky in the play area. They spared me a look before returning their focus to the abundance of toys, lost in the gleeful utopia. The interview with Clara already forgotten. I smiled and nodded at Clara. Her face was neutral, giving away nothing. I swallowed my despair and followed her into her office.

"Well, they are both lovely and open children," she said. "Poppy has made it very clear that she does not want to go to a jail to visit him. But they do want to see their grandparents again."

I slumped back on the couch. Even the children were against me. I wanted to give up.

I spent another hour crying, explaining to Clara I didn't trust Lyn and Greg. I had thought Greg was different, but he wouldn't stand up to Lyn or Julian. The whole conversation felt fruitless.

We drove home, my eyes stinging and swollen. The kids none the wiser. Unable to read the mood, they sat rehashing their excitement about all the toys in her waiting room.

Later that evening, once the children were safe in bed, I sought privacy in my room.

I tumbled into an even lower mood, convinced my future was bleak and I would be forced to stay in Darvo. My dream of a fresh start with Patrick on the other side of the country, overlooking a new ocean, seemed all but impossible. I'd have to send my children to sleepovers with Lyn, who I imagined would ferry them straight to the prison at her first opportunity.

When sleep finally claimed me, it was to return to the same hellish nightmares I'd dreamt of for so long. While Julian still chased me in some, they had changed somewhat since his conviction. Now my dreams were far less violent and infinitely more terrifying. Last night, I dreamt I'd come home to our old house and Julian sat there on the couch, watching television. Suddenly I was back in that relationship, unable to scramble away. My mind reeled as I walked to the kitchen, plotting my escape and he called out, "What's for dinner?"

I woke, unable to breathe.

I still couldn't escape him. Not even in my dreams.

———

# *Spring* 2019

Walking into the court was different than any other court day. My lawyer and barrister met us in the foyer and led us directly to the courtroom. It was empty except for our small parties. Legal teams outnumbered us. I'd learnt early on that a lawyer does not generally represent you in a court room. They most often brief a barrister to do the talking. Another expensive person to pay for. No other matters were heard in here today. This was our room, set aside for the next five days.

Julian's lawyer was at the bar table. No barrister next to him yet. The bar table outnumbered the gallery today.

I sat in between Patrick and Carrie. My heart rate spiked. It was about to start. The beginning of the end. The proper end this time.

We stood as our judge entered and sat in her central position.

The judge addressed the room. "I understand that we are here to make final orders in regards to the Rundell and Foster children, Poppy and Ricky."

"That's correct, Your Honour." Julian's lawyer stood addressing the judge. He cleared his throat. "I would like to advise the court that my client, Mr Julian Rundell, has decided to withdraw from proceedings on the proviso that ... er ... that there are no orders for costs."

My jaw dropped. Patrick and Carrie mirrored my expression. My lawyer turned his head towards me with a crooked smile. He handed me an excerpt from the family report:

*It is clear to the writer that after discussion with the father, he still maintains his innocence and feels he is being unfairly incarcerated. The father's negative narration of the mother is extreme: in his view, she could not do just about anything without him, and he raised, taught and cared for the children near independently. When the writer asked about his offending, he responded with: 'I have done nothing wrong.' He is of the belief he is an advocate and protective of women. Child abusers are notoriously patient and skilled with manipulation and grooming tactics. They wait and watch to see how the child will react to their actions. They pick their victims after careful and considered compliance testing, in this case, with many messages. Over time, they often use tactics such as offering small opportunities and perks to entice families with rewards, like special coaching sessions in this case, or opportunities on his coveted crew. The writer agrees with many statements made by Judge Cunningham in the sentencing remarks. The effects of child victimisation are deep and long lasting. The carefree nature of a child is forever changed by these heinous offences.*

*Due to the father's extreme negative narration of the mother, the writer is concerned that any time spent with the father could put the children at risk and affect their views. The concerns are the father could interfere with the ability for the mother to provide a stable and safe balanced home life. Therefore, the writer recommends no contact in any form with the father.*

I squeezed Carrie's hand. Finally, someone else saw Julian. She saw straight through him without even meeting him. A dangerous manipulator.

"Mr Love, is your client agreeable to no costs?" The judge asked.

My barrister turned to me, and I nodded with vigour.

"Yes, Your Honour."

The Judge nodded and continued to my barrister. "Mr Love, your client, Ms Jessica Foster is seeking final orders for sole parenting, permission to move interstate and no contact with the paternal family. Is that correct?"

Julian's lawyer had one eye on the door. Looking eager to get out of there. Was it the scathing family report that decided to rip Lyn and Greg's funding?

"That's correct, Your Honour," Mr Love answered.

The Judge rounded on Julian's lawyer again. "Just to clarify – Mr Rundell is withdrawing as long as there is no order as to costs?"

Julian's lawyer stood again. He adjusted his tie, clearing his throat nervously. Why did this guy become a lawyer if he couldn't hold it together in front of a judge? "Ah ..." He flipped through his folder. "That's correct, Your Honour."

"And I'm curious, what are the costs incurred by your client to date?"

"Uh ... well," He flicked wildly through the pages of the thick binder. "Ah ... okay ... Your Honour, I have that, if you can afford me a moment?" He kept flicking through the binder, his face now covered in a sheen of sweat. "Right, yes ... well ... it appears the bill er ... expenses to date are just short of one hundred thousand dollars."

The judge nodded, slow and controlled. There was no rush to this, it could last five days. The judge continued. "And who has funded that?" She leant forward on her bench, eyeing his lawyer, who shrunk away a little more.

"Ah ... the grandparents, Your Honour." He got out in a small voice with a tiny nod in the direction of Lyn and Greg. He wanted to leave and sold them off down the river.

The Judge's eyes flicked straight to Lyn and Greg. She didn't miss a beat. "Well, that doesn't look very good to the mother, does it?"

It wasn't a question.

The room remained silent, and I stifled a smile. Patrick squeezed my leg and Carrie, my hand.

The judge eyed Lyn and Greg before coming back to the centre of the room. "I will adjourn for a one-hour recess to see if the remaining parties are able to come to an agreement. But before we do. With the withdrawal of the applicant – the father – in this matter, the mother is afforded the order of sole parent. To be clear, it is essential that she – the mother – is *extremely* comfortable with any orders by consent."

She looked over her glasses at Lyn and Greg before glancing to me. I could have kissed her.

With court adjourned, my lawyer and barrister led us into a small conference room where they left us to meet all the legal parties in the halls for the chit chats. It wouldn't be a day in family court without some chit chat.

"I can't believe he's pulled out!" I exclaimed when we were alone.

"You read the report," Patrick said. "I think the parents have pulled the pin."

"Yes, I agree," Carrie said. "He would never back down if they kept funding him."

"How was that figure?" I said. "Bloody hell, the judge didn't seem impressed by all that money." I was still stunned by the amount.

Patrick looked amused. "No, and then they would have their own lawyers and barrister's fees on top of that!"

"Not to mention what they would have already spent on the criminal defence," said Carrie.

My barrister and lawyer returned to discuss the plan forward. There was some to and fro, but I held my ground. After sixteen years, I had a sliver of power back with that family report and the backing of the ICL. The tides were finally receding, and I might not drown after all.

Within an hour, an agreement for limited visits was found. I could move interstate and was formally listed as a sole parent.

Flanked by my best friend and loving partner, I signed the final orders with my lawyer. The trial ended where my family court journey started – in a dodgy little room of the family court building.

We walked out of the claustrophobic space as Lyn was leaving her own little room. She looked old, hugging her large handbag to her chest, head down with her cherry lipstick bleeding into her wrinkles. She walked towards the exit in defeat. Greg trailing a few feet behind.

I watched them leave, a weight lifting off my chest.

1196 days since I left him – I was finally free.

9

It was one of those perfect spring days. The morning air brisk, the breeze slight; due to pick up later in the day. Perfect for sailing. The sun unhindered, sprinkling dots of light along the river. I looked at the public marina and spotted the boat I was told would be here. There was no one else about, just a lone figure on a keel boat preparing for sail. The tall figure came into better focus as I neared the

364

end of the pier. I hugged my arms to my waist, anxious about how this would go.

I watched him tinkering before stopping, looking up, distracted by my movement. I was only twenty feet from him now. The man I thought supported the child abuser. Now, I didn't know how I felt about him, but I couldn't leave Darvo without doing this.

He stopped what he was doing, and looked to almost smile before turning serious again. His young, relaxed face long gone. Age had taught us all lessons with every line on our faces. No longer fresh-faced twenty-somethings.

He climbed from the boat and stood on the aged wooden jetty. I stopped a few feet from him. Not sure what to say after so long. It had been years since we had spoken. Not since that phone call when I thought he was taking Julian's side.

"Jess, I ..." He wiped his hands on his trousers and studied them.

"Hey," I said quietly. "Luke, I just wanted to say, we're leaving." I looked around at the boat, so I didn't have to meet his eye. "We're leaving. Today, actually. Moving away."

He nodded, still looking to his hands.

"I didn't want to leave," I said. "I mean ... not without ... I didn't want to go without giving you a chance to ..." Now I searched my own hands. "Fuck, I don't know. I want to know what happened."

I finally got the courage to look at him in the eyes. He pressed his lips together and looked at the river mouth before coming back to my eyes, looking like he might tear up.

"Fuck, Jess," he said. "It was all just so much shit, you know?"

I nodded but didn't let go of his eyes. "Why didn't you tell me you were a witness against him?"

"I tried to. Remember that phone call ... I was trying to warn you and you hung up on me."

He gestured towards the edge of the pier. I followed him and we sat, our feet dangling over, looking at the small fish feeding off growth on the pier below.

Luke continued, "I was told by Laura not to say anything to anyone. Fuck, at that stage, Julian thought I was still backing him."

"Why did you do it then? I mean ... if you knew, what took so long?"

He ran his fingers through his hair. "I used to look up to him a lot, you know. Like he could do no wrong. I was a bit younger than him and thought he was cool. I guess I saw his abuse of Kayla back then as a relationship. I thought she wanted to be with him."

I nodded and chipped away bits of splintered timber. Letting them drop into the water below.

"Jess, it wasn't until I had my own daughter and I had grown up a lot. I ... I looked at it different then. Like I knew how wrong it was after thinking about – what if it was my teenage daughter, you know?"

I gulped. Having children did bring a lot of clarity and growth with the challenges. And certainly, I'd never felt more protective over anything from the moment I knew I was pregnant.

"I understand." I said, watching another chip of wood fall.

"But even before then, I tried to warn people. Like I tried to warn Carrie to make sure he wasn't doing anything to her girls. I sent her that anonymous message."

"That was you? My god, I had no idea."

"Yeah. But Julian worked it out. Remember when you saw me all beat up in the club that day? I had broken ribs, a black eye and a real fat lip. I think you were pregnant with Poppy."

I winced. "I remember, you were black and blue. That was *Julian*?"

"Yeah."

"But you were his best friend."

"Yeah," he scoffed, raising his eyebrows. "Look it's complicated ... But when I heard about the messages to Emily, I thought, for fuck's sake, he's still doing it! Honestly, I thought that getting married and having children would level him out, you know, he might see things different, but ..."

"No," I said grimly.

He sighed, long and heavy. "Anyway, so I knew I had to do something, and I rang the detective. I spilled my guts to her. I'm just sorry I didn't do it sooner."

We sat in silence, staring upstream. The club we had spent so much time in years earlier stood across the river, bathed in morning light. It looked like any other innocent building, but I didn't like to see it now. "Luke, thank you," I eventually said.

He nodded, tears filling his eyes. Was he full of shame and regret too? Another victim of circumstance blaming themselves. Luke may have been his best friend, but I bet Julian lied and gave half-truths to him, too. I thought of Luke on the witness stand against his best friend. I was sure he'd describe it as, "trying to push shit uphill!". It must have been hard.

"So, you and Chloe were not supporting him?" I turned to him, wanting him to physically confirm the words.

"Fuck no," he grunted. "Chloe always thought he was a flog. Do you know, she told me only after all this came out that when we were first hooking up together, he had a crack at her one night?"

"What? Like came onto her?"

"Yeah. She couldn't stand him after that." He shook his head and we said nothing for a bit.

367

"How are Chloe and the kids?" I asked after a while.

"Great. She's pregnant with our third. It's a boy." A smile spread across his lips.

I echoed his smile. "Congratulations."

He cocked his head, looking proud. "Anyway, I better get this boat out."

"Yeah, I better get going too," I said. "Hey, nice to see you as the skipper by the way. It's about time."

"Yeah. Can you believe someone put me in charge of a boat?" His goofy smile from the old days shone through.

We both pushed ourselves to our feet and looked around again, rather than meet the others eye. He stepped forward and pulled me into his chest. The top of my head not reaching his shoulder.

"Take care, Jess."

I nodded and squeezed a bit tighter.

"Bye, Luke."

When I was halfway back along the pier towards the car park, I turned and watched him at the helm steering out of the river mouth towards the ocean. Unable to look away, for the last time I watched as the sail caught the wind, and he disappeared around the point.

# *Autumn* 2020

I turned to Carrie as she sat by my side on the deck of our new house, watching the sunset over the ocean. My new ocean. It had been four months since driving away from Darvo River. The constant roll of the waves into the sandy beach had become my metronome – my new beat in life. I woke to that sound each morning and could get on with my day from there.

Carrie, Jim, Meghan and Amelia were our first visitors other than Mum and Dad. I looked over the railing at Jim, Patrick, and the now adult Meghan and Amelia playing frisbee with the children on the beach below. Their faces pooled in warm orange and pink hues. It was no wonder photographers loved sunsets.

"So, they're all good?" I asked of her girls, stroking my now elderly Buffy, balled on my lap.

"Yeah, actually." Carrie smiled, looking at her daughters and sipped on her wine. "They're both loving life."

My smile was uncontained. I constantly asked for reassurance that Meghan and Amelia were okay, and she always allayed my fears. I kept in touch with them on social media, but these cherished visits were few and far between. I heard survivors often tended to either thrive or go down a road of self-destruction. My heart would break if the latter was our reality. We were the lucky ones.

"I've got to tell you ... I really don't know what you see in this place." Carrie smiled through her sarcasm.

Patrick tackled Ricky for the frisbee and they both ended up tumbling.

We chuckled as they wrestled on the sand. Jim and Poppy egging them on. Amelia sprinted forward and stole the frisbee from amongst the fracas. Her and Meghan's faces were rich with laughter.

Carrie and a handful of friends and family were the only things I still missed about Darvo. I was happy to try to forget most memories there; they all seemed tainted. Whenever I lost myself to memories, I felt like I was drowning; an internal chest burn I couldn't quell. I didn't want to feel that way. I didn't want to be damaged and bitter and jealous and untrusting. But that was my new reality. A constant internal battle.

Patrick had more than proven his loyalty to me, time and time again – and yet, my chest still constricted when he received a text message. If he touched me in a particular place, I recoiled involuntarily. Would I ever be normal again?

But if I was normal in my old life of ignorance and feeling powerless – would I ever choose that? I wouldn't trade who and where I was now for anything. I was damaged – but I was a work in progress. I was awake now.

"How's the practice going?" Carrie asked, as the game below resumed.

"Actually, it's getting busier each week," I said with a smile.

"Great." She smiled down at the beach as Jim spun the frisbee towards Ricky.

We sat in silence as a flock of birds darted in uniformed patterns across the orange sky. Their high-pitched chirps taking over the conversation for a time.

"I'm not coming back, you know," I said, following the flock with my eyes.

"I know," she said. I turned and we locked eyes. "And I'm okay with that. Our friendship survived Julian Rundell. So we can survive anything. Distance is *nothing*." She reached for my hand.

As the sun sank lower on the horizon, the frisbee game came to an end and they all started to make their way up from the beach. A content warmth spread through me looking at each exuberant face of those I loved climbing the final steps to the deck. I squeezed my best friend's hand.

All the agony and tortuous battle to get here – worth the fight.

# Acknowledgements

Domestic abuse may not always be physical or even verbal. But it always instigates fear. It is often a pattern of degradation and silent rules followed to keep the peace and avoid consequences. There are always consequences. Often beginning subtly; people don't even recognise it as abuse. The relationship starts with a flourish of love by a person so intoxicating, you cannot imagine your life without them. They profess love, security, safety, happiness and comfort. The world is promised. A future you crave.

Coercive control sneaks up. It is confounding. You can wake up one day, look in the mirror and hardly recognise who you have become. You can be empty internally and yet feel a relentless pressure in your chest – like you might burst. You yearn for comfort and behave the way you have learned to get the best reaction. Or at least to negate the worst. You may find yourself spending enormous energy, year after year living; placating, managing moods and unspoken rules. The rules you only learned existed when you broke them. This way of living becomes all-consuming and is utterly exhausting. That is where an abuser wants you.

It's on the day you realise how controlling the relationship is – the awakening. That's when the fear really settles in and nestles under your skin. You realise you are trapped. The day you realise that you don't recognise your once free spirited, optimistic self is when it dawns on you that there is no way out. It would be harder to leave than to stay.

The fear of leaving a coercively controlling abuser is genuine and valid. On average, one woman is killed in Australia each week by a current or former partner. A person who promised to love them and care for them. It is the ultimate betrayal. Many, many people are living in fear right now. Another woman somewhere was just murdered.

Child grooming and abuse can be equally as silent as coercive control. There is always a power imbalance. There is always shame and always fear. It may not even be fear of the perpetrator. Such skilful manipulation tactics can make the child feel worried for the abuser. The fear can be of what will happen to the perpetrator if the secret is told.

There are many parallels between coercive control and child grooming. Both are insidious and silent to the outside world and yet can happen in plain sight. Both are damaging and have lifelong effects on victim survivors.

As hard as these stories are to share and hear, the story telling is imperative for the dawn of change. A societal shift on a world platform is urgent. We can no longer sweep hard topics 'under the carpet'. We need to open our eyes and ears to the reality. Only then can we start to redress the perpetual cycles and commence healing.

Not discussing hard topics does not stop abuse from occurring, it only leaves victims and survivors isolated with their experiences. Silence is dangerous and only perpetuates further abuse.

To all victims, survivors and family members who have chosen to share their stories; thankyou. To those that are not ready; we are always listening if ever you choose. You are not alone; never forget your worth.

Some people expressed initial concern of the dark themes of this story. I was asked if it was marketable. Do people want to read about domestic abuse and child sexual abuse? The answer is probably not. But the question should be: can this story help somebody? I think it can. Even if just to help validate people's truth and show they are not alone.

Regina Lane saw the importance of Jess's story. Her support and guidance have been integral to this book coming to life. Never shy to share her honest opinion, even when it was hard to hear, driving me to write to the best of my ability. Our regular Zooms and feedback throughout writing this book were something I always looked forward to. The only thing more pleasurable than writing itself, was talking about writing. Regina has supported my vision from the beginning and helped steer me when I was feeling lost. I am forever grateful to you, Regina and Laneway Press.

Elizabeth Harrington may be sweet and demure natured but always strove to see the best in me and never pussy footed with feedback. Her regular coaching helped me beyond belief, always pushing for more and gave honesty when I was going off track. She was strong, clear and supportive, and never let me give up. Elizabeth, you are an amazing talent, and I cannot wait to read your future works.

I would also like to thank Lauren Webster for her detailed eye in the final stages of editing and proofreading. She picked up on errors missed a thousand times over.

I would like to thank my family for shaping the person I am today. I had a privileged upbringing and always had everything I needed. I am extremely grateful for all the help, guidance and support they have given me throughout my life. Thankyou Mum, Phil,

Dad, Coral, Lis and Kate.

To all the people I have been blessed to call my friends over the years, I would like to say a huge thank you. Near or far, you all know who you are. Even if I have lost contact with you, I will never forget who you are to me. Thank you.

To Gerard – my rock. You showed me what love is supposed to feel like. Without your undying support, this book never would have come to fruition. Many people would have laughed at me when I said I wanted to write a book, but not you. To never doubt in someone and support their passions is a quality foreign in many relationships. I am extremely lucky to have you in my life. Thank you for who you are and all you do.

To my beautiful children, Taylor and Harvey. Never was there a love as fierce and protective as what I feel for you. Thank you for your smiles that lighten my day, even when you challenge me the most. Raising good people is an enormous responsibility I do not take lightly. Your kindness and empathy are so apparent that I feel like I have won the battle already. Please never stop chasing your dreams, love hard, lead with kindness and be good examples. I will love and be there for you always.

Thank you to my dearest friend in the world. You are the epitome of what true friendship is. I have no doubt our friendship will endure eternity. Life may see people through a few long love affairs, partnerships or even marriages. But only one true B.F.F. I sometimes ponder if that is the ultimate love? Probably.

This book may not be an easy read. But it is my absolute honour and privilege to bring it to you. Thank you to everyone who picks it up and feels something ignite in them.

Thank you. Thank you. Thank you!

Printed in the USA
CPSIA information can be obtained
at www.ICGtesting.com
LVHW030438181223
766737LV00027B/2708